DEAD
DRY

ALSO BY SARAH ANDREWS

Earth Colors

Killer Dust

Fault Line

An Eye for Gold

Bone Hunter

Only Flesh and Bones

Mother Nature

A Fall in Denver

Tensleep

DEAD DRY

❖
❖
❖

Sarah Andrews

St. Martin's Minotaur ❧ NEW YORK

www.minotaurbooks.com

Library of Congress Cataloging-in-Publication Data

Andrews, Sarah.
    Dead dry / Sarah Andrews.—1st St. Martin's Minotaur ed.
       p.   cm.
    ISBN 0-312-34252-7
    EAN 978-0-312-34252-4
      1. Hansen, Em (Fictitious character)—Fiction.   2. Water-supply—Political aspects—Fiction.   3. Geologists—Crimes against—Fiction.   4. Government investigators—Fiction.   5. Salt Lake City (Utah)—Fiction.   6. Women geologists—Fiction.   I. Title.

PS3551.N4526D43 2005
813'.54—dc22   2005049404

First Edition: November 2005

10 9 8 7 6 5 4 3 2 1

With love and admiration
to Susan Landon,
Empress of Geology,
who blazed so much of the trail ahead of me,
and to Robbie Gries,
who walked that trail with Susan
and did so much to bring her back to us

ACKNOWLEDGMENTS

As with previous books in the Em Hansen series, this little monster was a collaborative work. My colleagues have been exceedingly generous and often passionate in bringing to my attention ideas and information that they feel the public needs to know about. I am, therefore, indebted to my entire profession for support in creating these stories.

In particular this time, I wish to thank geologist Robert G. Raynolds of the Denver Museum of Science and Nature for sharing his knowledge of the geology and ground water of the Denver Basin and for his technical review of this book. Everything I learned about Denver Basin aquifers (and a good deal more) appears in *Mountain Geologist: A Special Issue on Bedrock Aquifers of the Denver Basin* (October 2004, vol. 41, no. 4), edited by the incomparable and indispensable Susan Landon with guest editors Robert G. Raynolds (yeah, the same Bob Raynolds) and Michele L. Reynolds. I am especially grateful for insights provided in "Stratigraphy and Water Levels in the Arapahoe Aquifer, Douglas County Area, Denver Basin, Colorado," by Robert G. Raynolds (same guy again). Other texts that provided essential understandings for this book include *Ancient Denvers*, by Kirk R. Johnson and Robert G. Raynolds (beginning to get the drift about this Raynolds guy?); *A Field Guide to Dinosaur Ridge*, by Martin Lockley; *In Search of the Warrior Spirit*, by Richard Strozzi-Heckler; and *The Art of War*, by Sun Tzu.

Next on the hit parade of fabulously contributing colleagues comes (drum roll . . . dim the house lights and bring up the spot . . . a hush rolls over the crowd as men crane their necks, babies squeal, and women swoon . . . announcing . . . The stupendous! The magnificent! The astonishing!) Jim Reed of RockWare, Inc. Jim's technical review of the text provided lots of juicy forensic stuff. I am also forever indebted to Jim for making me laugh as hard as I ever have on the convention floor at the Geological Society of America.

Many thanks to the members of NecroSearch International, in particular the same Jim Reed, for their excellent investigations of clandestine gravesites, which provided a model for investigations described in this book.

Multitudinous thanks also to geologist and minerals economist Janie Chermak of the University of New Mexico for helping me understand ground water as a mineral commodity and for her technical review of this book.

Big kudos go to science historian Michele Aldrich for her winning bid and generous contribution to the Geological Society of America Foundation silent auction, thus allowing the use of her name for a character in this book. Michele Aldrich, the science historian, is real; Michele Aldrich, the Salt Lake County Sheriff's Department detective, is entirely fictional, but is inspired by one smart namesake.

The technical accuracy of this book was improved by input from a great many people in addition to those mentioned above. Heading the list is CDR Hugh Replogle, USN(Ret.) VA-165, VA-128, VA-115, and his many brothers in arms, especially those at the Intruder Association (www.intruderassociation.org). Additional essential information and/or colleague reviews of parts of the text were provided by geological engineer Edmund W. Medley of Exponent® Failure Analysis Associates; geologist Jan Dixon; Wisconsin State Geologist Jamie Robertson; San Francisco Fire Department Captain David Drabble; Salt Lake County Sheriff's Department Deputy Craig Meyer; geologist Marjorie Chan, Chair, Department of Geology, University of Utah; geologist Peter Modreski, U.S. Geological Survey, Denver; chemical engineer Karl Kaufmann, FMC Corporation; geologist John Dolson, Exploration Advisor, TNK-BP, Moscow; geologist William Siok, Executive Director, American Institute of Professional Geologists; attorney Chris Hayes;

John Rider; Million Air customer service representative Mary Jacobs; and bon vivant Paul Rest.

As always, I am indebted to Kelley Ragland and Deborah Schneider for their support and to the Golden Machetes critique group—Mary Hallock, Thea Castleman, Ken Dalton, and Norm Benson—for beating the goo out of me.

As I love to do, I save the last and deepest thanks to those without whose loving support and indulgence these books could not be written: my ever-patient husband (and geologist and pilot, who checks the pilot stuff), Damon Brown, and our ever-clever son, Duncan.

DEAD
DRY

◆
◆
◆

I AWOKE THAT MORNING IN THE BLISTERING HEAT OF SUMMER WITH something tickling my foot. At first I thought it was some kind of bug because I was sleeping in the backyard in the bed of my pickup truck where such creatures are not uncommon, but when kicking the sheet and wiggling my toes didn't make it go away I opened my eyes to see what it was.

"It" was Fritz Calder, a six-foot two-inch male of my own species who was smiling at me quite mischievously. Even though I had begun in recent months to grow quite fond of this male, I flinched with surprise. "Fritz!" I gasped. "Where did you come from?"

A shadow of worry swept across his face. "Sorry," he said. "Didn't mean to surprise you, I—"

"Out for your morning run?" I asked, quickly reassuring him with a smile. I didn't want him to go away. It was nice to see Fritz in the morning in his T-shirt and shorts, his cheeks flushed with exercise. He looked really good leaning against the side of my truck, the branches of the apple tree spreading out over him, the deep blue Utah sky winking between the green leaves and reddening fruit, but then, Fritz usually did have a way of looking good. In fact, in that moment, goodness suffused that tiny backyard, filling the intimate confines of the cedar fence and my landlady's tomato plants with a bucolic glow.

I had known Fritz for a year and a half now, and we had become good friends. Of late I had seen him mostly on evenings when one or the other of us thought up something nice to do together, such as a game of tennis (unbelievable, I know . . . cowgirl Em Hansen swinging a tennis racket) or a hike in the hills above the city or even a spin in the new airplane Fritz is developing. The plane needed exercise, too. It went like spit and Fritz knew I liked to zoom out across the desert landscape of Great Salt Lake and the Bonneville Salt Flats.

Fritz smiled back. "Up and at 'em, bright eyes. Seven A.M. and it's already eighty-five degrees out. Gonna be another scorcher."

"Pray for rain." I sat up and rubbed the sleep out of my eyes, hugging the sheet to myself with my elbows. I couldn't remember what I had on underneath it. A T-shirt was my standard sleep attire, but had I kept on much else in this heat?

"Too hot in the house?" he inquired.

"Yeah."

He looked up at the brick Victorian in which I rented an upstairs apartment. "I'll bet it roasts up there when it gets this hot, but isn't it a little unsafe to sleep outside like this? Salt Lake is the big city, Em. You're a long way from Wyoming. People might come by and see you here."

"Joggers, for instance. Renegade flyboys like yourself. No end to the depravity." I slid a hand under the sheet and discovered, to my relief, that I was indeed wearing a pair of athletic shorts and not just panties. I flicked off the sheet and was pleased that Fritz's gaze immediately dropped to my legs. "Breakfast?" I inquired.

Fritz's lips stretched into a grin. "Whatever you want to call it."

Fritz's jest tippled me into the wobbly sense of confusion in which I had been finding myself with increasing frequency around him. "I meant something like eggs and toast," I said.

Fritz's smile tightened and a scorching blush crept up his throat. "Well . . . ah . . ."

I was saved from thinking up my next volley by the arrival of a second healthy male of the species, good old Detective Thomas B. Raymond of the Salt Lake City PD. The gate squeaked shut behind him, bringing me to wonder how Fritz had come through it without waking me up.

Fritz turned to face Ray, his smile vanishing.

Ray nodded at Fritz, his expression equally unwelcoming.

I said, "Kinda early, Ray."

Ray said, "Sleeping in your truck again?"

"What do you mean, 'again'? You turning into a prowler or something?"

Ray's jaw muscles flexed.

Fritz's did, too.

I stood up, put a hand on the side of the truck bed, and vaulted out onto the gravel driveway. "Fritz and I were just getting ready for breakfast," I announced, realizing too late that saying this would make the collision even worse. "I suppose you've already eaten."

"Right." Ray's eyes were still on Fritz.

I sighed with irritation. "All right, what's up, Ray?"

Ray finally turned to me. "Fresh corpse. Still in place, just the way you like them. Nobody's touched it yet."

I stared at the ground, where I had a nice view of everybody's feet. "Circumstances?"

I saw Ray's weight shift in his shoes as he transferred his gaze back to Fritz. "Point of the Mountain. The gravel quarry. Employee just found it the hard way, with a front-end loader. All that's sticking out so far is one leg."

"That doesn't sound good."

"No, it is not. I warn you, this one's going to be bad."

I scratched my head. "So . . . a quarry wall collapse. Nailed by a few tons of falling gravel, right?"

Ray said nothing. I looked up at him. His eyes were closed and his eyebrows were beginning to jump. Not a good sign.

"A John Doe?" I asked.

Ray said, "Everyone who works there is accounted for, if that's what you're asking. It's not my jurisdiction. I'm just here to perform a courtesy."

"What's that?"

"I was asked to locate the state's forensic geologist, who's not answering her phone because she's sleeping in her truck."

"Who has the jurisdiction?" I asked, ignoring his barb.

"Salt Lake County Sheriff's Department."

"They have a homicide squad?"

Ray nodded.

I began to think out loud. "So they're wondering who the guy is and what he was doing wandering around a quarry in the middle of the night."

Ray's eyes snapped open. "That will be the sheriff's department's problem to figure out. Your job is to examine the . . . what do you call it?"

"Trace evidence."

"The trace evidence."

Fritz gave Ray a cocky smile. "The dirt in the dead man's shoes."

Ray's jaw muscles began to bunch again. He refused to look at Fritz as he told me, "You look at the dirt in his shoes, and then you go back to your office. Stay out of trouble. If you know how to do that." His scowl deepening, he said, "They need you *now*."

I said, "Give me ten minutes, Ray."

"No, *I'm* going back to my office," he said. "Identify yourself to the sheriff's deputy at the gate to the quarry. There is more than one quarry out there. You want the one on the west side of the highway. The others are part of Draper City's jurisdiction. Take whatever ID you have as a state employee, or they won't let you in."

"Oh, come on, Ray, you want to see this."

Ray closed his eyes again.

I said, "I'll follow you down there. That will make it quicker for me to get through the gate." I started toward the back door of the house, leaving Ray to make his decision.

Fritz fell in beside me on the walkway, bowing his head to get it closer to mine. "I don't have time for chow anyway," he said, keeping his voice down.

"I'm sorry, too," I said.

"I need to be at the airport in an hour. So this is it, your big chance, huh?"

I nodded. "Yeah. I've been trying to tell them to let me look at things before they yank the body. There's so much a geologist can learn from a clandestine gravesite. Tool marks, for instance, and—"

Fritz patted me on the head. "I know, I know. You've told me all about it. You gonna be okay with this guy?"

"Yeah. Ray's okay . . . just got dropped on his head too many times when he was a kid." I looked up at Fritz and impulsively gave him a squeeze. "Besides, it's you he doesn't like."

"I'll take that as a compliment."

I almost said *take it as a victory*, but instead asked, "You flying a charter this morning?"

"No, but Faye's got one, so I've got to run the shop while she's gone. It's challenging having a business partner."

"You mean it's challenging having *Faye* as a business partner."

"Right. You come out over your lunch hour. We could take a quick flight, get up above the heat for a while."

I smiled. "Sure. I'd like that. In exchange, I'll make you some dinner this evening. That way you still get something to eat out of the deal."

Fritz shook his head. "Can't do dinner."

"Is my cooking really that bad?"

"Cooking? Is that what you call that?"

I swatted him on the elbow.

"Nah, I love the way you char hot dogs, and your 'leftovers surprise' is the tops, but I have a charter later in the afternoon, soon as Faye gets back with the plane. That guy that likes to run back and forth to Denver all the time."

"Be gone overnight on a Friday? Doesn't that guy have a life?"

"He pays his bills on time."

"Gotcha. Noon it is."

Fritz gave me a quick one-armed squeeze, then turned himself around, gave Ray a serene little wave—barely a twiddling of the fingers—and jogged away.

Which left Ray standing a respectful but irritated ten feet away with one hand clamped on the nose of my truck as if he were about to crush it.

I let it pass. "Okay, I still have eight minutes. About time enough to get a quick shower and stuff some food into my mouth, okay?"

"I'll wait here," said Ray.

2

HALF AN HOUR LATER, I WAS STANDING BESIDE A BOOT THAT STILL
had a foot in it. The foot was attached to a battered and rather flattened
leg. I was sorry I had eaten after all.

We had driven down a long ramp road into the pit, following a con-
veyor belt constructed to carry gravel uphill to the sorting machines.
Loaders and ore trucks thundered away in the far reaches of the work-
ings, hauling away sand and gravel to make concrete for the foundations of the new housing that was quickly filling the Salt Lake Valley.

The sun was barely on it, but the gravel was already beginning to
cook, superheated air rolling off it like the breath of Cerberus. I wondered what that was going to do to the dead flesh that now lay exposed
to the desert air.

The bank of gravel that had fallen had been almost two stories tall.
Trying to abstract myself from the corpse, I stared up at what was left
of the bank. A mass at least twenty feet wide and perhaps ten feet deep
had collapsed. At 120 pounds per cubic foot, or a ton and a half to the
cubic yard, that would add up in a hurry.

"I can't figger out how it let go," the heavy equipment operator was
saying. "I work these faces all day long, so I know how to be careful. I
was just workin' this one yesserday, so I remember real good. I swear I
dint leave it too tall or over-steep, and you can see where all the rest of
them is fine."

A woman detective from the Salt Lake County Sheriff's Department was asking the questions. "Was it like this yesterday when you left?"

"No! Hell no! It was standing. I just thought it must of caved during the night."

"So whoever this is wasn't there when you left yesterday."

"I swear it! I tell ya, I got no idea who that is!"

In contrast to the equipment operator, who was clearly at the edge of his wits, the detective was cool and matter-of-fact. She was about thirty and very fit. She had a halo of strawberry blond hair and loads of freckles and the kind of ease about her that comes from knowing that men will find her appealing. She said, "What time did you say you came to work this morning?"

"Six," the operator said. "It's been so hot I like to get started early, and it keeps the dust down. Wind doesn't get strong for another couple hours."

I looked up over the brink of the quarry toward the mountain front. The constant winds were why the hang gliders liked this area. On any sunny day, there were always at least three hang gliders or parasailers hovering over the nose of rock known as Point of the Mountain. Had this man flown in over the fence?

The operator was apparently thinking along the same lines. "The place was locked up like always. Really. And them hang gliders stay on the other side of the highway. Just hover, like."

I thought of the scrawny fence we had passed coming in. I wasn't impressed by their security measures.

The woman nodded. "Okay, I got it. Funny thing that you should choose this pile first thing and find a leg sticking out."

The man's eyes shone with horror. "I went to it because it was all loose, like. Makes it easy to move the stuff. You gotta think of these things!"

"Just tell me what you saw."

"Nothin'! I tell ya, I saw nothin'! I was just backin' away from takin' my first load outta the pile and I saw . . . I saw . . . it's a boot, right? With a leg in it, for crissake!" The man's face was beginning to swell with a nasty cocktail of emotions.

Ray, who had conjured excuses to hang around, leaned toward me and mumbled, "Don't say I didn't warn you."

He was right, this one was bad. My stomach had gotten all spongy on me the instant I saw that boot sticking out from under the trailing edge of the pile of loose gravel. Geologists are too often exposed to unstable quarry and mine faces. But I didn't want Ray to think I couldn't take it. I had trained hard to do this job. It was time now to do it.

I crouched down and focused on the boot. It had old-fashioned hand-sewn welts. The edges to the rubber soles were worn completely round, and there were knots where the laces had broken. When new, the boot had obviously been expensive, but after years of wear it was about worn out, and after being subjected to catastrophic burial, it and the leg protruding from it looked like so much road kill. In fact, that's what the remains reminded me of most: a jackrabbit after it's been run over by three or four tractor-trailer rigs.

I took a deep breath. "Size 45," I read from the center of the arch. "European sizing." Knowing what size boots the dead man wore made him a little more real, and that increased my queasiness. I slipped into the kind of flippant, dark humor that can help separate the living from the dead. "Is our John Doe a Juan Gama?" I inquired, murdering a little Spanish.

The woman looked at me. "Nah, the Spanish make the cork sandals. That boot is from Switzerland or maybe Italy, so let's call him a Johannes Damhirschkuh or a Pinco Pallino."

I glanced up at her. The day had just improved immeasurably.

The woman held out a hand for me to shake. "We haven't met. I'm Michele Aldrich."

"Em Hansen."

"You're the geologist."

"Guilty as charged." I stood up, dug into my wallet, and handed her a business card. "I'm with the Utah Geological Survey. It's a state agency."

"What do you survey?"

"Huh? Oh, I get it. Yeah, a geological survey is literally that, a survey of the geological wealth and hazards of a state. Most states have one."

"And you are their forensics specialist?"

"Sort of. Most days I'm a mild-mannered, rank-and-file geologist evaluating mineral resources and such, but when a case like this comes in, I'm it."

Ray scowled for the second time that morning. He said, "Em, don't exaggerate. This is your first case."

Michele looked from me to Ray and back again with the micrometer eyes of a trained observer.

I counted to ten but said something defensive anyway. "While this is in fact my first murder case since coming to work for the Utah Geological Survey, it is my tenth overall. More often, forensic geology runs to civil cases."

"Civil cases?" Michele inquired.

"Sure. Someone puts expensive stone tile in a bathroom and it starts to fall apart right away. Did the contractor install actual Italian marble or was it Italian something else—serpentine, for instance? A common misperception. Not a gram of calcium carbonate in it. Or—"

"You lost me already."

"Sorry. Your command of foreign languages suggested—"

"I was a military brat. My dad was attached to a couple of different embassies. But rock-ese is not one of the languages they spoke there."

"Okay . . ." I turned my attention back to the gravel bank. It was bad enough being grilled for my bona fides by your average cop, but being fried by a smart, young, pretty one with abundant self-esteem had the potential to get downright unbearable. "I'll try to speak English."

"I wish I'd taken some geology," Michele said.

I winced, thinking that she was now trying to mollify or, worse yet, play me. Was I that much older than she? I had blown out the candles of my fortieth birthday cake, yes, but what did she think, I was her mother's age? I didn't like to be reminded of all the years that had stacked up around me, particularly because there were so many things I thought I'd have done by now. *Like marry, and yeah, become someone's mother,* I grumbled to myself, remembering what hadn't worked between Ray and me. "Geology's a good time," I said tersely.

"I can see that it might have been an addition to my criminal justice major," she said evenly.

She's not deferring, I decided. *No, she's setting the ground rules. You're there, I'm here, you do this, and I do that.*

Ray observed us intently, as if watching a good tennis match. I wanted to kick him in the shins.

"So what do you look for?" Michele inquired, turning her attention to the collapsed embankment. She had her pen poised, ready to take down evidence.

I decided grudgingly that I admired her style. "Geology has its own kind of clues," I said. I began wandering along the foot of the bank, examining it from a respectful distance. "Most of the landslides I've looked at—recent ones, anyway—will have a sharp edge to the top of the slide block. That's what we call the mass that fell. See? It rotated and flowed a bit as it came down. That's typical. The toe of the slide shoots out away from the cliff—in this case spreading into a loose fan—and the top kind of sits down on top of it, riding it down. But I look up there and I don't see a sharp edge to the cliff, so I wonder: Is this normal? Would sediment this loose hold its shape as it slides? Or did something other than gravity or the vibration of passing trucks set off the avalanche? When we've got an unexplained corpse lying underneath it, we have to ask these questions."

"You can tell if someone triggered this slide?" Michele asked.

"Maybe. It's gravel. Loose stuff." I shrugged my shoulders. "So I compare it to other gravel banks I've seen over the years. I look first at what looks right about this one, and then I can begin to spot the features that might have been changed by human activity."

Michele said, "The natural versus the unnatural."

"Well . . . we're part of the natural world, too, you know. But what you're saying is that we've learned to influence our surroundings by machine. Or explosives. But someone wanting to trigger a slide could've just stomped on the top of the cliff for all I know, although he'd be risking getting caught up in it himself. But we're getting ahead of ourselves here. We don't even know who our John Doe is. For all I know, he had every reason to be here and just got unlucky."

Michele raised a reddish eyebrow. "I somehow doubt that."

"Me, too."

"So what do you do next?"

"I look at the way the grains of gravel stacked up—what we call its bedding planes—and look at that pattern within the context of the greater geologic picture. You ask how the corpse got here, and I ask how this gravel got here."

"Okay, how did it get here?"

"It was deposited by rivers flowing out of canyons in the mountains."

Ray decided it was time to stick his nose into the conversation. "An alluvial fan," he said, returning one of the terms I'd taught him back when we were dating.

I nodded. "And in this particular case, the fan was building into a wide, deep lake."

Michele glanced around at the dry quarry walls that surrounded us. "There was a deep lake here. Okay . . ."

"No, really. Nowadays, the shore of Great Salt Lake is what, twenty miles from here? We call it 'Great,' but it's really just a little puddle next to what it was during the last Ice Age. You see, when the climate was cooler, things didn't evaporate as much, and Great Salt Lake grew much, much deeper and covered an area at least five times as big as today—and we called it Lake Bonneville. The glaciers that filled the valleys up in the mountains above here acted like great big bulldozers and sanding machines, grinding away at the valley walls and floors as they slid downhill under their own weight. As the glaciers melted, they left all the ground-up rock and gravel in the bottoms of the valleys. The rivers driven by the melt water carried the gravel out of the mountains, and where the rivers hit the lake, they dropped their load. When streams slow down, they can't carry as much sediment along." I pointed at the notch in the mountain front from which it flowed. "There was a great, rushing stream at this particular position, and it dumped a lot of gravel, as you can see."

Ray blinked.

Michele said, "Okay."

I turned toward the kill site, where that horrifying leg was sticking out from under a different geometry of gravel. I cleared my throat and forced myself to continue. "So because I know how this gravel was deposited, I know what the geometry of its bedding planes ought to look like." I pointed at the wall that had collapsed. "This gravel was deposited by a natural system, by moving water. It was wet, and the water was moving downhill from the mountains into the Salt Lake Valley . . . or, more accurately, into Lake Bonneville. Wet gravel has a lower angle of repose—the slope at which it will stack up—than dry. See those big lines running diagonally through the bank? Those are the bedding planes I'm talking about. Those formed as the gravel avalanched out of the foot of the river into the lake, one layer deposited on top of the next."

Now I pointed at a stockpile the heavy equipment operator had pushed together some other day. "That gravel was deposited in a heap by machines driven by humans. The machines drop dry gravel straight down from buckets. The gravel avalanches out every direction from a central point and stacks up at a much steeper angle of repose. See? The angle of repose of dry gravel is about twice that of wet."

I was beginning to run out of steam. Pretty soon we were just going to have to uncover the rest of that corpse, and I wasn't looking forward to it. I turned and faced the music—literally. The wind for which Point of the Mountain was famous was beginning to pick up, stirring the hot, rising air of the quarry. Little rivulets of dry sand cascaded down its walls and blew into my eyes.

Michele brushed grit from her face. She said, "Okay . . . wet, dry . . ."

"The bedding angles are stacked up like fallen dominoes. The tops of the dominoes show you where the surface of the lake was."

"Okay."

Out of the corner of my eye, I saw Ray shoot an amused look at Michele. Michele deftly lowered one eyelid and raised it again. This was all I needed: Ray making light of me to flirt with the sheriff's detective. I said, "Don't you have somewhere you need to be, Ray?"

"My shift ended half an hour ago."

"Just my luck."

I was trying not to look, but I saw him smile.

I pointed again at the bank. "This gravel is still standing because it's damp. As the quarry face dries, it will slowly become unstable, but the question is, how fast?"

Technicians had gathered around the jutting boot, taking photographs. Others were getting ready to dig.

I strode over to them. "While you're digging, I'd like to get some specific pictures," I called out, "and before you start, it's critically important to get a look at the top of the bank before anyone disturbs this ground. More could come down. Obviously, the static load alone is enough to crush a man, and you don't want to find out what a dynamic load can do."

"What?"

"Static means standing still. Dynamic equals moving."

The men who had been crouching by the pile quickly straightened up and stepped back.

Michele caught up with me. "Are you going up top now?"

"No, I'm not offering to hike up there and find out the hard way whether there are any cracks in the top of the bank. Damp gravel can stand a long time, but uh . . ." I waved a hand at the leg.

Michele said, "I'll get the equipment operator to bring that truck over here. You can stand on top of the cab."

The man brought the truck over, and I scrambled up. In the rising wind, the effort made my lungs feel like I was inhaling hot sandpaper, but I was able to see what I needed to see. The sunlight and shadow picked out slight depressions in the gravel, but were they footprints? I couldn't tell. I looked for the kind of cracks that would presage a thousand more yards of gravel about to tumble down into the site and saw none.

The stifling wind dried the sweat on my brow, gluing my hair to it and filling it with grit. From the top of the ore truck, I could just see the tops of the mountains to the east, and the first hang gliders beginning to hover. "What do you think?" I asked the equipment operator. "Does it look safe to you?"

The man tensed at the question. "I don't know . . . okay to work by machine, but I sit up high, where I don't get hit."

"Gotcha."

A second man joined us, and introduced himself as the quarry's safety officer. He said, "I don't see any immediate threat of another collapse, but still, we should proceed with caution. If your guys cut a bank more than a few feet high, it's too dangerous. That's all it takes to knock a man off his feet, and you'd suffocate before we could dig you out. So if it gets very deep at all, you'll need to bring in shores to hold it up. We don't want anyone else getting killed around here."

I nodded, and we climbed down to instruct the technicians. The men proceeded with shovels, taking it slowly, and, considering the weight of each shovelful and the quickly rising heat of the day, seemed glad to do it that way. It took an hour to completely uncover the body, given the interruptions for photographs.

I watched for bedding, evidence that the pile had in fact slid to the place we found it, rather than being shoveled into position. To do this, I had to dodge in and take close looks at the way individual pebbles had lodged against each other. The risk of further collapse of the bank kept me sweating even more than the heat.

At last the body—or what was left of it—was fully uncovered and more thoroughly photographed than a movie star on a red carpet. It was an odd sight: it lay—twisted and in most places decidedly flattened—on its side, facing the bank, with its knees brought up, as if in sleep. Wherever the skin was exposed it had been battered to a pulp by the avalanching gravel. There wasn't much left of the face.

"Looks like someone used a sledgehammer on him to get his teeth," one of the technicians declared. "That sure screws up chances for a dental ID. But there's relatively little blood anywhere else, which suggests that the man was dead before his body was crushed by the falling gravel."

Michele said, "Well, unless he somehow climbed the fence into the quarry and died of natural causes in the precise location a collapse would later happen to occur, he was killed somewhere else, brought here, dumped, and the avalanche was triggered to hide his corpse."

"I concur," I said. "His hands look weird. What's up with that?"

The technician lifted a hand with the end of his pen. "The flesh on the pads of the fingers have been removed. No fingerprints. Someone really did not want this guy identified."

"Someone who worked for the federal government or did military service," Michele said.

"How do you know that?" I asked.

She held out her own hand, palm up, and wiggled the thumb. "To get a driver's license, all you have to do is give a thumb print," she said. "So being this thorough—taking them all off—means our killer has had the experience of having all of his fingerprints taken as a set. The feds do that."

Ray said, "Or he's done time somewhere. That makes it a professional hit."

Michele said, "Who'd hire a pro who has a record? And smashing the face . . . that suggests anger. That's personal."

"Quick and dirty," said Ray. "Efficiency. That's a pro."

Michele asked, "What do you think, Em?"

I pondered a moment. "I agree that whoever did this was brutal. The fingerprints . . . maybe that argues ignorance of fingerprinting processes. But what interests me is what the corpse is wearing."

"Why?" she asked.

"Old-style hiking boots with knotted laces, outdoorsy slacks . . . that color was probably called 'mushroom,' very trendy . . . the fabric is that easy-clean, quick-dry stuff . . . I can just see them on page six of some catalog advertising togs for well-to-do travelers, captioned, 'Washable in your third-world adventure hotel sink or wash as you wear in your Balinese waterfall!' And that shirt looks like one of those ones that's supposed to screen out UV rays, or at least it would have before it was shorn to bits by the avalanche. This outfit cost money, except that the boots are past due for replacement."

Michele said, "You're good."

I added, "So I'm thinking he's someone who *had* money but doesn't anymore. And I'm thinking he's someone I would know."

"You do?"

I said, "He's dressed the way I am—or would be, if I had the cash. He's an outdoorsman who has used his boots as they were designed to be used: for hiking. They don't make boots like that anymore, and what's left of his hair is gray, consistent with buying boots like that new in his twenties. Let's say he's now in his late fifties, but his work still takes him outdoors. That's a geologist or perhaps a biologist. If he was a forester, he would have worn a different style of boots and some kind of uniform. An engineer would not have worn a shirt that style, and . . ." I broke off to address myself to the technicians, who were beginning to collect evidence. "Make sure you put plastic bags over his boots, okay? The welts and treads harbor soil and grit that might have come from somewhere else. And bag the hands, too, please, if you think there's anything left underneath those fingernails."

"Gotcha covered," one of the technicians said.

The other technician stepped forward to search the corpse for identification. He gently peeled back the collar. "No laundry marks," he said, "but this isn't the type of shirt you send out to the laundry. Not an obscure brand, so no reason for the killer to remove the label, I suppose."

Michele said, "I don't suppose he was kind enough to leave the wallet."

The technician rocked the body as he reached for the obvious first place to look—the back right pants pocket—giving the fabric a slight tug in the process. A large piece tore away, revealing the corpse's right buttock, which, having been turned away from the flying gravel, was intact, but at first glance still badly bruised.

The technician gingerly withdrew his hand. "No wallet," he said.

"Not fond of underwear," Michele said. "And what's that? A birthmark?" She stepped closer and bent to look. "Or . . . a tattoo?"

"A bruise from the assault, perhaps," said the technician. "If he's only been out here less than twelve hours, lividity won't have set in yet."

Now Ray got into the act. "No, that's a tattoo, all right. It looks like . . . a map or something. Like North America, only . . . it's cut in half on the diagonal."

I stepped into a position where I could see, too. It was indeed a map of North America, but as it had appeared during the Cretaceous Period one hundred million years ago, "cut in half" by the great shallow seaway that once stretched across the continent from northwest to southeast. Suddenly my head rang and felt light. "I know this man," I said, my voice coming out very small. "I've . . . I've seen this tattoo before."

"You do?" said Ray. "You have?"

"Who is it?" asked Michele.

All eyes turned to me just as I desperately needed privacy. I sat down on the edge of the shallow trench they had dug around the corpse and put my head between my knees, fighting a wave of nausea. I tried to make words, but they had somehow gotten thick, and my lips had turned to rubber. Even in the cloying heat, everything felt very cold and far away.

Michele put a hand on my shoulder. "Are you sure?" she asked. "Do you know his name?"

"Afton McWain," I said, trying to lift my head without it falling off my neck. "I knew him in the oil business. Denver." The ringing in my ears increased, and I pushed my head back toward the ground.

Michele went into a crouch. "Take your time," she said. "So you're sure this is him?"

I said, "Is there a little red star right where Denver would be? Look on the left shore of the seaway, about halfway up."

"The what?"

"The seaway . . . that split in the map. Is there a star?"

The technician said, "Yup, a five-pointer."

"That's our boy."

I started to shake. My mouth began to run, a poor attempt to eject the shock. "Afton is—was—famous, or infamous, depending on who you ask. Everyone knew him. He made sure of that. Big ego. But really

smart. Excellent geologist. Really knew his rocks. He discovered several oil fields. Regular wizard. Wanted to be the next Bob Weimer. You
don't know him, but he's the grand man of all that, and Afton worked
hard to try to match him."

I pointed a shaking finger toward the corpse. "That tattoo was kind
of a badge of honor, like he claimed the Cretaceous. That's how old the
rocks in the D-J Basin were. Are. Denver-Julesberg. It's—it's—a—
the—what you call the geology—the structure of the Denver area. Big
down-warp in the rocks, like a big dish. A basin. Am I making any
sense at all?"

Michele said, "You're doing fine. So . . . what? He was into skinny-
dipping or something?"

I realized that she was giving me an out, a reason for having seen
him naked. "I went on a field trip he led once. Colorado Scientific Society, five or six years ago, the western slope of Colorado. He was the big
cheese for the Cretaceous rocks. The trip wound up near some hot
springs, you see, and he . . . arranged for everyone to . . ."

"Quite the show-off," she said.

I said, "I'm from Wyoming where they teach us to keep our clothes
on at high altitudes, so we don't get sunburned."

Michele eased herself onto the bank next to me. "I'm thinking more
and more I missed something by not taking geology."

I was beginning to tremble. I knew that tears weren't far away. "Like
I said, geology is a good time . . ." I knew I was having a reaction to
the stress of trauma, but that didn't stop it from coming. I knew also
that the shock of seeing this particular old colleague squashed a few
inches thick was not all that was causing my reaction, and that made me
feel even more out of control. The tears began to spatter from my eyes.
"I didn't know him all that well, but his wife was a chum of m-mine. *Is*
a chum. Unless . . . unless she's under there somewhere."

The technician who had torn open the pants spoke. "I've checked the
rest of his pockets. Nothing but one bit of gravel."

Michele said in her matter-of-fact way, "Then the killer has never
been to the hot springs with him, or he'd have given him a buttectomy,
too."

I said, "Does he have a hand lens around his neck?"

The tech asked, "What's that?"

"It would be on a cord around his neck. He was that kind of geologist. Never took it off. It's a ten-power magnifying lens, what a jeweler would call a loupe."

The technician lifted the collar of the shirt. "No cord, but there is a line in his tan, or I can kind of make one out."

I said, "Well then, the killer knew that much about him. Knew the lens was a symbol of his profession."

Michele said, "You say he's from Denver?"

"Last I saw him. But it's been years."

The technician pointed at the tatters of silver hair that were still attached to Afton McWain's crushed head. "This gray hair is consistent with his age, then?"

"He was somewhere in his mid-fifties," I said. "He was already an established hotshot when I came to Denver. Already had more money than God from the oil he found back during the boom."

Michele said to no one in particular, "Well, it's off to the office for me. Time to make a few phone calls."

"Let me call the—the widow," I said, forcing my mouth around that final word. "I've known her since college; we took most of our geology classes together. She won't have suspected a thing yet. If her—that," I pointed at the remains of her husband, "if he's only been dead since sometime after this quarry closed yesterday afternoon, she won't know he's missing yet."

People were staring at me.

I said, "Not hearing from him one night won't necessarily seem out of the ordinary."

They continued to stare.

I began to feel defensive of my fellow geologists, a band of leave-me-aloners if there ever was one. "Either way, it'll be a terrible shock," I insisted.

In the continuing silence, I knew that my mouth had moved faster than my brain. It had been my intention, in getting a real job at the Utah Geological Survey and by starting to hang out with nice guys like

Fritz, to become less of a loner myself and to build a life with more of the good times and less of the stress. But I'm a slow learner. "In fact," I said, "I have a friend who's flying to Denver this afternoon. I'll hitch a ride and tell her in person."

3

MARY ANN NETTLETON SAT AT HER KITCHEN TABLE IN THE HOME she and her husband had bought in the Jarre Creek drainage southwest of Sedalia, Colorado. She stared at the estimate the water-well driller had just dropped off, unable to move. Thirty thousand dollars to drill a new well? And for what? Why should she have to buy something she already owned? And where had the water in the existing well gone? When you buy a house it comes with water, doesn't it?

She didn't have the money for a new well, and she didn't know where she could borrow it. Just six weeks earlier, the undertaker had taken all of her available cash to give her husband a decent burial. The burial insurance just hadn't been enough, and Mr. Entwhistle at the bank had explained that her husband had borrowed against his other life insurance to make the down payment on the house. Next to the well driller's estimate lay the latest mortgage statement, and it was not good. The banker had seemed so helpful when he explained that her mortgage had several payment options, allowing her to make a minimum payment, but that meant that she would be adding to what she owed on the principal. Money came from her husband's annuity, but that wasn't paying as well as it had back when he announced that they could afford to retire to this dream house. He had been so delighted at the deal he had gotten on it—a steal! And now he was dead, and she was alone in a nightmare that had three bathrooms, a kitchen, a wet bar, and an indoor laundry, but not a drop of water in its pipes.

Again and again her mind went back to the same spot and stalled: Why should she have to drill a new well in the first place? The existing well had water in it when they bought the house a year and a half ago, so it should be there now—shouldn't it? When Henry fell in love with the house she had not thought to ask where the water came from. That was a man's concern. Water had always been something that simply came out of the faucet when she turned it on.

Her head spun with a mixture of anxiety and indignation that was quickly mounting into rage. Within the dizziness of these emotions, she remembered a man who had come to the house predicting that the well would run dry. Henry had given him a beer and visited politely and when he left called him a raving utopian, an idiot with a Ph.D. But in the last months of his illness, as the daily yield of the well had indeed dwindled, Henry had asked him to return.

Mary Ann had remained politely in the kitchen while the men conferred in the living room. What had they discussed? And what was the man's name? McWherter? No, McWain. Alfred? No, something odd. Afton, that was it.

Well then, she'd invite this Dr. McWain to visit again. Ask his help. After all, he had offered to help Henry before he'd become too ill to listen, and she wasn't too proud to admit that they had misjudged him.

She opened the telephone book and searched for his number. There was no Afton McWain listed. She called information, but he was not listed there, either. How on earth could she get in touch with the man?

Mary Ann suddenly recalled the file of notes her late husband had made as he sat there in the living room, his oxygen cannula strapped to his waxen nose, listening to McWain. Perhaps he'd written down the man's phone number.

She opened the file and turned over one page after another, trying to find it, but the only phone numbers Henry had written down were for their real-estate agent, banker, and a lawyer. Then it came to her: Dr. McWain had no phone. No phone, no power lines, no sewer. He had said that he lived "off the grid"—bragged, even, as if that were some badge of honor—beyond the reach of the wires that bound the rest of humanity in sensible electronic communion.

Mary Ann began to look through the notes, turning the pages more slowly now, looking for notations that might make sense to her. The first page concerned their real-estate agent, Hugo Attabury. Mr. Attabury was such a nice man; he'd worked so hard to get them that loan from the bank so that they could just squeak in on their fixed income and afford to move here.

And there was the banker's name on the second page of notes: Wayne Entwhistle. Mr. Entwhistle was very earnest. Mr. Attabury had guided Henry to choose Castle Rock Savings and Loan because it was right there in Castle Rock. And Henry wouldn't have it any other way. Dear departed Henry had always liked to do business with local enterprises, and Mr. Entwhistle's bank had a nice, modest look to it, not like those big banks up in Denver that didn't give such personal service. And Mr. Entwhistle hired such nice girls to work at the counter.

The third page was headed with another name and profession: Todd Upton, real-estate lawyer. Mary Ann hadn't met Mr. Upton, but she could see how a lawyer might come in handy if she indeed had to go forward with drilling a new well. She shifted that page a bit to the right, so it would be easy to find again.

The next page listed a name she certainly did recognize: Bart Johnson. He owned a ranch nearby. Henry had explained that Mr. Johnson used to own the parcel that had been subdivided to build their home and the other lovely homes around it. Henry had commented that Mr. Johnson didn't seem to work his ranch anymore. He had a health problem of some sort, poor man.

Why was there a page in this file for Mr. Johnson? She tried to make out her husband's cryptic notes. "Beef down, land up, arthritis," he'd written. That much she could make out—though she was not certain of its meaning—but some of the other terms Henry had dutifully inscribed below that were completely foreign to her, or at least the way they were put together: "Aquifer. Alluvial fan. Recharge. Mining."

Tears began to well up in Mary Ann's eyes, and not just because she missed her wonderful, intelligent, companionable husband. How wretched that Henry wasn't here to explain it all to her, to protect her and their investment, to make it all better. He had tried to explain the finances to her, because he had known he was dying. Luckily he had set things up for her with the bank so that at least the major bills were getting paid on time, like the mortgage on this house.

Would she be able to keep the house?

What would she do if she couldn't?

One thing was clear, either way she'd have to drill this well, because without water, she could not continue to live here, and no one would buy this house from her. Having water delivered by truck was getting ridiculously expensive, especially for washing dishes! She had to take her laundry to the coin-op in town. That did not fit within the dream retirement she and Henry had planned.

Laundry. She felt stupid; no, selfish. Even with no water in her pipes, she had so much more than most people in this world. But then again, if she had to sell the house at a loss, there would be no other house, and she had no children to take her in; she and Henry had simply not been blessed with heirs, and that was why it had seemed reasonable to spend so much on this house. "We can't take it with us," he had told her, "and we have no one to leave it to, so let's spend it!" It just wasn't fair!

The whirl of grief over her lost dream of a long, happy retirement with her husband rose up again and slapped Mary Ann's brain into motion. The tears dried on her face. She picked up the telephone and began to dial the numbers her husband had so neatly annotated beneath each name. Attabury. Entwhistle. Upton. Surely one of them could put her in touch with Afton McWain.

4

MICHELE LIKED MY IDEA OF VISITING McWAIN'S WIDOW. "LET'S GO to my office and make plans," she said and, without waiting for my acquiescence, added, "Are you going to ride with me, or are you stuck on Ray?"

"No, thanks. I've got my truck right here."

As I followed her car, I phoned Fritz on my cell phone to make sure I could tag along with him to Denver. I explained my errand.

"Sure," he said, "as long as you don't mind pretending you're my copilot. I've got to keep up appearances with my paying passenger. You can't actually take the controls while I'm flying for hire though, not until you get your twin-engine rating and your commercial license." He chuckled. "But that day will come."

"What time?"

"Can you make it by noon? Faye's getting back early, and the client's ready and raring to go. He wants to get into the air before it gets too choppy."

"Weak stomach?"

"No, just nervous. Hard-charging young exec. Type-A personality."

"You mean he likes to be in control. Bouncy air suggests to him that he is not."

Fritz chuckled again. "You said it, not I. So, noon?"

"Ah . . . sure. Yeah, I have nothing pressing after I get some evidence samples into the analysis pipeline."

"Good. We can have dinner together." When I didn't answer immediately, he added hastily, "That is, if you're in the mood after your conversation."

I paused. "Well, ah . . ."

"Ship's Tavern, Brown Palace Hotel. Prime rib."

"That's hard to pass up."

"Then don't."

"Okay. Thanks, I'd like that."

"Done. I'll tell Faye you need to borrow one of her flight uniforms."

"It would never fit! I'd have to roll the pant legs up a yard!"

I broke off the conversation to the sound of Fritz's appreciative laughter. Michele was pulling into a parking lot.

The Salt Lake County Sheriff's Department occupies modern buildings at the corner of 3300 South and 900 West. Once ensconced in the jumble of coffee mugs and case files that was Michele's office, I used her computer to look for a phone number for Julia McWain. The McWains' home number wasn't listed, but she wouldn't be at home, anyway. I selected the number for McWain Geological Consultants on Court Street. Memories of my oil-patch days started to flow back as I remembered the offices she and Afton kept in a funny little building in downtown Denver, above an Irish bar called Duffy's. I used to get a green tongue from drinking beer at Duffy's on St. Patrick's Day and danced in the narrow hallways of the offices upstairs, in which a tribe of renegade geologists like Afton held forth.

Using Michele's phone, I punched in the number and took a couple of deep breaths while it rang. Michele lifted an extension to listen.

Julia picked up on the second ring. "McWain Consulting," she said crisply.

"Hey, Julia, you'll never guess who this is."

"What? I'd know that cowgirl twang anywhere. Em Hansen! What the hey! It's been years! You ran off to Utah with that cop—what's his name? Ray somebody?"

I turned a shoulder to Michele so she couldn't see my face, which was beginning to feel hot. "Uh, that was then, this is now."

"Well, I should have known," Julia said. "The last of the great holdouts. Marriage is too good for you, girl. What's up? Are you in town or something?"

"No, but I will be. I was wondering if I could drop by your office."

"Sure. I'll be here until five. Hey, it'll be great to see you!"

I hurried off the phone before my voice began to waver.

Michele punched a button on a recording machine and played the conversation back, her eyes blank as she listened intently.

"Hey!" I said. "I didn't know you were recording that!"

"Sorry. I didn't think to trip the record button until it was already ringing. Don't worry, it's not admissable as evidence."

"You think Julia McWain would kill her own husband?"

"Never met the lady. Would she?"

"Never. Afton was a handful, but not that kind of handful."

"What kind of handful was he?"

"Aw, shit, he had an ego the size of the Ritz. You saw that tattoo. He was brash and opinionated and didn't care whose toes he stepped on, but he was good to Julia."

"Was he?"

"Well . . . I never heard otherwise. They led a charmed existence, really."

"You don't sound so sure."

"Well, *I* wouldn't have lived with him, but he was the big catch. Back before Julia and I got into the game, he made huge oil discoveries in the Denver Basin, and he had a royalty on every barrel produced. I don't even know why they kept working. He was rolling in it."

Michele listened intently. When I was done with my explanation, she said, "I'd like to have you record your visit with her." She opened a drawer and pulled out a digital voice recorder.

"I—" I stopped with my mouth open, catching flies, as my mother used to say. "Record a conversation in which I tell a woman her husband has been brutally murdered? No way."

"Then I'd better come along," she said.

My stomach felt like I'd just taken a bungee jump. "No."

Michele glanced at her watch. "I can catch a noon flight. Would you prefer I spoke with her first?"

"No. . . ."

"Well, then. I'll meet you . . . where?"

I glared at her.

She gazed back at me, impassive.

Through tight jaws, I said, "In the lobby of the Brown Palace Hotel. It's across the street from their office." For a moment, I considered backing out of the whole deal. Let Michele be a jerk all by herself. But I knew I had to go. Julia was a friend. I could comfort her, perhaps soften the impact of having a detective walk into her office and announce the death of her spouse.

Michele said, "Something the matter?"

I opened my mouth to say something—anything—but changed my mind. Better to just ride it out. I told myself: *Talk to Julia, ditch Michele, and then meet Fritz for dinner. How bad can it be?*

I STOPPED BY my office at the Utah Geological Survey just long enough to explain where I'd been, sign out for the rest of the day, and leave my car in the lot. Michele swung by and gave me a lift the rest of the way to the airport, which is just a few miles west of the UGS, and dropped me outside of Fritz and Faye's place of business before continuing around to the main commercial terminal on the other side of the airport.

Fritz and Faye run an FBO, which is pilot-ese for "fixed-base operation." Theirs was a fledgling operation, to use an apt metaphor. There's not much more than a desk, a couch, a flight computer, and, outside on the ramp, a string of airplanes. They have two Katanas they use to teach flying, two Piper Aeros and a Beechcraft Duchess to rent, and Faye's big twin-engine Piper Cheyenne II Turbine, which they use to fly charters. Fritz's prototype sits out there, too. It also has two engines, but one is in front and the other is in back. He lets me fly it sometimes, after we're airborne and before we land. I am only licensed to fly single-engine craft, but he's a certified instructor, and the fore-and-aft in-line configuration of the propellers on his craft make it relatively easy to handle.

Fritz grinned when he saw me. "Em! You'd better get rigged up."

I was right, Faye's uniform pants were way too long for me. She about busted a gut laughing at me when I pulled them on. I was standing on four inches of fabric but my butt filled the seat.

"Em," she said, "you're such a clown."

"Thanks for nothing."

She bent to the floor and began wrestling the excess. "Here, I'll tuck them under. Get off the cuffs, you're getting them dirty."

I lost my balance and began to fall over against the sink.

Faye's toddler, Sloane Renee, started to giggle. "Auntie Emmy funny," she said.

"Thanks for nothing, Sloanie," I said. Then, feeling bad about my sourness, I tousled her hair. It was soft and gave off a scent that always made me feel all warm and fuzzy.

Sloane grabbed my hand and cheerily twisted my fingers, giggling uproariously. She always loved a party.

Extracting my fingers quickly before they required medical attention, I asked her mother, "Does the shirt fit okay?"

Faye expertly finger-pressed the bottoms of the pant legs to their new length and straightened up to assay the effect. "Mmm . . . not like a tailor did it, but you'll pass. Suck in your gut."

"Screw you."

"There are children present, foul-mouth."

I felt awkward doing this close "girl" stuff with Faye. I had never been good at it, and I had fallen out of synch with her in particular. I had once lived at her house, helping her with Sloane Renee when she was an infant and Faye was newly widowed, but of late I had been working long hours and Faye had made friends with other moms.

Faye straightened up and took a look at her work and started laughing again. "Just let Fritz do all the flying, okay? We can't afford to lose that plane."

"Yeah, yeah."

She arranged the gathers at the bottom of the shirt front, making them blouse properly, then gave me a friendly pat on one cheek. "There. How can Fritz resist you now? Of course, it isn't Fritz who's doing the resisting."

I knit my eyebrows into a scowl. "Faye . . ."

"Really, Em, how long are you going to torture the guy?"

"I am not torturing Fritz. We're good friends."

Faye grabbed me by the epaulets and gave me a shake. "He's a good man, Em. Why not give him a chance to move beyond the 'good friends' stage?"

"What in hell's name are you talking about? Fritz is dating . . . what's her name."

"Fritz would date *you* if you let him."

"You keep saying this, but the man has never so much as . . ."

"As what? What do you need? An engraved invitation? Try putting both arms around him next time you idiots hug each other, okay?"

I showed her my teeth.

She rolled her eyes.

I bent to give Sloane a squeeze, then straightened up, pushed past Faye, and banged the door open on my way out through the flight service office and went onto the tarmac. I didn't like to be rude, but I didn't have an answer for her, or at least, not one that I understood myself.

The door swung open again behind me. I heard Faye call, "Give it a chance, Em. And stay out of trouble, okay? I mean it."

"Sure," I said, through clenched teeth.

"And look me up when you get back? It's been too long."

I stopped and took a breath. Without turning to face her, I said, "Okay."

◇

WE LIFTED OFF from Salt Lake International, banked east over the Wasatch front, and left Salt Lake City and the heat of the land behind us. Faye's Piper had a lot of oomph, so in no time at all we had put Flaming Gorge Reservoir to our left and were crossing into Colorado over Dinosaur National Park. Unfortunately, the morning's cumulus clouds were quickly gathering into thunderstorms, and the ride began to get bumpy. I glanced back at the passenger to see how he was taking it. His grip on his armrest seemed a bit severe.

Fritz spoke to him over the intercom. "Mr. Reed? I don't think I mentioned that in her other life, my copilot is a geologist. Would you like her to give you a natural history travelogue?"

"Sure," he said, his voice thick with tension.

I rolled my eyes toward Fritz.

He grinned and poked at my arm.

"Okay," I said. I turned around and faced Trevor Reed, a nice young multimillionaire, and gave him my best tour-guide smile. "Colorado is divided into three parts," I began, wondering if I sounded like the beginning of my high school Latin text. "West to east, one-third plateau country, one-third peaks, and one-third plains. The plateaus are big old layers of sedimentary rock that have been carved up by the river drainages. Below us is Dinosaur National Park. You can see that the rock layers have been bent into a big hump—the geological term is anticline—and the Green and Yampa Rivers have cut down through it, exposing the older layers below. See the big white layer? That's the Weber Sandstone. It was laid down hundreds of millions of years ago when this region was a big, sandy desert much like the Sahara. Up ahead, we'll fly over the Rocky Mountains, a whole bunch of metamorphic and igneous terrain that's pushed up and been eroded into peaks."

Mr. Reed looked studiously out the window. "Sandstone, I think I understand. Metamorphic and igneous, these are types of rocks also?"

"The three main categories of rocks are igneous, metamorphic, and sedimentary," I replied, ticking them off on my fingers, "and sandstone is a type in the sedimentary category. Sedimentary rocks, as you might imagine, are formed when sediments like sand or silt, or the exoskeletons of marine creatures such as corals are deposited and get cemented together. They are children of the surface of the earth. Igneous rocks are born at great depth as molten masses of the raw stuff of which minerals are made. As the masses—we call them plutons—rise toward the surface, they cool and start sorting themselves into minerals that crystallize out. Minerals freeze from liquid to solid, just like water. If the mass flows all the way out onto the surface before it cools, we call it a volcano. Volcanic rocks cool so quickly that you can't see the individual crystals in the rock. Most of the time you have the right chemistry in the molten mass to form basalts, or lighter-colored rocks called andesite or rhyolite."

"Igneous, sedimentary, metamorphic," Reed said back to me, concentrating. "Basalt, andesite, rhyolite."

"You've a quick memory! If the molten mass cools downstairs the freeze happens more slowly, and the atoms have time to sort themselves into larger crystals, big enough to see with the naked eye. Most of the time you have the right chemistry to form a type of rock called granite. Granites are rich in silica, which makes them lighter, both in color and density. Because they're less dense than the basalts and even heavier, deeper rocks called peridotites, they want to rise up like marshmallows floating in your cocoa. Or course, that's one horrendous oversimplification of the process—mountains rise for a number of interrelated reasons—but less dense stuff rising gives you a place to start thinking about it."

Trevor Reed's face actually relaxed enough to form a smile. "I'd prefer to have a more substantial image to hang onto than a marshmallow."

"Okay. The Earth's crust is solid, but it buckles up and down a lot and slides around on a thick, molten layer beneath it. You like that better?"

"That will have to do."

I said, "The granites of the Rockies have been rising for hundreds of millions of years—in pulses—and as they rise they're also being eroded down. The eroded rubble forms big aprons of sediment around the granite cores, and these sediments get cemented into sedimentary rocks like sandstones, shales, and conglomerates."

Just then the turbulent air through which we were traveling gave the airplane a particularly dramatic bounce, but while our passenger braced himself, he did not stiffen as much as he had for lesser jolts earlier. Smiling wryly, he asked, "The granites rise in . . . what did you say? Pulses?"

"Yes. The granite that forms Pikes Peak and surrounding mountains, for instance, started cooling and rising about a billion years ago. About half a billion years ago, it stopped or maybe even sank for a while. Then around three hundred million years ago, it began to rise again, forming what we call the ancestral Rockies. About sixty-five million years ago the whole region started to rise a third time. It rose for about thirty million years and then stopped. Everything eroded down flat, but it didn't sink; it just looked like Kansas for a while. Just smallish granite knobs sticking out of surrounding aprons of rubble eroded from the earlier peaks. Then ten million years ago the elevator started up a fourth time, and the rivers began to cut down again. They always want to cut things down toward sea level. So they eroded canyons through the rubble blanket and cut back into the granite core. Voilà, modern Rockies."

I paused to see if Mr. Reed had questions. He asked, "What about the metamorphic rocks?"

I was impressed. He obviously had a mind built for ticking down lists, and I'd left one item on the list un-ticked. "They're formed where other kinds of rocks are heated or squashed to the point where the minerals in the rock recrystallize and need to adjust to come into equilibrium with the new . . . ah, temperature and pressure regime. Here in the Rockies, metamorphic rocks have been formed as the hot igneous plutons intrude up into the sedimentary rocks, squeezing and cooking them into metamorphics like marble and gneiss. Then they catch a ride up to the surface with all those rising granites."

Our passenger was smiling now, enjoying my story and all but ignoring the bumps. "You've told me about the mountains. Now tell me about the flat parts."

"The eastern third of Colorado is made of sedimentary rocks, all in layers, like a cake. As the Rockies rose up—remember they shed sediments to both sides—they shed layers that became sandstones and conglomerates. From times when the whole works was under water, so we also have shales and limestones."

"Colorado was under water? When was this?" He feigned alarm, as if there was an important memo that had not crossed his desk.

"Well, the last time Colorado was below sea level was about seventy million years ago, towards the end of Cretaceous time. The center of our continent kind of buckled, like the hood of your car during a huge fender-bender, except it went downward rather than up, and we had a shallow sea that stretched from Alaska clear down to the Gulf of Mexico." I continued to smile, but now it was forced. Thinking about the Cretaceous seaway reminded me all too acutely of the tattooed map I had seen only a few hours before. I felt slightly faint.

He said, "Are you alright?"

"I'm fine," I insisted. I focused even harder on my storytelling, hurling myself into the task. "Imagine giant marine reptiles—mosasaurs, ichthyosaurs, plesiosaurs—swimming in a warm ocean. Imagine bony fish fifteen feet long, giant clams, and ammonites—squid-like creatures with spirally curled shells—the size of cartwheels. Where today we'd have pelicans, imagine pterosaurs—flying reptiles that survive on fish but don't like to light on the water because they might in turn be dinner for a big, hungry mosasaur." I held out my arms like the upper and lower jaws of that ancient behemoth, but they suddenly felt frail.

Mr. Reed observed me with the practiced eye of one used to gauging his opponents across a boardroom table but continued to make small talk. "All that against a background of the Rocky Mountains? Beautiful. I'll have my real-estate division start buying beachfront property."

"No, the modern Rockies hadn't risen yet. We'd had the ancestral Rockies, but they'd worn down. The place had been flat as Kansas for two hundred million years. The pulse of mountain-building that formed the modern Rockies started to rise about the end of the Cretaceous—sixty-five million years ago. That's when you wanted to buy your Denver real estate. It would have looked like parts of Florida: palm trees, gingers, ferns. But you wouldn't have liked the mud flats; they would have stank."

Fritz said, "Is 'stank' correct? Or is it 'stunk'?"

"You just fly the plane," I told him, beginning to regain my edge. "We're talking swamps and bogs here."

The passenger laughed. "You two are quite a pair."

Fritz grinned and wiggled his eyebrows at me, a sort of 'how about it?' dance.

I dove back into the story. "Of course, you might sell your Cretaceous Denver real estate as a theme park. Once that downwarp let go and the seaway drained away—"

"We sent the continent out to the body shop," Mr. Reed said dryly.

"Yeah. Anyway, then there were dinosaurs by the peck and the bushel. Oh, and before the Cretaceous seaway, too. The Jurassic was their heyday."

"Ah, dinosaurs," said the passenger. "Now we're talking. Big ones or the little chicken-sized ones I've read about?"

"Will *Tyrannosaurus rex* do? The first footprint of that fellah was found on the Colorado-New Mexico border by a geologist named Chuck Pilmore. And we've got *Triceratops* for you, curb weight five tons. Then there's *Pachycephalosaurus,* the lizard with a head like a battering ram, and *Ankylosaurus,* which would have looked like a Hummer fringed with thorns, sporting a tail like a caveman's club. They all left bones and footprints in the beaches and riverbeds."

"The meat-eaters might make it tough to get insurance for that theme park," Reed commented.

"No problem," I said. "Sixty-five million years ago, insurance hadn't been invented, which was a good thing because if it had been, every insurance company on Earth would have gone bust when the asteroid hit."

He snorted. "Asteroid?"

"Yeah, that's probably what killed the dinosaurs. Armageddon never had it so good. Imagine a chunk of rock the size of San Francisco hitting the Yucatan. That sucker blew a crater 125 miles in diameter. Everything inside the crater was atomized, and it set off tidal waves hundreds of feet high. The shock wave alone was a killer, but then the molten spherules of atomized rock rained down, and the Earth was encircled with fire and smoke. Forests clear on the other side of the world were incinerated. But somehow, just enough creatures survived to repopulate our world. In Colorado, these luckiest creatures were perhaps tucked in the lee of the growing mountain peaks, and before long Colorado was lush with forests and swamps and, after a while, rain forests."

"Rain forests in Denver."

"Hard to imagine, I know. Nowadays, Denver is semi-arid. What does it get, fourteen inches of rainfall a year?"

Mr. Reed shifted in his seat, his eyes on the mountaintops that were gliding by beneath us. "How do you know all this? Or is it really just speculation?"

I thought for a moment before I answered. "*I* don't know all of this, not really. As a scientist, I rely on the collected knowledge of a great many people. Tens of thousands of geologists and as many climatologists, botanists, and paleontologists . . . and physicists, chemists, astrophysicists . . . you get the picture."

"No, I don't, in fact. I've never understood how you arrive at your conclusions."

I began to wonder what philosophical tradition my listener was coming from. Was he a religious fundamentalist? "Excuse me," I said. "I didn't mean to presume. Do you adhere to a literal interpretation of the Bible?"

"No, but what would that be?"

"That the Earth is only a little over six thousand years old."

Mr. Reed smiled in a friendly way. "Six thousand? I have no idea how old it is. I've never studied these things."

"What have you studied?"

"I'm an investment banker."

"Then you studied finance?"

"I have a bachelor's degree in finance, yes, and an MBA in financial management."

"Then you know numbers."

"Yes."

"Do you trust them?"

"Yes. As long as I trust the people who gave them to me."

"Well, I trust my scientific colleagues. But like you, I put limits on how well I trust them. Science is designed to be questioned; that's what the scientific method is, a system of questioning. As our knowledge grows, some of our earlier assumptions and interpretations prove false, or too limited. Others hold. Scientists are hard-wired to question findings, especially our own, and we are not shy about challenging our colleagues. In this way, we build our knowledge as a community."

Mr. Reed folded his arms and leaned back in his seat with his jaw tilted up, indicating a challenge. "Put numbers to that."

I grinned. "Hmm . . . geology doesn't quantify easily, but I'll try. There are about one hundred fifty thousand geologists working in the United States, and each works two thousand hours a year. In reality, we work more—in fact, we never stop working because we never stop observing the world around us, but using the standard forty-hour week, fifty-week year builds some conservatism into this estimate. That's three hundred million man-hours per year in the United States alone. Now, to be equally conservative, let's multiply that number by two to get the number of man-hours for geologists worldwide, although a factor of three would probably be more accurate. That gives us six hundred million hours per year dedicated to understanding the Earth.

"Now let's factor that over the number of years geology has formally been a science. It's just a baby; let's call it 150 years. We didn't start out with half a million geologists, so let's just cut that number by two-thirds, to again build in some conservatism, and we get thirty billion man-hours. That's a three with ten zeros after it. Thirty billion man-hours it's taken to develop the understanding of the history and dynamics of the Earth, from which I just abstracted that story of the Colorado Rockies. Now, if you add in those physicists, geophysicists, chemists, geochemists, botanists, paleoecologists . . ."

"I get your point. Your billions quickly become trillions. But do you trust these people? And if so, how far?"

I smiled. "Some of us are brighter than others, and the occasional jackass or congenital idiot or pathological liar sneaks in and drives everyone nuts. But the thing I trust is this: On the whole, scientists prefer knowledge over ignorance. If they preferred lies, they could have saved themselves all those years in school, eating mac and cheese out of a box and living in crummy apartments."

Reed's eyes narrowed with thought. "Don't you ever get someone who tries to cover up the facts?"

"What do you have in mind?"

"Surely there are practitioners of your art who find themselves in a conflict of interest."

"Ah, you mean like someone who's trying to sell a prospect. A gold property or a place to drill for oil or gas." I laughed. "Yeah, sometimes a con artist gets into the game, but usually it's more a matter of optimism. To explore, you have to be optimistic."

"Are you an optimist?"

"No, I'm more of a pessimist. When I worked in oil and gas, I specialized in maximizing the production of known reserves. I was always pissing management off by showing that there was less oil in place than they had hoped."

Mr. Reed laughed. "I could use someone like you on my assessments staff."

"Well, Mr. Reed, I—"

"You can call me Trevor."

Fritz raised an eyebrow. He had his back to the client, but I saw it.

"That goes for you, too, Fritz," Trevor said, as if he had seen.

Fritz nodded, but I noted that his back had gone especially straight. I wondered what was up. I'd been having trouble calling the passenger Mister; the guy had to be at least five years my junior.

A short while later, we entered the landing pattern for Jefferson County Airport, which is in the suburbs just northwest of Denver. As we approached, the granite peaks gave way to the plains. Reed was watching. "I see fins of rock along the foothills," he said. "Are those igneous, metamorphic, or sedimentary?"

"Those are the edges of layers of sedimentary rock that got bent up when the granites pushed up. See those red ones? That's the famous Flatirons behind the city of Boulder. Lyons Sandstone. The ones closest to the mountains are Fountain Formation. Remember I told you about aprons of rubble fanning off the mountains? The Fountain Formation was one of those aprons, three hundred million years ago."

"Amazing." He shook his head.

Fritz brought the plane in for one of his silky smooth landings and taxied to the terminal. We stepped out into wilting heat. Denver was even hotter than Salt Lake City.

Reed had a car waiting to whisk him away. "So, Fritz," he began, as Fritz handed his client's leather-bound luggage over to the driver, "you have the keys to the condo and you have my cell phone number if you need to reach me. I'll be ready to head back about noon tomorrow.

Earlier if I can get away sooner." His smile became a wry grimace. "Avoid the thunderstorms." He turned to me. "Although I enjoyed the dissertation on the Rockies, Ms. . . ." He stared at me, trying to get my attention.

I was staring into space. It had not occurred to me that I would be spending the night in Denver. This caused certain problems, such as where I was going to sleep, and I hadn't brought a change of clothes. I glanced down at Faye's uniform. For that matter, I hadn't even brought something to wear into Denver. What was I thinking? *Had* I been thinking?

Fritz said, "I'm sorry, Mr. Reed, but I forgot to introduce you. This is Ms. Hansen."

I snapped my brain into focus. "You can call me Em," I said awkwardly. "Short for Emily." I thought of giving him my hand to shake, but for some reason, the uniform I was wearing stopped me.

He gave me a nod. To Fritz, he said, "Tomorrow at noon, then."

Fritz said, "Yes, Mr. Reed."

"Trevor."

"T—uh . . . yes, I'll be here."

Reed studied Fritz in detail for a moment, then sat down into his car. The driver closed the door for him, climbed into the driver's seat, and the low black car slithered away.

Fritz stayed where he was, watching it go.

"Can I ask?" I inquired.

He turned to me and blinked. "Ask what?"

"Why you can't call him Trevor? Or Trev? Or how about T-revor rex?"

Fritz's face went cloudy. "No, I'm not subservient, if that's what you're asking. I'm the pilot in command of that aircraft. That guy may be paying the bills, but he's not calling the shots. If the weather gets truly bad or he shows up with ten pals and I only have seats for six, I need absolute control over fly or no fly. It's just easier if the relationship stays one hundred percent professional."

I looked down at my shirt front again. "I was wondering if it had something to do with wearing a uniform."

Fritz got a faraway look in his eye. He raised one shoulder a notch and then let it drop. "Well . . . I may have left the navy, but I suppose it hasn't entirely left me. I've always flown planes where I'm calling the shots, but maybe you're right, once we're on the tarmac, it's easier if the chain of command is clear." He shook his head, stared at the mountains a moment, and then snagged his own satchel out of the baggage compartment. "Didn't you bring anything?" he inquired.

I stared at the tarmac. "I was so busy swapping shots with Faye, I forgot."

Fritz tousled my hair and led the way to the terminal. "Don't worry," he said. "I can loan you one of my T-shirts to sleep in." He chuckled. "And unless you're going to find yourself a hotel room, you're welcome to model it in T-revor rex's place in Denver. He'll be staying up in the foothills somewhere after a late meeting. Okay?"

"Sure." I took a deep breath and followed him, wondering what I'd gotten myself into this time.

5

As planned, I met Michele Aldrich in the lobby of the Brown Palace Hotel. It's a splendid place with an anachronistic air, and I never tire of finding excuses to hang out in its lobby. You can order high tea there, and maids in black uniforms and white aprons will bring out multi-tiered platters studded with cakes and petits fours, or, later on, you can listen to a man in a tuxedo play a grand piano while you have a drink. I was indulging myself in an early gin and tonic, getting up the Dutch courage to tell Julia McWain what I needed to tell her, when Michele arrived.

Michele's eyes danced as she took in the many balconies and stained-glass ceiling above us. "Nice place," she said, summing it up in two words. Then she looked me over, top to bottom. "What's with the pilot's uniform?"

I couldn't help stiffening. Michele had changed from her early morning slacks and blouse into a summer frock, a pale celadon green that set off her ginger hair. It brought out her freckles, and if anything, she looked even younger. I felt absurd in Faye's blue slacks and epaulets next to Michele's curvaceous sleekness, and for the first time in I don't know how long, I wished I knew how to dress like that. "It's a long story," I said. I knocked back the last of my G and T and stood up. "Julia McWain's office is just across Seventeenth Street from here," I said. "Follow me."

The Brown Palace sits at the intersection of Seventeenth and Broadway, at the eastern end of Denver's business downtown. It was built at the end of the nineteenth century, and Denver had grown up all around it, adding chunks of building every other decade, following the nation's various booms and busts. Now, glass-clad skyscrapers completely surrounded the old brownstone hotel and a small handful of other structures from bygone eras, including the Navarre (a former house of ill repute that used to connect to the Brown Palace via a handy tunnel that ran underneath Tremont Street) and Duffy's Bar, which lay beyond Seventeenth Street to the south. Duffy had been offered big bucks throughout the 1980s to sell out to make way for another high-rise, but he'd refused, much to the delight of his clientele, who helped razz the developers by raising steins of the infamous green beer to the surrounding construction mess each St. Patrick's Day.

As I passed the entrance to Duffy's on my way to the door that accesses the offices upstairs, I reminisced on the high points of my friendship with Julia McWain, sitting on adjoining barstools and swapping Celtic jokes until our tongues were the color of a leprechaun's britches. I counted Julia a friend because I had known her forever, professionally speaking. As I said, we had gone to the same college at the same time. We had fetched up in Denver working in the oil business at the same time. But from there, she had taken a path that had differed from mine, marrying and having children. Afton had been a real leg-up for her in the profession. When I repeatedly found myself out of work with the ups and downs of the oil and gas industry, she had managed to inch forward, and she had been able to hang in there while I had wandered off into forensic work and public-sector employment.

The rabbit warren of offices upstairs from Duffy's is ironically known, among the diehard petroleum geologists who inhabit them, as Duffy's Petroleum Tower, in honor of its low-rise stature and unpretentious air. The offices are accessed via a small elevator that rises from a vestibule right off the sidewalk next door to the entrance to the bar. Michele and I got in, and I punched the button for the third floor. When we got out, we moved down a narrow corridor past a row of small offices that looked like they hadn't been upgraded since the 1950s, which is perhaps when the building was erected. Each office is heralded by only a plain door with a funky old name plate overhead sticking out perpendicular to the wall. To a trove of geologists who preferred to thumb their noses at the physical trappings of progress, this was heaven.

The door to McWain Geological Consultants was the second to the last on the right. I peeked in the door to see if Julia was there.

She was seated behind an old battered oak partner desk, tapping at a computer keyboard. The computer's two monstrous screens, cordless keyboard, and processor were the only things in view that weren't old enough to vote, and Julia blended in with the rest, decked out as she was in a comfortable old skirt and a turtleneck sweater. Now shot with gray, her hair was still fashioned the way she had worn it when I first met her in college, and even then the style had looked like a holdover from high school. A soft light streamed in the city-grimed window, surrounding her with an atmosphere of serenity. I hated to bring it to an end.

I leaned up against the door jamb and said, "Hey there."

Julia jumped up and came around the desk to give me a hug. "Emmy! What fun! Hey, what's the difference between Mick Jagger and a Scottish shepherd?"

"You got me," I told her, returning the force of her hug.

"Mick Jagger says, 'Hey, you! Get offa my cloud!' and a Scottish shepherd says, 'Hey, McCleod! Get offa my ewe!'"

"Eeeww . . ."

"Thank you. Thank you. A man goes into a bar, and—"

I put out a hand to stop her. "Sorry, Julia, this really isn't the moment." I glanced at Michele.

She blinked. "What's with the pilot's uniform?"

"Long story."

"Does it involve a man?"

"Yes."

"Knew I could count on you. What brings you to Denver? And who's your friend?"

I said, "This is Michele Aldrich. She's a detective with the Salt Lake County Sheriff's Department. We have some bad news."

Julia's eyes went sharply alert. "News? What news?"

"Your husband is dead."

Julia cocked her head to one side, her expression a sudden tangle of emotions. "I don't *have* a husband," she said. "What the hell is this, some kind of a joke?"

My mouth dropped open. "You mean you and Afton . . ."

Julia had backed away from the hug, planting her hands on her hips in fists. "Didn't you hear? Mr. Wonderful took off two years ago! Divorced me. Dumped me *and* the kids. Split the sheets. Gone. *Sayonara. Kaput!*" She sliced the air with one hand. She's a tall woman, and the gesture was more than a little intimidating.

"I didn't know." I shifted uncomfortably. This was not what I had expected, not at all.

"Yeah, well, now you do. So what's this shit about he's dead?" She was beginning to tremble.

I shook my head with regret. "Well, he is. We found him this morning. He was—"

Michele put a hand on my arm to stop me. "I'd like to take it from here if I could, Em." She turned to Julia and showed her a face that was placid and patient. "Had Mr. McWain moved away from Denver, ma'am?"

Julia fixed a look on Michele that would freeze water. "Ma'am? Suddenly I'm *ma'am*? What kind of—"

"I'm sorry," said Michele. "We've come a long way to talk to you. Clearly this is a shock to you, but it's true. Em here spotted an identifying mark on the . . . remains that we understand was a positive ID."

Julia looked from her to me and back again. She smiled warily, offered a chuckle. "Oh, I get it, this is a joke about Afton, right? So what's the gag, has he been showing off his ass again?"

I stared at the floor, remembering what that joke had looked like lying on the quarry floor. "Not exactly, Julia."

Her face darkened. "Or did someone finally do me a favor and *shoot* the bastard?"

I couldn't let her talk this way in front of Michele. "You don't mean that, Julia."

Julia whimpered, "Dead? Afton isn't dead, Em, he's just ducking me! What kind of a game is this? Tell me that, Em. Tell me this is a joke. Please!"

I said, "Julia, he's dead. Very, very dead. He won't be troubling you anymore."

Julia began to cry, a piteous hiccupping sob. "But the children . . ."

This was a better way for Julia to be talking in front of the witness. Helping her build on this sympathetic ground, I asked, "How old are they now, Julia?"

"Samantha's . . . um . . . ten, and Timothy's . . . he's . . . um . . . eight."

Michele asked, "When was the last time you saw Mr. McWain?"

Julia stopped crying abruptly and fixed a tear-rimmed glare on her. "Why? Who needs to know?"

Michele said, "To find out who killed him, I have to establish certain things. Why he was in Utah, for instance, and how long he'd been there." She gave a tiny, encouraging smile. "You understand."

"It would help the investigation. Anything you could tell us," I added.

Julia sat down and averted her gaze. Finally she looked at me. "This really happened?"

"Yes," I said. "Afton is really, truly dead."

She took several long, ragged breaths. "The last time I heard from him was two weeks ago today. He was supposed to take the kids for the weekend, but he bailed on them. The last time I saw him was two weeks before that, when he actually showed up for a custody date. I have no idea why he was in Utah. I had no idea he was there. In fact, I have not been privy to his movements, or his motivations, or diddly squat, for quite a long time. Do you get the picture?"

Michele said, "Then you expected him today to take the children for the weekend? He had them every other week?"

Julia leaned back in her chair. She folded one arm across her stomach and used the other hand to cover her eyes. "I've quit making plans around him. If he shows up, fine, if . . ." Her shoulders heaved violently, twice. "Though I suppose what you're telling me is he won't be showing up again. Ever."

I said, "No, he won't."

Michele pursued her point. "So you hadn't heard from him in the past few days."

Julia dropped the hand from her eyes and glared at Michele. "Are you deaf?"

Unphased, Michele moved on to her next question. "Where had Mr. McWain been living?"

"It's *Doctor* McWain—he had a Ph.D., for crap's sake—and he had been living . . . near Sedalia."

I turned to Michele. "That's about an hour's drive south of here."

Julia said, "He moved down to the ranch a couple years ago."

I said, "The ranch?"

Julia let out a mirthless laugh. "Yeah, the ranch. My, my, Emmy, you have been out of touch. He—we—bought a nice little spread down there three years back. The idea was to move down there and raise the kids off the grid. Hah. It wasn't long before he started staying down there—said he was working on the ranch house, trying to make it 'green,' he said—but somehow it was never 'the right moment' to take the kids there. Said it was 'hazardous' for us to show up. I let myself believe it was because of the construction. After three or four months of that, seeing him only when he condescended to stop by the house, I decided to drive down there myself and see what the fascination was." She stared at the floor a while. "Well, you can just guess what I found."

Michele said, "Another woman?"

"He called her 'Nature Girl.' Shee-it. Nature doesn't come with ninety-dollar haircuts."

I gave up on trying to keep Julia from incriminating herself. I had not seen her go off like this in perhaps a decade, but I remembered a tirade or two in college that were doozies. I said, "Someone finally turned his head? I thought he was smarter than that." Seeing the insensitivity in my remark, I quickly added, "Besides, Julia, he had *you*."

"He had me, all right! Lock, stock, barrel, and two kids, he had me.

That and this consulting firm. That's what I got out of the deal: the McWain name, for what it's worth."

"But you kept the house?"

"I . . . had to give him something on that, too, even though he managed to take the whole ranch. He had the books so cooked, this business looked like a Fortune 500 corporation, and the ranch was a liability. He was supposed to pay some child support. I don't know. . . ."

I said, "But all those overriding royalties he had from his oil strikes here in the DJ Basin, what of those?"

She gave me a rueful smile. "He managed to get those appraised at the bottom of the price swing."

"Are those assets part of this business?" Michele asked.

Julia turned her eyes on the detective. "Oh, no, no, no . . . he made those strikes back in the late seventies and early eighties, back when he was a hotshot working for Davis Oil." She turned her head away. "Back before Saint Julia the Idiot took a shine to the map of North America in the Cretaceous."

Trying to be kind, I said, "It was a nice map, Julia."

"Sure, he was a stud. So I managed to rationalize all that stuff about his first wife, who got cashiered out with a pittance. I told myself that we were soul mates, that it took another geologist to truly understand him."

"Maybe it did."

She hung her head. "God, I've gotten bitter in my old age."

I said, "We're not that old, are we?"

"I feel old."

Michele cleared her throat. "Can you tell me how to find the ranch? And this, um, ah, third wife? What did you say her name was?"

Julia rolled her head like her neck hurt. "I don't think he even bothers to marry them anymore. Her name is Gilda something. The ranch is down past Sedalia, near Wildcat Mountain."

"Off Highway 85?" I asked.

Julia said, "I can draw you a map. Give Gilda my heartfelt howdy, will ya?"

"What's the phone number at the ranch?" asked Michele.

Julia said, "There is no phone at the ranch. Ol' Afton honest-to-gosh went off the grid. Doesn't even drive a car anymore. No electric power, except from solar cells and windmills. Everything bona fide, certified *au natural,* 'with no obligation,' as he put it, 'to the man.' He isn't even sure bicycles are above suspicion."

"How does he get around?" Michele asked, slipping into Julia's present tense.

"He mooches. Hitchhikes. Catches rides. He thinks it's more saintly. *Thought* it was more saintly."

"Then there's no way to get hold of this Gilda without actually going to the ranch."

Julia said, "She has a cell phone. God knows where she gets the battery recharged."

"So you *are* in touch with Gilda," Michele said.

I was beginning to read Michele's tricks. She had a way of keeping people talking, either by asking leading questions, or just by saying things so innocuous that there seemed no reason not to answer her. And she asked some questions over again, in different ways.

"No, *she's* in touch with *me,*" Julia said. "It seems she had a hard time keeping track of him, too." She pushed a hand against her face. "Well, I'd better fold it up here and go tell . . . the kids." Her lips writhed, and a tear slid down to her chin.

It was time to get Michele out of there quick while Julia looked more pitiable than hostile. I reached toward the phone. "Is there someone I can call, Julia? I don't like to leave you alone."

Michele turned to me. "Are you going somewhere?"

"Yes, out the door with *you,*" I said.

"We're leaving?"

"Yes, we are. You need me to find this Gilda person, and it's getting late. Julia, is Tina Wentworth still around?"

Julia's lips quivered and her voice came out a half-octave high. "She's right downstairs. Boy, won't this be a surprise for her. She was going to take the kids this weekend so I could go to a conference." She sniffed. "In Utah."

Michele pounced, "So you knew he wouldn't be showing up this weekend."

Julia's face turned dark with anger. "I quit depending on him for *anything!* Do you need semaphores or something, or should I write that out in Braille?"

Michele said, "And you were going to Utah, you say?"

"Is this one of those fucking 'I should have my lawyer present' pieces of crap?"

"Just checking a few facts," said Michele.

"Well, then, don't get excited, honey! I've got an alibi for the ages: I go from this office to the kids' school and pick them up. I am then home with them until the next morning—every morning—until I drop them at school, at which point I come straight back here. There are people all up and down this hallway that can vouch for me. Now get out of my life!"

"Julia, draw us that map!" I cried in a last ditch effort to keep her out of trouble. I grabbed the Rolodex next to Julia's phone and found Tina's number, dialed, explained what was going on, and begged her to hurry.

Julia obeyed me. She plopped heavily into her swivel chair and began to draw, holding the pencil in a very tight grip, accomplishing what geologists do best: rendering information into graphical language, preparing a quick, concise map that would direct us to Afton McWain's ill-gotten ranch.

As she worked, her tears dried. Work is the cure-all; just screw the brain into the socket and the world goes away.

As Julia shoved the map toward us, she muttered, "You'll want to get a move on. They're working on the highway; it's Friday, so every moron and his brother is heading out early for the mountains to get out of this heat, and the traffic's even worse than you'll remember."

Michele looked like she was opening her mouth to ask another question, so I cut in and changed the subject. "I haven't even asked after the kids."

"They're fine, or at least they are until they get your news, Hansen."

Wincing, I jumped in with another question before Michele could get on her again. "Working on anything interesting?" I asked.

"Sure, work's just all sunshine and happiness." Julia's jaws clenched rhythmically with rage. "I switched to ground water. I gave up trying to make a buck at oil and gas two wars and an economic slump ago. The price was in the shitter so long."

"It's back up now, isn't it?"

"Yeah. Most of the gang jumped back on the bandwagon, but I'm sticking with ground water. It's more important. Besides, it's all just getting juice out of rocks." She grabbed the map back again, affixed a north arrow to it, and spun it around for me to read.

She'd labeled the essential cities and towns "D" for Denver, "CR" for Castle Rock, and "S" for Sedalia, had put highway numbers inside of circles—Interstate 25 south to the cutoff to U.S. Highway 85 to Sedalia, then southwest onto state Route 67—and now tapped her finger to point out important secondary roads. "This is Rampart Acres Trail, or some such, and this gravel goat track is Castle View Estates Boulevard, some horny developer's wet dream."

She had marked the drainages—Jarre Creek, Plum Creek, Indian Creek—although I didn't need such detail. She knew she didn't even have to put in the Interstate or 85—I could have found my way to Sedalia with no map in a driving blizzard—but as one geologist making a map for another, there was a certain pride and communion to be addressed. She had even drawn a little X labeled RANCH and had made a small notation which read, TURN AT THE BARKING DOG.

I heard Tina approaching down the hallway. I gave Julia a quick squeeze and whispered an apology into her ear. "Sorry. It was the best I could do."

"I know you," was all she said in reply. Having run out of something to do, she was beginning to contract into a smaller version of herself.

Tina hove into view. "Jesus, Em! What's with the pilot's uniform?"

"Long story," I said, giving Tina a quick hug. "I'll check in later this evening, okay?"

"Yeah, sure, Em. We know you. Always off somewhere." She elbowed me affectionately out of the way and put her arms around Julia.

To Michele, I said, "Where's your car?"

"Down Tremont, past Sixteenth Street."

"Let's get moving." I grabbed the sheriff's detective by the shoulder and pulled. "You've worn out your welcome. This woman needs comfort more than she needs a cop, and I need to be back in Denver by dinnertime."

6

RAY DRIBBLED THE BASKETBALL HARD, DRIPPING WITH SWEAT, grinding with inwardly-directed anger. How could he have slipped so far off his program that he could make such an ass of himself around Em? And worse yet, around that friend of hers. Who was he? *More importantly,* Ray wondered, *who is he to Em? No! I don't want to know! I'm done with that!*

He pounded the ball up and down the court four more times, working his body until it began to relax out of simple fatigue. Then he stood at the foul line, bouncing the ball rhythmically, four bounces with his right hand, four with his left, his eyes on the basket, focus, focus.

He lifted the ball into two hands, flexed his knees, and rose up. Feeling his body extend, he rotated the ball and pushed off with his right hand, sending the sphere into perfect flight. It crested the rim, arced, and slipped through, touching nothing but net. Thus redeemed, Ray fell into a softer, more liquid transit of the court, feeling the ball rise up under his hand, arriving exactly where it belonged, sending the pleasure of physical poetry through every muscle and nerve and into his soul. As he moved, he recited the Twelve Steps of Alcoholics Anonymous inside his head, one for each transit of the court, saying each as it appeared in the book and then modifying it as he went:

Step One: We admitted we were powerless over alcohol, that our lives had become unmanageable. I admit that I am powerless over Em Hansen, that my life with her had become unmanageable.

Bounce, bounce, bounce—shoot! Another perfect basket.

Step Two: Came to believe that a Power greater than ourselves can re-store us to sanity. I've never had any problem with that one, Ray assured himself. *Heavenly Father has always been with me. I shall let him guide me. I feel his sanity growing within me.*

Bounce, bounce, bounce—shoot! A little rim, but it went in.

Step Three: Made a decision to turn our will and our lives over to the care of God as we understood Him. No problem. Done that. Now do it again . . . and again.

Bounce, shoot! Nothing but net.

Step Four: Made a searching and fearless moral inventory of ourselves.

Here Ray began to lose his rhythm. He couldn't understand where he was going wrong. *I've worked the Steps twice. I've made amends to Em. I've admitted that I can't carry the woes of the world single-handedly . . .* Bounce, shoot! The ball skidded off the backboard and bounced chaotically out of his control.

Control. That's what it always comes down to.

Ray retrieved the ball and dribbled it up and down the court two more times before he gave up, broke for the bench where he had left his gym bag. He dug out his cell phone and dialed.

"Hey there, Ray," Ray's Al-Anon sponsor answered.

His lungs still working like a bellows, Ray gasped. "I saw Em this morning. I behaved badly."

"Mm-hm. What happened?"

"I had to get her for a job. She was sleeping in her truck again. Like I told you. I messed up and told her that I knew she did this some-times."

"Wild woman. So what's the deal? You're embarrassed that you care about her? That you watch over her like an angel?" The man laughed cheerfully, trying to loosen Ray up. "Of course, we did talk about how this was a bit co-dependent, Ray."

"I know, I know. But I just check on her."

Another laugh. "I'm sure it doesn't hurt to check on her. I'd surely appreciate it if God sent someone to look after me if I was doing any-thing that foolish."

"Well, she's not really that foolish or reckless," Ray argued. "She doesn't live in such a bad neighborhood, and she's inside a fenced yard, and in fact you'd have to look into the truck to even know she's there."

"So what's really the problem, then?"

Ray paused. "She knows I was watching."

"Right. So let's cut to the chase. What really gets hurt when she knows you care about her?"

Ray was quiet for a moment. A drop of sweat accumulated on his nose and dripped into the cell phone. "I suppose it's my self-esteem."

"Right. Why?"

Ray's jaw muscles bunched. "Because I'm afraid she doesn't care about me as much."

"Once again, louder, please? I couldn't quite hear that."

"I'm afraid she doesn't care about me as much as I care about her."

"And maybe she doesn't. But who does care about you?"

"God does."

"And do *you* care about you?"

"I'm working on it."

"Good. What else happened?" The sponsor chuckled kindly. "I'm guessing you aren't telling me everything, Ray."

Ray squeezed his eyes shut. He counted his heartbeats, which had almost recovered to resting pace. Ten . . . eleven . . . twelve. "There was another guy visiting her."

"Ouch."

"I've seen him before a couple of times. Around town. They play tennis together. I . . . I jumped to the conclusion that he'd been there all night. But now I realize that he probably hadn't." Ray wanted to swallow the words he had just spoken, make them and the story they told not exist. He still struggled against clamming up whenever he got upset. "There was only one small camp mat in the truck, so she must have slept alone, but she got mad at me, made it sound different."

"Ray, why are you focusing on her? Come on, focus on you."

Ray straightened up, realizing that he had been bent over, facing the ground as if in shame. He now gazed up at the wide blue sky, beseeching God to rain mercy upon him. "I've gotten too lonely again."

"Right. The old bugaboo. Too tired, too hungry, or too lonely. So, which of your old friends haven't you looked up lately? And what other young women have caught your eye? Come on, I know you, you like to hide behind this caring you have for Em."

"Right." *What other women . . .* The image of the ginger-haired Salt Lake County detective floated into his mind. What was her name? "Well, there was one . . ."

"And meanwhile, give your mom a call. How's Ava?"

Ray suddenly grinned. "Now, don't go on about my mother. I know where you're going with that one. You want to know her better yourself!"

The sponsor chuckled. "You're so right. What a lovely person she is."

Ray's grin widened further. "Now, don't get your hopes up. She's picky. No one's ever been able to measure up to my father."

"It's too bad he died. Such a woman should not be alone."

"She's not alone. She has all of us kids, half a dozen grandkids, and half a dozen hounds like you howling at her back door."

"Really? The grandkids howl at her back door?"

"You know what I mean."

"Okay, then. What are you going to do about this thing with Em?"

Ray sighed. "I'm going to work my steps."

"Good man. Let go and let God. You okay now? I gotta get back to work. My job, I mean—not The Work."

"Sure. Thanks."

Ray switched off his phone and turned his attention back to the basketball court. He lifted the ball, aimed, and watched with satisfaction as it lifted off from his fingers almost like a cloud and fell noiselessly through the net. *Now all I have to do is figure out how to do that with Em,* he decided, as he recovered the ball, palmed it, and pounded it back down the court.

7

As I stalked down the sidewalk, I heard Michele say from somewhere behind me, "I suppose you thought my questioning a bit callous," she said.

"Yes." I didn't slow down.

"I'm sorry. It has to be done. I've been through a special training. We learn to repeat a question three different ways, just to make sure." Her voice came from closer behind me. She was catching up.

I slowed down a little. "I suppose."

"And Julia's a friend of yours. Not to put too fine a point on it, when you're busy hugging people, you don't watch for their reactions to information."

I stopped and waited until she caught up with me.

She said, "It's a good system. We're taught to be polite and considerate, so that the subject gains confidence in us, and that way if they have something on their chest, well then, they'll spill it."

"You mean like maybe a confession to murder. You want to know why I was in such a hurry to get out of there? Because I wanted you out of there. It wasn't fair to put her through that much pressure. Because I know Julia. I've known her for twenty-two years. I know her well enough to know that she shoots her mouth off, but that's *all* she does. I have never, *ever* seen her get physical. Never!"

"Well, then, just for the record, your friend passed the test."

"The test," I hissed. "What am I doing, helping you administer sainthood tests to friends who have already walked through hell?"

Michele's tone remained as even as ever. "I mean I don't think she knew anything about Dr. McWain's murder before we arrived."

I stood there on the sidewalk on Tremont Street watching pigeons peck at bits of junk food that had been dropped by passing humans. "I could have told you that. Remember, I spoke to her earlier to make sure she'd be there. I would have noticed." I felt like a Judas, even though I hadn't actually gotten Julia into trouble. I hoped.

Michele said, "Anyway, in the future, I'd sure like it if you let me do the questioning."

"Fine. I'll dial this Gilda creature. But you talk to her."

"Thank you."

I started walking again. "Find out whether we can even *find* her before we go running all the way down there."

Michele stopped to dig her cell phone out of the small shoulder bag she was carrying. "As long as we're putting things on the record, why are you really coming with me?"

I stopped in the middle of the sidewalk. "Okay, fine!" I shouted. "I had to . . . get out of there. And get you out of there before you tore my friend apart!"

"Just as long as we're clear on that. I'm glad of your company. We're both public employees, just doing our job."

I said, "Maybe I can match the clays we found on Afton's boots. It's probably from the dooryard of that ranch, don't you think?"

"You're the expert on that."

Why was I deferring to her? I read off the phone number Julia had written on the margin of the map, and Michele punched it into her cell phone. I leaned close so I could hear. After just a few rings, a connection was made, and a soft female voice came out of the tiny speaker. Background noise—some honking country and western music—poured out around it.

"Hello," Michele said. "Is this Gilda? Hi, my name is Michele Aldrich, and I have a message for you regarding Dr. McWain. I'll be passing through Castle Rock in a little while. Could I stop off and give it to you?"

Ooo, I thought. *Smooth as a baby's butt.*

The voice on the cell phone was too soft to make out, but Michele was apparently asked to provide more information. "I'm sorry, you're brea—ing u—," she replied, making herself sound like a bad connection. "Ca—you—peat that?"

The voice on the phone grew louder. "Who did you say you were?"

"Mi—Al—rich," she replied. "I'm just in fr——alt La——ity. Where can I fi—you?"

I made a mental note not to mess with Michele Aldrich, not ever.

The voice on the phone shouted, "Meet me in Sedalia. Do you know where that is?"

Michele glanced at me. I nodded. "Sure."

"There's a place there. The Sedalia Grill."

I mouthed, you can't miss it.

Michele said, "I'll be there in . . ."

I flashed fingers at her; both hands four times, then my right hand alone once.

Michele said, ". . . in forty-five minutes. How will I know you?"

"That won't be a problem, just get here," she said, and ended the connection.

Michele glanced at me. "She said 'here.' That means she's already at the meeting place."

"Maybe that's where she plugs in her phone to recharge it," I said dryly and swept a hand to one side to indicate that she should lead the way to her car.

DURING MOST OF the drive, I stared straight ahead at the traffic, which was already bunching up in the Friday afternoon scramble for cooler elevations. We were driving along the edge of the plains third of Colorado that I'd pointed out to Trevor Reed during our flight from Salt Lake City, about ten or fifteen miles from where the plains meet the mountainous third of Colorado. The air was clear and the view was gorgeous. Great billowing clouds were lining up for the afternoon's thunderstorms, a view I can never get tired of—as long as I'm not just down a narrow gully from where the clouds squeeze out their water. Flash floods and gully-washers are exciting but no fun.

As the traffic continued to thicken, I began to wonder if we'd get back to Denver in time for my dinner date with Fritz. I didn't want to have to phone him and delay. That wouldn't show him how I felt about him, however that was.

I was so preoccupied with Fritz that I momentarily lost track of where we were. As we passed the turnoffs for Highlands Ranch, I sucked in my breath.

"What is it?" Michele asked.

"It's grown even bigger!" I said.

"What has?"

"This housing development." I gazed in horrified fascination out across the sea of houses. They were huge houses painted pale shades of gray and packed impossibly close together. The development flowed away from the highway over the rolling plains toward the majestic peaks of Colorado's Front Range, which, with the lingering drought and summer's heat, were naked of snow. I rummaged through my file of mental images, trying to decide what it all looked like. The only match that came to mind was an ice floe riding coldly over a frigid sea. *Wrong,* said my brain. *It's almost one hundred degrees out there, remember? And why do they call it Highlands Ranch when it's down here on the lowlands?*

Michele said, "More things man does with his machines, huh?"

"Huh. I wonder where they get enough water to flush all those toilets. Hell, even if this drought were to end tomorrow, this ecosystem couldn't sustain this many people."

"What's the population out here, anyway?"

"Damned if I know. Metro Denver crested a million a while ago. And everyone wants to live here. Good-bye grazing land. Good-bye winter wheat. The land's worth more as house lots, I guess."

"Somehow I don't think you really believe that."

"No. I am the opposite of a cynic."

"What do you mean?"

" 'A cynic,' according to Oscar Wilde, 'is someone who knows the price of everything but the value of nothing.' This land has a high price—too high to graze cattle on it now—but I look at something like this, and it has little value for me."

"But at what price?" she said, cheerfully twisting my words.

I was trying to understand that myself. I was forty and single and childless, owned no home, barely owned a truck. In fact the bank owned more of that truck than I did. Was I taking my values too far? Was there a home on a nice piece of land with the right man and a bundle of joy waiting out there for me somewhere? And why, if I wanted all that so much, had I not found it yet?

Michele broke into my thoughts. "You're getting awfully quiet again."

"My thoughts cost more than a penny," I muttered. I glared at the housing development. Down among those streets lay not happiness, but capitulation. I could never be happy in a place like that, and I knew it. Shaking these thoughts out of my head, I said, "I was just wondering where the resources for this housing development came from."

"Resources? What do you mean?"

"All the lumber and the gypsum for the sheetrock, the latex for the paint. And the water. Where do they get their water? It takes a lot of water to fill all those pipes."

Michele shrugged. "From a reservoir?"

"Maybe. But where did the water come from that filled the reservoir?"

"Rain?"

"This part of Colorado gets maybe fourteen inches of rain per year. There are two sources of drinking water: precipitation and ground water. Either way, it's a reservoir. A surface-water reservoir is easy to understand; it fills a lake. A ground-water reservoir is more subtle."

"I've heard of underground rivers," Michele said, "but not underground lakes."

"Neither term is accurate. Ground water resides in the tiny spaces between the grains of sand in sandstone, or in fractures in crystalline rocks like granite. Or in partially dissolved limestones it can be in small caverns."

"How does it get to the well? Through the underground river?"

"You drill the well right into the reservoir rock," I said. "Ground water does move, but the term 'underground river' is a misperception. It moves very slowly and flows through the whole layer of rock." I smiled. "Denver has a true underground river called the Roberts Tunnel. It's twenty-three miles long. Denver ran short of water years ago. It now gets its water from a network of reservoirs on the western side of the Continental Divide that flow through the tunnel."

"What do the people on the W side drink?" Michele asked.

I waved a hand westward to indicate the far side of the Front Range of the Rockies. "Well, Denver doesn't take it all, but you're right, what Denver diverts to the eastern slope doesn't make it into the Pacific Ocean. The Colorado River starts just the other side of the divide and runs westward down through Utah, Arizona, and the corners of Nevada and California."

"But don't people downstream need that water?" Michele asked.

"Sure. People . . . raccoons, fish, bacteria, birds . . ."

"I did study ecology in school," Michele said, a little defensively.

"It's tough thinking these things through," I said. "It's not like we're aliens who just landed here to exploit the planet. We do manipulate our environment more than a raccoon or a fish does, but we're part of the ecosystem, too. We know how to treat the water so that the bacteria don't give us diarrhea, and we know how to dispose of our wastes in ways that don't foul the water. So more of us live to grow up than used to—in countries with poor sanitation, infant mortality skyrockets, and it's usually intestinal disease that gets them. But in places like this, we not only live to grow up, we live to grow old."

"Which is a good thing."

"Yes," I said, "and we've learned how to build machines that can move earth resources all over the place, bringing the gypsum for all the sheet-rock walls in all those houses in over the mountains and bringing the two-by-fours in from Oregon and the nails in from Michigan, or from wherever the iron mines send their raw resources to have them formed into nails . . . maybe somewhere in China now, for all I know."

"So our population keeps increasing, which is a bad thing."

Probably not a Mormon, I decided. "Yeah, and we've developed medicines that can kill bacteria even if we do screw up and drink fouled water, and we can keep people alive who have all sorts of diseases that used to kill them, which is good, but it means that there are more and more of us, which I agree is a bad thing, because we are using up resources, living long enough to think up new ways of polluting, and crowding out other species."

Michele said, "But we have effective means of birth control now."

Definitely not a Mormon. "Yes, we have birth control. But we also have huge appetites for comfort, which is only natural, so we build these huge houses, and we move in from Cincinnati where they have lawns, so we plant lawns here, too, and we have bigger closets now to hold all the clothes that were made for pennies over in China and we have to wash them all, and . . . well, getting back to that tunnel, all that uses a lot of water."

Michele said, "I'm glad I'm a homicide detective. There, things are black and white. Killing is bad. Figuring out who killed the dead person and putting them in jail is good. End of discussion."

I said, "But what if Afton McWain deserved to be killed?"

"Did he?"

"I don't think so, but you've already had a taste of how royally he could piss people off."

Michele contemplated this a moment. "I don't think anyone should get so mad he flattens someone an inch thick."

"We'll be in Castle Rock in ten or fifteen minutes," I said, changing the subject.

Michele glanced at me. "You know this area well?" she asked, deciding to change the subject.

"Well enough. I grew up in Chugwater, Wyoming, a couple hours north of here along this interstate highway. I went to college in Colorado Springs, which is forty-five minutes south of here, also just off the highway. So yes, I've been through here a few times." I watched the soft contours of the prairie open up now that we were escaping the buildup of homes. It was a landscape painted in the pale greens and yellows of sage and rabbit brush, broken by dry washes and stunted bluffs out into the country rock. How I loved the short-grass prairie in all its moods.

Beyond us to the west, the high peaks of the Rockies danced in the summer's heat, gathering up thunderheads with which to cool themselves in the coming hours. Call me romantic, but I love the drama of a good, pounding thunderstorm growling and flashing and hurling stones of ice—except of course if I'm caught out in it on horseback. "You turn off at the next exit and head west to Sedalia," I told Michele.

She piloted the rental car off the highway and headed along the two-lane blacktop toward our target. We passed a jolt of outlet stores—one of those clever streamers of modern consumer culture that attach themselves like remora on modest neighborhoods—but then the landscape grew increasingly rural, following the lower reaches of Plum Creek, where it was little more than a dry swale between undulating, tawny hills. Presently, we rounded a curve and came upon the Sedalia Grill. Michele turned left into the parking lot, nestled the rental car in amongst a crowd of motorcycles, and shut down the engine.

The structure was as vernacular as the outlet stores had been alien: patriotic to a fault and decidedly—nay, elaborately—rustic, with signs indicating that this was one whopping good place to get victuals, and, the pièce de résistance, the wall nearest to the parking lot was painted up as a gigantic American flag.

I let Michele lead the way into the building. Inside we found all the trimmings of your basic wayside Western watering hole: pool tables to the left, a well-stocked bar in the center, and to the right, a dining room packed with varnished rustic pine tables set into booths made from benches that featured hefty peeled and varnished pine logs for trim. Sad sucker songs twanging out of the juke box. Neon advertising Coors. Illuminated plastic sign displaying the Budweiser beer wagon and Clydesdales. Framed pictures of motorcycles. Menu listing jalapeño burgers. Local boys with tattoos and pool cues and summer cowboy hats with brims artistically bent and the sleeves of their cowboy shirts cut off. Ye-haw.

It wasn't difficult to figure out which member of the clientele was Gilda. She was the only woman in the place. Moreover, she glowed in the dark, or should I say she glowed in the carefully modulated gloom of the establishment. Gilda was golden. Her electric blond hair curled like a corona around her head, collecting and reflecting light the way clouds do at sunset. Her skin was smooth and creamy and seemed lit from within, and her eyes emitted the emotionless, glassy stare of an antique doll. She was dressed in an ankle-length, rose-colored knit chemise that draped like a million dollars. A necklace made of thin gold chains and tiny faceted gems lay across the oiled perfection of her neck, and on the patrician feet that extended from the hem of that dress, she wore the kind of sandals that come over trade routes on camel's backs.

But *this* was *Nature Girl?* Okay, maybe that dress was made of organic cotton, and she *was* drinking tea instead of the alcohol her companions preferred, and instead of hamburger, she had opened a lunch box filled with bean sprouts and, but really, now . . . *Nature Girl?* I calculated that she'd last about five seconds on a cattle drive, and if those pampered feet had ever stepped more than ten inches off a beaten path, I'd eat my Stetson.

As we approached the table, she extended a delicate hand that had never gripped any tool heavier than a silver spoon, but instead of offering it to be shaken, she raised it up and ran it lovingly through her hair. "Michele?" she said in a breathy, ethereal voice.

Michele gave her a nod that almost edged into a bow. "Yes, I'm Michele Aldrich. I'm sorry to interrupt your party. Who are your friends?" She indicated the men who had arrayed themselves around Gilda at the table.

"Oh . . ." said Gilda, as if she hadn't noticed them until Michele pointed them out to her. "Yes . . . may I introduce Hugo Attabury, Todd Upton, Bart Johnson, and . . ." She thought for a moment. ". . . Wayne Entwhistle." She stopped to breathe after this effort of mental acuity, her small but shapely breasts rising and falling slowly. She raised one eloquent eyebrow and glanced briefly at me. "Whoever you are, it seems you bring your own pilot."

I stuffed my hands into my pockets in a subtly insolent way and took a long squint at Gilda. I'll make no bones that I wasn't liking her very much. There was something funny about her, the kind of funny you don't want to laugh at. Nature Girl, my ass.

I tried to reckon her age. Were those the first crow's feet of advancing years I saw beside those dazzlingly spacy eyes, or was that just a shadow cast by her artfully arranged hair? I decided that she was my age or perhaps a bit younger. One never knows, when surgery can play such tricks.

After letting the conversation hang until the tension had built to a point of ripeness, Michele offered a smile but said only, "This is Em Hansen."

I measured the three men who were seated around Gilda. Only one of them, Bart Johnson, looked like he belonged in a cowboy bar. He looked like a cattle rancher who'd been reprocessed through an upscale Western-wear shop. He was considerably older than the rest, and, under the fancy pearl-snapped shirt and greased-back tatters of silvered hair, he was considerably more beat-up. He sat stiffly, and the one hand I could see was bent with osteoarthritis.

Hugo Attabury was a big, meaty fellow with a brush of colorless hair and a forty-dollar polo shirt, who was drinking an American beer out of a bottle. His arms crowded the tabletop, and his burgeoning paunch pressed against its edge.

Wayne Entwhistle had his beer in a glass. He wore wire-rimmed glasses and a short-sleeved dress shirt and looked like he'd been worked over with furniture polish along every inch of his rather globular body, including his caterpillar-like mustache. He had an over-compacted look to him that suggested to me that he was trying to go unnoticed.

Todd Upton sat under an antique sign with a bucking bronco that advertized explosives and blasting caps. He had a highball in front of him, serious drinking for so early in the afternoon. He was tall but built narrow and wiry, like a ferret. He had dark eyes that took in but emitted no light, and his thin shellac of hair had forsaken the crest of his skull. He wore a pressed, blue pinpoint cotton shirt with button-down collar, and one knuckle of his left hand was encrusted with a heavy gold class ring. I thought at first that the ring didn't go with the shirt but then glanced at Attabury's and Entwhistle's hands and spotted matching jewelry, right down to the color of the faux stones. Home-town boys. Judging by the variation in clothing, each had gone his own way for a while after high school but had returned to the fold and had fleeced it for a good living.

"What do you fly?" Hugo Attabury asked me, his tone an odd mixture of aggression and charm.

I locked eyes with him long enough to say, "Piper Cheyenne II," then returned my gaze to Gilda. Out of the corner of my eye, I saw him purse his lips appraisingly. Faye's plane is a fast, sleek, twin-engine job. If the big guy knew what a Cheyenne II was, that meant he was a pilot, too. But apparently a rude pilot: neither he nor any of his friends had gotten to his feet on our arrival or offered us seats.

Still standing, Michele got down to business. "Thank you for meeting with me. I'm afraid I bring bad news."

No one moved. Gilda did not even blink. The men stared at Michele like so many parts of one big animal, tense and ready to spring.

Michele took her time looking each in the eye, then announced, "I am with the Salt Lake County Sheriff's Department. Afton McWain was found dead this morning."

Nobody moved.

The moaning, groaning music from the jukebox, some sodden she-done-left-me song, flowed through the scene like molasses.

Michele put her hands on her hips. I realized that there was no place under that thin summer dress where she could have hidden a gun. Her slender body suddenly looked vulnerable, even as her face hardened.

Gilda began blinking at a hypnotically slow rate. Her great long eyelashes floated up and down like the peacock feather fans Indian servants wave over sahibs in B movies.

Several more long moments passed before Michele again dropped words into the strangely non-reactive tableau. "You are Mr. McWain's . . . ah . . ."

Michele at a loss for words? This was new.

Gilda opened her perfect lips and pronounced, "*Doctor* McWain."

"Did you hear what I said, ma'am?"

I felt blood pounding in my temples.

Gilda said nothing. One of the men cleared his throat. I think it was Todd Upton. Hugo Attabury began to shift his bulk in his seat, like a whale attempting to remove barnacles. Wayne Entwhistle chewed at one corner of his mustache, his eyes darting from one face to another.

I was ready to start kicking over tables when somebody finally opened his mouth and said something. It was the big guy, Hugo Attabury. He said, "Surely there's been some mistake." The line sounded hideously contrived. He blushed angrily.

Michele said, "No, Mr. Attabury, there has not. Did you know the deceased?"

Attabury erupted into a relative frenzy of motion, swiveling his huge frame from side to side like the whale was now trying to stand on its tail. "Sure, we all knew Afton."

Knew.

Michele's body tensed. She had heard it, too.

Attabury read her posture loud and clear. He said, "I mean, you just said he was dead, right?"

Todd Upton spoke for the first time. His voice had a kind of nervy restraint to it that was decidedly unpleasant, and his eyes twitched into slits as he spoke, which exaggerated the narrowness of his face. "I think we should see some identification, Ms. Aldrich."

Michele whipped out her badge, showed it around, replaced it in her pocketbook. I realized that she'd had her thumb on it, ready for the question. She waited, watching each person's moves. When the tension reached a level where it could have blistered paint, she said, "What have you been discussing here today?"

No one answered.

Michele asked the question again in a different way. "May I know what you've been talking about?"

Gilda said, "The weather. There's a drought on, you know. We were wondering if it might rain."

Wayne Entwhistle pushed his plate away as if the French fries on it had turned to worms. Bart Johnson shifted stiffly in his seat. Hugo Attabury put a thick hand to his lips as if trying to protect them. Todd Upton did not even blink.

Michele said, "So, okay, the weather. And what else?"

Bart Johnson said, "Michele, honey, we've just had some bad news here. You want to take it easy on us?"

Michele opened her mouth to continue her interrogation, but just then Gilda swooned. I mean she slid back in her seat and laid a slender wrist across her forehead and groaned, the most delicate little groan you ever did hear.

The men crowded forward to her aid.

I wondered what kind of performance I was watching. This woman was either off her bean or on some kind of drug or she was blowing a smokescreen around a lack of real surprise in hearing that her lover was dead, and I was willing to bet on option three.

A blur of activity that erupted around the table rendered Gilda onto her feet and out into the parking lot, where she stood wavering in the afternoon heat. In the full glare of the sun she looked peaked, even shocky, and I began to wonder if my prior judgment of her character might have been too harsh.

She turned to Michele. "Do you have a car?" she asked. "Yes, of course you have a car. Take me to the ranch."

Todd Upton put out a hand to stop her. "I'll take you there, Gilda." He gestured toward a late-model BMW, beetle black with black leather seats.

She turned and looked at him as if surprised to find him there, and said quite firmly, "No, Todd. This lady will run me home."

"But as your lawyer, I really think I should be there."

"No, I want to go without you."

He grasped her arm. "Don't say anything," he insisted.

Gilda wrenched herself free and walked toward the parked vehicles. The men headed to their cars. Johnson headed to an old truck, Entwhistle and Attabury headed to the shiniest and newest SUVs, and Upton stalked off toward the black BMW.

Michele unlocked the door of her rental car and hustled Gilda into it. "You just get yourself comfortable there and I'll get you home straightaway," she said.

I hopped into the backseat and settled in to eavesdrop, but was disappointed. Apart from giving vague directions, Gilda said absolutely nothing all the way to the ranch. Neither did she ask any questions. I had a nice view of the back of her head, period.

I followed Julia's map as we turned off the highway and started up a paved road past a jarring eruption of swanky new three-bedroom ranchettes and then turned onto a graded gravel road that grew increasingly rustic. I didn't have a good view of the odometer and was about to ask Michele where the turn to the ranch was when, just as Julia had indicated, a big, neurotic dog came barreling out of nowhere, barking its fool head off as it banked its trajectory to follow us along the far side of the obligatory barbed-wire fence. I saw flashes of fang and needed only a glimpse of the twin cowlicks of hair that ran the length of its back to know its breed. "A Rhodesian Ridgeback," I said. "Weird."

Gilda rolled her head laconically toward the dog. "Fucking psychotic," she told the animal crooningly, and to Michele she said, "You turn here."

Michele turned onto a rutted pair of tracks that led over a very bashed-up cattle guard and then headed off to the left, taking us away from the now-slathering hound. The rental car bottomed out repeatedly. Clearly, Afton McWain had put no money into grading his entry road. It had more washouts than an Ivy League college.

The ranch was a nice spread of grass and stands of Gambel oak tucked in among the hogbacks of red sandstone that flank the Front Range and I could see the first fists of the granites beyond them. It was a geologist's dream—the layers of upturned rock spanned hundreds of millions of years. For such an easy drive from a decent place to buy hamburgers and shoot pool, it felt wonderfully remote, having neither pavement nor power lines coming in from the road.

We came around a turn and into a small grove of cottonwoods, and there stood a strange assortment of small buildings: an old log cabin, a new prefabricated barn, a rickety privy, and a yurt. I hadn't seen one of those fabric yak-herder's tents in years, not since the last time I spent a weekend with chums from college who had been trying to have a commune. This layout seemed a bit more high-tech, in an eclectic sort of way. The log cabin had been retrofitted with solar panels, a satellite dish, and a glass lean-to filled with black fifty-five gallon drums, no doubt for passive solar heating. A wild system of pipes led out of a big, black water tank up the hill, feeding what I presumed to be a solar shower and what I was certain was a bathtub for fresh-air fiends. And, most classy among these features, a very expensive-looking windmill stood hooked up to the first piece of electrical cable I'd seen since we had left the gravel road.

"Just pull up by the house. I'll hop out," Gilda said.

"Can I use your rest room?" Michele inquired.

Gilda gave her a once-over. "I'd rather be alone. Can't you pee along the road on your way out?"

Michele gave her a broad grin. "That must be your outhouse over there. I won't be but a moment." Michele slapped the car into park and shut down the engine. She got out and headed for the little shack with the crescent moon on the door.

I took my cue and got out, too. I began to wander around, my hands stuck deep in my pockets like I was browsing in an antiques shop.

Gilda got out and stared at me. "Am I under arrest or something?"

"Should you be?" I inquired.

She shook her head, more like she was trying to snap out of a fog than to answer in the negative. "I just can't believe this."

"What?"

"Are you guys for real? I mean, I'm sitting minding my own business in a nice café, and you two drive up and tell me Afton's dead. Am I really supposed to believe this? It's not really true, is it?"

I stopped wandering and watched her. "I knew Afton," I said. "I may look like a pilot—well, I know how to fly an airplane, but not professionally, I don't have a commercial license—but in fact, I'm a geologist."

Gilda blinked. She kept watching me, her face limp.

"I knew Afton in Denver. I'm a friend of Julia's."

Gilda waved a hand dismissively. "Oh. Julia."

"Yeah. I haven't seen the kids since they were really little." I was getting really angry at this woman. Why? Because she'd just insulted my friend? Surely I had more compassion than that; a woman in shock over a loss of this magnitude could be forgiven for a lapse of manners, but the beauty-parlor hair, the expensive "nothing" dress, the exotic sandals, and the air of privilege had gotten under my skin. I struggled to get a grip on myself. "Was Afton still doing any geology?" I asked.

Gilda waved a hand toward the log cabin. "As long as you two aren't going to take no for an answer, it's up there," she said as she disappeared into the yurt, closing the canvas door behind her.

I headed over to the cabin double-quick. The door was locked, but I was able to see what I needed to see through the windows.

The one-room structure was neat as a pin but was clearly a site where work was being done. Two walls were lined with bookcases filled with geological texts. There was a flat file for maps and an old-fashioned drafting table and stool with plenty of work laid out on it. Proudly displayed on top of an old-fashioned oak file cabinet rested a four-inch tricone drill bit that had been bronzed. I recognized it from his office in Denver years earlier, when it had sat on his desk there. It was the completion bit from his discovery well, which had made Afton McWain a millionaire.

The remaining two walls were papered with geologic cross-sections, a type of diagram that geologists create to examine how layers of rock connect from one location to another. They represent vertical slices into the Earth. If you cut a chocolate cake in half and just looked at the inside, you'd get the same sort of view, except that rock doesn't tend to come in quite such tidy layers, and in fact, "layer-cake geology" is a term reserved for places where the rock layers are unusually flat and continuous.

Judging by the labels he had put on them, Afton McWain's cross-sections transected the Denver Basin north to south and west to east. Next to the "N" for "North" he'd also written "Greeley," which is a city at the north edge of the basin, and next to "S" for "South" he'd inscribed "Colorado Springs," which lies at the south. Instead of a town's name by "W" for "West," he'd written "Wildcat Mountain," which was apparently a topographic feature somewhere nearby, as just to the right of that he'd written "Sedalia." "E" for "East" was tagged "Last Chance," a town on the eastern plains of Colorado, about as far from civilization as you'd ever want to get a flat tire. I ought to know, I've done it, driving a cattle trailer for my dad back when he was selling off some bulls.

Remembering my cattle ranch beginnings was something that was bound to happen as I stood there staring into that log cabin. The original part of the house I grew up in on my father's ranch wasn't much bigger than this one, but Dad had kept it up proudly, leaving the insides of the logs showing as well as the outside, just as Afton McWain had done.

Looking into his workspace, I began to remember the parts of Afton that I'd enjoyed knowing, the same parts that Julia first noticed: his intelligence and his fastidiousness and his interest in the quality of life. On that same field trip where he'd showed off his buttocks, he had also made sure that everyone ate well, a detail that escapes a lot of field-trip organizers. Instead of hustling the ubiquitous box lunches with gummy white bread sandwiches and tiny packets of potato chips, he'd supplied deli breads, whole hams that he'd had run through a slicer, bricks of cheese, nice lettuces, and crocks of condiments. He'd understood that to get his point across, we had to be capable of learning, and a well-fed troop is a troop agreeable to paying attention. And he had indeed been a damned good geologist.

Michele came up behind me, fighting a smile that was clearly getting away from her.

"What's so funny?" I asked.

"Oh, it's that outhouse," she said. "It's like a shrine to rustic elimination. They've got the old corncob in the glass case marked IN CASE OF EMERGENCY BREAK GLASS, a 1962 Montgomery Ward's catalog, and, the pièce de résistance, the toilet seat is lined with rabbit fur."

"No pucky!"

"I sure couldn't. Man!"

"Well, Afton always was a sensualist," I said. "I wonder what Ms. Glamorpuss thinks of all that?"

"Oh, she left her mark. There's a big, square candle with "om" in Sanskrit, some very artistic sprays of sagebrush flowers, a signed photograph of some guru, and the aroma has a strong overprint of *eau de boudoir*."

I said, "The guru might be Afton's if he really got his butt enlightened."

Michele tried the door.

"It's locked," I said. "I already tried it."

Michele peered in the window. "What are you looking at?" she asked.

"I was just trying to figure out what Afton's been working on. It looks like the good old Denver-Julesburg Basin, just like old times."

"What do those diagrams tell you?"

I tried to sort out what might have any relevance to his murder. "On the face of it, these charts tell me about the thicknesses of sedimentary rock layers around here and how they vary from place to place. See that layer at the bottom, labeled 'Pierre Shale'? That's a mudstone layer five thousand feet thick in places. Next up, the Fox Hills Sandstone, which is a stack of shales interlayered with sandstones. Then above that, you've got the Laramie Formation. Swamps that got squished down to make coal beds and such."

"Really?"

"Sure. Above that, more sandstones—the Arapahoe, Denver, and Dawson. Some of those have more continuous sandstones. It looks like the Arapahoe is by far the best."

My geology lesson was interrupted by a sound from across the yard, a demure, "Shit!" We both turned to see Gilda emerging from the barn. She had a small satchel slung over one shoulder and grappled a cosmetics case in the opposite hand. "Good, you're still here," she called out. "I need a ride back to town."

Michele said, "Why?"

"Because my cart has insufficient charge."

"Your cart?" We crossed the yard to join her at the barn. Inside, we saw what looked like the big sister of a golf cart. It was clad in white Fiberglas, had a silly roof, and looked like it could carry two passengers plus a few parcels. I was reminded of what certain characters in cartoons from my childhood drove, a kind of latter-day tin lizzie.

Gilda's cheeks flushed with anger. "*That* is my cart. My *electric* cart. It is not much, but it can make it to Castle Rock and in fact has, on many occasions." She put down her case and pointed at the windmill.

"But *that* thing has not been turning enough to charge it. Do you understand English? The wind has not been blowing. When the wind does not blow, the blades do not turn. When the blades do not turn, the batteries do not charge. When the batteries do not charge, my cart does not make it to the nearest pavement, let alone as far as Castle Rock." She stamped her elegant little foot. "So I need a fucking ride, get it?"

Michele looked past the electric cart at a big, white truck parked behind it and asked, in her matter-of-fact way, "Why don't you take that truck?"

I added, "There's a loading dock just outside the barn here. I'd be glad to help you push that electric cart up onto the ramp and into the back of that truck. Then you can take it to town and plug it into the house current at the Sedalia Grill."

Gilda said, "That truck runs on *gas*. We don't use *fossil fuels* on this ranch! And the electricity at the Sedalia Grill is generated by coal-fired turbines, *another* unscrupulous waste of fossil fuel!"

I had to hand it to her, she had her consumption of the Earth's resources spot-on. I began to wonder if she had, in fact, adopted a low-impact lifestyle and wasn't just freeloading off of a rich man. Was every last cosmetic in the case she was carrying environmentally friendly? Or was there a little petrolatum hiding in one of her tubes or jars? I said, "I hate to tell you, but the resins in the Fiberglas your cart is made out of probably came out of an oil well."

Gilda opened her mouth to deliver additional invective, but she hung fire in mid-curse, her eyes going blank with thought. Suddenly her brow unkinked and her cosseted lips softened into an O. In the blink of an eye, her manner changed from shrewish to polite, even winsome. Fetching. Coquettish. "Wait a minute," she said. "Why don't I just ride with you to Salt Lake City in your airplane?"

Michele said, "I flew commercially. It's Em here that came by private plane."

Without missing a beat, Gilda turned and focused her charm on me. "Oh, then can I hitch a ride to Salt Lake City with you?"

I glanced at Michele, hoping for a cue as to how she wanted me to play this. "I, uh . . . don't own the airplane. I was flying a charter, see, and—"

Gilda's charm evaporated as quickly as it had appeared. "Then just into town will have to do. Unless you're going as far as Denver, in which case you can drop me there. Shall we go?"

It was Michele's turn to put on a winning smile. "What do you need in Salt Lake City?" she inquired. "Perhaps I can save you the trip."

Gilda gave her a "you dummy" look, then quickly transformed it into one of bereavement. "The sad task I must do can only be done by me," she said. "You see,"—she paused for dramatic emphasis—"I have to claim my husband's body."

Michele said cheerily, "I didn't realize you and Dr. McWain were married."

Gilda raised her chin regally. "Common law, my dear. We were man and wife under Colorado common law. Now, will you be so kind as to give me a ride to town . . . from *my* ranch."

8

MARY ANN NETTLETON DROVE DOWN THE ROAD IN SEARCH OF retribution. None of the men she had telephoned had returned her calls, and that made her angry, and that anger was now all mixed up in the anger she felt about her well going dry.

If they couldn't return her calls, she would pay calls on them.

She would go first to Hugo Attabury, the real-estate agent who had helped her and her dear Henry purchase the now waterless property, and, if she didn't get the answers she needed from him, she'd go to Todd Upton, the real-estate lawyer, and if that did not bear fruit, she would visit her banker, Wayne Entwhistle, at Castle Rock Savings and Loan. She did not know much about how these things worked—that had always been dear, departed Henry's domain—but it seemed reasonable to her that a purchase as expensive as real estate should come with some sort of guarantee, and if that guarantee was not backed by the real-estate agent who showed them the property and helped them sign all those papers that tied up their life's savings to purchase it, why then, a lawyer could tell her who was responsible, and if the lawyer was no help, then surely the banker would understand that it was in his interest as much as hers that she be able maintain the value of the property. Thirty thousand dollars to drill a well—ridiculous! She needed every penny she had just to make the payments on the mortgage!

Mary Ann hit the button to raise the windows of her SUV now that the air-conditioning unit had blown out the cauldron of hot air that had formed in it as it stood waiting for her in front of the garage with its windows up. The world around her receded as her rolling bubble of separation enveloped her with its steel- and vinyl-encrusted sense of well-being. She made the turn onto the two-lane blacktopped highway that connected her with the town, barely tucking in ahead of an oncoming truck. She glanced into her rearview mirror, wondering where it had come from so suddenly!

The truck behind her cruised up close to her back bumper and hung there for a while, then finally backed off a few lengths. Really, where did such monsters come from! Just driving to town was such a torment these days, since her wonderful Henry had gone to his great reward. How she needed him. How she missed him. They had had the perfect marriage: He had worked and made the money, and she had kept the home—kept it neat as a pin, as he used to say. What a daily pleasure it had been to make his favorite foods and have the house just perfect for him when he came home, his gin and tonic and a little plate with crackers and cheese waiting for him on the table next to his favorite chair, right next to the paper, which she thoughtfully laid on top of all those nasty bills. Henry would sit down and raise the footrest of the chair, sip his drink, nibble his cheeses, and read the paper. Only when the last cube of ice had spun down to the bottom of the glass and every crumb of cracker was dabbed from the plate with those great, thick fingers he'd lick to show her how much he loved her attentions, would he give her that wink of his and take the mail and walk into his study, where he'd lay out the invoices and write the checks. What a strong man. What a good man.

In the months before his death, he'd tried to show her how to turn on the computer and scroll through the electronic records of the checking account and the brokerage accounts that held their monies. He'd tried, and she'd tried, but it wasn't her forte, and she was so upset by everything that was happening—the trips to the doctors, his increasing dependency on her. She had never driven farther than the grocery store before, and suddenly she was driving him clear to Denver for treatments! No matter, Banker Entwhistle was taking care of all that now, he and his marvelous staff. Henry had seen to that in his last days.

The road led between the low bluffs, now dipping in near the bottomlands where a few willows grew. It was pretty, all this wilderness, but Mary Ann had to admit that a few doubts now came unbidden, now that Henry was not here to anchor this dream in place. Might she not be happier in a smaller house in a large town somewhere? She could move back to suburban Denver and be nearer her sister and friends, even walk to the store.

But none of this could happen if she had no water. No one would buy her property if they had to cart water from town even to wash their hands or take a drink, let alone flush a toilet or do the laundry! All allegiance to Henry's dream of a rural retirement was moot if it was rendered worthless by a lack of water!

These thoughts grew like thunderclouds in her head as she drove the last miles into Castle Rock and idled uncertainly by the traffic light, trying to remember which way to turn to get to Mr. Attabury's office. She looked left and right and finally spotted it. Well, that was one good point for living in a small town, everything was right there and easy to find! Feeling a flickering of hopefulness for the first time that day, Mary Ann turned the wheel and piloted the vehicle toward her goal.

She maneuvered the SUV into a parking space, turned off the engine, stepped down onto the blistering hot pavement, closed the door, and pressed the locking button on her key fob—beep, beep. Waves of heat enveloped her. Her new-found confidence leaching through the soles of her shoes, she climbed the five steps into the real estate office. She was surprised to see Hugo Attabury's inner office door click shut just as she entered the reception area. Always before, he had stepped out to greet her.

She gave her name to the receptionist. She waited while that young woman first turned to call through what was usually an open doorway and then, finding it closed, dialed and spoke into the phone, announcing Mary Ann's presence.

The receptionist's eyes widened at something being said to her through the earpiece. Putting down the phone, she informed Mary Ann that Mr. Attabury was in a meeting just now, and could she come back another day?

Mary Ann stood by the receptionist's desk, trying to think. It had never occurred to her that Mr. Attabury—that *Hugo* Attabury, good heavens, he must be two decades younger than she, young enough to be her son—would not be available, only that he might not know how to help. Certainly he had been amply available every other time she had been to this office, when they were first looking for property, when they were negotiating to purchase it, and when they came to sign the countless, confusing papers that made it their own and that obligated them—her—to pay for it.

Mary Ann Nettleton, who had until that moment never in her life raised her voice to anyone except in jest, opened her mouth and shouted, "What could possibly be more important than getting water to my house! The house he sold us! The house where I live!"

The receptionist goggled at her.

The door to Hugo Attabury's office remained closed.

Mary Ann Nettleton suddenly felt chilled to the bone. Her hands trembled. Overwhelmed with the enormity of her outburst, she turned and hastened back out the front door of the office, down the five steps, into her car—beep, beep to unlock—turned on the engine, and drove home, where there was not a drop to drink.

9

You may think that being packed into a car with a woman for nearly an hour—the time it took to bounce back down the ranch road from Afton McWain's ranch, wind our way back to the pavement, follow that pavement to I-25, and then to the first exit that would lead her to a major highway heading west—that we would have gotten some kind of information out of the amazing Gilda. But no. *Nada. Bobkes.* We got nothing. She barely spoke, except to say, "That turnoff will do nicely."

"Don't you want us to take you to the bus station? Or perhaps the airport?"

She shook her head. It was clear that she intended to extend her shapely thumb and catch a ride with the first tractor-trailer rig going her way, as her eyes were now fixed on a clutch of them that were huddled around a truck stop.

Michele pulled up and got out. She walked up to a group of truck drivers and said, "You know anyone who's going to Salt Lake today?"

"I am, baby," one driver said. "Can I give you a ride or *something?*" He was a big guy who looked like he knew how to order deep-fried cholesterol in five dialects and liked it served by waitresses with big tits. His buddies laughed sheepishly.

"No, but my friend here is." Michele pointed at Gilda.

The man's capacious lower lip hung even lower and grew shiny with saliva. "Sure . . ." he growled.

"Which rig is yours?" Gilda inquired.

The man pointed at a shiny Kenwood that was hitched to a moving van.

Michele looked toward Gilda. Gilda nodded an okay. Michele flipped her badge out of her pocketbook and showed it to the driver. "Great. What a nice man you are. Now, take Gilda to Salt Lake and drop her at this address." She handed him her business card, which gave the address of the Salt Lake County Sheriff's Department. "If you have any trouble along the way, you just show the patrolman my card." She gave one to Gilda, too. "But be a good boy, or we'll all be asking what happened to the driver of . . ." she glanced again at his rig—"Colorado license plate number JR–2623. Do I make myself clear?"

The driver pursed his lips. His fingers moved like he was playing a tiny piano. "Clear as glass."

Michele gave Gilda a wink. "Have a nice ride, lovey."

We watched as the big guy handed Gilda up into the shotgun seat of the rig, climbed up himself, buckled his belt around his girth, and revved his engine. The flap valves on his exhaust pipes jumped merrily, the modern-day equivalent of the knight's stallion rearing up in readiness. He engaged his automatic transmission, gave us a wave, and was off.

"What do you suppose that lady is all about?" I asked, as the rig climbed the ramp toward the highway.

Michele made a show of scratching her head. "Got me, but it's ornate."

"Oh, well," I said, "I guess it's not my problem anymore. I've done my bit."

"What do you mean?"

"I was done by lunchtime today. Or I could have been. All I need to do is write up my report, and you guys do the rest. The investigation, I mean. I could do a little more research about how long gravel quarry walls can stand without being disturbed, but other than that, I'm done."

Michele got a kind of puckery smile on her lips. "You sound like you'd like to do more."

"Well, some soil samples . . ." I laughed. "Yeah, sure, the old war horse smelling battle and all that. But I've learned my lesson: If I want to have a nice life, or much of a life at all, I'll stick within my specialty."

"I hear tell your specialty is broader than just gravel quarries."

"Oh, sure. I used to get myself into some scrapes. I'm content to leave all that to you cops now."

"Okay . . ."

"No, really."

"But if I have any questions?"

"Well, questions . . ."

"The man was in your profession. Geology. There have to be some connections I wouldn't know to make."

"Sure . . . that's the broad end of forensic geology: knowing the professional context. That's why I looked in the window at what he was working on."

"And what do you think?"

"I don't know."

"But you'll ask around."

"Okay." I was suddenly feeling less and less sure about much of anything, but I smiled and gave her a nod.

"Well, I've got to get back down to Castle Rock and make some more inquiries, but . . ." She looked at her wristwatch. "I'll drop you the rest of the way into Denver first. You'll have twenty minutes to spare. The Brown Palace, wasn't it?"

I nodded.

She laughed. "Want me to lend you a dress? I think we're about the same size."

I turned to her and put a hand across my heart. "Sister," I crooned.

THE DRESS FIT just fine, which is kind of amazing, considering that Michele and I were not built alike, and double-considering that I am not a wearer of dresses. The occasional skirt and blouse are within my sartorial lexicon, or, in the case of a five-star professional turnout, even a suit, but never a dress. I did not own one. I am a tomboy. I wear blue jeans by choice, and the fact is . . . if you put a dress on me, I feel like some kind of cross-dresser. But for some reason I could not quite identify, this one felt good. And it looked quite nice, even I could see that.

I slithered into it in the ladies' room just off the lobby in the hotel. It's a Rolls-Royce of powder rooms, featuring private rooms, not stalls, for your peeing pleasure and cloth hand towels that you use once and toss into an elegant hamper. I made good use of that room, primping as best I could with the materials that came to hand. For once in my life, I even wished I had a dab of lipstick, but native looks were going to have to do, just like always.

The dress was good, like I said. It was a lightweight, appealingly flimsy cotton in a kind of periwinkle blue that managed to put roses in my cheeks. In fact, the roses had found their ways there all by themselves. My pulse was pumping. I realized that I was truly looking forward to this dinner with Fritz.

He was waiting for me in the lobby, standing near the double doors that lead in off Tremont Street. I saw him an instant before he saw me, so I had the pleasure of gauging his reaction. His eyebrows jumped and he smiled warmly, a smile that spread into a grin.

He stood straight, his shoulders back but just a tad higher than usual. He's tall and handsome, in a down-home sort of way, and he looked marvelous in a linen suit jacket I'd never seen before, a crisp, white button-down shirt, and gray summer-weight wool slacks that draped his firm torso and muscular legs to good advantage. His hair was still damp from a shower. The effect was delicious.

"Hello," I said. "Looking for anyone in particular?"

With two long strides, Fritz came up next to me, but then he stopped awkwardly and gave me one of his trademark one-armed hugs. Or at least, this is what he had always given *me* for a hug. When he hugged Brendan, his son by his former wife, or little Sloane Renee—Faye's daughter—he used both arms with robust affection and kissed a cheek or nuzzled as the situation warranted, but what I got was a quick sidewinder, firm but brief. "M'lady," he said, now offering me his arm.

I slid my hand up into the warmth of his elbow and let him lead me into the restaurant.

The Ship's Tavern is done up to look like the aft galley of an old schooner. It's a comfortable place that serves nice steaks and other tried-and-true repasts, with just the right degree of the gourmet for a ranch kid like myself. Fritz had the maitre d' seat us over to the side under the windows where we'd have a little privacy, although the acoustics of the place preclude the subtlety of whispering. He ordered prime rib for each of us and offered me a drink, which I eschewed in honor of keeping him company. The standard pilot's motto of "eight hours from bottle to throttle" is considered prudent, and he had at least sixteen hours before lift off, but Fritz was not your average pilot. He wouldn't drink so much as a beer within twenty-four hours of taking to the sky.

Over iced tea and salads we talked about flying and where we thought we'd go hiking next. Over the main course we talked about his son Brendan, who was just about to turn eleven. I liked the kid. He was bookish and a bit of a couch potato in comparison to his father, but the two found plenty to do together. Fritz took him to the library a lot, and the two had become aficionados of Saturday morning garage sales.

"What does a boy that age want for his birthday?" I inquired, as dessert arrived.

"A little brother," Fritz said succinctly.

I choked on my after-dinner coffee.

"Don't worry," he murmured. "If you won't marry me and help me make him a sibling, I can always get him a dog."

By this point I was hacking into my linen napkin. When I finally pulled myself together enough to speak, I asked, "Doesn't your ex-wife have a handle on the baby production department?"

Fritz gave me a wolfish grin. He seemed to be enjoying putting me on edge. "Who, Marsha? Don't wait up."

"But she's remarried."

Fritz leaned onto the table with both elbows and studied me carefully. "I was truly enjoying this meal. Can't we talk about someone . . . or something . . . else?"

"I'm sorry. Has Marsha been misbehaving?"

"I'd rather not talk about it."

"I'm sorry."

Fritz's gaze dropped to the tabletop. "She and her new husband are thinking of moving out of the state."

"You're kidding! She can't do that, can she?"

"It's complicated."

"Tell me."

He took a deep breath. "Some things I shouldn't fight."

"But Brendan loves you."

"And I love him. And his stepfather has a career to look after. And that is important to Marsha." Quickly changing the subject, he said, "Do you want any dessert?"

"No. The waiter already brought it, remember?"

"I was thinking of another kind," he said.

"Of what?"

"Of . . ." He blushed. "Never mind. I'm out of line."

When I didn't reply, the look on his face faded from embarrassed mischief to concern.

I shook my head. "I'm sorry," I said. "It's been a long day."

"I meant to ask you about that. How did things go?"

"Okay, I guess."

"This was a friend of yours who was killed."

"A colleague. A friend's husband, or ex-husband, as it turns out."

"Did you find who killed him?"

"No. And I'm not going to. It's not my job." I found that I couldn't look him in the eye anymore. I stared instead into my coffee.

Fritz reached out a hand and covered mine with it. It was warm and dry. "What you saw this morning was a shock."

"Yes, it was."

"Do you have more work to do on it?"

"No, not really."

"Thank heaven for that. How did your friend take the news?"

"Shook her up."

"Of course."

Fritz signed the check and pocketed his credit card. "Come with me," he said.

We headed out to the lobby. Fritz handed his claim check to the doorman, who called the valet to bring his car, or should I say the black, late-model SUV that Trevor Reed kept at his condo in case he decided to go skiing. Fritz had told me about this condo. It wasn't far away, just at the other end of downtown in a reviving neighborhood called LoDo, where antique brick buildings stood side by side with newer, more earthquake-resistant renditions of the style. He said, "I brought the car in case there was anywhere you wanted to go." He guided the vehicle around the block to Eighteenth Street, from which he could access either LoDo or the highways. "We could run out to Golden and unscrew the light bulbs on the Colorado School of Mines 'M' if you like."

I laughed. "Been there and done that. It's a good way to get your ass kicked by the Blue Key Club. Besides, I'm not, uh . . . dressed for a guerrilla raid."

"Okay, we'll skip that then."

I said, "There's not much of anywhere to take a walk around here at night, unless you walk to where you're going instead of driving."

"Well, I screwed that up by bringing the car."

"I'm kind of tired, anyway. It's been . . ." The events of the day flipped past my eyes like a deck of cards being shuffled. "I'm just tired."

"Then we'll just call it a night. I'm assuming you'd like to stay at the condo?"

"I . . . yes, I'd appreciate that. I hadn't made other arrangements."

Fritz zipped into the subterranean parking garage. We stowed the vehicle and got out.

Fritz stood tossing the keys up and down in one hand. "I guess we haven't actually worked out the terms of . . ."

"Of, ah . . ."

He blushed. "Well, this is a one-bedroom unit. I'll take the couch in the living room. I checked. It folds out."

I felt my face growing hot, too. "No, I can take the couch. You've been too kind already. Bringing me here with your client was a risk, and dinner was great."

"It was my pleasure. And my client is not stupid." Fritz winked at me. "He likes to keep his pilot happy."

My face was now red hot. And Fritz looked really, really good in that jacket and crisp white shirt and gray slacks. And we were far away from everything I liked to use to orient myself and too close to the haunts where I used to jump in bed first and try to sort it out later.

"Come take a look," said Fritz. He placed a hand at the small of my back to guide me toward the elevator. It sent a thrill up my spine. Eighteen months I'd known this man, chumming around with him, enjoying his friendship, watching him date other women, avoiding thinking about how much I'd grown to like him, and never had he touched me like this. Like a woman. Always before it was that half-hug, quick and athletic, not warm and sensuous. I noticed that I wasn't breathing below my ribs.

At the top floor, Fritz turned a special key in the elevator and the door opened into a spacious bachelor retreat. Reed had a taste for the heavily masculine, trendy end of classiness and was clearly bent on accumulating the symbols that went with it, including in this case a loft with a view of the mountains and lots of empty space, stainless steel, exposed brick, and polished black stone. Folks call it black granite, except that it's another igneous stone entirely called gabbro, but either way you call it, it makes damned gorgeous countertops, and I found myself staring at it for something to train my eyes on.

Fritz took off his jacket and slung it over the back of a tall stool that fringed the galley counter and leaned back onto that twenty-foot expanse of shiny black stone. "Can I get you a drink?" he inquired.

"No, thanks."

"Coffee?"

"I'll be up all night peeing as it is." *Good one, Hansen,* I told myself. *Real romantic. In fact, stellar.* And thinking this thought, I realized: *I want to be romantic with him. A lot. And that scares me. A lot.*

Fritz tipped his head to one side and smiled softly. It occurred to me that it was my move. I knew what I wanted that move to be.

I asked myself why I was feeling as I was. Did I simply need to affirm life in a day in which I'd seen such absolute death?

Fritz waited, his hands out wide to each side, his strong fingers curled down around the edge of the counter, as still as the stone on which he was leaning. This was Fritz: a man of patience, of quietness of being, and yet a vision of strength and readiness. And I was his opposite: impatient, roiling with a need for action, unable to hold still for an instant.

I stepped toward him, stopped halfway.

He didn't move.

I said, "Thanks for dinner and for bringing me here. Very much. I appreciate it."

His hands tightened their grip. I could see the knuckles blanch.

I moved forward quickly, put one arm around him for that quick half-hug. He leaned into it, tucking his head down next to mine, cheek to cheek, but did not release his grip on the countertop.

I thought of bringing my other arm up to complete the embrace, but let go and stepped back. "Thanks," I said. "Thanks." I pointed over my shoulder at the couch. "I—really, I'd be glad to take the couch."

"No, that's okay," Fritz said slowly, still gripping the stone. "It's better that you take the bedroom. And—close the door."

I turned and started toward the bedroom.

He said, "And Em . . ."

"Yes?"

"You look really nice tonight. I like the dress."

10

RAY RAYMOND SLAPPED A FRESH MAGAZINE INTO THE GRIP OF HIS .40 Sig Sauer, pulled back the slide to chamber a round, and took aim at the silhouette target he had set up ten yards down the firing range. Imagining that the hulking shape was a man who was raising his own pistol to shoot him, he squeezed off four rounds in rapid succession, stitching the target neatly in the center ring.

The officer in the next station on the range leaned around the partition and spoke to him. "Nice shooting," he said. He raised his voice to be heard over the ear protection both were wearing.

Ray startled. "Eddie! I—I didn't know anyone else was here this late." He exhaled slowly, trying to let off the steam that was still building within him. Failing to relax, he turned back to the target and emptied the rest of his clip, released it, popped in another one, and emptied that one, too. Then, nostrils flared and lips tight, he packed up his gear and started toward the door.

Eddie set down his pistol and fell into step beside him. As the two came to the doorway, he put a hand on Ray's shoulder and stopped him. "What's eating you, Ray? You've always been a good shot, but today you were fuckin' *motivated*."

Ray shrugged.

Eddie mirrored the gesture. "Okay then, I'll drop it. You don't drink, so I won't invite you for a beer, but I see someone steaming like this and I think, hell, you ought to rethink your religious strictures and find something that can let you relax a little."

Ray stared at the floor.

"It's that Em Hansen, ain't it. I heard you had to go get her and take her to that bad kill at the quarry." He gave Ray a friendly punch in the shoulder. "Forget her, man. Besides, ain't she hanging out with Fritz Calder?"

Ray's eyes went bright with concentration. "Tall guy? Stands like a soldier?"

"That's my man. He was a flyboy for the navy in the Gulf War. Drove an A-6. Nice guy. You'd like him. Relax, he's okay."

"How do you know him?"

"We play racquetball together sometimes. Us ex-military stick together. Hey, how about that Michele Aldrich? I hear she's available."

Ray said, "A bit young for me, don't you think?"

Eddie pursed his lips appraisingly. "Personally, I like 'em tender, but to each his own. But you're right, she's probably trouble anyway."

"What do you mean?"

"Oh, haven't you heard? She got crosswise with the chief, and he's gunning for her. She wasn't his hire. Someone else's pet. When he took over the section, he found her a little too young and cocksure for his liking. He has no use for her a 'tall. So he's hung her out to dry on this job. Her partner's laid up in the hospital, but the chief went ahead and sent her to Colorado without a replacement."

"She went *alone?* On a job that dirty? That had organized crime written all over it!"

"You know that, and I know that, but she don't. She reported in a couple hours ago and was all hot about some scene with a bunch of local boys in a biker bar somewhere, says she's sure one of them is our dream date."

"She walked into a *biker* bar? *Alone?*"

Eddie shook his head. "Don't worry, Michele ain't alone. Your Em Hansen went along with her."

Ray squeezed his eyes shut. "That was all I needed to hear."

"What is it with you, Ray? That woman can take care of herself. Or at least, if she wants to get her ass in a crack on every case, she can the hell take responsibility for it. Squeegee her out of your mind, man."

Ray shifted uncomfortably from foot to foot. "But I saw Em's truck parked at—" He caught himself and clammed up.

"She musta caught a ride with Fritz. She coulda rode over to Colorado with him on that charter he was flying. I guess I shouldn't be telling you all this, huh."

"Huh."

"Sorry, man."

Ray pushed the door open and started down the hall. "See you around, Eddie."

The other man stayed by the door. "Hey, I'll keep it to myself next time, honest."

Ray turned and looked at him, now backing away. "Eddie, you are a fountain of information. Keep me informed."

"Okay. You want in on the pool how many chunks they come home in? It's five bucks."

Ray turned his back quickly on Eddie so the man couldn't see his face.

Eddie called after him, "Hey, sorry, man. I was just kidding!" But Ray was already slamming another door between them.

Ray leaned forward and quickened his pace, but he knew he could not outrun his fears.

11

I DIDN'T REST WELL IN TREVOR REED'S BIG BACHELOR PAD BED. I felt lost in the wide expanse of satin sheets and weirdly alone, even though, when I cracked the door quietly and listened carefully, I could hear Fritz's deep, rhythmic breathing in the next room.

It was still dark out when I gave up on sleeping, having awakened from a dream filled with falling gravel and parched ranches gobbled up by houses that floated like corks on a sea of dust. The unwelcome image of Afton McWain's corpse kept flashing across my consciousness, and I kept thinking about Julia and the kids. And then there was the puzzle of Gilda, who, all her beauty and style aside, had to be about the oddest woman I had met in a month of Sundays. I wondered if she had made it to Salt Lake City yet or if she was stuck in some truck stop somewhere staving off the advances of the big guy Michele had chosen for her.

Even as the warm light of dawn filled the room, it was too early to see if Fritz was awake, so I grabbed the phone off the bedside table and dialed up my old friend Carlos Ortega, figuring that a cop would know to shut off the phone if he didn't want calls at odd hours.

Carlos picked up on the third ring. "*Hola,*" he said sleepily.

"*Hola,* yourself. This is Em."

"Emmmily! *¿Qué pasa, Chiquita? ¿Y dónde estás?*"

"*Estoy bien, gracias, ¿y tu? Estoy en Denver.*"

"*¡Qué bien! ¿Desayuno? Un momentito . . . ¿es sábado, verdad?*"

"Yes, it's Saturday. You don't have to work, do you?"

"No. Come on, have breakfast with me."

"*Desayuno* would be great."

"Where are you? I'll come get you."

"I'm . . ." Just then, I heard a knock at the door. *"Momentito,"* I told Carlos, and to Fritz, I said, "I'm awake."

"Do you want some breakfast?" Fritz inquired from behind the door.

"Sure . . . ah . . . hey, I'm on the phone with an old friend here. Carlos Ortega, he's on the Denver homicide squad. He knows some great little breakfast joints. What say ye?"

There was a pause, then, "Sure. Um, do I have time for a run? And a shower?"

"Yes."

"See you in thirty, then." I heard the elevator call button ding.

To Carlos, I said, "I have someone I want you to meet. All three of us for breakfast?"

Carlos laughed mischievously. *"¿Un hombre?"*

"Sí, un hombre. Es muy nice guy. You be nice, too, okay?"

Carlos's laugh became a deep chuckle. "Always you can depend on the proud Mexican."

AN HOUR LATER, Carlos pulled up in front of Trevor Reed's swanky condo building in a beat-up Toyota sedan. I jumped into the backseat and gave him a squeeze from behind his neck, and Fritz folded himself into the front. The two men shook hands, Carlos's chubby, dark digits an interesting contrast to Fritz's long, pale ones.

"Nice to meet you," Fritz told Carlos.

"Mucho gusto," Carlos replied. "Aieee, Emily, too many years!"

"Verdad, Carlito. *¿Y dónde está el desayuno?"*

Carlos laughed. "You lost your sense of smell, *mi corazón?"*

I sniffed. Indeed, I caught the whiff of *chiles, queso, frijoles,* and *salsa,* but I connect such aromas with Carlos, so it hadn't occurred to me that he'd brought food with him. "Where is it? Gimme some!"

"In the trunk. In the cooler, staying hot." He laughed again.

I leaned back and inhaled. "Smells glorious. So what's the deal? Are we going on a picnic or something?"

"*Sí*. I feed you, you inform me. *¿Está bien?*"

"What do I look like, an informant?"

"A teacher, then. You can cure me of my ignorance."

I slapped my hand across my chest in mock agony. "What? My old teacher wants me to teach *him* something?"

He chuckled. "Today, the information flows only one way: First, tell me why you're in Denver."

"Never! You'll pry it from my cold, dead fingers."

"We have methods, *Cariño*. These are the *finest* burritos."

I leaned back, considering a way to counter his game. "Okay, drive out toward Morrison, and I'll show you what I'm up to."

He launched into a question-and-answer session that took us from my exodus to Utah to maybe marry Ray, to the eventual and inevitable breakup, to grad school, to my current status as a geologist with the Utah Geological Survey. Carlos is good at interrogation.

When I leaned on him for news, he reciprocated in his coy way, giving me as few clues to his personal life as possible except for updates on his many siblings and other family members. Little Salvador was through high school and in the navy—where did the years go?—and Esperanza was pregnant with number three. And so forth. It was a pleasant reunion.

As we gabbed about Carlos's family, he tooled westward along the Sixth Avenue highway through Lakewood and turned south on Union Street, just west of the Federal Center, taking the scenic route toward Morrison. He turned right on Alameda Parkway and headed west around Green Mountain—which by Colorado standards is a glorified hill—and headed into the valley that lay along the foothills. Running down the center of the valley was a fin of rock four miles long that rose up from the valley like a great wave breaking westward.

"So, Emmy, you were going to tell me what brings you to Colorado."

"No, I was going to show you. I'm your teacher today, remember?"

"Okay, what's on the syllabus?"

"Dinosaurs."

"Oh, terrible lizards. Very appetizing. Then I stop at the ridge, *¿ver-dad?*"

"*Sí, bueno.*"

Fritz was looking back and forth between the two of us, as if watching a tennis match over his shoulder. "Can I be in on the joke?"

Waving a hand at the landform in front of us, I said, "This hogback is called Dinosaur Ridge."

"Hogback," said Fritz.

I said, "So-called because it stands up from the surrounding lands like the spine of a razorback hog. A hogback forms when the layers of rock are tilted up—like I was telling T-revor rex—and the more resistant layers stand proud while the softer rocks are eroded into valleys. This resistant layer is called the Dakota Sandstone. It stands up between the mudstones of the Morrison Formation and the Benton Shale."

Fritz said, "Your riverbed sandbars and beaches laid down when the continent got bent in the middle and the sea came through from Texas to Alaska."

My jaw dropped. "And I thought you were just flying the plane yesterday."

"You explained it well," he said. "A smart pilot always listens to his B/N."

"His what?"

"Bombardier-navigator."

"But most people can't sort out all those names that quickly, let alone remember the sequences of the rock layers!"

Fritz gave me a satisfied smirk. Man, did he have my attention!

We neared the hogback. It had been a few years since I'd been out to Dinosaur Ridge, and I was pleased to see that Rooney Ranch was still there, the oldest continually run family-owned ranch—or just call it open space—in the Denver area. The ranch house was built of Dakota Sandstone back in the early 1860s, when the 200-acre ranch was homesteaded by Alexander Rooney, and it's now occupied by his great-grandson Otis. A second house, which Otis and his brother Al built back in 1952, had been converted into a small museum. We drove past several life-sized models of *Stegosaurus*—the Colorado state fossil—sporting wild paint jobs, from American flag livery to renditions of modern art. People were having fun with science.

I had Carlos drive over to the other side of the hogback—the older side, geologically speaking—so we could examine the rock layers in the order they were deposited. We parked the car and, carrying the picnic cooler and a jug of coffee, started up the interpretive trail that follows along the displays by the roadside, stopping here and there to admire the dark fragments of dinosaur bone that protruded from the rock. Presently, Carlos sat down in the shade of one of the interpretive signs, opened the cooler and pulled out the wonderful-smelling burritos. "You must eat. You need your strength to teach someone as thickheaded as me."

"Oh. Yeah. I keep forgetting that you are *estupido*." I dropped down next to him and greedily bit in. The big flour tortilla was filled with *chorizo* and *huevos revueltos* with all the trimmings. The luscious juice of kidney beans cooked long and low with just the right spices and rich with sour cream swept through my mouth and warmed my heart. The *jalapeños* bit hard, and the sun was already heating the rocks, but in that moment I loved heat in any form.

Carlos said, "So why are you here?"

I said, "I'm eating."

Fritz let out an appreciative "Mmm," as he swallowed his first mouthful, then said, "She hitched a ride with me to tell an old friend that her former husband had been murdered. You know Em, she knows how to party."

I swatted him on the knee.

Fritz bit into his burrito again and moaned with delight. "This is the best burrito I've had in ages!"

I thought, *I like this is a whole lot better than playing tennis.*

Carlos said, "You and I are going to be friends, Fritz. So tell me about this dead former *esposo de tu amiga,* Emmy."

I did. I gave him the whole nine yards, right down to the calculated weight of the gravel and the resultant thickness of the corpse, just to pay Fritz back for spilling my story. "But you didn't hear any of this, Fritz."

"Any of what?"

Carlos furrowed his brow. "You shouldn't be talking about a case this freely, Em."

I nodded. "You're right, of course. But Fritz has a high-security clearance. If I can't trust him, who can I trust?"

Carlos shook his head and averted his eyes. He went back to eating, something he did for both pleasure and therapy.

He was right, I had made a mistake. Was I showing off for Fritz? I quit talking and ate.

Carlos licked the juice off his fingers. "I should put you in touch with Tim Osner. He investigates clandestine gravesites. He's a geologist, like you. He volunteers his expertise to the police and sheriff's departments here in Colorado. When we find a buried body—or can't find a burial we know has to be out there—we always call him in. We get so much more information, tighter cases. Always before, we just looked at the corpse, mostly, but Tim finds information for us by the way the corpse was buried."

"Such as," said Fritz.

Carlos opened a jug of coffee and poured some for each of us. "Actually, I've never worked directly with them," he said. Unlike me, Carlos knew how to keep his mouth shut.

I said, "Such as . . . how deep is the grave? That gives a clue about whether the killer was in a hurry, and there are others just in the way the grave is dug. Here's an example from a case that we can discuss: a young woman was found buried in a shallow grave in the dirt floor of the crawl space underneath her family home. Her brother confessed to the murder but said it was a crime of passion, said she was shaming the family by threatening to marry outside their faith, and that someone had to set her straight. After the coroner removed the body, the investigators carefully removed the soil until they had the bottom of the grave. And they noticed they had desiccation cracks in the soil."

Fritz tipped his head to indicate that I should explain.

I said, "Desiccation means drying. If you have a lot of clay in the soil, it will shrink as it dries and crack, just like a mud flat. They have archaeologists in their crew as well as geologists. And biologists, and all sorts of specialties. So what do the geologists on the team say? 'Move over five feet and dig another grave, just alike. Time how long it takes the cracks to form.'"

Fritz said, "And how long did it take?"

I raised my coffee cup in a toast. "Seven days! A full week. Some crime of passion, eh? He'd been passionately waiting for a week for her to come home and get murdered."

Carlos waved his hand dismissively, then licked his thumb. "Murder two became murder one."

I slurped my coffee appreciatively. It was piping hot and laced with cinnamon.

Carlos said, "Now, about this teaching . . ."

"Okay," I said, standing up so I could address my little schoolroom. "What we have here is not unlike what your Tim Osner does. You see, the rock tells just as much of the story of what happened here as the bones do. Paleontologists learned that lesson the hard way. When these rocks were first quarried for bones back in 1877, they just blasted the bones out of the rock—they used dynamite—and left as much rock behind as possible. They considered it waste." I pointed up the rock face in front of us. "Look what they missed."

Fritz said, "It's all clouds to me, B/N. What am I looking at?"

I said, "Those bulges in the rock. What do you think they are?"

Fritz shook his head. "I don't know. Are they anything special?"

I nodded. "They're dinosaur footprints."

"No." He got up and stuck his nose quite close to the rock. "Where?"

"Look at the way the sandstone protrudes down into the layer of mudstone below it. Something heavy stepped in the mud, and then it was filled in with sand."

"I never would have noticed that," he said.

"And I can't fly a jet the way you can. There's a great deal more information here. The way the rocks are interlayered—sand, mud, sand—tells a story, too. And if you follow the Morrison Formation rocks along the mountain front, you'll discover that although the whole thing's bent up into a hogback now, it was once as flat as a pancake. And if you follow it far enough, you'll find the plant fossils that represent what the animals ate. All this tells the story of what life was like then. And then there's the story of the animals' death. That's right here in front of us."

Fritz and Carlos both squinted at the rock.

"No," I said, "it's not something tiny. In fact, you've got to step back and sweep your eyes left and right to see it. See how far apart the bones are scattered? And the way they're in the sandstone rather than the mud layers? Think it through. Mud settles out of slow-moving water; sand, by contrast, equals fast equals flood. These are the bones of animals that came apart after death and got dumped along a sandbar in a river. It must have been one hell of a flood."

Carlos sighed. *"Magnifico."*

I continued with my lecture. "In other dinosaur quarries, you'll find the bones still articulated. Those were dinosaurs that lay down and died without getting swept away and torn apart. Other places you'll find the bones have been chewed before they fossilized. The kinds of clues are endless."

"¡Qué bueno!"

"Here's something else you'll like: In some kinds of fossil remains in particular—oyster beds or fossil trees—we sometimes find the fossilized organisms arranged as they were found in life. A whole fossilized reef, for instance, that was suddenly covered by sand during a huge storm but not displaced. That's called a life assemblage. Other places, like this, the creatures were swept away from their life zone and dumped in a disorganized heap. This, my dear Carlos, is a death assemblage."

Carlos laughed merrily as I led the way up over the crest of the hogback and down the other side.

Fritz asked, "What kind of dinosaur were we looking at?"

"Several kinds," I said. "As I recall, they were your big long-neck guys—*Diplodocus* and *Apatosaurus*—and some *Stegosaurs* and maybe an *Allosaurus* or two. The first time I saw this hogback, none of these interpretive displays were here. I came with a field trip for my freshman geology class."

Fritz winked at me. "Eighteen-year-old Emmy. Now, that would be interesting."

"It's a classic teaching site," I said, feeling my face grow hotter than the day dictated.

We walked on until we faced an immense slab of rock that was rhythmically pitted by impressions the size of dinner plates and larger. Fritz said, "Okay, this time I don't have to be told: These are more footprints, right?"

"Yes, that's a whole dinosaur trackway. On the other side of the ridge, we were looking at footprints in cross-section. Here, they're in map view."

Fritz held a hand out parallel to the rock, which the forces of mountain building had bent up at least thirty degrees off the horizontal. "But this rock wasn't at this angle then."

"Imagine a gently sloping beach that went on for miles along a sleepy ocean."

Fritz stood with mouth agape, like a big kid. "Dinosaurs coming down to swim."

"No, probably dinosaurs using the beach as a highway. They may have been migrating from south to north and back again. It's late Cretaceous, so the plants were flowering."

"Plants didn't flower before the Cretaceous?"

"Flowering plants evolved sometime in the Jurassic, after those dinosaurs died and left their bones back there and before these dinosaurs walked by over here. I forget the exact date."

Carlos said, "It was a Thursday, wasn't it?"

I laughed at myself. "No, if you adhere to a literal interpretation of the Bible, I think flowering plants showed up on the third day, which would have been Tuesday, or perhaps Wednesday, depending on whether you count Sunday as the first day or the seventh, and . . . or how about *español*? *En el dia de tres, Los Dios creatár los árboles y todos los otros vegetales y los flores, y todos están bueno.*"

Carlos laughed so hard that tears ran down his cheeks. "Oh, Emmy, I've missed you so! Your Spanish is so awful!"

"*Gracias, Carlito.*" I pointed at the nearest track, a three-pronged, two-inch-deep concavity in the sandstone, about a foot or so long. "That's some sort of ornithopod, an herbivore who walked on all fours most of the time. Maybe she could rise onto her hind legs to forage for juicy flowers. It's thought to have been something like an *Iguanodon,* your ol' duckbill gal. Over there," I pointed at a narrower, pointier track, only nine inches long, "that guy was some kind of carnivore. Perhaps *Ornithomimus.*"

Carlos said, "And the point is that police investigators often miss much of the evidence that is right in front of them."

I nodded. *"Exactamente.* Nowadays, paleontologists know to examine the sediments the bones are found in, because it's full of trace fossils like these footprints, not to mention microfossils, and the minerals themselves say much about the environment the animals lived in."

Fritz said, "It tells us not only how they lived, but often how they died."

I nodded. "So that, Carlos, *mi corazón,* is what I've been up to, continuing to use the techniques I have learned as a geologist in the service of crime investigations." I added, "You were good students today. You both get A's."

As we retraced our steps to the Toyota, Carlos said, "I've missed you."

I put an arm around him, drawing him close. "And I've missed you, Carlos."

Fritz had wandered ahead a little ways. Carlos put his lips close to my ear and whispered, "I like this one, Emmy. Don't let him get away."

❖

THE AIR OVER Colorado and eastern Utah was calm, making for a gentle ride home over the mountains to Salt Lake City. T-revor rex snoozed in his seat until the air grew choppy as we came over the Wasatch. Tall clouds were building, portending an afternoon of thunder and lightning.

Fritz was quiet, except for the requirements of radio communications. He listened to the frequency for Denver Center until that controller handed him over to Salt Lake Center and from there he was handed to Salt Lake Approach, which lined him up for a straight-in approach on Runway 35. This took us within spitting distance of Point of the Mountain. Far below us, several hang gliders floated in the mid-day heat, oblivious to the scene of carnage beneath their feet. I wished I could see back in time, to know who had taken my old colleague to that death assemblage. The image of Afton McWain's corpse returned to my mind's eye with sudden force, and I shifted my gaze abruptly to my pilot and friend.

He was flying with only his left hand on the yoke. The growing turbulence might have seemed jarring to our passenger, but to a pilot trained to fly a two-seat jet off an aircraft carrier into the worst kinds of weather through anti-aircraft barrages, it was nothing. Between slight adjustments to the throttles and an occasional tweak of the electric trim switch on the yoke, his right hand lay calmly on his thigh, only inches from mine.

An urge rose within me. I thought about it for only a moment before I acted on it. Looking straight forward, as if nothing interested me more than the view out the windshield, I laid my hand on top of his.

Out of the corner of my eye, I saw Fritz smile. He curled his thumb around to give my hand a brief squeeze, then lifted his hand to put the flaps down to their final notch for landing.

12

By the time I had the plane tied down, the clouds were growing dark with rain. "Now that I'm on the ground," Trevor Reed said, "I'm glad the clouds are building. It'll cool things off this afternoon, and I've got a tennis date this evening." He turned to me. "I checked you out with some of my contacts this morning. You're not *just* a geologist."

This startled me. "What did you hear?" I blurted.

"That you work for the Utah Geological Survey. That you are a forensic investigator." He raised his eyebrows impishly. "And that you weren't just along for the ride yesterday. You were on a case."

I cocked my head to one side. "Who were you talking to?"

Reed grinned. "A smart man never exposes his sources. But let me know if I can ever help. To an investments specialist, information is everything. I do a little detective work myself some days."

I watched dumbfounded as he hopped into his car and drove away.

Fritz was in something of a hurry, as he was due to pick up Brendan in under an hour. Dropping me at the UGS parking lot, where I had left my car, he got out and gave me his patented one-armed hug but bent into it a little more, giving me the full expanse of his chest. I matched his hug, and then brought up my other arm, hesitated only a fraction of a second, and put it around the other side of him.

He broke the hug without reciprocating and backed away, smiling inscrutably.

Had I misunderstood his gestures over the past twenty-four hours? I did my best not to show my uncertainty.

Fritz turned and strode away toward his car. As he reached it, he turned, facing me fully for just an instant, but in that moment he brought his right hand up to his heart, touched it gently to his chest, and then turned it toward me. With one last smile and nod, he got into his car and drove away.

I drove quickly home, ran upstairs, unlocked the door to my apartment, dove inside, and slammed the door behind me. For what reason was such adrenaline pumping through me? Fritz was my friend, someone I could trust. I knew I could trust him. And yet I had no idea what he was trying to tell me through his gestures. I had hoped that he would squeeze me close, even kiss me. Had he decided that he saw me only as a friend, just as I was beginning to realize that I wanted more?

I told myself to calm down and forget what had happened over the last thirty-six hours, but I was tired and wired at the same time. I asked myself again if my growing desire for Fritz was just a reaction to seeing another friend brutally murdered.

Who had killed Afton McWain, and why? I shuddered, once again reliving the sight of his mashed body. Whoever had done that was deeply angry with him or felt nothing for humanity in general. Was it one of the men at that bar in Sedalia? I mentally scanned their faces, trying to decide which among them might have been covering his native brutality. Even in the heat of the day, I felt cold at the thought.

A light was flashing on my telephone answering machine. I turned to it, anxious for something else to think about, and punched the PLAY button.

A familiar voice crackled out of the speaker. "Em, this is Ray. Uh . . . this is Saturday, and . . . I'm down at the station, and . . . well, there's a woman here who says she knows you and that you're going to give her a place to sleep. Her name is Gilda. Didn't say Gilda who, just Gilda. Said you'd know. Um . . ." His voice grew increasingly discomforted. "Uh . . . either way could you please give me a call? If not here—I'm off at four—then, uh, at home?"

I punched in Ray's direct number at the police station. When he realized it was me, he sounded extremely relieved. "So can I bring her to you?"

"Well, I think so, but how'd she get to you? Michele Aldrich gave her a card, so shouldn't she be at the sheriff's department?"

"Oh, she was there, all right, but Michele wasn't. They wanted to question her, but she's not their dream date." The pitch of his voice was rising.

"Ray, old pal, you don't have to explain. I got a dose of that woman yesterday, so I read you loud and clear. She's persistent. Let me guess: She couldn't find Michele, who I take it isn't back from Colorado yet, so she's going after me, and they handed her to you. Ray, my dear, she is an accomplished mooch. So tell me: What did she want from the sheriff's department?"

"Can't talk just now, your friend is returning from the ladies' room." He sounded almost giddy, as if the woman was tickling him, which is not something Ray Raymond would enjoy. That would be too much like not being in control of what was happening to him.

I looked out the window at the dark clouds that hung all moist and threatening over the mountains. The scene was set for trouble. "Bring her over," I said.

We signed off and I hung up the phone. I stared at it a moment, relieved to find myself in the middle of an emergency, especially as long as it was something as ludicrous as this. The heap of energy I'd brought home now had a place to run.

TWENTY MINUTES LATER, Gilda stood in the middle of my glorified one-room apartment, her head swiveling this way and that, taking in the lay of the land. She had walked in like a customer checking into a hotel, dropping her satchel in the middle of the floor. If I'd had a little desk bell for her to ring, I'm sure she would have rung it. Ray had set her cosmetic case next to her, releasing the handle as if it were made of something sticky.

"Hi, Gilda," I said. "How was your trip?"

DEAD DRY ◆ 107

"Terrible. Do you have any filtered water?"

"No."

"Can you *boil* some water, then? Perhaps with an inch of raw ginger root in it. If you have organic." She examined my habitation inch by inch. When her gaze panned onto a print of a Remington poster I'd put on the wall, she scrunched her nose up into a tiny sniff.

Snob, I thought. I considered showing her the door, but curiosity won out over irritation. In my best East Coast lockjaw accent, I said, "I'll put the kettle on. Why don't you take a seat?" I pointed at the only chair in the room, which was right next to the only table. The matching chair was out on the tiny sun porch.

I switched on the gas under the kettle and stepped out onto the porch to get the other chair. A gust of wind from the coming storm slammed the door shut. Ray opened it for me, in a panic to not be left alone with Gilda an instant longer.

I thought, *He's down past monosyllables, all the way to hand gestures. This woman really freaks him out.*

Without waiting for an invitation, Gilda picked up her gear, wandered into my bathroom, and closed the door behind her.

Ray burst into action. He whipped out a pen and grabbed a piece of scrap paper off the table. Leaning it against the wall, he scribbled, *Please remember everything you can get out of her. The sheriff likes her.*

I nodded. "Likes her" meant "thinks she killed him."

Ray crumpled the note and stuffed it into the kitchen trash, making sure it was buried underneath something wet. Then he froze in the middle of the room with his mouth open, as if there was something else he wanted desperately to say.

"Don't worry," I said, keeping my voice down to a whisper. Then I mouthed, *I'll call you.*

Ray nodded, glanced once toward the bathroom door, and beat a hasty retreat down the stairs.

The kettle whistled. I switched off the gas and pulled a coffee mug down out of a cupboard and put it on the table.

The sound of water escaping the toilet, followed by more water swishing down the sink, emanated from the bathroom. I thought she'd be coming out then, but I heard still a third water sound now. The shower.

I considered going through her gear but she had taken it in with her.

I sat down and waited. Ten minutes passed, and the water kept running. I supposed that if I'd been up all night riding in a semi with some guy who hadn't bathed recently, I'd be ready for a shower, too, but it annoyed me plenty that she hadn't asked, and it downright smoked me that she was using up so much water. They don't call Utah a desert for nothing.

Fifteen minutes later, the water finally stopped running. I wondered sourly if she'd simply run out of hot.

The door opened. Gilda emerged, her hair wet, rubbing it with one of my towels.

We looked at each other.

She said, "Don't you have a hair dryer?"

"No," I said, although this wasn't true. It was in a suitcase in my storage area in the basement, but I was damned if I was going to go get it for her.

I gestured toward the mug. "The water already boiled," I said. "The kettle's over there on the stove."

She approached the table and inspected the mug without touching it.

"It's clean," I said.

She nodded but looked doubtful. "How long did you leave it boiling?"

"It boiled. I turned it off. That was fifteen minutes ago, while you were showering."

"Would you turn it back on and this time leave the kettle boiling for a few minutes, please."

I considered telling her to take a walk through a cactus patch but instead reached over and switched the thing back on and flipped up the gadget so it wouldn't scream. "I suppose you need something to eat, too," I said.

Gilda stared at me. "I have things in my bag," she said. She opened it and pulled out a plastic container. She selected a small health-food bar featuring flax seeds and set it on the table next to the mug, her hand hovering for a moment as if she wasn't quite certain it was safe to set it on my table even if it was still fully wrapped. As if finally noticing the rudeness of her manner, she said, "These are rich in anti-oxidants. I have to maintain my skin." She then returned to the bathroom, which she had left strewn with tubes of cosmetics, combs, hairbrush, and lotions.

My anger swelled like a balloon and then popped. Suddenly, I felt sorry for her. She had only one bit of merchandise to take to market, and it had a pitifully finite shelf life.

Gilda folded her legs carefully to position herself over her satchel, dug through it, and produced a ceramic tea ball and a tin of tea marked with Chinese characters. She came back out into the room, busied herself about the task of decanting exactly one teaspoonful into the ball, screwed that shut, and set it gingerly into the mug. She stared at the kettle for a moment, then faced me again and addressed me as if I were an assistant attending her in surgery. "I suppose that's long enough," she said.

My sympathy evaporated. Glaring at her, I sat down, leaving the pot boiling.

Two pink spots appeared on her cheeks. She stared at me until she felt she had made her point—which was, no doubt, that I was a hideous host and cruelly lacking in compassion—and then picked up the kettle and poured. When she was done, she set the kettle down straight on the tabletop—no trivet—and sat down to dunk her tea ball.

"Holy shit!" I shouted, jumping up to move the hot kettle back to the stove before it burned a mark into the wood. "What, can't you—"

I realized that she was crying.

I sat down again. "Sorry," I said.

As if in mockery of her tears, rain began to pound the windows, great thudding drops that hit almost as loud as hail.

I said, "I suppose you've been through a lot in the past twenty-four hours."

She swiped delicately at her nose with one fragile hand, not quite touching the nostrils, for that would be uncouth.

I hoisted myself to my feet and found her a box of Kleenex. I sat down again and said, "So how'd it go down at the county?" I'm not subtle, but I figured that if I asked, she might say something.

"Th—they wouldn't let me see Afton," she whimpered.

I almost said, *You wouldn't want to see Afton,* but I managed to quell the urge. Instead, I asked, "Why not?"

"I'm—I have no record . . . of our . . . I have to present proof that I'm next of kin."

"Ah."

I waited, hoping she'd say more. Minutes slithered past, and she sipped her tea, keeping her eyes on the tabletop the entire time.

I said, "Do you plan to keep the ranch?"

She stopped and stared at me as if I'd just asked if the sky was blue. "Yes, of course."

"But that's a lot of work for . . . well, you see, I grew up on a ranch, so I know a bit about how much work it is to live so far from town, and . . ."

"Afton taught me to appreciate the land," she said primly. Then she went back to sipping. When she was done with the tea, she removed the tea ball, emptied the spent leaves from it—into the cup—and stood up.

I wondered what to do next. Was I supposed to keep an eye on her? I decided that such a task wouldn't be difficult, as she would no doubt ask me to drive her wherever she wanted to go next, but she surprised me yet again. "I'll just lie down for a while," she said and without further ceremony walked over to my bed and stretched out on it. She turned once and looked at me expectantly. "It's rather cold with that breeze blowing in," she said, and added, rather accusingly, "My hair's still wet."

At least she hadn't presumed to climb in between my sheets, but then again, she probably found them lacking.

I took in a long, slow breath and let it out. Then I got up and found her a blanket.

13

THE PHONE RANG AT 5 P.M. GILDA STIRRED, OPENED HER EYES briefly, and then closed them again. I was amazed that she could sleep that long in a strange room and under that blanket. Thundershowers had cooled the neighborhood, but it was still pretty warm in that room.

It had stopped raining, so I took the phone out onto the porch. It was Michele on her way in from the airport. "I have a visitor," I told her.

"I know," she said. "I've been in communication with my office, and they put me through to Ray. What have you gotten out of her? Anything?"

"She's been asleep. I take it she was up all night."

"Rough way to travel," Michele said. "So we can presume that the lady has no available cash."

"Perhaps it's a part of the green lifestyle. Don't waste resources. The truck is going through anyway so it can carry me, too."

"Nah, I'm calling her broke. So you think she killed him for his money?"

"You like that diagram?" I asked.

"What? Oh, I get it, you're speaking in metaphor in case she's listening."

"Yeah."

"No, I don't think she's the heavy lifter in this job, but I think she's got a part in it."

"Tell me more."

"Oh, as in, what did I learn after I dropped you in Denver?"

"Yeah."

"Not much, at first. It took me until this morning to get a warrant, and when I got back up to the ranch, there wasn't much to see."

"Nothing there?" I asked.

"Nothing at all. Well, the yurt just had clothes and stuff, nothing of interest, but McWain's office had been stripped."

"No shit!"

"None whatsoever. The question is of course who did that and, as importantly, why, and that's your department. Who wanted that geological information he had there? Why was it important? Or worth killing and then breaking and entering to get?"

I said, "Gotcha. I'm on it. But there's another way to ask that question."

"Which one?"

"The 'Who wanted it?' one. You can want the stuff, or you can want the stuff to go away."

"Ah."

"So what else can you tell me?"

Michele hummed into the phone, thinking. "I can give you this: All four men we met at the Sedalia Grill had alibis. Or shall we say, I haven't been able to bust them yet."

"And?"

"And tell you more?"

"Yeah!"

Gilda opened one eye and looked at me. I offered her an apologetic grin and, after a moment, she sighed and turned her back to me.

Michele said, "Well, I didn't question them all myself, so what can I say? Ernie Mayhew—the sheriff's deputy there—he questioned two of them without me present and he came along with me for the other two. That was pretty messy."

"How so?"

"Well, like you told me as we were driving down there yesterday, the place until recently was a very small town. So they all knew each other. Seems all of those men played football together at Castle Rock High, along with Mayhew. It was almost like a social occasion, like, 'Let's all humor the female from Utah.' "

"And you were spoiling their party with the questions you asked."

"Precisely. Mayhew as much as suggested that whatever happened to McWain happened in Utah and had nothing to do with anybody in Colorado."

"Could be."

"And pigs have wings."

I asked, "Which ones did you see personally?"

"Upton and Attabury. The latter was particularly tight with Mayhew."

"Wait, of the other two, you say they *all* were on the team?"

Michele said, "What? Oh, I get what you're saying. No, Bart Johnson wasn't on the team, but his son, Zachary, was. You didn't meet him. He's a hapless sort, pours drinks at a place in Sedalia called Bud's Bar. And so you don't have to figure out how to ask me, yes, it's just the two of them—Bart and Zach—out there on that ranch. Mrs. Johnson is dead, and you'll recall that Bart hasn't much time left himself, by the looks of him."

"Okay. So what's their beef?"

"Ah, a cattle ranching joke, huh?"

I smiled. "Don't mess with me."

"Okay, here's who those guys were: Attabury, the big one—"

"Who knows something about flying," I interjected.

"He does? Yeah, well, Attabury is a Realtor. I asked him if he sold McWain his ranch, or rather, if he was the broker on that transaction, but he said no, and he seemed grouchy about that."

"He's local?"

"They all are, like I said. Anyway, uh, let's see . . . Upton, the preppie guy with the narrow face and the BMW, he's a lawyer. Specializes in real-estate law, estates, that kind of stuff. Then there's Entwhistle. He has the local savings and loan, holds a lot of local mortgages."

"Belonging to anybody we know?"

"I couldn't find out about McWain's ranch, whether that was mortgaged or not, but I'm working on it. I had hoped to get those records from his office, but as I said, by the time I got there, they weren't."

"Ah."

"The last guy was Bart Johnson. He owns the adjoining ranch to the north."

"The one with . . ."

"The barking dog. You'll love this. The dog's name is Barker."

"Perfect. And?"

"And what?"

"Gossip?"

Michele didn't say anything for a moment. Just when I thought we'd lost the connection, she said, "A woman at the ice cream shop in Sedalia says Attabury and Johnson are involved in a development project called Wildcat Estates, and that McWain is part of a citizen's group that opposes it. I'll bet—hey!" She broke off and hollered at someone who was cutting her off in traffic. Then, she said, "So I'll come over to your house, okay?"

I looked back into the room. Sleeping Beauty's eyes were open and she was looking at me. "Fine. Let me give you directions."

Michele chuckled. "I know where you live. I'm a cop, remember?"

"WHAT WAS DR. McWain doing in Salt Lake County?" Michele asked Gilda.

Michele had asked her this in the car as we drove her to Denver the day before, and Gilda had stonewalled us. Today, she was merely uninformative. "I don't really know," she said, infusing her voice with the deep, breathy tone of the tragic heroine.

Michele decided to be blunt. She said, "You know, Gilda, there's some mutual back-scratching to be done here. You give me information and I'll see if I can open doors for you at the morgue. You understand?"

Gilda put a hand to her heart. "*Would* you take me there?" she cried.

Michele raised an eyebrow. "Surely he said something to you. How long he'd be gone, who he'd be with?"

Gilda turned both palms upward in a poetic gesture of innocence. "He just said, 'See you in a few. Hold down the fort.'"

"A few days? A few hours?"

"You know men." Gilda sighed. It was quite a performance. She was playing the We-Poor-Girls chip. "Afton was a . . . a free spirit."

That was an image for the ages. *Nature Girl meets Free Spirit, coming to a theater near you.* I asked, "Was he out here to do geology? I mean, was it a professional trip?"

"He really didn't do much of that anymore."

"He'd given up geology?"

"Pretty much."

I said, "But when I looked in the windows of his study I saw that he had work spread out. It looked to me like he was working on something."

She shrugged her shoulders. "He fiddled around a little, I suppose. There's not much to do on a ranch with no electricity or running water, you know."

I suppressed a derisive smile. *Sure, nothing to do but water the stock, keep the buildings and fences repaired, cook three meals a day . . .*

Michele asked, "Did Dr. McWain take any luggage with him when he left home?"

Gilda waxed prim. She was sitting on the edge of my bed with one leg folded over the other, and she now drew herself up narrow and steepled her fingers over her knee. "Such as?"

"A suitcase with a change of clothes," Michele said. She managed to keep her voice even through this ridiculous question.

Gilda blinked glassily.

I said, "How about an attaché or a small backpack? Surely he had to carry notes or field gear."

Gilda's eyes widened ever so slightly, but both Michele and I saw it. She said, a bit too emphatically, "Afton never took anything with him, anywhere."

"Why?"

She hesitated, then said daintily, "Afton had taken a vow against consumerism."

Michele said, "A vow?"

"Yes. One should not purchase that which is being cast off as waste."

"Wow," I said, "I'd like to see the other nine commandments on that list. So you mean he was into scrounging pens and paper if he needed to write something down."

Gilda fluttered her lavish eyelashes and waited for the next question.

In the afternoon light that was coming in the west windows of my room, I took a good look at her. Yes, there were decided crow's feet forming around those genteelly made-up eyes, and the skin underneath her jawline was just starting to soften. What did that make her, forty-five? Had she ever actually married, or was she just an itinerant opportunist who moved in with wealthy men to the detriment of their marriages? She couldn't play that game forever. She must be feeling the need to nail down a nest egg before her flesh descended any further.

Michele asked, "So does that mean he was into hitching rides the way you do?"

"Oh, yes," Gilda said. "In fact, he taught me that ethic."

Ethic? This was an ethic?

Michele said, "So then, is that how he got to Salt Lake County? We've checked all the public transit for the past several days and have come up dry. And you say he didn't own a car."

Gilda raised her bird-like shoulders in a tiny shrug. "He hitched a ride, I imagine."

"In a truck, like you did?"

I had to be paying very close attention to catch the ever-so-slight tensing that whipped through Gilda's body. How I would have liked to have her wired up to a polygraph machine.

Michele let silence hang for a full minute. She had seen Gilda's lapse, too. She asked her question again in two different forms, but Gilda had seen her error in this chess game and had moved her queen back into the defense of her king, whoever that might be now that Afton was dead.

At length, Michele said, "Why was he dressed the way he was dressed?"

Gilda countered with, "How exactly was he dressed?"

While Michele pondered her next move, my mind tumbled down a rabbit hole of speculation. What had someone as vain and arrogant as Afton McWain been doing wearing worn-out clothes? It didn't jibe with the prosperous Afton I remembered strutting his masculine stuff in the hot springs and lavishing his field trips with top-end foods. Where had his money gone? And what had drawn him away from his professional circle to a run-down ranch?

Something about that ranch was bothering me. A ranch is a small economy unto itself, a closely-managed system of resources, especially one that is "off the grid." I said, "Hey, Gilda, where were you guys getting your water out there at the ranch?"

Gilda froze like a pin-ball machine that has just gone TILT.

Had I asked something important? Or was she one of those creatures who knew absolutely nothing about the origins of the natural resources she consumed in such quantity? I said, "I mean the water you drank. What you washed in."

Irritably, she said, "From the tap." As in, *where else, silly?*

"And how did the water get into the tap?"

She began to look a little insulted, as if I were making fun of her. "Why, out of a pipe, of course. Afton was in charge of all of that."

Michele said, "Why do you ask, Em?"

"Oh, it's nothing. It's just this drought. It's the worst I can remember, and yet even in lesser droughts, there were years when we were hauling water from the creek to water the horses. So I was just wondering, what with this green lifestyle stuff and not driving a car or that truck in the barn, how you got your water."

Gilda said, "I do not know," enunciating the words sharply, as if they were separate sentences.

Michele let the silence widen again. Finally, she said, "So now, Gilda. I understand that you came here for a purpose, and that perhaps your purpose has not been completed. How can I help?"

Gilda's response was explosive. "I need to see his body!" she cried, flailing her hands. "I need to have . . . have . . ."

Michele shot me a warning glance. *Don't finish her sentence for her,* her eyes told me.

I clamped my lips together and waited.

Gilda looked back and forth between us, measuring our response to her performance. "I need *closure*," she said finally.

"Okey-dokey," Michele said, getting up from the straight-backed chair in which she'd been sitting. "Get your satchel and cosmetic case, honey, and let's have us a visit to the morgue."

14

About ten minutes later, I made a colossal mistake. I phoned Fritz and invited him to dinner. This was a mistake because he wasn't alone. In fact, he didn't answer the phone. A friend of his did. A woman friend. "Hello?" she said, in a mellifluous voice.

"Oh, I must have the wrong number," I told her.

"Are you calling Fritz?"

"Yes."

"I'm just answering for him. He's in the shower." She laughed, as if there were some joke I should understand.

"I don't mean to interrupt," I said.

"Who shall I say called?"

"Nobody. I mean—"

"Wait, here he is!" she said triumphantly.

There was a short pause, during which I dearly wish I'd broken the connection, but I couldn't remember if I'd given my name.

Fritz came on the line. "Hello, who is this?"

"Oh, it's Em. Sorry to interrupt. I didn't know you had company."

He paused awkwardly. "Um, that's uh, okay. What's up? I mean, I'm sort of busy now, but is there something you need?"

"Want to go for a hike tomorrow?" I asked, trying to sound like good old hiking pal Em.

"Uh, no. Tomorrow's kind of booked."

I heard the woman's voice in the background again. "Fritz! Dinner's getting *cold*, Big Guy!"

Big Guy? "I'll let you go," I said.

"Okay. I'll give you a call."

"Great."

"See ya 'round."

"Ten-four." As I hung up the phone the world went all dim around me.

IT'S ALWAYS SAID that if a horse bucks you off, it's best to get right back on, but in this case, the horse in question was busy, so the only solution was to get busy, myself.

The only thing busy enough to take my mind off of what was going on at Fritz's house was Afton McWain's murder. Afton's murder got me to thinking about Julia's reaction to the news, and thinking about Julia reminded me that she had been planning on coming to Utah for some kind of convention. Any convention Julia would attend would be geological in nature, so why couldn't Afton have been here for the same reason?

I reached for my laptop computer, fired up a search engine and screened for SALT LAKE CITY, the date, and CONVENTION, which gave me the schedule for the Salt Palace Convention Center. Unfortunately, there was nothing listed that might even remotely have drawn the likes of Afton McWain—or Julia, for that matter.

I got out her number and dialed.

"Hello," she said, her voice heavy with dejection.

"Julia, it's Em," I said, already matching her tone. "I'm sorry I took off so quickly yesterday. I wanted to . . . to find out how things are going."

"That's okay, Em," she said, an edge working into her tone. "I was getting kind of worked up, so why stick around?"

"I deserve that."

Silence, then, "I'm . . . just . . . so *mad* at Afton, going and getting himself killed! I mean, what was he thinking? Sure, he hadn't done dick for the kids for a year or more, let alone have the decency to communicate with *me* unless it suited him, but really, getting himself flattened under ten tons of gravel!"

My stomach about dropped out of my body. "H-how did you know that, Julia?"

"What?"

"Where he was found."

"The gravel quarry? Under a collapsed bank?" she said. "Shit, Senator White just phoned half an hour ago, told me all about it. Wanted particulars for her eulogy, in case she can get some air time out of it."

"Who's Senator—"

"She's a Colorado state senator. Serves on some sort of commission or committee. Apparently Afton got her to appoint him to a task force. What a roast. 'Task force' is one of the most meaningless buzz-terms government hacks have to offer the world, right up there with 'stakeholder' and 'we'll review this and then revisit our decision.' Just the sort of thing Afton was into these past few years."

"What do you mean?"

"Always looking for something noble to do so he could qualify for canonization. Afton, the geology saint. Shit."

Afton McWain involved in politics? His ego was big enough, but geologists typically stay out of such frustrating wrangles. "What task force, exactly?"

"Ground water."

"What about ground water?"

"More like, 'What ground water?' We're running out of it, in case you hadn't noticed."

"But how did Senator White hear about the quarry?"

"An investigative reporter for the *Denver Post* called her for a comment. She told me all the grisly details, said it was going to be in tomorrow's paper."

"Wait, *investigative* reporter? Why—"

Julia laughed derisively. "You didn't know about Afton's involvement with the Clearwaters Project?"

"No . . . what's that?"

"Shit, Em, you really have been gone from Colorado for a while. Clearwaters was a proposed development down along Jackson Creek, south of Afton's blessed ranch. Afton advised the citizen's group that opposed it."

"But why investigative . . . that makes it sound like there was some dirty doings," I said grabbing a piece of paper and a pen so I could take notes. Michele had to hear about this, and soon.

"There's been a lot of speculation. Rumors of unmarked black helicopters coming and going from there, and one promoter had a record of swindling in another state. Afton and his pals hired a private investigator who used to work for the FBI, and he said there were maybe connections to the Chinese mafia or something. They managed to block the development, which would have turned a 2,400-acre ranch into a country-club-style setup with over a hundred luxury homes, half as many cottages, and who knows how many holes of golf."

"Not my idea of ecosystem conservation, no."

"They *said* they were going to leave two-thirds of it in open space, but a promise like that is no comfort once the camel's nose is under the edge of the tent, and you've got a bunch of pampered fat cats driving golf carts around the wild plum trees and chokecherries and scaring off the game. And besides, where's the water for all those spas and steam rooms and golf greens? The whole thing looked like a big drug-running and money-laundering scheme to Afton. He wanted to 'leave the dry-lands for the coyotes'—I think that was his personal slogan."

"Coyotes. That sounds like him. But let's get back to this investigative reporter. How did *he* hear that Afton was dead?"

"He quoted the guy who drove the front-end loader and found the body." A fresh wave of rage swept over Julia, and she tried to take me with her. "So why didn't you tell me this? Huh? You left me to get it the hard way!"

"I was ordered not to talk about it," I said guiltily, biting my tongue before I could add, *You didn't have to see what I saw.*

Julia decided to use her advantage to grill me for further details. "So, how'd you like the lovely Gilda?"

"Well . . ."

Julia said, "Okay, so she's a looker. Ha, ha, ha on Julia."

I said, "Come on, Jules . . ."

"I think I'll take up drinking. Don't you think? A nice fifth of vodka might really cheer me up about now."

I said firmly, "Booze didn't work for my mother. Or her children."

Silence. Then, trying to pull herself together, she said, "Well, nice of you to call."

"Not all that nice. In fact, I'm looking for information."

She laughed raggedly. "Well, at least you're honest. Good old honest Em. Okay, let 'er rip, Sherlock."

"That conference you were coming here to attend. Where was that being held?"

"Snowbird. Why, you want to get into the ground water game?"

"No, just chasing down some possibilities. We're trying to figure out why Afton was in Utah. Maybe as part of that task force he—"

"Could have been," she said. "Trust him to not tell me he's going to be out of the state on a child custody weekend *and* make it to a conference I myself was *going* to attend."

I said, "Julia, get a grip! This is beneath you."

Silence.

I said, "What is it they say in Al-Anon? 'Resentment is like taking poison and expecting someone else to die'?"

Nearly spitting with frustration, she said, "What, are you a Twelve-Stepper now?"

"An old boyfriend's into it. It's not hard to memorize their slogans, and there's wisdom in them even if they grate on the nerves."

She was silent for a while, then sighed. "You're right, I should get off my pity pot. So tell me, do you think I'm obligated to throw the man a funeral? Or do I get to leave that to Gilda?"

"I don't know. Who's his next of kin?"

Julia said, "The kids are."

"Then you do right by your children. Schedule that memorial service. Have all your old buddies from the oil patch attend, and I mean 'your' plural; they're your buddies, too. You'll get closure, and the kids will get a view of their father in his prime, because you know? Lots of people held him in high esteem."

She sighed again. "You're right," she said, and suddenly she caved through her anger into her pain and began to weep for the man she had loved.

MY NEXT INTERNET search delivered me to a meeting of a group of regional ground-water societies, which were holding a summit in Snowbird starting the next morning. It was my experience of such meetings that if they were in session on Sunday, they'd have registration open Saturday evening.

I telephoned Ray. *He* at least had the decency to be home alone. "Hey," I said. "I need to run up to Snowbird and find out if Afton McWain was here to attend a meeting there. Want to come?"

"Well . . . why do you need my help with that?"

"Why? Oh, come on, Ray, meetings at Snowbird are 'for old time's sake' with you and me. Besides, if I go in there and flash my Utah Geological Survey ID it's going to mean nothing to them, and I need to get into their records. I thought a cop would get them moving."

"Shouldn't you ask Michele instead? This murder isn't my jurisdiction, Em."

"Michele's down at the morgue with Miss Wonderful."

Ray laughed nervously.

I was making progress. "Pretty please?"

"Okay," he said. "I'll be there in fifteen minutes."

◆

IT WAS GETTING on past dinnertime, so I got Ray to stop at the Lone Star Taqueria for take-out fish tacos, which we managed to drip all over ourselves as we drove up the tight curves of Little Cottonwood Canyon. We were laughing and getting pretty well relaxed by the time we pulled into the lot at the Snowbird resort.

"What's the conference about this time?" Ray asked, as we got out of the car and started toward the conference hall. "The last time we were here for one of these, it was all about dinosaurs."

"Ground water," I said.

"Right." He pushed open the door to the conference hall. "Whatever."

Everything went smoothly. Ray flashed his badge at the appropriate moments, and the lady at the registration tapped into the electronic list of attendees. Sure enough, there were two McWains: A for Afton and J for Julia. "Your Afton McWain is scheduled to speak at the plenary session tomorrow afternoon. Is there anything else we can do to help?" she asked, looking nervously at Ray.

I said, "Would you be so kind as to issue me a complimentary pass, just for tomorrow?"

The woman jumped on it. Anything to get rid of the fuzz, I suppose.

Before heading hack to his car, Ray and I took a walk along Little Cottonwood Creek, reluctant to give up the cooler air that rested at that elevation. Evening was quickly descending, and with it, the scented air of even higher slopes. The first few golden leaves twinkled on aspen trees high above, and a crescent moon hung on the western horizon.

"So how's life been treating you, Ray?" I inquired, making small talk.

"Okay."

"Ooo! A one-word answer! Something's bugging you, old friend."

"Emily . . ." He hunched his shoulders and dug his hands deeper into his pockets.

"I'm sorry. I seem to be stepping on your toes lately."

"No, you're not," he said, too quickly. He stopped walking and squared his shoulders as if preparing to make a speech. "It's I . . . I'm stepping on yours."

"Nonsense," I said. "What do you mean?"

Ray flung his hands wide. "It's none of my business who you sleep with!"

My jaw about hit my toes. *"What?"*

He held out a hand in panic. "That didn't come out right."

"You're damned straight that didn't come out right! And just who in hell's name do you think I'm sleeping with, smart guy?"

His face flushed with embarrassment and anger. "The man you were with yesterday morning?"

I exploded. *"Fritz?* You think I'm sleeping with *Fritz?* Oh, bull*shit* I'm sleeping with Fritz! He's . . ." What was Fritz to me anymore? "He's just a friend," I said firmly, then, with defiance, added, "But maybe I would sleep with him, if he'd have me. So what's it to you?"

"Just . . . just be careful!" he said, his voice cracking.

I stared at him. "What's eating you, Ray? It's not like you to butt in like this."

"Well . . . what if you're . . . pro-choice," he said miserably. "You could get into—"

"I *am* pro-choice, Ray! The government has no right to say what goes on inside my body, and as importantly, populations stabilize and societies flourish when a woman has control over her reproductive choices and *not* just because she can end a pregnancy if it's going to ruin her life and those of everyone around her! I'm for *preventing* unwanted pregnancies before they happen. That's because I'm pro-life as well. Abortion is a damned ignorant, last-ditch way of dealing with things, but you either respect every last one of my choices or you don't really respect me at all. It's all one ball of wax, Ray. A woman has to keep the keys to the castle or it becomes a prison." I ran out of steam. "Now tell me why we're having this conversation."

"Because you should be protected from . . . from . . ."

I shook my head. "Ray, old friend, I'm living my life as responsibly as I know how."

Ray squeezed his eyes shut in frustration. "I know . . ."

My anger spent, I looked on my friend and felt instead his concern. "Ray," I said gently, "You grew your beliefs from the outside in— received them from your family and your church—and if that works for you, I'm glad for you. But I get my wisdom from the inside out, by living and making my mistakes and learning from them, and by doing things that work better the next time and then learning from that. So no, I'm not sleeping with anyone—euphemism for having sex, Ray, making *love*, creating something, but if I was, part of that something would be making children."

"But you've been with men *before*!" Ray said.

It occurred to me that Ray saw himself as more of a father to me than an old boyfriend, which was kind of sweet. "That's right," I said. "I guess I'm not the saint you are. I'm forty years old, and you're right, I'm not a virgin. I got curious about sex just like everybody else, and you know what? A body has needs, and good sex is one of them. So burn me at the stake, Ray, but I'm damned well going to live my life by my conscience and not yours." When this still did not seem to satisfy him, I whispered, "A life means more to me now than it did when I was younger, Ray, and I'm finally ready to take that to the place it needs to go. The next time I make love with anyone, it will be because I'm going to love him for the rest of my life, and have children with him."

I noticed that Ray had turned very pale.

I said, "This isn't really about me, is it."

Ray could not find his voice.

"Your wife's been dead how long?"

He stared now at the ground. "Five years."

"That's rough," I said.

He raised his indigo blue eyes to the mountains, where the last glow of daylight played along the peaks.

I poked him in the ribs. "Some days I think I liked you better before you learned to talk."

He lifted his head. "And other days?"

"I like the new, more communicative Ray."

He nodded, then put a hand on my shoulder in a tender sort of way and walked with me back to his car.

15

News of Afton McWain's death was not only in the news-papers Sunday morning, it was out on the grapevine.

As the outside temperatures in Salt Lake City again rose to the wilting point, a couple of old friends from the oil patch started phoning to reminisce about our departed colleague and to fish for grisly details. We talked about his former life as a hard-driven petroleum geologist who made buckets of money with big strikes in the D-J Basin and mused over his sudden departure into parts unknown. The caller who barely knew Afton eventually sidled up to the matter of the setting in which his corpse had been found, wondering askance if I could offer any juicy tidbits. The one who knew him well asked more directly, trying to deal with a sense of shock.

I told them that I couldn't say much about the circumstances of Afton's death—apart from truly not knowing much about its causation, it was incumbent on me, I explained, to keep what we could of the mechanics of his demise out of the pool of general knowledge, so that anyone who *did* have such knowledge would be easily identified as his *killer*. I indulged in a little dramatic flair in delivering that last, suitably horrifying word.

"That's how it's done on the cop shows," the first caller said. "So hey, are those things accurate or what?"

I said, "In my experience cops aren't usually as glamorous as you see on TV, and they don't go waving their pistols in bad guys' faces if they can possibly help it. That's a good way to get your gun turned on yourself. And cops are trained to aim a gun only on the way to using it."

"Cool."

"I suppose so. But just like us geologists, police detectives deal with incomplete data. So just like us, they often have no idea who did what and why. But on TV, every crime is solved within sixty minutes or less with three breaks for commercials."

"Emmy . . ."

Michele phoned at ten. "Have you had any additional thoughts about any of the evidence?" she inquired.

I told her what I had learned in Snowbird, then asked, "How badly does it hurt the case that everybody now knows that the body was found mashed flat by a gravel slide in a quarry?"

"That doesn't help the process." She didn't sound happy about it. Not at all.

Carlos phoned at eleven with the forensic geology referral he had promised. The contact's name was Tim Osner.

I remembered Tim vaguely from my Denver days. He had worked for one of the mid-sized oil companies for a while, and now was teaching part-time at a couple of different schools, eking out a living as geologists so often find themselves doing. It's always the same story. People want oil? We'll find oil until it gluts the market and people think they don't need us anymore. Folks got ground-water contamination to clean up or landfills to be built to ensure that additional ground water isn't fouled? We'll all jump on that until that's done, and folks think they're done spilling things, and again we're out of a job. Humankind wants to be safe from earthquakes? We'll map the fault lines and advise legislatures until public policy is enough improved that everyone forgets what we did for them lately and . . . yeah, same story, we fall prey to the next budget cut. Folks don't comprehend how long it takes to build such knowledge, and how quickly it can be lost.

I wrote down Tim's number so I could phone him from my office.

By noon, it was almost 100 degrees Fahrenheit out. I was dripping with sweat again and more than ready to escape up the canyon to cooler elevations and the ground-water conference. I arrived at one, put on my complimentary name badge, and slithered into the gathering of ground-water geologists, hoping to look and smell like a sheep rather than a wolf.

I immediately ran into someone I knew. It's a small world for geologists, a prime example of my first theorem, which is that regardless of how many billions of people there are in the world, only one hundred thousand of them get around, and ten thousand of those are geologists. The person I bumped into was George Hadley, another old Denver oil patch survivor who, like Julia, had retrofitted his knowledge to serve the issues of ground water.

"Hey, Emmy," he said, as he sidled over with his free cup of coffee and mashed a hug on me. "What's the haps?"

"Oh, not much, Georgie boy. Just slummin'. Seein' what you H_2O freaks are up to."

"It's all just getting juice out of the rocks, Emmy." He showed me a little smile and took a swig of his coffee. "My God, this stuff's foul. So you getting rich, or what?"

"Not me, boss. Just keeping out of trouble as best I can. So I hear where Afton McWain's one of the keynote speakers at the plenary session. Wow." I phrased it such that if he had heard that Afton was dead, it would sound like I was speaking about him in the past tense, and if not he could say whatever occurred to him. It was just possible that the Coloradoans attending the conference had been in transit when the news broke, and would not yet know. News of the corpse in the quarry had already washed through the Salt Lake newspapers, and the Denver papers would be waiting on their doorsteps back home. And certainly neither Gilda nor Julia would have informed the conference of his death.

"McWain. Oh yeah, McWain. Folks are asking where the fuck he was, like they expected to see him here last night or something." George's face creased with a pompous display of mock concern. "I even heard a rumor that someone bumped him off. I wouldn't be surprised. He's been such a flake lately."

"Why, what's up?"

"Afton's gone and got hisself in a bit of a bramble down in Douglas County."

"How so?"

"Stay tuned. I mean, do stay tuned. He's gonna deliver one corker of a talk here today, even by his standards. Or that's the scuttlebutt."

"Really."

"Yeah. He's been working on that Denver Basin stuff. Hell, we've all been working the Denver Basin. It's the hot topic, but he's gonna blow it all out in the open."

"Wow. What Denver Basin stuff?"

"Man, Emmy, you really have been out of touch. It's like war out there. Oh, hi there, Hugh . . ." He turned to someone who was just sidling up to him hollering something about the increased girth of George's stomach. When George was done defending his paunch, another pal of his had wandered up, and another, and there was no getting back on the topic. As the crowd started to funnel into the ballroom for the plenary session, I buttonholed him, but he'd forgotten what he was talking about. "Shit," he said. "I've got such a hangover. Bunch of us partied hard when we got in yesterday. I barely woke up in time for this session."

"You were telling me about Afton."

"Old Afton?" he said. "Don't mind me. You know I was always jealous he got in before they quit handing out the overrides." He spotted someone else he wanted to talk to. "Hey Freddie!"

I found my way into the ballroom where the talks were being presented and chose a seat near the back, where I could observe as many people as possible and also leave early, if the talks began to put me to sleep.

Two moderators took their seats at the raised dais and shuffled their notes. The program indicated that one was from California and the other was from Nevada, so they might not have known the dead man personally. Presently, one of them stood up and made a general statement about the purpose of the session, showing a few PowerPoint slides that listed the talks about to be given—Afton McWain's was scheduled third—and then introduced the first speaker. So it was official: they didn't know that Afton would not be speaking that day, unless it was from the far side of the morgue.

I settled in to learn a little hydrogeology.

The first talk was given by Jim Connor, a consultant from Arizona. He discussed the way water was valued—or undervalued—in our society. As an example, he described the Central Arizona Project, an immense system of aqueducts, tunnels, and pumping stations that had been built in order to mitigate the over-pumping of ground water by delivering surface water from Lake Meade.

He described the political maneuvering that had beleaguered the project. "Farmers, who are the main consumers of ground water outside of our rapidly growing municipalities, think they should get a break on the cost, because why should they pay more for water than the price of running the pumps on their wells? And the municipalities wonder why they should pay more than farmers. Meanwhile, they've pumped so much water out of the ground that the ground has cracked and subsided as much as twelve feet.

"Now, you all know from your freshman geology classes that once an aquifer has collapsed, it's a dead aquifer, but the average citizen does not understand that water is part of what holds the ground up. As the grains of sediment are deposited, water fills the tiny spaces between the grains. The water can flow through the rock, but, being a non-compressible liquid, it actually helps support the sediments, even when, over time, they become deeply buried. But if water is pumped out faster than it is replaced, there is nothing to support the weight of overlying sediments. The pore spaces compress and collapse. They no longer exist. Water can never fill them again."

Connor intoned, "We are, in effect, mining the water, and the resource is going away and cannot be regenerated. Water must now be piped in from elsewhere, and now we all pay the cost, an increasingly higher cost. Okay, so today I'm preaching to the choir. So how do we educate the public and our servants, the lawmakers?"

As Connor was speaking, one moderator peered repeatedly at the entrance door. Was he watching for Afton McWain? A woman appeared at the door and raised her shoulders and turned up her palms in the universal "who knows?" signal. The moderator drummed his fingers nervously on the desk.

The second speaker, Janet Terry, presented a summary of the ages of ground water in aquifers around the West. "Why is the age of the water we are drinking important? Simple. If we're drinking ground water that filtered into the ground during the last ice age—or earlier—we know that this aquifer is not recharging. We are instead mining it, as Jim explained, whether we're collapsing soft sediments or just draining rock."

Terry was a specialist in finding the age of water by isotopes dating. When she talked about the Denver Basin aquifers, I sat up and took notice. The water in the Arapahoe aquifer—which I had seen delineated on Afton McWain's office wall, and whose depiction had now mysteriously vanished—was 30,000 years old. Older than the last ice age. Mammoths that are now extinct had watched it fall from the sky as snow.

"This is vintage water," she told us. "The water Douglas County residents are drinking found its way into the ground 30,000 years ago. That means that rain that falls today on the aquifer's recharge area along the foothills of the Rampart Range is not migrating into the ground fast enough to replace the water residents are pumping out."

The Rampart Range. She was talking about the foothills at the edge of Afton McWain's ranch, which, even as she spoke, lay searing in the prairie heat in the worst drought on record. I was beginning to see why Afton had developed an interest in the rocks that lay beneath his feet.

As the isotope specialist showed us one alarming slide after another, the woman who had shrugged her shoulders in the doorway reappeared, briskly approached the dais, and handed a note up to the moderators. As they read it, their eyebrows shot up. Anxiety played across their faces. They looked back and forth at each other and around the room. They put their heads together and whispered urgently, then looked down at a woman who was sitting in the front row. One of the moderators got out of his seat and hastened down to talk to her, keeping his head low so he didn't form a silhouette on the projection screen.

Terry finished her talk and left the lectern. The time for Afton McWain's presentation had arrived.

One of the moderators stood up. He adjusted his glasses, cleared his throat, ducked his face awkwardly toward the microphone, and said,

"Uh, we're going to, ah . . . change the order of, ah . . . the talks here a bit. We'll move next to, uh, Karen Brown, who will present the economic model for ground-water development. Uh, thank you for being flexible, Karen." Having introduced her, he left the hall and did not return until the end of her talk.

Karen Brown was a minerals economist from New Mexico who strode to the podium on athletic legs and delivered a high-speed summary of water economics as it is practiced in the American West. She pointed out that American consumers treat water as a free commodity because it falls out of the sky but that few have any comprehension of the nature of ground water—how it gets into the ground, what happens when we begin to take it out, and most importantly, the fact that, if it is pumped out faster than it percolates in, it is a finite resource.

She said, "What is the price of ground water? Typically, we pay the cost to lift it out of the ground or have it piped to us but give it no per-volume value unless we put it into bottles and sell it in grocery stores. Water drawn from rivers or reservoirs, by contrast, has a volume value because it is reckoned by the acre-foot if you are a farmer or by the gallon if you are a homeowner in places where it is metered or rationed, but even then it is usually based on the cost to deliver, and the valuation is a matter of apportionment. We talk of water rights but rarely do we discuss a per-unit cost of water. We know the price of a gallon of gas to the penny, but what is the price of a gallon of water?"

Brown pumped the remote, firing rapidly through her PowerPoint presentation. "Trying to say who owns the water in the ground is unclear in most states," she explained. "Surface water is typically governed by a system of prior claim. First in line, first in priority. The oldest claim is satisfied first, and if the stream is sucked dry before the newest claim is satisfied, that's that person's tough luck. Again, this is not regulation, this is apportionment. In some places we have meters on water wells, but this is not to regulate consumption but instead to create a tax revenue stream. It's the tragedy of the commons. We degrade that which we own in common, each taking what we can before it can be taken by someone else."

Brown went on to present some graphs that showed what happens when a community on private wells runs out of water and needs to start importing it from other areas. "We typically turn to a government agency and expect them to 'fix' our problem. The government agency puts in a community-wide system that delivers water from another source—sometimes hundreds of miles distant. The agency must charge to provide O and M—operations and maintenance—and that puts them in a subtle conflict of interest. If they stop delivering water, they're out of a job, and anything a government provides has to be paid for. It is therefore in the government's interest that the citizens consume water. They tend not to regulate consumption even if that were the purpose of the agency. Ration, maybe; regulate, rarely."

The question-and-answer period after Dr. Brown's talk was lively because, it seemed, there were a few journalists present. One asked, "What do you think of the statistics published by Senator White of the Colorado state senate subcommittee on water supplies stating that there is plenty of water to be had to support development in the south Denver metro area?" he inquired. "I refer to Arapahoe and Douglas counties, which are expected to gain 400,000 citizens by the year 2050."

Brown replied, "Well, as you know, there are several kinds of lies. There are lies, damned lies, and then there are statistics. I'd have to ask Senator White if these additional citizens are going to learn some extreme measures of conservation."

Someone asked her why Senator White and the rest of the subcommittee might have conjured these numbers.

Brown replied, "Any elected official in any western state is well aware that to mention the reduction of water resources in a public forum is a sure way to avoid reelection, so having the temerity to actually do anything about it is tantamount to political hara-kiri."

Laughter ensued. As the child of a ranching family, I rolled my eyes in agreement. In Wyoming, ranchers have been known to invite any official that foolish to a barbecue, and they wouldn't be serving beef. In the semi-arid West, a ranch needed a certain number of irrigated acres to grow enough alfalfa to get the herd through the winter or they'd have to cut the herd. Having to purchase feed could tip the economic scale from profit to loss.

I raised my hand and asked, "This may be off the point, but while I've worked in a commodities-based industry—oil and gas—I've never taken economics, and I'm wondering, how do you tell when an economy is in a state of decline? What are the symptoms?" I was asking for two reasons: first, to better understand what had happened to my heritage, and second, to find out whether it was happening, in perhaps a different way, to the community around Castle Rock, Colorado.

"It becomes stagnant," Brown replied.

"You mean it quits growing?"

"Yes. Most economies are based on growth."

"Then how can an economy stay healthy, if it's eventually going to run up against the exhaustion of its finite resources, such as ground water?"

Brown said, "Then, as I said, they have to import the resource, and the governing limit becomes cost or the balance of trade."

A journalist asked, "Then you're saying that an economy is only healthy if it's growing."

"That is usually the case," she replied, "at least, from a Western capitalistic viewpoint. The new thing is to try to figure out how to make economies and the resources that they rely on sustainable, but the way most economies work is that populations either grow, level off, or decline, and with them goes demand. Most often, populations grow."

"Then is there a way for a growing population to continue to prosper if it's dependant on a finite resource like water?" another journalist asked.

Brown replied, "Well, you can change the mix of industries or the technological base of the community, but that's difficult to engineer. So on the whole, I have three answers for that question: yes, no, and it depends."

The audience laughed, but I didn't. No one understood conservation of water resources better than a ranch child who had grown up helping her father cycle the same acre-foot of water downhill through three fields of alfalfa so there'd be enough left over to cycle through the bodies of their livestock. Ranchers knew to keep the water near the bottomlands, irrigating only near the creeks and saturated ground whence the water was lifted and leaving the dry lands to the short grasses of the prairie for grazing. Long gone was the era when excess people and cattle died directly of drought. Instead, the human species was now increasing its numbers and standard of living, now subdividing the ranches, building houses on the rolling prairie, and raising water from the ground to flush toilets and water lawns, always figuring we would find one more source of water, and another, and another . . .

Brown's lecture was followed by the announcement I knew was coming: the moderator returned to the dais with the chairman of the association that was hosting the conference, and, after the briefest of introductions, turned the microphone over to him. The chairman came to the microphone, hands trembling so strikingly that the piece of paper he held shook visibly, and said, "I am sorry to have to deliver some painful news. Afton McWain, who was going to deliver his talk on the aquifers of the Denver Basin here today, has been . . . we are advised by the police . . . that he's been found dead."

The room burst into a rumble of sound. Geologists are not shy about opening their mouths and making noise when something surprises them, and in three-quarters of a second at least nine-tenths of the people in that room were talking at once. I glanced around the room, looking to see who was *not* surprised. The journalists were not, and were scanning the crowd as carefully as I was. Among the others, it was hard to tell. There were a lot of poker faces.

The chairman waved his hands for quiet. "I'm—I don't have any details. This is a terrible loss to the profession. As you know, Dr. McWain has . . . *had* a career spanning three decades, and his contributions to our understanding of Denver Basin stratigraphy are monumental. Would you all please join me in standing for a moment of silence?"

The audience stumbled to its feet. Isolated coughs and astonished glances among colleagues punctuated a long half minute. Awkwardly, people began to settle back into their chairs. The chairman cleared his throat again and said, "Now, Afton's talk was important to this meeting, so we've, uh, asked Bob Raynolds to step in for him. Now, Bob can't just speak from Afton's slides, and um, we don't have those anyway, so . . . this is all very shocking. We were concerned when he didn't check in with us, and we'd heard rumors, but as you all know, he's . . . was . . . a bit unusual in his ways of doing things, and we figured he'd show. But Bob Raynolds is here and has his slides from that wonderful talk he gave on the Denver Basin last year, and he edited that volume in *The Mountain Geologist* on the Denver Basin, so, ah, here's Bob."

As Raynolds took his place on the stage, you could have heard a pin drop. He was a slender, raw-boned man with an endearing mixture of intellectuality and disarming charm, which was lucky, considering that he had to grasp and hold the audience's attention after such an announcement. But he succeeded magnificently. Hitting the switch to kill the overhead lights, he brought up the first slide and went to town.

He spoke to us intimately, even confidentially. He got down and gritty about the rocks of the Denver Basin in general and the Arapahoe aquifer in particular. He showed evidence that the rocks had been deposited as great fans of sand by streams running onto the plains from the growing mountains. He gave examples of similar fans being deposited today along the sides of the southern Andes. It was a brilliant, classical presentation of what geologists do like few can: He took obscure and largely buried data about ancient rocks, compared it to modern deposits, and built it into a predictive model.

"And here's why this is important," he said. "The previous estimates of how much water was in the Arapahoe aquifer were grossly inaccurate. They were wildly high. What happened was this: Engineers measured the porosity of the aquifer rocks—the percentage of void space—at the apex of one of the fans because that was the part of the rock that was sticking out of the ground as a hogback along the Rampart Range, where it could be easily studied. Engineers are engineers, not scientists; it's not their job to know how rock varies. They just apply formulae to the numbers available to them and crunch them into more numbers, and where they lack numbers going in, they make assumptions. Because they could not see how the rock varied underground, they assumed that the porosity of the rock stays the same all the way down into the ground, where that layer becomes deeply buried, and continues the same as that layer extends under the eastern plains toward Kansas.

"But that assumption was incorrect. They knew nothing of the architecture of the rock. At the outcrop where they measured it, at the apex of the alluvial fan, they found a high-quality aquifer, but they did not know that with every mile eastward, the quality of the rock drops precipitously. As the streams carrying the sediments that would become the sandstone of the Arapahoe aquifer burst from the steep slopes of the youthful Rocky Mountains, choked with gravel and sand and silt and clay, they hit a shallower slope and dropped the coarsest grains in their load of grit, but the smaller particles tumbled onward, and the finest sediments—the silts and clays—enjoyed the ride farther before the slope became so shallow that these least permeable also dropped to the bottom. Thus the rock has yielded copiously near the outcrop, but just a few miles downstream, it tightens down to something less productive than a brick.

"I say *has* yielded. Early wells in the area yielded abundantly for decades. Now, they decline quickly and many are going dry. Add that to the miscalculation that the engineers made. Their estimates of water available to be pumped out and run through taps in kitchens and bathrooms and horse troughs and car washes and laundries and garden hoses in all the existing homes and businesses and ranches, and in all the homes and businesses under construction has been cut by 30 or 40 percent. Those homes and businesses and ranches were dependent on well water drawn from that aquifer. And the rate at which the water is disappearing is accelerating.

"Homeowners had been assured they had over one hundred years of water supply," Raynolds said. "But this promised water is not really there. It is 'paper water.' Simply drilling more wells will not be a solution because although each new well briefly yields a small local supply, the cost per gallon produced becomes prohibitive.

"On average," he said, "the water table in the Arapahoe aquifer is dropping one inch per day. That's thirty feet per year, in an aquifer that is only four hundred feet thick. Where will these people get their water when it's gone? They'll have to import it, but from where? All the surrounding water rights are going fast, and hundreds of thousands of people are projected to move into Douglas County in the coming decades." He looked from face to face within the audience. With evident pain he said, "Douglas County proudly advertises itself as one of the fastest-growing counties in America."

Raynolds set down his pointer. "We have time for a few questions," he said.

A hand shot up. "Dr. Raynolds, can you comment on the fact that Afton McWain was scheduled to testify against the proposed Wildcat Estates development? Is that lawsuit going to go forward?"

My ears pricked to attention. Wildcat Estates was the name of the project Michele had mentioned. What lawsuit? And who was involved?

The question was way off the scientific basis of Raynolds' talk, and no scientific colleague would have addressed him as "Doctor." By simple deduction, I guessed that the question had been asked by one of the journalists in attendance, and not just a science journalist, but an investigative journalist, the kind that digs into malfeasance and corporate misconduct. I couldn't believe that the Salt Lake City papers would have sent a reporter to cover a development in Colorado, so that meant it had to be someone from the *Denver Post* or the *Rocky Mountain News*.

In the jumble of events of the past two and a half days, this bit of information had slid past me, but now it clicked into place with the rest: Johnson had a ranch to sell, Attabury could sell or perhaps develop it, Entwhistle could handle the loans, and Upton would push the paperwork.

And Gilda? What was her part in the deal? It had to be more than a coincidence that we had found them all together.

And these high-powered journalists were circling like sharks. And that meant that there was more stuck to Afton's murder and the Wildcat Estates project than four men and a woman sitting in a roadside bar.

As I pondered this new view of the puzzle, Raynolds stared at the top of the lectern, composing a response. "For those of you who are unfamiliar with this situation," he said finally, "citizens have brought a landmark lawsuit against a group of people who have proposed yet another housing development in the Castle Rock area—ironically named Wildcat Estates after the small mountain that forms the apex of the Arapahoe aquifer fan. The wells for Wildcat Estates would of course tap this already over-drafted aquifer. The suit will test the rights of defendant landowners to build at certain densities if they are dependent on ground water to supply their houses, and the rights of the plaintiffs—existing homeowners—to demand that their dwindling water supplies not be further tapped. As expert witness, Afton McWain's testimony was expected to be pivotal. I shall be watching the fate of this lawsuit with acute interest."

Like so much boiling oatmeal, a hubbub of conversations broke out around the room. I felt an itch to stand up and announce that someone had emptied every last shred of paper out of Afton's log-cabin office, just to really get everyone riled, but I managed to stay in my seat.

The questioner asked, "But didn't McWain have a conflict of interest in this case?"

Raynolds replied, "I assume you refer to the fact that Afton owned the adjoining ranch, which makes him a stakeholder in the outcome of the case."

"Yes."

"Is it a conflict of interest to tell the truth? Next question."

Someone asked, "Why is his testimony so important?"

Raynolds said, "Because Afton McWain was, first and last, a scientist of peerless reputation. And he was unimpeachable on the witness stand. If anyone could make the claimants' arguments stick, he could."

Another journalist asked the next question. "Can you comment on the plaintiffs' assertions that the money behind this proposed development has ties to organized crime? Do you think Dr. McWain's killers were sending a message?"

Raynolds smiled sadly. "That would be a matter for a different sort of an investigator than I am. I study rocks and the modern landforms that are the keys to understanding them, while you are asking me to shed light on human interactions." He shook his head. "I cannot comprehend murder. You're asking the wrong man."

I began to squirm in my chair. Perhaps the killer had sent a message. He had bashed in a face and cut off fingertips, and burying the corpse in that quarry almost guaranteed that it would be located. The West was riddled with lonely stream banks and abandoned mines where a body could rest for eternity without being found.

For an instant, I imagined my own body lying six feet underground, grown cold and damp in a place no one ever visited. The image of such loneliness seeped into my bones, and I fought back the urge to phone Fritz and beg him to put that second arm around me and touch me again in that way that had made me feel alive. Instead, I got up from my chair, hurried to my truck, and drove down the canyon to the solitude of my apartment and the loneliness of my bed.

16

RAY RAYMOND SAT ON A ROCK BESIDE THE TRAIL THAT LED UP CITY Creek, trying to decide what to do with himself. After the previous evening's miserable trip up Little Cottonwood Canyon, he had gone to a late Al-Anon meeting and in the morning had attended church with his mother, but even these comforts had failed to set his soul at ease. Em was in danger, and he blamed himself. By fetching her Friday morning, he had done his job but had gone against some deeper principle. By bringing Gilda to her Saturday afternoon, and then through the tacit encouragement of letting her use his badge to gain information at that conference, he had abandoned her even more deeply to her fate.

Now the McWain case was all over the Denver papers, totally blowing what little cover Em had enjoyed during her rash rush to Colorado. He had to do something to warn her, to stop her, to protect her, but he knew there was nothing.

Ray shook his head ruefully. Em was her own woman, she had made that clear time and again. Why did her care and protection hang over him like this? Each time she came into his life, everything became a sweet but terrifying chaos, and when he closed his eyes in prayer to try to bring order, Em was right there like a shard of light, ripping at his heart, telling him something he could not bear to know.

The jagged edges of the rock he was sitting on dug into the palms of Ray's hands, but he welcomed the sensation, trying desperately to feel his own body.

Suddenly he rose to his feet. This time he would settle things with Em, with her help or without it.

❖

MARY ANN NETTLETON'S sister decanted bottled water into a pan and turned on the LP gas underneath it. "There," she said, "a little tea is just the thing after an experience like that. It'll be ready in a minute."

"Don't pour too much, Rita Mae. That bottle is all I've got until the delivery man comes."

"When exactly did your well run dry?"

Mary Ann heaved a shuddering sigh that hovered on the raw edge of tears. "It never did well, but about a month after Henry died I began to run out when I was doing the laundry. Sand would come out into the machine. Then I'd have my hair all soaped in the morning, and it would go to a dribble. Now, I can run the faucet only two minutes a day at a trickle." She sniffled a bit, daubed at her nose with a crumpled tissue. "It was so nice of you to drive down here to be with me."

"Sisters have to stick together. Besides, it's nice to get away from Denver for a while. So you need a new well. So you'll get a new well, and then you'll be fine."

Mary Ann hung her head. "Somehow I don't think that will be the end of it, Rita Mae."

"Mr. Upton seemed to feel that you can get Mr. Attabury to pay for it, or at least get you a discount through his development firm."

Mary Ann twisted her tissue into a knot. "I just couldn't believe what Mr. Upton had to say about Mr. Attabury! I'd always thought Mr. Attabury was such a nice man."

Rita Mae patted her sister on the shoulder. It was an easy gesture, one she'd made many times in their long life, but now she noticed how frail Mary Ann had become. How old was she now? Sixty-eight? "Well, I didn't like hearing what he had to say either, dear, but sometimes we have to take our medicine even when we didn't ask to catch the disease. It was nice of him to see you on a Sunday. He came into his office just for you, opened it himself, just to be nice because he couldn't attend to your message earlier. He didn't even have a secretary there to look after him."

"He called Mr. Attabury a 'shady dealer.' Imagine!"

"Well, he did say he's known him all his life. You've known Mr. Attabury less than a year, and he wanted your business. Anybody can seem sweet and nice that long."

"But to say he was cheating people clear back in high school! He called him a swindler!"

The water boiled, and Rita Mae poured it over the tea bags she had set in the two nice china cups. "I think you should sue him."

Mary Ann said, "Mr. Upton seemed hesitant to do that."

"His hesitancy had more to do with his conflict of interest than anything else."

"Rita Mae, I don't understand these things."

"Well, dear, a conflict of interest means that Mr. Attabury is also his client. So he can't represent one client in suing another. That's all it means."

"But if Mr. Attabury is a dishonorable man, why does he represent him?"

Rita Mae shook her head. "I don't know, dear, but when you've known someone since high school, things get complicated. Men are difficult to understand sometimes." She arched her eyebrows knowingly. "So we'll just find someone competent for you up in Denver, and that will make it nice and clean."

"Meanwhile, I don't have any water. And how am I to afford hiring a lawyer in the first place?"

Rita Mae set the cups down on the table and got the half and half out of the refrigerator. "You need a new well. You'll drill the well and then take the bill to Mr. Attabury. Mr. Upton says he must have known there was no water when he sold the property to you. I'm sure there's a law about that kind of thing. Or there should be."

Rita Mae tapped the file of notes that Henry Nettleton had made when Afton McWain came to visit him. "Meanwhile, I'll put on my thinking cap and see if I can make heads or tails out of all this information."

Mary Ann cuddled the hot teacup between her aging hands. She felt chilled to the bone even in the terrible heat of the day. "All right," she said. "But if we find out that Mr. Attabury swindled my dear departed Henry, he's going to be sorry he was ever born!"

17

MICHELE PHONED AS I WAS MAKING MYSELF A DINNER OF COTTAGE cheese and yogurt, a favorite when it's hot out and I just can't conjure anything worth eating. After I told her what I had learned at the conference, she said, "So you're saying that McWain's expert witness testimony was key to the upcoming lawsuit. So killing McWain is killing the star witness. That puts the spotlight on . . . well, each one of them had a stake in the outcome of that case. Even Gilda. I don't believe this pap about wanting to stay on that ranch, not after the performance we saw when she couldn't get her cart to run. She's into this case up to her eye sockets."

"Either that or she's next in line to find herself two inches thick," I said. "This case smells more and more like organized crime. Give it over to the feds, Michele. Stay alive."

"So what are you going to do next?" she asked, ignoring any advice.

"Me? I'm going to analyze what little trace evidence we got off that body—and there wasn't much, Michele, so don't pin any hopes on my results—and I'm going to write up my report and fax it to you. Then I'm going to go back to the work I was doing before Friday, with a smile on my face and a song in my heart."

"Sure you are. This guy's a friend of yours. You want to know who killed him even more than I do."

Michele was beginning to get on my nerves. "He was a colleague, not a friend. And if he had been a friend, all the more reason to bow out of the case. Give me your fax number, so I can send you my results, then find someone else to be an idiot, if you want a partner for this case."

I wrote down her number and hurried off the phone. Focused my eyes on a book, though it would not cooperate and hold my attention. Turned out the light and tried to sleep. At length, succeeded. Got up the next morning and headed to the sheriff's department evidence room, where I examined the following items collected at the crime scene:

1. Reddish clay soil collected from the welts and treads of the corpse's boots. (I was beginning to have trouble connecting my departed colleague's name with his remains.)

2. A sack of sand and gravel taken from the quarry site immediately surrounding the corpse.

3. Residue taken from underneath the corpse's few undisturbed fingernails.

4. A pebble found deep inside a pocket in what was left of the deceased's pants.

The pebble was the easy part. It was a two-inch-long, sub-oval bit of chert, which is a quartz mineral, and as such very common on the face of the Earth, and I do specifically mean the face, because quartz is one of those less-dense, silica-rich minerals that "float" on certain others, as I had explained to Trevor Reed. Having a low freezing temperature, quartz is the common mineral that forms near the surface of the Earth and has a sturdy crystal structure. It is stable and durable. Grinding by glaciers and tumbling by wind and water do little more than wear away the corners of its crystal laths. In the case of this pebble—which I held in a gloved hand as I examined it underneath a ten-power hand lens—it had traveled far enough to become delectably smooth, which was probably why it was in Afton McWain's pocket. A Ph.D. in geology he might have had, but he would have carried this stone in his pocket simply because it was nice to touch. Now it was sealed in a plastic bag that was marked with chain-of-custody and evidence ID numbers. A pity.

I set the pebble back in the evidence tray and turned to the dirt from his boots. This was mostly a fine, red clay, but there were tiny bits of silt and fine sand there as well. It was markedly different from the sand and gravel from the quarry, which was monochromatically gray and totally lacking in red clays as viewed through the lens. The gunk found under McWain's fingernails looked more animal and vegetable than mineral, but I would do my best to identify it once I got it under the far more powerful eye of the scanning electron microscope, or SEM, at the university.

After signing the chain-of-custody document in the sight of a proper witness and taking splits of the samples, I drove up to the University of Utah to log some time on that SEM. When I got there, I discovered that someone with a higher priority than mine had a gob of analyses to run, and I'd have to come back tomorrow.

Having the brakes jammed on like that hit me like a brick. I realized in a flash that Michele was right, I didn't want to go back to other tasks. I wanted to stay on this one. So much for being able to walk away from the case.

Restless for something to do but determined to get it done, I put the various samples under a binocular microscope and picked through them with a stainless steel probe that had a wooden dowel for a handle. I selected a few representative clods of clay and prepped them for a trip through the SEM. The SEM would unmask the minute platy structures of the clays, and I could identify the bits of grit, helping me evaluate whether or not the soils from which those samples came could be fingerprinted or at least narrowed to a state, county, or municipality. But even if that could be established, which was unlikely, it might be indicative of exactly nothing. A man as adventuresome as Afton McWain might have picked up that clay years earlier on a safari to Africa, for all I knew, and could have left the boots in the back of his yurt until the day he was murdered.

Which got me to thinking about those boots again. Hand-sewn welts were almost a thing of the past, having been largely replaced by the glued-on soles that were coming out of China. Whoever stripped the body of its identifying marks had not thought the boots unusual. That would argue for someone old enough to have worn boots like that himself. Whoever had dumped his body at the quarry—and presumably performed the murder, as well—had taken a lot of trouble to obscure the corpse's identity. Teeth and face smashed, fingerprints gone.

But this brutal killer had not known about the tattoo. This eliminated Gilda from the list of suspects, unless she was smart enough to make the murder look like the work of someone who hadn't ever gotten naked with the victim. And I couldn't see someone who took such care with her own manicure cutting off her lover's fingertips, let alone finding the strength to swing a sledge into his face.

I realized that I was skating mighty close to breaking my resolution about not getting any more involved in this case, so I jotted a few notes about what I had surmised, took the samples to lockup at the sheriff's department, and headed back to my office to concentrate on other work.

IT WAS ONLY 11 A.M. I was soon drumming my fingers on my desk, restless as a mare with a burr under her saddle, and by eleven thirty I was all but walking around on the ceiling. When the phone rang, I jumped to answer it.

It was Faye, calling from the airport. "Can you look after Sloane over your lunch hour?" she asked. "I know it's short notice, but I've got a student who wants desperately to go up and shoot some touch-and-goes."

The idea delighted me but not the venue. "Is Fritz there?"

"No," she said. "He's flying Mr. Reed to Reno. Why?"

"Just curious. I'll be there in ten."

"What a pal."

The Utah Geological Survey is on West North Temple, about two-thirds of the way from downtown out to the airport. I stopped by the deli at the local supermarket and grabbed a turkey-and-Swiss sandwich and a big bottle of mineral water for me and a box of animal crackers for Sloane. When I arrived, Sloane ran up to the door to hug my legs, and I hoisted her up for a cheek-to-cheek nuzzle. She ferreted the cookies out of my pocket before I could ask Faye's permission to give them to her. "Sorry," I said. "They're organic anyway."

"She'll burn it off. Hey, you're a peach. The phones are pretty quiet today. No one wants to fly a low-horsepower trainer in this heat except old Barfie there." She indicated the rather wan-looking young man who was waiting by one of the two-seat Katanas Faye and Fritz had on the line. "Oh, that reminds me," she said, and pulled a half dozen barf bags out of a cupboard to take with her to the plane.

I said, "Imagine that. Your weakest stomach wants to go up on a high density altitude day."

"That's what he says."

"When's he going to make his solo flight?"

"Never, at the rate he's going. He has almost a hundred hours already."

"He must just have a crush on you."

"That's it. He has a weak stomach, so he goes after women twice his age."

"You still have your come-hither, Faye."

"Yeah, that's why the kid barfs every time we go up. Okay, you know the drill: Stay awake, make notes of any calls, and keep Sloane from making any calls to her bookie."

"Gotcha."

Such was the tenor of our friendship. We were like an old married couple some days. I had helped her raise Sloane from birth to eighteen months, and since I'd moved out and Faye and Fritz started the business, I had still looked after the little girl once or twice a week over lunch hours and some evenings after work. Faye got the odd bit of child care, and I got pure love.

Now Sloane Renee skipped over to me where I was sitting on a stool by the phones and patted my knee, an old signal meaning that she wanted to get up. I lifted her into my arms and hugged her again. Exuding the intimate aroma of child, she sat cross-legged on my lap, her back braced against the counter, arranging the animal cookies along her legs. She had on bright red pants and wore tiny moccasins. I touched her soft cheek and drifted into a moment of peace.

Two minutes later, the phone rang. It was Fritz. "Oh, hi, Em. Where's Faye?"

"She and Barfie are touring the pattern."

"The Barfs? What a man. Would you give Faye a message for me?"

"Certainly."

I could hear Trevor Reed calling to him from the background. Something about being in a hurry. Fritz said, "Please tell her that I'll be back there by two. Mr. Reed wants home quicker than we thought."

"Check."

"Thanks, Em," he said brusquely. "See ya. Oh, wait—"

"What?" A flutter of hopefulness tickled my heart.

"Mr. Reed wants to talk to you." He passed the phone to his client.

"This is Em?"

"Yes, Mr. . . . . Trevor."

"I read the papers yesterday. Did your quick flight to Colorado Friday have anything to do with that corpse the sheriff found in that gravel quarry down near Point of the Mountain?"

I considered denying this but decided against it. I wanted to hear what he had to say. "Yes, it was," I replied.

"My contacts in the investment banking business tell me that McWain was trying to block development down in Douglas County."

"That's what I hear."

"Want me to look into it on my side of the fence?"

"That . . . would be fine. But perhaps I should introduce you to the sheriff's detective who's on that case."

"If she's as smart as you are, I'd be delighted."

"How'd you know she was a she?"

He laughed. "I have my ways. I'm handing you back to Fritz."

Fritz came back on the line. "Just tell Faye I'll be back sooner," he said again, then the connection went dead.

"Over and out," I told the phone. To Sloane I said, "That's us, Sloany my dear, just one big family, where we're all single and no one's getting hugged but you." I sat hugging her for a while, but even during these fine moments, my mind managed to slither back to the case. I found myself contemplating Trevor Reed's offer. So I wrote him a note.

Dear Trevor,

What can you tell me—and Michele Aldrich of the SLCo Sheriff's Dept—about a Realtor named Hugo Attabury and his proposed development of a ranch belonging to Bart Johnson near Sedalia? It's called the Wildcat Estates Project or something like that. The bank of record may be Castle Rock S&L, and I think the head of that is named Entwhistle. On the QT, *por favor* . . . need I point out that someone who might be connected to this crew has gotten very rough? Thanks,

Em Hansen

I read it back several times to gauge whether or not I had made the connections between the named parties and organizations sufficiently vague. Satisfied, I added my office phone number and Michele's, put the note in an envelope, licked it and stuck it shut, and left it with Faye to await Trevor Reed's return from Reno.

TUESDAY MORNING, TO my immense relief, I managed to get my mind back on other work for a while. I'd been assigned to help update a database of dimensional building stones quarried from the state of Utah. So I was fiddling with a map trying to locate some of the more obscure quarries of the Navajo Sandstone when, at noon, I got a call from the SEM lab up at the university telling me that the machine was available now if I wanted to run my samples.

I dropped everything and headed back to the sheriff's department to pick up the evidence. I signed for it and hurried back out the door. As I walked through the gathering heat of the parking lot toward my truck, I bumped into Michele, who was just walking in. "How goes the hot pursuit?" I inquired.

"The only thing that's hot today is this weather," she replied. "You know and I know what the story is there in Colorado: Those guys at the Sedalia Grill are cold as ice. They were having a business meeting, sizing Gilda up for an heir to the throne who will do their bidding. Attabury and Entwhistle both have money on the line already invested in that development project, and Johnson loses big time if it doesn't go through. And if Upton hasn't figured out how to get a sizeable bite out of the deal, I'm not sure how good a lawyer he is. So we've got motive galore—good old greed—but I can't prove an opportunity to save my life. They all swear they were snug as little bugs in their little bitty beds last Thursday night."

"Better you than me," I said. "I'm just going to go commune with these bits of muck."

"Get me something I can hang someone with, will you?"

"Emmy's the name, dirt's my game. Just gonna go crawl off into a nice, cool laboratory and stay out of trouble."

She glanced at me over the tops of her sunglasses. "You? Stay out of trouble? You're as big an adrenaline junkie as the worst cop on the line."

I stopped and stared at her. "What's that supposed to mean?"

"Come on, everybody in law enforcement in Salt Lake County, if not in the state of Utah, knows that you're—how should I say this?— very enthusiastic about your work."

I stood there weighing possible comebacks. Phrases like, *That was when I was as young and stupid as you are* came to mind, but I settled for, "Man, you've sure got your undies in a bundle."

To which she replied, "So you have absolutely nothing else to tell me."

"Me? Not a single, solitary thing. But if you'll get off my case, I'll put you in touch with an investment banker who might be able to dig up some inside information for you."

Michele smiled wickedly. "You've got it bad."

I argued with her in my head all the way up the hill to the university.

A SCANNING ELECTRON microscope works by bombarding each sample with electrons like radar. You can watch the results on a TV screen. It can enlarge a sample by tens of thousands of diameters, and it comes with an electron microprobe, which is a gizmo that can focus on one tiny part of the picture and tell you what it's made of. The results print out as an image and a graph. It's a great tool to use when analyzing clays and other trace evidence. Each type of clay has a different and recognizable appearance—illite, montmorillonite, kaolinite, and on and on—and the microprobe graph shows both the elements present and their relative proportions.

Best of all, in a heat wave like Salt Lake City was having, SEMs are kept in a refrigerated, interior room with no windows.

My time in the cool room told me that the red clay sample had mixed bentonite and kaolinite clays with considerable limonite staining (a fancy term for iron oxide, or rust). Under the intense magnification of the SEM, bentonite appears fibrous while kaolinite is revealed to be a stack of thin plates. Together they are about as common geologically as . . . well, dirt.

Bentonite and kaolinite are common along the eastern plains of Colorado. Finding these minerals in the evidence samples told me almost exactly nothing, except that the dirt on the dead man's shoes did not come from the quarry in which he was found, which, being geologically somewhat peculiar, was mostly gravel. Which was why it made a good quarry, if gravel happened to be what you were wanting.

The fingernail goo was similarly unexciting. It was mineralogically nearly identical to what was on his shoes. All that told me was that he had put his hands in the same dirt he had stepped in and hadn't washed since.

I dropped the samples back at the sheriff's department—cleverly nipping in the back way so I wouldn't have to go anywhere near Michele's office—and took the results back to my own office where I could set to work writing my report.

I didn't have much to say. Afton McWain had had clay on his boots and dirt underneath his fingernails that didn't match the sand and gravel in the quarry. Not surprising, considering that all evidence said that he had been murdered before being taken to the quarry. He'd had a pebble in his pocket. Whoopee.

I wrote up these results, printed it out on a piece of Utah Geological Survey letterhead and signed it, then faxed it over to the sheriff's department to Michele's attention and put the hard copy in the mail and a photocopy in the proper file. Then I sat back down at my desk and promised myself that that was that.

Feeling let down that my involvement in the case had ended so anticlimactically, I telephoned Tim Osner, Carlos Ortega's contact—mostly to add him to my professional network, I told myself.

Tim answered on the first ring. "Osner," he said, in a bored voice.

"Hey, Tim, this is Em Hansen. Calling from Utah."

"Oh yeah, Carlos said you'd be calling. Didn't you work for Blackfeet Oil back in the before times?"

"Yeah, for a couple years."

"Those were the days. So you've got a road kill in Utah that belongs in Colorado."

"A road—oh, I get you."

"Sorry, my sense of humor gets out of hand rather easily."

"No, it's just . . . well, I happened to know the guy."

"Ooo! Bad luck! So how can I help you?"

"Well, I'm mostly making contact. Us forensic geologists have got to stick together."

"Yeah, we're rare as hen's teeth. So, you working on anything? Carlos suggested you might be."

"I've got some red clays as trace evidence. Do you guys have an index of Colorado soils or clays lying around loose?"

Tim Osner laughed. "No, sorry, but I'd love to play 'where's the clay' any Saturday. Sorry if it dulls my luster, but the rest of the week I mostly fly a desk. Ninety-nine percent of the time I'm staring into a computer. My forensic work is on a volunteer basis. I don't get paid for it, but it sure gets the blood running in the veins."

"Tell me how that works."

"Well, a couple of chums and I have an association with the law enforcement detectives. When they have a missing corpse, someone's gone and gotten lost in a river or drowned in a lake, and the job is to find the body, they give us a call. We use geological tools and logic to figure out where it is. I narrow the search by using geological computer software—RockWare—to plot probabilities in three and four dimensions. Say you're trying to figure out where the body (a three-dimensional object in three-dimensional space) went (moved through time, the fourth dimension). I tickle the software into crunching a bunch of coordinates and running a wad of probability algorithms and then plotting the whole mess on the computer screen or a sheet of paper, all color-coded to indicate hot spots of likelihood."

"Sounds like fun," I said.

"It's a blast. We call up our buddies: Geologists, geophysicists, biologists, botanists, psychologists, anthropologists, meteorologists, criminologists, and use cadaver dogs, software, telemetry, you name it. All week long I plug away at my boring little life, but on Saturday if the police have a job for us, I charge on out to the site and I'm . . . some-*body*!"

"A regular Walter Mitty."

"In person. At your service, ma'am. Which way to the self-help session on hero self-worship?"

We fell into a fit of giggles. I knew I'd have no trouble getting along with the likes of Tim Osner.

"So when are we going looking for red dirt?" he inquired. "I'm free tonight."

"I'm calling from Utah, friend. And sorry, I've already made my run to Colorado with this case, but may I call you if I have any questions in the future?"

"Sure. Ciao, baby."

MICHELE PHONED TEN minutes later. She had read my fax. "That's *all*?"

"My, you are cranky! Okay, so it's nothing very helpful, not without something to stick it to on the other end."

"What does that mean, specifically?" The surge of hope in her voice was intense and immediate. I began to wonder what she had riding on this case.

"I have limonite-stained kaolinite on the man's boots. He had a chert pebble in his pocket, probably a worry stone. The—"

"A what stone?"

"A worry stone. You know, something smooth you fiddle with. So far as I know, he could have carried it in his pocket since he was nine or something."

"I was hoping for some clue about where he'd been during the days he was missing."

"Missing? How long is he unaccounted for?"

"Not missing as in reported to the police, but no one can say where he was, or *will* say where he was since Wednesday afternoon. He was found at the quarry Friday morning. Attabury said he saw him in Castle Rock on Tuesday. Upton said he wasn't sure the last time he'd seen him, it could have been weeks. Entwhistle said it had been late the week before but wasn't sure of the date. Johnson said he'd been out of town himself. Gilda—"

"So you finally got something out of Gilda? What did you do, nail both of her feet to the floor and threaten her with a greasy French fry?"

"No. She has issued a statement. Through Todd Upton, who is apparently her lawyer. She states that she was away when McWain left—down in Colorado Springs getting her skin exfoliated, but why that takes two days I don't understand—so she didn't know when he left the ranch. She last saw him on Tuesday, or so she states. She was only just returning from Colorado Springs when she stopped at the Sedalia Grill to use the bathroom and 'just happened' to run into the men."

"So how did McWain get to Utah?"

"I've searched all the airlines and bus lines, and I've asked everyone at the ground-water conference who drove over from Colorado if anyone gave him a ride and they all said no. He must have hitched a ride. Looking for someone who gave a ride to a hitchhiker is like trying to find a needle in a haystack. I may have to put a plea out on TV. But on the other hand, if one or more of our star suspects is lying, and one of them drove him over here and killed him, well . . . I'm going to have to figure out how to prove it. I'm trying to run their credit cards, to see if any of them charged gas in, say, Grand Junction or Green River, but so far, nothing."

"So where did you get that Wednesday time fix?"

"Bart Johnson's son Zachary picked him up on the road and gave him a lift as far as Bud's Bar in Sedalia, where he works."

"So Afton told him he was leaving town? Did he get any more out of him?"

"No, it's just the last fix I could get on him. Zachary said McWain used to hitch rides with him a lot, because otherwise it's a five-mile hike to town."

"Was he carrying anything? A backpack or anything? As if he was leaving town for a while?"

"No, he was just dressed 'as always.' Slacks and a long-sleeved shirt, hiking boots. That was it."

"I'll bet he was just going into town for some reason. He didn't have to be in Utah until Sunday. Why would he leave early?"

"But he did leave early," Michele pointed out. "He was here by Thursday night."

"Yeah. So what are the alibis you're trying to crack? Where were the four men Thursday and Friday?"

"Oh, they've got some good lines. Gilda was at that spa," she said, beginning to tick off a list.

"Oh, it was a *spa.*"

"All very tidy, eh? She checked into a spa so she would have plenty of witnesses that she was a good little girl. Upton was in his law office from 9 A.M. to 7 P.M. or later every day last week except Thursday, when he took off a little early to play golf. Bart Johnson was looking after his cattle up on his ranch, and Zachary vouches for him, so Zachary and Bart have each other covered."

I said, "Sounds like you're putting a lot of stock in this Zachary, in his word."

"I am not. I don't trust him. He's the type who'll tell you what he believes in, rather than what is accurate."

"I know the type."

"Except Zachary Johnson is not bright enough to start a war. No one would follow him into battle."

"But perhaps they'd send him to do battle for them. Anyway, what about Entwhistle, the banker?"

"Entwhistle was at his bank during the days and home with his wife at night. And Attabury was likewise at his real-estate office, and he was Upton's golf partner on Thursday evening."

"That's pretty tight," I said. "It's over five hundred miles by road from Castle Rock to Salt Lake City. That's an eight-hour run each way, let alone what it takes to break into a gravel quarry, dump a body, and set off a landslide to cover it. And then of course there's the time it takes to strip the body of its identifying marks, although if you have two guys in the car, one driving and one working at a corpse with a knife and a pair of pliers in the backseat, but then that would be kind of messy, and . . ."

"Nah," Michele said, "it just doesn't work. I've got to go back to Colorado and dig for someone else who's pissed at this guy, or figure out what's staring me right in the face on this end. My boss thought Gilda did it."

"Why?"

"Because she hitchhiked over here to identify the body, when she wasn't even next of kin. He figured that was a big performance to make it look like she was deeply aggrieved and show everyone how long it takes to hitchhike back and forth. Sort of like doing it with the judges watching."

"There's some merit in that argument. It did seem odd to me that she came over here."

"Yeah. But now that she's presented her alibi, my boss thinks McWain got mugged and dumped."

"That seems pretty far-fetched. And it still doesn't explain why he arrived in Salt Lake City ahead of the conference."

"So what do you think?" Michele asked. "Would there be someone at that conference in Snowbird who's got a gripe?"

I said, "That's a long shot. The opportunity might be there, but there would be no motive. Intellectually, scientists have rivalries all over the place, but they don't go around killing each other over them. That would end the game; it's much more fun to keep it going. And besides, you know the old saw that murder is usually about money or sex. Well, science doesn't pay well, and it sure isn't sexy. And speaking of sex, McWain was only boffing Gilda—or have you checked out that angle?—and he wasn't in contention for jobs that have a price tag to them anymore. He'd left the oil patch. He'd left the profession entirely, until he dove back in on his quest to save the aquifers. But that presents the motive: People like Attabury and Entwhistle or his neighbor Johnson would not want someone as persuasive as Afton McWain campaigning against them."

"Campaigning. An interesting choice of words," Michele commented. "That reminds me to look into the political arm of this situation. What was that state senator's name?"

"White. Good idea, because these people who did not appear to be surprised by news of Afton's death and who had a reason to want him quiet, each have an alibi. Maybe they know someone else who did it. Some other Realtor who had a piece of the action, or something like that. Man, this is frustrating!"

Michele said, "Welcome to my world. They all feel like this if they hang on more than forty-eight hours."

"Why forty-eight?"

"Because the crimes you solve faster than that are the easy, obvious ones. There's an adage that if it goes on for more than two days it's going to be a difficult one because someone's actually done a halfway decent job of covering his tracks." She sighed. She sounded tired. "Do you have anything else for me? Anything at all?"

"No."

"Have you talked to Julia again?"

I said, "You don't have to ask me three different times in three different ways. I have nothing else. Zip. I'm done."

"Yeah. Sure."

I didn't even argue this time. I knew she was right.

18

After their evening meal, Rita Mae sat at her sister Mary Ann's dining table with a pad of paper, making notes. Across the table lay sheets of paper that she had pulled from Henry Nettleton's file labeled MCWAIN. She took a sip of tea and cleared her throat. "It's a mess, but I think I understand it now," she said. "I'm glad Henry held onto this." She held up a sheet of notes entitled CITIZENS' GROUP, and pointed at the telephone number that Henry had underlined three times. "That woman we telephoned will be along shortly now."

Mary Ann looked up from the sock she was knitting. She had been knitting all day and knitting with a fury she had not previously brought to that activity. The yarn was wrapped so tightly around her aging fingers that it was polishing her thin skin to a shine. "All right, I'm ready to hear it."

"This man McWain, he did a lot of research," Rita Mae began. "There's all this science he did, for instance. It took me a while to understand any of it, but it seems that the water comes out of the rock, not an underground river as the well drillers told you."

"Out of rock? How can that be?"

Rita Mae looked at her sister over the tops of her reading glasses. She loved Mary Ann and knew her to be highly competent at the tasks she liked to do, but it had always been clear that other jobs were best left to someone who had other talents. It took all kinds to make a world, and Mary Ann was simply not the analytical type. "Just take that on faith," she said. "The thing is, some kinds of rock can hold more water than others."

Mary Ann set down her knitting and held her hands together to make a cup. She looked up at Rita Mae with a pathetic glimmering of hope in her eyes.

Rita Mae said, "No, Mary Ann. Think of it like a sort of sponge. Like in your kitchen here, some materials will soak up the water and then let you wring it out more easily than others."

The dawning of comprehension softened the lines on Mary Ann's forehead. "You mean the way a good cotton terry makes a better towel than polyester."

Rita Mae said, "Something like that, Mary Ann. But for the moment, think of it like a nice, big bucket. You stick your straw in there and have yourself a drink. You can drink for quite a while before the water runs out. And then maybe there's a tiny little trickle of water coming back in from somewhere—drip by drip—but if you're drinking from that straw and your neighbor's got a straw going, too, and his neighbor . . . well, you see, it's just coming out faster than it's going in, and you're out of water."

"So you're saying we can't share like our dear father taught us to."

"I'm saying there are more people in this world than there used to be, so there's not enough to go around."

Mary Ann said, "That's frightening, Rita Mae. I don't like thinking about that."

"I understand, Mary Ann, but this time you don't have a choice. You can refuse to think about it, but the facts don't change." She cocked an ear to the sound of a car approaching in the driveway. "Ah. That will be her now."

The doorbell rang, and Mary Ann got up to answer it.

At the door was a woman carrying a well-worn accordion file tied up with black ribon. "I'm Helga Olsen," she announced. "I'm so glad to meet you at last."

"Come in, Mrs. Olsen. This is my sister, Rita Mae Jones."

When they were all settled at the kitchen table with fresh cups of tea, and Mary Ann had once again resumed her frantic knitting, Mrs. Olsen opened her file and began to take out papers. "As you may know, a group of us have formed a citizens' alliance to stop development in this area. Now, I know that sounds like, 'I've got mine, now the rest of you stay away,' because few of us grew up here, but I see it differently. We have our investments to protect, and we also prefer that anyone who might be thinking of moving in here not get swindled by purchasing a house that's going to run out of water in jig time."

Helga extracted a stack of newspaper clippings and laid them out on the table. "These articles may have a lot of unfamiliar words in them, but the thrust of the matter is clear enough: Colorado doesn't have enough water for all the people who are being born here, let alone the people who are moving in from other places. In the northern and western parts of Colorado, the water supply is pulled from the rivers mostly, but down here in the southeast, most of it has to come out of the ground. And there just isn't enough water in the ground, so municipalities like Denver and surrounding cities have begun buying up the water rights from the farmers." She pointed at a sidebar that summarized the facts. "Thousands of acres per year—even tens of thousands—are being pulled out of production so the water can be piped to the cities."

Mary Ann said, "Well then, our municipality should be looking after this!"

"No, dear, you don't live in a municipality. You are on a private well. You're out here on thirty-five acres, and you have to find your own water."

Mary Ann's knitting needles clacked faster and faster. "You're telling me that this is widely known. That there have been articles published in . . . in a newspaper or something and that people know this and they didn't tell Henry or me."

"That appears to be the fact."

"What newspaper was that article in?"

Rita Mae looked at the margins of the papers. "It's the *Denver Post*, sister. And this one's in your local paper here in Castle Rock." She tipped her head forward and studied Helga Olsen over the tops of her glasses. "Now, I imagine that if it was in that paper, it would have been the talk of this whole county."

Helga opened another section of her accordion file. "And here's a whole packet of articles about a development some people from out of state wanted to put in just south of here, that would have pulled the water out of our ground even faster. Luckily, we've put a stop to that one, for the time being. But there's one more thing you need to know, Mary Ann."

"What's that? I can barely stand this!"

Helga turned another page in the sheaf of notes. "This is a photocopy of the permit to drill a well on your property."

Mary Ann's face knit with angry confusion. "I don't understand. What are you trying to tell me? Do I need a permit to drill my new well? Or does it already exist?"

Helga shook her head. "You do need a permit, but this is not it. This is the permit for your existing well, drilled one month before you purchased this property. And this . . ." She turned the next page. "This is the permit for the original well drilled on this property two years before that, when the house was built."

"I've got two wells? Where's the other one?"

Helga turned a sad face toward her neighbor. "No, dear, you have just the one. It appears that the first one is just a hole in the ground, and it's dead dry." She tapped that page. "The people who first lived in this house ran out of water, too. They knew there was almost none left, so they drilled themselves another well and quick sold the property to you."

"Then . . . I have to drill deeper yet?"

"No, it looks like you're already clear to the bottom of the aquifer. You see, the water here is all but gone. Each new well is lucky if it hits a tiny part of the rock that just didn't get drained yet, and those wells don't make water but a little while. But Mr. Attabury's company wants to build more houses out here anyway."

Mary Ann thrust the knitting down into her lap. "The nerve of these men! This is fraud!"

"Yes, it is. Your Realtor knew all about it, and so did the banker who made your loan."

"Mr. Entwhistle! Why ever would he engage in something like this? He could lose his bank!"

Helga opened her hands palms up. "There's an old saying about bankers, my dear: 'If you owe the bank a hundred dollars, you've got a problem. If you owe the bank a million dollars, the *bank* has a problem.'" She tapped one of the papers in her file. "Entwhistle's bank has loaned money to finance most of the homes in this valley, and it has a great deal more money out to Hugo Attabury's even bigger plans."

Mary Ann shook her head. "This can't be. I can't believe these men would purposefully set out to steal from people."

Helga leaned back in her chair. "I don't suppose they woke up one morning and said, 'Let's find someone to fleece.' I think they got in the habit of making money in a certain way, just as we're in the habit of getting water out a faucet. It's hard to stop doing something you've always done, even when it becomes obvious that it doesn't work anymore. The kindest thing I can say about these men is that they aren't yet ready to notice that they are doing something wrong."

Rita Mae said, "Henry's notes from his conversations with Dr. McWain suggest that the land along these creeks used to be cattle ranches."

"That's correct," said Helga. "Developers have been buying up and subdividing the old ranches all around here. They built your house. Attabury wanted the ranch that Afton McWain bought, but the man who owned it didn't want it subdivided, so he sold it to Afton instead. Bart Johnson is ready to go in with them on their grand scheme, but they need an easement across Afton's ranch to meet the county code." She rapped a knuckle on a list of figures. "But I can't see anyone investing money if they hear about the problem with the water."

Mary Ann let out an angry snort. "*We* invested."

"I know, dear."

Rita Mae said, "We'll have Mr. Upton refer us to a good lawyer."

Helga did not mince words. "Todd Upton knows all about this situation."

Rita Mae said, "But he sounded so surprised when he met with us!"

"He even came to his office on a Sunday," Mary Ann added. "He opened the office himself. His secretary wasn't even there."

Helga said, "Well now, he wouldn't want to meet on a day when there would be witnesses to your conversation, would he? Some people think the world exists for them to make a living, and I do believe your Mr. Upton is one of them. And then there's the man who supplies the cement for the foundations, and the owner of the lumberyard, and so on and so forth. It's not news to a one of them that these wells are going dry. Just ask the well drillers! They all play poker together. None of them wanted you to know you were buying a pig in a poke. They're all making too much money drilling new wells."

Tears swam in Mary Ann's eyes. "Then how . . . you mean . . ."

Helga said, "People don't like knowing that the comfortable life they've been living can't go on like it's been going." She gestured around the kitchen, at the dishwasher, at the clothes washer, at the sink. "These houses are built for a water-consuming lifestyle, so we're just going to have to change how we do things."

"What can we do?"

Rita Mae noted this small change in her sister's attitude: She had said 'we.' She no longer saw herself alone.

Helga said, "We can vote. We can hold our elected officials accountable and work to get more balanced policies in place that don't just follow the election campaign fund money, and think a little smaller than we have. And we can vote with every penny we spend. We can spend our money with people who supply products and services that will help us conserve, and we don't have to buy from people who encourage a throwaway lifestyle. For instance, we can think locally. All those outlet stores down by the freeway don't have their hearts and minds on local lifestyles, now do they? Decisions about what is sold in those stores are made in corporate offices in some other state, and the goods are manufactured on another continent. They sure aren't worrying themselves about what is happening here. They don't even know."

Rita Mae said, "Aren't you getting a bit off the point? They're just shops, after all."

Helga said, "I look at them as symptoms of the disease. We've all gotten so used to looking at *price* that we no longer know how to look at *cost*. When we build a house this way just because it's how we've always done it, we set ourselves up for just the sort of financial disaster your sister is now facing."

Rita Mae said, "But how is Mary Ann supposed to live out here with no water?"

Helga sighed heavily. "It's going to be tough, but we've set up a course at the community center that could help, if you're interested. We bring in specialists each week to teach us how to conserve, and we have a geologist who teaches us about our Earth systems, so we don't stay so ignorant. It's an interesting topic, once you get started."

Mary Ann turned her face to look out the window at the marvelous, open landscape that Henry had so loved. The setting sun was picking out each rock and shrub with rosy light, but the very sight of it sickened her now. Her voice quavered as she said, "So what you're saying is that even if I can find a way to pay for a new well, and even if it happens to have water in it, it's only a matter of time before the new well will go dry, too. And that means that if I drill the well just to put the house on the market, I'll be passing the fraud right along to the next poor person."

"I'm afraid so."

"I can't do that."

Rita Mae studied the way the light played across her sister's face. "Of course not, dear. You're not that kind of person."

Mary Ann stared out the window for quite a while longer before she said, "I can't believe Henry knew this and didn't tell me."

Rita Mae said, "Put it out of your mind, dear. He was desperately ill. A man can't bear to let his wife down."

Helga patted her wrist. "And he may not have known quite everything, dear. But you're not alone now. Alone, we are kittens. Together, we are like a pride of lions."

Mary Ann closed her eyes, dislodging a tear. "Doesn't Dr. McWain offer any hope?"

Helga cleared her throat. When she spoke again, her voice had gone husky. "He made some suggestions. He believed in a policy of collecting rainwater for personal use, but that, sadly, is against the law. All surface waters in the state of Colorado are already owned and apportioned."

"Then we should invite him over for dinner and get acquainted," Mary Ann declared, popping her eyes open and stiffening her lips.

Helga said, "I'm afraid that's not possible, dear."

"Why not? He was pleased to come once, so he'll come again, I'm sure of it!"

Helga closed her eyes. "I'm sorry to tell you that he's been murdered."

RAY SAT AT the table in his house, listening to the sounds of evening through windows left open in the hope of a breeze. Physically, he was alone, as he had been in all the years since his wife had died, but in his heart he reached out to the company of a great many people. He stared at a framed photograph of himself as a boy, posed in the house he had lived in then, with his parents and all of his sisters. In his mind, he assembled the support offered by his sponsor and all of the people who attended Al-Anon meetings with him. To this list he added his mother, who smiled brightly in the photograph, all of her children right there in front of her, healthy, happy, safe. Sitting next to her was his father, the first taints of the illness that would take this man from them already carved at his face. He lived on by the strong example he had set. And to his mental gathering Ray added Em Hansen, about as strong a woman as he had ever met. *Or maybe just hard-headed,* Ray decided angrily. *Hard-headed and uncompromising.*

Ray squeezed his eyes shut and bowed his head in frustration. *There it goes again, my frustration coloring my judgment. Because she doesn't share my beliefs, I decide that she's wrong.*

A car passed in the street. A dog barked. From somewhere down the block, a child shrieked.

I need to write a Tenth Step, Ray told himself. *Acknowledge where I'm going wrong. How tough can that be?* He flipped open *The Twelve Steps* of *Alcoholics Anonymous*, and read aloud: "Step Ten: Continued to take personal inventory, and when we were wrong, promptly admitted it."

What did I do wrong? he asked himself in frustration. All his hard, painful work of two years in the Program seemed to vanish like sand washing out from under his feet, swept away by the flood of his emotions. Ray stared down at the book that lay on the table in front of him. He set it aside and laid a sheet of paper in its place. On that clean white plane he evoked God as he understood Him. A kind and loving God. An all-powerful God. A God capable of hard choices.

Ray's heart raced with anxiety and confusion. *Heavenly Father, you never make mistakes. You are divine. I am human, and full of error. Please, let me know Your will for me.*

The page shone brighter.

Ray wrote: *I judged Em Hansen harshly. I decided that she was a bad person, someone who is fornicating, having sex outside of marriage. I didn't ask for the facts. I got angry without even knowing the truth.*

Ray sat up straight and read his words over a few times. One side of his brain cheered him, telling him how good he was being. The other side of his brain growled like a chained dog. *It doesn't take a genius to read that picture,* the dog snarled. *She's lying to you. She's sleeping with that guy, plain and simple. She's just another fornicating gentile, deviling God's plan for her, making it tougher for the rest of us. Serves her right if she gets in trouble trying to be a detective, when she's really just a geologist.*

Ray tightened his grip on his pencil, trying to focus on the next thing he was supposed to do. Follow the Steps, as the Program and his sponsor had taught him. His sponsor was a good man, a devout Mormon with a Temple Recommend. It wasn't his fault his wife had turned to drink.

Ray felt the room start to tilt. *I must hang onto my wits,* Ray told himself. *I'm judging again! And where does judgment take me? Straight to hell.*

He drove the pencil tip into the paper, writing as if he were trying to inscribe the words in stone: *When people don't do things my way, I feel insecure.*

Ray closed his eyes and stared at the ghostly after-image of the page. Moments ticked past.

He opened his eyes and wrote: *When Em follows her will, not mine, it hurts my self-esteem, and I get angry so I don't have to feel that hurt. My anger is so strong that it feels like the Will of God to me, but it is not.*

Ray dropped the pencil, snapped his hands together, and said the only Twelve-Step prayer he could think of: "God, help me not be angry at Em Hansen. She is a sick woman."

As the words slithered out, he knew they were not right. Like a drowning man, he grabbed for another life ring, another prayer: "God grant me the serenity to accept the things I cannot change, the courage to change the things I can, and the wisdom to know the difference!"

The words rang against the naked walls of the room. The four naked walls. The walls that he had uncovered when his wife died. He had taken down her pictures—not just the photographs of her, and of himself and her together, smiling, looking fit and prosperous in God's light—but also the other, more decorative pictures she had hung on the walls to make their house a home. Their home, this house that should have had her in it, and the children that had somehow never come to them.

His aloneness crowded in on him again, aloneness that followed him everywhere like a wolf, gaunt and hungry, dining on every shred of happiness that came his way.

Ray yanked his wallet out of his back pocket and dug through it feverishly, prizing up the tiny school photographs of his nieces and nephews that he kept there. Their little faces smiled out at him, needing him, loving him. He lined their photographs up on the tabletop and brought nearer the big, framed photograph of his boyhood family. He peered in at himself as a ten-year-old and found a face intent with seriousness mixed with pride and terror, for he was the only son with so many to look after if—when—his father died. And now, as a forty-two-year-old man, Ray arranged all the photographs around his confessional sheet of paper, pulling together all the strength he could muster, adding the mental image of his sponsor.

The phone rang. He answered it. The welcome voice of his sponsor filled the line. "How's it going, Ray?"

"Terrible," Ray said, no longer surprised that this man somehow always knew when to call.

"Sounds like progress. I always thought you got through the first round of this program too easily." He chuckled affectionately. "You mowed through the Steps first time like an Eagle Scout collecting merit badges."

"Thanks."

The jocular tone in the sponsor's voice vanished, replaced by concern. "Oh, sorry . . . you're down to one-word answers. You're truly upset."

"You know me well."

"So, what have you written so far?"

Ray read the words to his sponsor.

The sponsor reflected back. "Security. Self-esteem. A powerful mixture. We all need them. What else?"

"I fell into self-pity."

"Because . . ."

Ray's voice escaped him. Em had put her finger right on it. She was terrifyingly smart. He opened his mouth several times but could not push out even a single word. Finally, on the fourth try, he whispered, "I miss my wife."

"Yes."

Ray's voice cracked as he said, "Now *you're* using single words."

"How did she die, Ray?"

"Car crash."

"Who was driving?"

The room went cold.

The sponsor whispered, "Who was driving, Ray?"

"I was." The words drew out of him like a knife so sharp it cuts its scabbard.

"Was it your fault?"

"They . . . the officers that came to the scene . . . say it wasn't. The other driver was drunk. They say he came out of a side street doing sixty. I never saw him."

"Well, then."

"But I told Em . . ." Ray's face felt cold again, then his neck, then his chest, even in the heat of summer. It was as if his life was bleeding out of him, just as life had left his precious, innocent, beautiful wife in a steady, uncontrollable ooze.

"What did you tell Em?" the sponsor asked, when the silence had grown too long.

Ray yanked himself back from the image of his wife's face turning gray even as she looked up into his eyes, a farewell lifting from her face without words. "I told her that . . . I wasn't involved. Not there. I tell people she was alone." A great sob broke loose from Ray's chest, and in a voice as tiny and frightened as a child's, he said, "She may as well have been. I have my whole family lying for me!"

"What's Step One, Ray?"

"I admit—powerless—" Ray shifted the phone's handset from his ear to his forehead and rapped it sharply against his skull. His face writhed, turned dark red with holding his breath in an effort to stanch the images. Pain shot through him like an arrow, bringing in its wake the whole chaotic night it happened— the sirens of approaching police, the hot ride to the hospital in the cruiser, trailing the ambulance, the looks of terror and heartbreak on the faces of everyone in his family, the blur that filled the days that followed. The void, the emptiness.

Then Em . . . Emily Bradstreet Hansen, the first face strong enough to dredge his heart and mind up from the past and into the present. A woman so much the same as him and yet so different—a match yet not a match, enough conundrum to last a lifetime. A woman he had almost killed in his pursuit of her. A woman who forgave him and offered him her rebellious friendship even after all of that.

"Ray?" His sponsor's voice was a tiny bee in the earpiece.

Ray returned the phone to his ear and let his breath out in a long, ragged stream. "I'm here."

19

WEDNESDAY I WAS AT MY DESK AT THE UGS EXAMINING SOME UTAH marbles—iron concretions from the Navajo Sandstone, which geologist Marjorie Chan noted in the journal *Nature* are remarkably similar to the "blueberries" found by the Mars rover Opportunity—when Fritz phoned.

"Want to come for a spin after work?" he asked.

"Uh . . . well . . ."

"Come on, I'll take you across the Bonneville Salt Flats a hundred feet off the deck. A little low-level zooming always improves the blood flow."

"I'm kind of busy tonight," I said, though I wasn't. I stared at the marble in my hand. Was I losing the ones in my head?

"Okay," he said. He sounded doubtful. "Maybe a hike this Saturday?"

I wanted to ask, *Are you sure you'll be available Saturday? What if you sleep in with whoever answered the phone at your house Saturday night?* My heart contracted around that thought, telling me that the problem was there, not in my head. How could I tell him that I no longer wanted to be his pal, when I wanted to be so much more? But if I kept saying no, I wouldn't see him at all, and that was unacceptable, too. "Call me as the week progresses," I mumbled.

"Sure," he said, his voice flat.

I remembered the touch of his hand against my back as we returned from dinner that Friday in Denver. Had that feeling flowed only one way?

Fritz didn't say anything for several moments. Then, with concern in his voice, he asked, "Did they figure out who killed your friend?"

"No," I said, glad to have something I could talk about that wasn't about us. "We don't even know how he got here from Colorado. He didn't come on the airlines and ditto, public bus. It's kind of difficult to track a hitchhiker, unless maybe he rode a truck like . . ." I stopped abruptly, wanting to kick myself for speaking so freely. I had very nearly spilled essential information.

Fritz said, "Maybe he hitched a ride on a private plane, like you did."

The idea hit me like a brick. "Fritz, you might have something there. If someone was going to do that, where would he have to go from Sedalia, Colorado, to get a flight to Salt Lake City?"

"You mean, where was the nearest airport?"

"Yeah."

"Give me a minute." I could hear rustling as he unfolded an air chart. "Where is Sedalia, exactly?"

"It's south of Denver, about three or four miles northwest of Castle Rock, which is the biggest town between metro Denver and metro Colorado Springs."

"Okay, got it. There's an airport there in Castle Rock. No, wait, there isn't. Well, there are several private airstrips around there, and then there's Centennial, which is halfway to Denver, and then Colorado Springs International. Let's see . . ." Now I heard him tapping computer keys. "Centennial is fully IFR, and of course C Springs has the juice . . ."

"You're saying which airport you'd keep a plane at."

"Exactly."

"How would the police find out if someone had flown a passenger from there to here?"

"They'd subpoena the FAA for information about flight plans or go for the tower records. All those guys who track aircraft keep records of one kind or another. The towers keep tapes. Even if they left from, say, Colorado Springs and landed in Provo, there'd be a record of one type or another. And, as you'll recall from your own pilot training, the flight plan would list the passengers though not by name."

"Right," I said. "But it would list the pilot's name."

"Yes, it would list both the pilot and the aircraft. But there's an easier method for finding out who was aboard."

"What's that?" I asked, my excitement rising.

"If they landed at Salt Lake International, they'd tie down at one of the FBOs out here, and we pay plenty of attention to who comes and goes. It's a security requirement. All doors and gates are kept locked and we have people who'll stop anyone who tries to get out on the ramp without a clearance. We keep records of the tail numbers, and when someone buys gas and pays for the tie-down, we've got their credit card receipt. And even if your pilot doesn't buy gas or stop long enough to tie down, he might own the aircraft. You can go online to look up aircraft ownership."

"How do I do that?"

"The FAA site has a cross-reference. You can look up by owner's name, or by tail number."

I was so excited that I jumped to my feet. "Thanks, Fritz. You're brilliant. Gotta go."

"Wait! What's the hurry?"

"I think you just turned the key. Really, I've got to report this right away."

"Well, call me. There's something I'd like to talk—"

"Sure," I said, but I already had my hand on the button, cutting off the connection, and my eyes were scanning my desktop for Michele's card. I found it and dialed.

When she picked up the line, I said, "Bet you dollars to doughnuts Hugo Attabury is a pilot. That means he might have a plane. Hell, a small-time tycoon like him—"

Michele was laughing at me again. "A what?"

"He's got 'hustler' written all over him."

"So wait, what's this got to do with . . . ohhh, you think he flew McWain over here and bashed his head in and threw him in the quarry and flew home."

"Could have been, huh?"

"It's a long shot."

"But easy to check out. First you'd get on with the FAA to find out if he owns a plane. Wait, I'll do that myself." I turned to the computer on my desk and brought up the FAA Web site. A few keystrokes later, I was into the aircraft registry. As I typed in HUGO ATTABURY, I said, "He doesn't have to own it, he could rent one, and there you'd just go to the FAA anyway because the flight plan would be in his name. Just search backward from Friday—wait!" The site spat back my answer.

"What did you find?"

"Here it is: Beechcraft B55. Our boy flies a nice, fast little twin."

"What's a . . . oh, you mean two engines?"

"Exactly. A B55 is a Baron. It'll cruise at, say 180 knots. That's over 200 miles per hour. Even against a headwind coming over the mountains, he could leave Thursday afternoon, be here from Centennial in two hours, do his dirty work, and be back in Colorado in time for a nightcap. If he landed at Salt Lake International, he'd probably have parked at Million Air; that's the FBO that receives most of the transient general aviation aircraft. They have guys out on the line who gas the planes, and they see the pilots and passengers, too. They are responsible for security just like on the commercial side of the airport. You can't come and go through there without being clicked through locked doors and gates by a guard. They'd have a log you could subpoena, and there are people at the desk who are trained to make personable contact with everyone who comes through there. Their job is to remember individuals, not like the cattle processing that goes on at the commercial aviation side. People think that general aviation is a security sieve, but an FBO will be able to tell you not only names but also what each passenger looks like, and how he took his coffee."

"So he wouldn't even have to kill McWain here. He could kill him in Colorado and fly him here dead."

"He'd have killed him here. The boys on the ramp would notice if someone offloaded a bloody corpse. Besides, a man who owns his own Baron would bring the meat in on the hoof. The last thing he'd do is dispose of a nice plane like that just because he got a little blood in the cargo bay."

"And he killed him why?"

"Ah . . . because the stiff knew he didn't have any water for that big subdivision he has planned with Bart Johnson. They couldn't let him live; he was going to keep them from overstepping their ecological footprint."

"Overstep their footprint. I like that."

"Don't snicker at me. Get on the horn and subpoena those tower records."

"Will do, cap'n," she said, her sardonic laugh growing thicker.

"What's so damned funny?"

"You just called your old colleague a stiff. In your mind, he's changed from a human being to a piece in a puzzle. You're in this for the excitement. As I said, Em, you're hooked."

"Have it your way, Michele."

"You—" I heard a buzzer sound on her end of the line. "Hold a sec." When she came back on the line, she said, "Who's this Trevor Reed, and why is he calling me? He says he knows you."

"Investment banker. Didn't I tell you? I asked him to run down the Wildcat Estates development for us. Inside information."

"Oh. Okay, then meet me at his office downtown in about fifteen minutes."

"I'm on my way."

"And, Em? Thanks."

◈

Trevor Reed lounged back in his cushy leather swivel chair, examining me with the interest of a tailor examining his work. His office was huge and lined with exotic hardwoods, and his chair was imposingly large, too. It all but swallowed him, and exaggerated his youth.

Having eyed me to his satisfaction, he settled on a longer look at Michele. He obviously liked what he saw. "Thanks for running over so quickly," he said. "I don't have all that much to report, but I thought I should get it to you right away."

"Fire when ready," said Michele. She sat in one of the capacious side chairs, pen poised over a tablet.

"I have this: The Wildcat Estates project is in trouble. Their investors have been very unhappy with them because they have not come through with the promised requisites for the project."

"Are we talking about the water?" I asked. "Or lack thereof?"

Reed momentarily looked blank. "No, my sources mentioned an easement."

"What kind of easement?" Michele asked, narrowing her eyes in concentration.

Reed shifted in his chair. He fiddled with a pen. The corners of his mouth flickered into a smile. I realized that he was nervous in the way men get when they meet a woman they find particularly attractive.

I settled back to watch.

Reed leaned forward, putting his elbows on his desk. "The county plan requires that a development of that size have two routes of egress," he began. "Bart Johnson's ranch is sufficiently large to make the project go—fiscally speaking—but it lacks a second way out. This is required in case of needing to move emergency equipment in, things like that. The problem is that his ranch is sort of pie-shaped, with just the narrow point connecting up to the one road. He needs to connect to another road on the far side of the hill, but he would have to cross the neighboring ranch, belonging to your murdered man, McWain. McWain wouldn't give him an easement. To make things even more contentious, it seems that McWain purchased his ranch from Johnson's brother. Another way of saying this is that Johnson's brother sold it to McWain *instead* of Johnson."

Michele said, "No easement, no development. No development, no cash flow."

"Not only no cash flowing in, but lots of invested money going away. And Entwhistle's bank could go under."

"And you were able to find this out from your contacts."

"Easily. A lot of investors are quite angry with the promoters of this project."

Michele gave him a beaming smile as a reward. Reed actually blushed.

She tapped her pen on her tablet. "Anything else?"

The pleasurable embarrassment dissolved from Trevor Reed's face. "Just this: I am aware of who these angry investors are. They are not the sort of people I'll do business with."

"What kind of people are they?" Michele inquired.

"The last time they wanted something from a rancher who hesitated about cooperating, they landed an unmarked helicopter on her spread and shot all her horses."

I DROVE OVER to the Salt Lake City Police Department. I needed to talk to a male friend, and Ray was going to have to do.

Ray startled when he saw me, his hands jolting outward as if to get his balance. He brought them in again as quickly, trying to cover his reaction. "Em," he said. "What's up?"

"Got a moment?"

He looked right and left. "Sure . . ."

"Maybe we could walk around the block?"

"Let's walk to the north and east a ways, where at least there's some shade."

I nodded, and we set out. When we were a block and a half from the police station, I said, "I need your advice."

"Here comes trouble."

"I'm sorry, Ray, but I don't know who else to ask."

"All right, shoot."

Now I didn't know what to say. What was troubling me was gray and nebulous, like a cloud. "This case I'm assigned to," I began.

"The corpse in the quarry?"

"Yeah."

"You can ask to be removed from the case. Any time."

I was taken aback. "Why would I want that?"

"Because you knew the guy. Always best not to be involved. They'll understand. In fact, they'll prefer it."

I stopped walking and stared at him.

His face had gone all stormy. "You asked for my advice."

I stared into his dark blue eyes and saw a whole lot of worry shining back. "Do you know something I don't, Ray?"

He looked away. "No . . ."

"Well, there's another part to this, anyway."

"What's that?"

We began walking again, the heat of the pavement rolling in under the shade of the spreading trees. "Well, it's kind of personal, but maybe related. It's about . . . well, why are men so protective of women, Ray?"

He laughed nervously. "It's our job to protect you."

I tipped my head at him. "You know that's not what I mean. I'm not looking for what it says in the Good Book or anything like that. I mean . . . well, I'm trying to understand why some men are protective and some aren't."

"Men who don't protect their women should be shot," he said.

"Well, now we're narrowing down the topic. I'm talking about men who are protective of a woman who isn't their woman."

Ray blushed deeply. "Who exactly are we talking about?"

"A hypothetical guy," I said. "I know you, and I used to be . . . well, I'm not talking about you, okay? And, well, I've got to talk to a friend about this! I know this guy, see, and he's always around kind of looking after me, and I like that fine, but other friends are telling me he likes me, see . . . *likes* me likes me, but I don't see that, so I'm just trying to understand."

Ray began to chuckle, as if savoring a private joke.

"Damn it, Ray, what's so funny about that? Can't I be interesting to someone?"

He patted my shoulder. "It's okay, Em. Okay, I see what you're asking. Well, men are protective of women, yes. And that's a good thing. Speaking for myself, I'm protective of my mother and my sisters and all of my nieces and girl cousins and, as a policeman, I'm protective of every woman in Salt Lake City. But you're talking about something different from that. Something additional."

"I suppose so."

We walked onward. "So what's your question?"

"I already said!"

He laughed again. "Just teasing, Em. Okay, I'll tell you, from personal experience, what it's like to feel protective of you. It's awful."

I punched him on the arm.

"Em, part of what's attractive about you is that you can look after yourself. That's what drew *me* to you. There are men who need a woman to be more helpless than you are, and then there are men who like their women strong."

"Okay . . ."

He said, "But there's a conundrum to that. Because you're strong, you take on jobs that other women wouldn't, and then you're at risk. *Really* at risk. We're not talking 'Let me carry that for you, ma'am,' or 'Do you need me to build a shelter over you.' You walk right out there where people want to kill you."

We had turned and were heading back toward the police station now. "So you're saying that men who are attracted to me are also put off. I'm a bad investment."

He nodded. "In a manner of speaking. I mean no offense, but if you were looking for someone to have babies with, would you choose someone who might get shot by a criminal?"

I gave him a look. "I chose you . . ."

He nodded. "But I'm the man. Babies don't die if the dad dies. Not right away." Before I could start arguing modern sociology with him, he added, "I'm talking hard wiring here, Em. Men don't consult some book or something when they find themselves attracted to a woman."

"Okay, but if he's feeling protective, does that mean he's attracted? And how would he show that he's feeling protective, and, um . . ."

Ray strolled along, eyes on the sidewalk in front of him, hands folded behind his back. "Em, remember when you and I were really close?"

"Yes . . ."

"We had a connection."

"Yes, well, ah . . ."

"I mean a very deep connection, Em, and parts of it are still there, so I know you know what I mean. I'm not talking about sex. I'm talking about the Spirit."

"Oh. Well, there you know more than I do, with all your church stuff."

He laughed again. "You are one of the most spiritual women I've ever met, Em, so we're really just arguing terms. Do you remember that time you saved my life? What am I talking about? You've saved me again and again!" He stopped and stared up into the trees, his arms wide with happy supplication. "That's it! Now I get it!"

"Get what?"

"Why I still feel so protective of you! I *owe* you, Em!"

"You owe me nothing, Ray."

He waved a hand, indicating that I couldn't possibly understand. "Don't worry. It's okay. It's okay . . ." Suddenly he fixed his eyes on me, sharply. "But what I'm saying is true, Em. Connection from one spirit to the next, it's a true and real thing and very, very precious. If you ever need me, *ever*, you just put up that antenna of yours and say, 'Ray, help me!' Okay? I'll hear you!" He reached out and grabbed me by both shoulders. "Do you hear me, Em?"

"Yes." I was so startled that I spoke like a little girl trying to be good.

He searched my face. "Because we're back to your original topic now, Em. This case you're on. It's a bad one. I advise you to write up your report and stop right there."

"I did."

He dropped his hands in frustration. "I've just done the dumbest thing in the world."

"What?"

"Told you not to do something. Now you'll take that as a challenge."

"No, I won't. Honest. I've been trying to get out of this case, but Michele—"

"*Damn* Michele!"

"Ray, I've never heard you swear. Never."

He jammed his hands into his pockets and hurried back toward the police station. On his athletic legs he was pulling ahead of me, fast.

"Ray, wait up!"

Without turning to face me, he shouted, "Just promise me you'll watch your back this time, Em. Please! Just watch your back."

MICHELE AND RAY were right, I couldn't stay out of it. As soon as I got back to my office I phoned Julia.

She was roaring. "That bitch!" she howled.

"What bitch? Me?"

"Nature Girl!" she shrieked, giving the name an ear-splitting nasal sing-song. "That black-hearted, weaseling, gold-digging *monster!*"

I could hear a lot of conversation in the background. One loud voice was telling Julia to keep her voice down and not say anything she didn't want repeated back to her, grossly distorted, in a court of law.

"Have I called at an inopportune time?" I inquired.

Julia struggled to get her voice under control. "That's my dear friend Angie in the background. She happens to also be my lawyer. She is over here trying to keep me from taking a shotgun and *shooting* the freaking beauty queen *impostor—*" Here she took another breath and screamed, "RIGHT IN HER SHRIVELED, RANCID, BUSH-LEAGUE EXCUSE FOR A *HEART!*"

"And the shriveled . . . whatzit has done *what* to get you this excited?"

"She has filed in court to be recognized as Afton's next of kin!"

"And her excuse is . . . oh yeah, she styles herself his common-law wife."

"That *is* her fantasy."

"So she's really going to press that claim."

Julia shrieked, "You *knew* about this? And you didn't *tell* me? What kind of a friend *are* you?"

I closed my eyes. I said, "I'm sorry, Julia. Truly. I am working on this case and because of that I have to stay quiet about a great many things."

"So what *else* haven't you told me?"

I winced. I'd always gotten along with Julia—in spite of her coarse language and penchant for self-pity—precisely because she was candid, but candor was too slim a virtue to mitigate the bad cocktail of emotions that was sluicing around inside her just now. I counted to ten, struggling to keep my own in check.

Julia said, "You show up in my office pretending to be my friend, but you're just an adrenaline junkie! Or worse, you're a ghoul!"

Julia's words stabbed into me. Perhaps because this was the third time I had heard this accusation in one day, I looked down into my heart and saw nothing but a dried-up loner who couldn't figure out how else to have a life with the people around her. I was hiding in my work, and work like this was a drug to numb my aloneness, just like smack.

You're forty years old and pretend you want a man and a baby, but you've been hiding in an arm's-length relationship with a man who considers you his buddy, I told myself.

But there are those wonderful moments with Sloane, I argued. *Or the times I go to dinner at Faye's . . .*

When was the last time you did that? my internal critic sneered.

My mind wandered back to the realities of the moment. Julia's voice was still going off in my ear. ". . . and if you can't be honest with me, go do your damned cowgirl Em Hansen thing. Go to hell, okay? I mean, life is too short to hang out with people on a trip like yours, you know?" She was crying now.

"You're right," I said, in a voice as thin as vapor. "You're absolutely right, I've been playing hero again, and you need me to just be your friend." I took a deep breath. "Please forgive me, Julia."

MICHELE PHONED AGAIN just before it was time for me to quit for the day and go home. In the wake of my conversation with Julia, I had been on a downward spiral into that dark place that lurks underneath daily routines and the other businesses of life. "What do you have for me?"

I asked, meaning *Do you have something that can fill the next hour, let alone the rest of my existence?*

"I have a plane ticket to Colorado, unless you've got another hitch-hiker's pass with your friend."

"What?"

"Your idea about the airplane hit the jackpot," she said, her voice going all juicy with satisfaction. "We've got an FAA record of a Beechcraft Baron belonging to a Hugo Attabury taking off from Centennial last Thursday at 5 P.M. and returning during the night. The flight plan gave a different name—George Lewis—but we've got an eyewitness at Million Air who saw two white males getting off that plane. One answers close enough to a description of Hugo Attabury, and the other was dressed just like our corpse. They were met by another man who was waiting for them. The car came back at 2 A.M. I don't have an eyewitness yet who saw how many people were in it, but we'll have that as soon as their night crew comes on shift. We're subpoenaing the tower tapes to nail Attabury's voice."

"So you're going back to Colorado to interrogate him again?"

"Right."

"If you're so close to a collar, what do you need me for?"

"You're the one who understands this ground water thing. If he was so afraid of McWain's testimony that he'd kill him—and if McWain got off that plane alive, who else killed him, hmm?—then finding out I've got a geologist backing me up will loosen him up quite nicely."

She was right. Forensic geology was a double-edged knife. One edge looked at microscopic evidence of Earth materials. The other edge was much broader: The contexts and connections under which the profession of geology was carried out. "With the evidence you have, he'll probably go down like a house of cards. Anyone can file a flight plan under a false name, and his alibi is a lawyer who also stood to gain from McWain's death," I said.

"All right," Michele grumbled. "But if Attabury can prove it wasn't him at the controls of that airplane, I'm back at it with the shovel again. So stay close to the phone, okay?"

"Sure. Hey, you've got a backup going into it with Attabury, right?"

"The locals are ready and waiting."

"Good. See ya."

"I have a nasty feeling you will."

20

TO PROVE TO MYSELF THAT I HAD A LIFE OUTSIDE MY WORK, I phoned Faye and invited her and Sloane to come to my apartment for dinner. When they arrived, I had hot dogs for Sloane and a nice bit of steak for us grownups, and some cold cooked potatoes fried up with red onions. Faye brought a salad. We sat out on my little balcony in the shade of the elm tree and caught the evening breezes, enjoying a cup of decaf after the meal and waiting for the air to cool and the sky to go pink over the Oquirrhs.

"How's that case coming?" she asked.

"I'm standing by for a phone call," I told her. "I might need to go back to Colorado tomorrow."

"Are you going with Fritz?" she asked. "I thought he wasn't going back until the weekend."

"No, that's okay," I replied. "The sheriff's department will pay for me to fly commercially."

"But Fritz will be going over there again tomorrow or the next day for Mr. Reed. Why would you want to fly commercial when you can go general aviation? No waiting at the gate, no long lines anywhere, you go into a more convenient airport and to an FBO where people treat you like something smarter than cattle, and besides, you get to ride with Fritz. And Mr. Reed really enjoyed your travelogue."

"That's nice to hear," I said noncommittally.

Sloane had climbed up onto my lap. "Horsy ride," she begged, pulling on my thumbs as if they were reins.

I jiggled her up and down gently and sang, "This is the way the ladies ride, trippity-trot, trippity-trot . . ."

"Are you and Fritz having a fight or something?" Faye asked.

"No."

"Then why are you avoiding him?"

"Am I?" I tried to deflect Faye's scrutiny by looking the little girl in the eye, wondering if the horsy seemed lame to Sloane, too. Shifting to a faster gait, I said, "This is the way the gentlemen ride, gallopy-trot, gallopy-trot . . ."

"He said you turned him down for a low-level flight in his plane. That sounds serious to me."

"Cowboy!" Sloane cried, giggling with glee.

Faye said, "Em, fess up; something's bothering you. Come on, you can't hide it from—" she shot out a hand and jabbed me in the ribs, a rough tickle, "—the claws of Faye!"

"Ouch!" I shrieked.

Sloane squealed with glee. "Cowboy! Cowboy!" She rocked forward and back maniacally, almost dislocating my thumbs.

Bouncing Sloane right into the air, I cried, "This is the way the cowboys ride, gallopy-gallop, gallopy-gallop!"

Faye raised her arm for another strike.

Panting, I said, "Fritz is busy."

"Busy doing what?"

"Dating what's-her-name."

"What's-her-name? Who's what's-her-name? Fritz hasn't spent time with anyone but you in months."

"Well then, who was that in . . ." Cringing, I slammed on the verbal brakes, but I had already said too much.

Sloane twisted and wiggled with delight. "Farmer! Farmer! C'mon Auntie Emmy! Farmer!"

I began to lift one knee and then the other, rolling her from side to side. "This is the way the farmers ride, hobblety-hoy, hobblety-hoy . . ."

Faye gave me her you-cannot-avoid-the-piercing-mind-of-Faye look. "Spare me the twenty questions this time, will you?"

I tried unsuccessfully to quell a whiny tone that crept into my voice, but failed. "There was somebody at his house Saturday night. A woman answered the phone."

"Oh yeah. Marsha."

"That was *Marsha*?" I felt like a total fool. "What was his ex-wife doing answering the phone?"

"She was there to drop off Brendan and discuss their situation. Which is serious. Did he tell you she wants to move out of state?"

"Yes . . ."

"Yeah, well she can't do it without his say-so, I don't think, so she's there putting pressure on him. It's been awful for him. He could really use your support just now."

I pulled Sloane into a tight hug and buried my face against her shoulder.

Faye asked, "What's troubling you so, Em? Come on, you can tell me. I won't bite."

"It's nothing."

"It's Fritz."

"No, it's not."

"You can lie to yourself, Em, but you can't lie to me. Why are you hiding from him? Because Marsha answered the phone? Wait . . . I get it! You *like* him! Well, he's *nuts* about you!"

"How do you *know* that?"

Faye stared at me, really squinted, as if I were some odd bug she had never seen before. "You two really are a pair. Just like you, he misses half the social clues that are thrown at him and misconstrues the others. In his case, it makes him easy to get along with because, while he doesn't hear half of the compliments, he's also deaf to three-quarters of the insults. But with you, it somehow just makes you ornery."

"So you're saying we're not suited for each other."

"I'm not saying that at all. What's not to like? He's Mister Nice Guy. Amiable. Decent. Keeps his nonsense to himself. He doesn't take things personally, and he'd never, ever push himself on you. Besides that, he's smart about a great many things— good at business, good with clients for all the reasons I've just mentioned, and a wizard at anything to do with aircraft or flying. And he's damned fine to look at, he takes care of his body, he loves kids, and hey—featurette!—he's deeply moral. What is your problem?"

"I—" What *was* my problem? "I don't know. He's so calm all the time. I get to feeling agitated around him. I can't hold still. I feel like an idiot sometimes."

Faye shook her head. "He's a good man, Em. Try letting him be the calm one so you can do the wiggly stuff."

I seized the opportunity to change the subject from me to her. "It sounds like you like him a lot. I shouldn't get in the way."

"He has eyes for you, toots, not me. Trust Mama Faye."

"But what if I weren't here? Wouldn't he then like you?"

"I doubt that."

"But would you like him to?"

"Like him to what?" Faye asked.

"To like you?"

"He does like me. We're very good friends and successful business partners, and that is exactly how we both like it. Trust me, we've even . . . drum roll . . . discussed this."

"But wouldn't you like him to *love* you? As a woman?"

"No, I would not like that."

"Then you don't really—"

"What are you looking for? My stamp of approval? Didn't I just give that to you?"

"If you approve of him, why aren't you interested in him?"

"Because it would ruin everything."

"How so?"

"Because then he would be a frustrated business partner who wanted to be my lover, which I don't want."

"Why not?"

"Because I'm not his type, and he's not my type."

"What is your type?"

Faye's gaze drifted to the sunset and grew dreamy. "You knew him. Tom was my type. Tom really, truly did it for me." She shook herself as if waking from a trance. "Fritz does *not* do it for me."

"But do you do it for him?"

"I already said—oh, I get it, you don't want to be second best. Don't worry about that, Em. Fritz has never even so much as given me the once-over. I think he saw you and that was that. The women he's been dating since he met you have been just . . . well, companions. He's been waiting for you."

"How do you know this? Has he told you this?"

Faye was beginning to lose patience. "No, but it's as clear as the nose on his face. Every time he looks at you he gets kind of . . . well, his cheeks get rosy; haven't you ever noticed?"

"I thought that was just how Fritz's face was put together."

"That's because you're there each and every time you look at him. Try sneaking up on him some time. In fact, try not ignoring him; he'll get even redder."

Sloane had turned around in my lap and rested her head against my chest. She was getting sleepy with all this adult chitchat.

And I was getting agitated again. The subject was swinging back to me like a twenty-millimeter gun that had snapped an anchoring pin. I kicked it back her way. "But you need a husband, a father for Sloane."

The little girl's eyelids were growing heavy, and her neck was damp with baby sweat from being so close to me. I wanted to hold her forever.

Faye said, "I may need a father for Sloane, but I do not need a husband."

"You don't?"

"No. I don't. Em, not every woman needs a husband. When Tom came along, that was great—while it lasted. In my own peculiar way, I'm kind of a one-man woman. But that's gone. Over. He's dead."

"I know, but if he'd lived?"

"Then I hope we could have kept it going, at least for Sloane's sake. But neither of us was really built for the good ol' settled-down bit."

"Am I?"

"I doubt it."

"Then why—?"

"Because you want a man! It's written all over you. You've got 'I need a man and a baby' tattooed on your forehead. Or maybe on some other part of your anatomy."

"But you've just said I'm not built for settling down."

"You aren't. Damn it, Em, dynamic people do not settle down!"

"*I'm* dynamic?"

Faye flopped back in her chair. "Woman, you are the dynamo itself. Or make that feminine—you're a dynama."

"So—"

"So you find someone who doesn't require that you settle down. What is this, rocket science? You want to be miserable, go find some chump who's looking for a house frau. That is not you. Bon-bons and daytime soaps just ain't gonna keep your heart pumping. You're like a horse that needs plenty of exercise. And a very big pasture to run in."

"No," I said. "I'm the rider. And no fences or I'll jump them."

"I rest my case."

"But Fritz wants . . . a woman who'll settle down?"

Faye said, "Yeah, what does Fritz want? Let's see if you can figure that out. Em, you are so thick!"

"He makes jokes about wanting a wife and babies. Doesn't that mean settling down?"

Faye shook her head. "Fritz is not the type who makes jokes about such things, except maybe to hide his intentions in plain sight."

"How do you know so much about him?"

"I work with the man every day." She shrugged. "And it's a lot easier to see these things when you're not hiding from the man. Em, take it easy on him. Look what he's going through now. Ol' Marsha wants to take his one baby somewhere where he couldn't see even as much of him as he's seeing now. I think the man's a saint that he's not taking a meat ax to her or even cussing about her. Most men who go through such things come up with nasty names or just refer to their former wives harshly as 'the ex.' But Fritz doesn't have a mean bone in him."

"So how's he doing with all that?" I asked with embarrassment. She was right, I should have been a support to him.

"Oh . . . well . . . I asked him how he felt, and he said it hurt but that life wasn't simple. He said he'd made his choices, and she was making hers, and he had to think it through and figure out what was best for Brendan, time with his dad or too much time with a frustrated mother. Call him, Em."

"Okay," I said. "Okay, I'll call him, get him out for a hike. He always looks happier after a little exercise."

"I'll bet. He gets those roses in his cheeks every time." She stared at the clouds that had gathered over the Oquirrhs. "You've done such a good job of asking me questions that I haven't gotten to ask you the obvious one. Do you want him?"

Sloane was out cold, or should I say, out warm in my lap. Softly, I said, "I don't know, Faye. How do you know when you've met the right man?"

Faye let out a long sigh. "Sometimes you find out the hard way."

21

MICHELE PHONED FROM COLORADO JUST AFTER THE LAST LIGHT OF sunset had faded. "Attabury's tougher than I thought," she said.

"What happened?" I asked. "When I didn't hear, I figured you had it sewn up."

"I got him down for questioning, but he got Upton on me so fast my head was ringing. He admitted that the plane was his but said if it's been to Salt Lake City in the past three years it was without him. He showed us a long, narrow black book like that should prove to us he wasn't there."

"His Pilot Log Book," I said. "And he has a point there. They're like a religious article . . . what do you call them, that name Catholics have for bones of the saints."

"Holy relics. Anyway, it was quite a performance. Upton said to come back when we had something stronger than 'a bunch of hearsay from a government agency.'"

"He was referring to the FAA."

"The same."

"A pilot not writing his hours down in his log book, that's cold. But it didn't worry them just a bit that eyewitnesses at Million Air had him and McWain on the ground at Salt Lake International last Thursday?"

"No, it did not. Whoever flew that plane paid cash for the tie-down. And I couldn't make McWain stick, because I haven't put McWain's mug shot in front of the ground crew, have I, because I don't have a picture of what he looked like alive, do I? Upton too accurately pointed out that 'white male in hiking boots' was a rather broad categorization. So now I'm cooling my heels at the Motel No-Tell again, waiting for daylight, a judge, and the hope of subpoenas, so I can get at that airplane. I just hope he doesn't have any football buddies on the bench, or I could be here a while."

"Tough luck."

"Yeah. But of course if he was a whiner I would have had him last Friday at the Sedalia Grill. So anyway, can you come out here? The longer this takes, the colder the trail and the more time Mister Wonderful has to cover his tracks. Maybe you can subpoena *his* shoes and get some damned clay off of them."

"What you'd want is some gravel from Point of the Mountain Quarry."

"That would do nicely. Can you do that?"

I shook my head at the phone. "I think you're getting things backward here. Remember, I'm a scientist at heart. I like my evidence straight up, not cooked."

Michele growled, "I wasn't suggesting that you salt him."

"But you were thinking it."

"*You* try sleeping in this motel. The walls are as thin as cardboard. I can hear the couple next door—"

"Spare me! And you want me to come sleep there, too?"

"Well, I thought a smart scientist like you could crack this case before lunchtime. You'll be home for dinner with that pilot of yours."

"Leave Fritz out of this."

"Give me my dress back."

"Sorry. I meant to launder it first."

"Keep it a while. It might help you get lucky. And try smiling once in a while, it makes you look human."

I realized that I was grinning. Michele and I were having fun cussing each other out. "Okay, firebrand, I'll see you there as soon as I can get a flight."

"I already made a reservation for you. It's the red-eye. You can just make it."

"You think of all the amenities."

"Rent a car at the airport, and get your butt down here. I'm going out for a while to keep Attabury under surveillance. If I'm out when you get here, call me on my cell phone. If I'm here, I'll no doubt be awake unless Mister Olympus on the other side of the wall runs out of steam."

◈

THERE'S A BIG five-pointed star all done up in lights that glows on the top of the butte that Castle Rock is named after, and when it hove into view later that night I began to feel my fatigue. It was not only the hour but the year. I had seen that star so many times as I drove to college and back again that it was like a splinter in my psyche digging deeper with every year.

I pulled into the lot by the motel at 2:30 A.M. under a starry sky that had faded under the pollution of too many security lights left on around too many buildings.

The light was on in room 201, so I tapped on it softly and Michele opened the door. She was not only awake, she was still dressed. "Thanks for coming," she said.

"Think nothing of it." I yawned. "I left messages for my old friend Carlos Ortega of the Denver homicide squad before I got on the plane, as well as Tim Osner, who's another kind of forensic geologist, just to give them a head's up. In case we need some mystery moves. You know what I mean."

"Yeah. We could use a magician right now. Bet you dollars to dough-nuts our boy's gone in the morning."

"You think your pigeon will fly the coop?"

"Yeah."

"Then why aren't you parked by Centennial Airport where you can get a photograph of him leaving? Didn't you give him the old, 'don't leave town' lecture?"

"I did. I dropped by Centennial on my way down here and the smart boy had already moved the plane somewhere else."

"And let me guess. He didn't file a flight plan."

"No, ma'am."

"So it could be anywhere. In any of half a dozen private airstrips around here, tucked into a hangar where you'd never see it, or even across the border in Mexico by now."

"Yeah, with him in it. He did a real nice job of giving me the slip half an hour after I called you. That boy knows escape and evasion driving."

"No shit."

"None whatsoever. I lost him on I-25. He pulled the old on-off trick."

"Down one ramp and up the other to see if you were following him."

"And I was. And there's all that construction. And a stoplight that he hit just as it changed, and some old biddie between us slammed on her brakes like the good citizen she was. He's good."

"Damn."

"Douglas County put an APB out on him. Hopefully, the state patrol will spot his car."

"So where was your backup?"

"We're out here in the tules, it would seem. I thought we were close to Denver, but this is a different county altogether. I was following him in the rental car. He was driving a BMW."

"Well then, they'll spot it easily enough."

"Oh yeah? You want to know how many assholes drive that make and model along the Front Range of Colorado?"

As common as cow flops on a feedlot came to mind, but I said, "Well, get some sleep." I went to my room, locked and chained the door, and got into the T-shirt I liked to sleep in. The air conditioner was noisy, so I turned it off, but then the highway noise started to grind on me, so I turned it back on. I turned out the lights and stared into the dark, or should I say half-gloom, considering all the light that was leaking around the curtains. After half an hour contemplating how correct Michele was about this motel, I switched on my cell phone to see what time it was and saw that there was a message waiting for me. I punched in the code to listen to it.

It was Fritz. "Hi, Em. Hey, Faye just phoned to tell me you were on your way back to Colorado. T-revor Rex wants me to fly him there to-morrow evening, so if you're still around, why not give me a call? You know where I'll be. In fact, *please* give me a call. Thanks. Good-bye for now."

I listened to the message again, then turned off the phone and closed my eyes. The light and noise didn't bother me half as much now. I fell asleep quickly and rested well.

◆

THURSDAY MORNING, HUGO Attabury was nowhere to be found. He had not returned from his drive the evening before. He was not answering his home phone, his office phone, or his cell phone. His wife had not seen him. His office manager had not heard from him. His cell phone rolled over to its messenger service instantly, indicating that it was not even switched on.

"This won't help his case," Michele said.

"If you find him," I replied. We were eating breakfast at one of those archaic places just off the interstate that serve overcooked eggs, dispirited hash browns, greasy toast, and burnt coffee to people with too much inertia and too little gastronomic insight to drive a block further off their route. "So I'll get to work anyway. I thought I'd give Julia a call and ask her if she can fill me in on some of the politics around the Arapahoe aquifer."

"Just don't tell her anything she could repeat. We don't want that angle out on the grapevine. Understand?"

"Yes, ma'am. And what about Gilda? Where is she in all of this?"

"I forgot to tell you. She's disappeared, too."

"What *is* it with these people? You mean *disappeared* disappeared, or just not at home?"

"I've been up to the ranch looking for her and her golf cart's there, but she's not. And no one's seen her, or at least, no one who's seen her since Tuesday is talking."

"What are you thinking?"

Michele shook her head. "I can't quite figure it. She told *you*—not me, I don't rate—that she wasn't going to sell the ranch for development, but

I don't believe that for a minute. But if she wants to win her lawsuit that would make her the heir, then you'd think she'd be sitting on that place like it was the golden egg."

I said, "Well, what about all the rumors that organized crime is behind all this? The moves they make don't always make sense to people like you and me."

Michele made a gesture like she was swatting flies. "Everybody keeps saying that, and yes, the FBI has been looking at the Wildcat Estates development project, but that's because they were looking at that earlier development project that was voted down, and they're thinking that some of the same money is behind this one. But still I think it's the local muscle that killed McWain. They're all covering for each other, and we've got Attabury red-handed saying he wasn't in Utah when we know he was. So how complicated does this have to be? Attabury flew him there and killed him and flew home. Gilda's probably racked out in a health spa somewhere getting her cellulite gold-plated. She'll be back."

Fatigue settled in around my brain like lead. I was not feeling as positive about things as I had been the night before. I looked out the window to the sky. "Well then, leave a message on her cell phone and wait for her to come to you. You don't want to go out to that ranch in anything less than a four-wheel-drive today. It's not looking good out there. The clouds are building up."

"So it might rain. So what?"

"The soils are riddled with bentonite. That's a swelling clay. You get it wet, and it turns to grease." I pointed south along the mountains, as if we could see past the buildings. "And it's too early for the thunderheads to be building. These mountains form what's called an orographic high. The way the air rises and condenses around them, they seed their own clouds. You can about set your watch by the afternoon thunderstorms around Pikes Peak, which is less than fifty miles away. But this is different. These clouds are rising too early; it looks like some kind of front, which can make things messy, eh? So wherever you or I go today, we should keep in touch, because it won't take very much rain to turn that road to snot and spin you into a ditch. Check in every hour by cell phone, okay?"

"Whatever."

I stared at her. Had she slept at all? "Why didn't the Salt Lake County Sheriff's Department send someone out here with you?" I asked.

"*You're* here."

"That's not enough, and you know it. They sent you out alone last Friday, too. Is that standard procedure?"

"No. My partner's in the hospital, and the other two detectives are on that big LDS case. The one with the missing girls. The church finds it embarrassing and—"

I nodded. "Wants it solved fast. So a wayward gentile geologist from Colorado isn't considered all that important, and they sent—" I managed to shut my mouth before I said any more, but Michele finished my sentence for me.

"The rookie. Not to put too fine a point on it."

"Sorry. Well, where are you off to?"

Michele glanced at her watch. "The county courthouse opens in five minutes. I'm off to find a warrant." She grabbed the check and headed to the counter.

I dialed Carlos Ortega again but got his answering machine. I tried Tim Osner's office, which was the only number I had for him. He was not in yet. I left a message saying that I was in Castle Rock wondering if he was up for a red clay hunt. As long as I had some waiting to do, I figured I might as well do what I was actually trained to do, collect trace evidence and analyze it.

Then I phoned Julia.

"You sound like you're on a cell phone this time," she said. "Does that mean you're back in Colorado?"

"I'm in Castle Rock," I said.

"What are you doing there?"

"I have some forensic samples to try to match. I was wondering if you could tell me how to find a few things."

Julia seemed hesitant. "What did you have in mind?"

"I figured to drive out near the ranch, get my samples, and then if I follow the creeks out toward the canyon, I can find out where the Arapahoe outcrops, and—"

"You are no doubt driving a rental car," she said irritably. "You can't go where you need to go with that. I'll bring the Jeep. Just stay there in Castle Rock. Where I can find you? I'll be there in an hour."

◆

THE SUN BEAT down on my head and shoulders like a renegade masseuse as Julia and I climbed the odd, conical hill known as Wildcat Mountain. The air was stifling hot and weirdly humid and still. A few miles to the west, the clouds continued to rise along the peaks like a great, gray fleece, growing darker by the hour. The birds had stopped singing. I made a mental note to get off the high, rocky protuberance of Wildcat's summit before the tops of the clouds blew over into thunderheads.

Julia led the way up the trail through chokecherries and wild plum trees, her long legs carrying her with an elastic stride. She wore an old pair of boots with hand-sewn welts of the same make and vintage as her departed former husband, beat-up khaki pants, and a short-sleeved cotton shirt, and her hair was tucked up underneath her cap to leave the back of her neck open to the scant breeze she made by moving through the air. "This is the key to the whole mess," she was telling me. "Right here. See how big the pore throats are in this stuff?" She pointed at the red sandstone that outcropped all along the top of the hill, which was in fact a hogback like so many other ridges along the mountain front, but in this case a hog with a very short back.

As we reached the summit, we could see the long train of hogbacks that ran all the way up to Dinosaur Ridge. I said, "What I don't get is why this hogback doesn't go very far. It's just a point instead of a long ridge."

Julia gave me a tight smile. "You always were observant, Hansen. You've asked the hundred-million-dollar question." She swept her arms out to take in the trend of the mountain front. "Here we stand at the end of the Cretaceous. The Rocky Mountains are rising, and the rivers are eroding the granites and carrying all that nice, fresh, coarse sediment downhill to the east. Right here, a river breaks out of the mountains and onto the flats, just like today, right out of a nice, narrow valley, say." She raised both arms to form a V. "So now tell me, what are we standing on?"

"We have the apex of the fan," I said. "Are you telling me that this is the original morphology of this sandstone? I thought it had been eroded into this shape."

Julia dropped her arms to her sides. "Bob Raynolds figured this out. He came down here with his wife and his kids and their pet potbellied pig and saw all the thrust faults along here between Wildcat and the foothills, and he saw the stacked channel deposits, and he said, 'Must be synorogenic deposition!' "

"Syn . . ."

"Synorogenic. It means 'sediments deposited same time as the mountains were building.' "

"As opposed to . . ."

She shrugged her shoulders. "I don't know . . . sometimes there's erosion going on but the sediments are washed clear away to some other place." She began to gesture with her hands. "See, as the mountains came up to the west, the fan was able to grow and grow and grow to the east, stacking up on top of itself like books loading onto one of those spring-loaded carts under the book-return chute in the public library." She dropped her hands and looked around at the scenery, remembering earlier visits. "Bob brought Afton down here, and Afton brought me and the kids."

"Then is this where the water recharges the aquifer?" I asked. "The snow-melt from the mountains, seeping down into the sandstone right here?" I knew the answer to this, but wanted to hear what she would say.

She shook her head. "That's where the whole thing falls apart, see. It'd be a great system if that were happening, but people take water out in human time spans—damned quickly—and it seeps back in geologic time—slooooooowwwwly. It's the tortoise and the hare story all over again. Except this time, nobody wins."

"And this is the best aquifer in the Denver Basin," I said.

"It's certainly the best one in Douglas County. It's what's filling all the bathtubs around here. Round numbers? About 200,000 people living on the south side of Denver here—Douglas and Arapahoe counties— depend on ground water for their water supply. The engineers have calculated that those people are pulling 53,000 acre-feet *per year* out of these rocks." She patted the stone. "Do the math. That's over seventeen *billion* gallons—375,000 boxcar loads—"

"Boxcars don't hold water," I said ironically. "They'd leak like a sieve."

"Don't mess with me, Hansen. One and a half boxcars per year for every man, woman, and child—and that's a conservative calculation. Others double the numbers. She swept a hand out toward the eastern plains. "And the developers want to build and build and build." She stared out across the dry landscape that was baking in the sun. "We're in the middle of the worst drought in recorded history, and the speculation is that the population of this county is going to triple in the next forty years. Things have sure changed around here since we were in college."

"Yes, they have. There weren't as many of us, not by half, and we didn't feel we needed such fancy homes. We didn't have as many private swimming pools, or have as many clothes to wash, or . . . or anything else that goes into the luxury developments like Wildcat Estates," I said, beginning to fish for information about the local developers.

"Why is it that developers want to build such water-intensive fantasies?" Julia mused.

"Because that's what people will buy? Because we're all feeling so crowded that we need to isolate ourselves in a fantasy life of luxury? Because we've always preferred to pamper ourselves rather than contemplate our frailty? I guess we all try to find our space one way or another." Before she could get going on Afton's death and her losses, I asked, "What do you know about that development, Julia?"

Julia picked up a pebble and threw it out over the hillside, where it dropped noisily into the low, scrubby oaks. "Wildcat will be voted down. It has to, like they voted down that other development."

"Where was that other one?"

She pointed to the south along the fetch of the foothills. "Just down there, a bunch of yay-hoos from Louisiana—*Louisiana*, damn it, where they've got so much water they have to build dikes to keep it off New Orleans—decided they were going to build heaven on Earth for all the golfing bozos. You know how much water your average golf course drinks, especially out here in ninety-degree heat and twenty percent humidity and fourteen inches annual rainfall?"

"I have no idea."

"Eighty-eight million gallons per year—another two thousand boxcar loads just to grow *sod*, thank you very much, so some boys from the country club can wear pastel knits and knock little white balls around. They were going to cram in over one hundred deluxe homes and fifty cottages for transient guests from places where people don't know what 'drought' means. Hey, let's fly our personal jet up to Colorado for the weekend and loll around in our hot tubs, why don't we?"

"How did that get voted down?"

"A local citizens' group managed to convince the county commissioners to stop it, at least for the present. You won't believe this, but they managed to get someone elected who understands the realities of this situation. Shocking, huh?"

"Someone who's not just out for the deepest pockets so he can get reelected? I didn't know that anyone like that made it into office anymore. That's wonderful. And I'm glad they were able to stop that development. It sounds crazy."

"They stopped it for a while, you mean. You know what the developers said when the gavel fell with a 'no' vote in the county commissioners' meeting? 'I am at a loss to understand why anyone would oppose this plan. It's not reasonable to think this property is going to stay as it is forever.' It's insidious. The developers will just hold onto it for a few years or sell it to some other scoundrel, and they'll wait until the county commissioners swing toward development again, and off we are to the races again."

"What about those houses?" I asked, gesturing toward the little ranchettes that studded the landscape to the east.

"They're running out of water."

"I hear the latest thing is for municipalities to buy up water rights from the farmers. I wonder where the water will come from to grow food."

Julia's gaze settled into a million-mile stare. "You mean like out by Rocky Ford, out there on the eastern plains? The farmers had been using the water to grow melons. Do you know how much water it takes to grow just one melon?"

"I have no idea, Julia. You're the numbers girl."

"One hundred and twenty gallons," she said, without skipping a beat. Julia ran her hands over the rock, as if soothing it. "The last good time we had together was here."

"With Afton?"

"We brought the kids," she said, a faint smile playing across her face. "Had PB&Js and squashed bananas. The kids ran around on these rocks like a couple of mountain goats." The smile drained from her face. "It was later that day that he first showed me the ranch. Said he wanted to buy it. And I thought we were just taking a little field trip."

"Wait, Afton knew the water was drying up in this aquifer before he bought the ranch?"

"Sure. He figured no one could develop around him because there wouldn't be enough water. He thought he'd found heaven on earth, close enough to Denver to drop in on the real world when he felt like it but far enough out and sufficiently drought-stricken that he wouldn't have many neighbors. Of course, then he had to figure out how to live on a patch of land that had no water, but you know Afton, he had a brain and a will to go with it."

I said, "So that's how he got into this green business? The old geologist's imperative of being away from it all?"

She nodded. "And of course one thing led to another. He bought a dry ranch to be alone, but learning how to live on it took him to some pretty quirky conferences with people who see life as a spiritual crisis."

"I can't see how that would appeal to him," I said, remembering him as the wild man with the presumptuous tattoo.

"You know how he could be—driven. Happiest when he had a new idea to screw his brain into. But then he decided that these green people weren't all that smart, and he was of course nothing short of brilliant, so he had to save them all. He started to work with legislators to save the arid lands for aridity, or something like that. First it was the Colorado state congress and then the federal. He developed quite a name for himself in certain circles quite quickly." She laughed mirthlessly.

"And somewhere in there, he developed a name for himself with Gilda." I could just see Gilda working the room at some conference for firebrands and policymakers. People of power. People with their hands on money. "Gilda is an opportunist," I said.

"I—I don't want to talk about her," she said.

A low rumbling reverberated across the landscape.

Julia looked up toward the mountain front as if watching for approaching Valkyries.

I said, " Let's head down toward the creek. I saw some red clays in the soils along a cut bank."

"No!" She suddenly seemed unnerved by the towering clouds. "We should leave. Get to shelter."

"I've been watching those clouds, too, Julia. I saw the flash before the thunder and I counted, and it's at least five miles off. And those clouds don't look like they're moving."

"No. Field trip over for today, okay?"

"Okay," I said, "but first I've got to grab a soil sample."

"What for?" Julia asked.

I knew that Julia could help me know where to look, if I could get Michele's permission. I pulled out my cell phone and punched in Michele's number. The call rolled over to her message service, which indicated that she was somewhere where she was receiving no signal. I put my phone away. "Roll with me on this," I said. "I've been looking for red clays."

Julia shook her head impatiently and pointed at the darkening sky over the Rampart Range. "Em, *really*! This is *bad*. Just look at the tops of those clouds. They've been getting bigger, and now they're bulging out toward us."

"But there's still no wind," I said. I had been watching the sky like any good ranch-bred person would, checking to make sure the clouds weren't moving our way. Now I realized that she was right, there was something very wrong about these clouds. "You're right, let's get out of here," I said. "Then just one quick stop along the creek, and I'm done."

Julia started moving.

We hurried down off the conical hill, slowing only to glance ahead when we had to jump down over rocks, to make sure we didn't roust out any rattlesnakes who might be sunning themselves before the storm. Another crash of thunder surprised Julia just as she made one of her leaps. She missed her footing and landed like a sack of potatoes.

I rushed to her side. "Are you hurt?" I asked breathlessly, winded from our sprint.

Julia rolled over clutching her knee in a tight embrace, her face twisted with pain. "Oh, no . . ." she moaned.

I said, "Can you get up?"

"I—I don't know." Gingerly, she extended her leg and set a hand down to brace herself.

I bent to help her. "Should I go for help?"

"No. I can make it, and we shouldn't stay." She grabbed my hands and hoisted herself up. She grimaced in pain, but her leg held her weight well enough to hobble along. "So much for hurrying," she said. "But we're almost to the Jeep."

The Jeep was an older, red, practicality-only model with MCWAIN GE-OLOGICAL CONSULTING emblazoned on both front doors. I said, "I'll drive."

"No, I can drive."

"Bullshit, you'll drive."

"Okay, I'll give you the keys if we can just get us the hell away from that storm," she said.

"Okay, okay!" I loaded her into the passenger's seat and climbed in behind the steering wheel. I steered the Jeep down the hill, balancing haste with caution as I retraced our route down the track to the road we had come in on.

Before turning onto the highway, I tried Michele's number again. This time I had no signal.

"Who do you keep trying to call?" Julia asked.

"I'm trying to reach the sheriff's detective so she can meet us for lunch," I explained. "She can meet us in Sedalia at that roadhouse there. The jalapeño burgers looked mighty good."

"No!" she said.

I gave her a quizzical look.

She said, "Those burgers are to die for, but tell her Castle Rock."

"Why? Sedalia's closer. We need to get some ice on that knee of yours."

Julia's agitation was increasing. "Do you remember the Big Thompson flood?"

We had reached a junction among dirt trails. I waited while several mountain bikers passed, all pedaling madly away from the mountains ahead of the storm, then followed them. "How could I forget?" I said. "I was only about ten years old when it happened, but it was all anyone talked about for weeks. Over a hundred people died."

"One hundred forty-four," Julia said. "Do you remember what set it off?"

"Well, rain, but—" I bumped over a sharp rock that was sticking up in the middle of the dirt track. "Oops! Sorry about your tires."

"Watch it!" Julia said. "It was not just your ordinary rain. It was about this time of year. I've seen pictures, and it was a cloud that looked just like that," she said, jabbing a finger toward the heavens.

"You're right," I said. "A front stalled out along the Front Range. My dad was down in Denver that day. He said you could see the thunderheads from Pueblo clear up past Fort Collins. And they were tens of thousands of feet tall."

"Yes. Cumulonimbus usually don't grow that tall. They develop the classic anvil head as the winds aloft whip them sideways. *And* those winds usually push the storm along. The day of the Big Thompson flood, they sat still and grew higher and higher, just like these are doing."

I said, "They were forty thousand feet tall over Big Thompson Canyon, and when they finally ripped loose and rained, they dropped six inches in an hour, something astronomical like that. And they hit a watershed that fed into a tight drainage, and that tight drainage had—"

"—Big Thompson Reservoir in it, which had a dirt dam, and that dam was hit by all that water arriving so quickly, and it failed," Julia said. "And it came down the canyon like the fury of hell."

I glanced at Julia, who knew all about fury. "I remember the stories. People didn't know to climb to safety. They saw that the creek was rising and tried to outrun the flood by getting in their cars and driving down-canyon."

"Bits of them were found clear out to Loveland," Julia said. "One guy had gotten his family into the car and ran back up to get one more thing out of their vacation cottage. The wall of water came through and swept away the car, killing his wife and all the kids. And it took away their little signs that hung one underneath another, one for each name, leaving just his at the top."

I could only imagine what that story meant to her now. "You're right," I said. "This is bad." I opened my cell phone again. It was showing a signal but there were no missed messages from Michele. A heavy feeling settled into the pit of my stomach.

I came to the end of the dirt track that led down from the mountain and turned onto a well-graded, gravel road that led out past several new thirty-five-acre homesteads that, given the lack of water in that aquifer, probably shouldn't have been there. I had driven a quarter mile down this road when we heard a *thud* and the vehicle lurched. Gripping the steering wheel tightly, I piloted the Jeep successfully to the edge of the road and got out to see what I could see.

Julia lumbered out the opposite side, leaning against the vehicle to spare her hurt knee. "Damn!" I heard her yell and saw the vehicle shake slightly as she kicked what was left of the tire on that quarter.

I came around to take a look. The tire was not only punctured, it was ruined, a tatter of thin rubberized shreds. "Where's the spare?" I asked. "Is it underneath that gear box in the back?"

Julia stood beside the offending mass of rubber, one hand against her face, the other arm wrapped tightly across her chest. Her shoulders shook spasmodically. She was crying.

I put an arm around her. "What is it, Jules?"

"The spare," she whimpered.

"What about it?"

"I don't have one."

My last shred of sympathy for Julia snapped like an old rubber band. "This isn't like you, Julia! First you blast your knee and now you're out doing fieldwork without a spare! What were you thinking?"

"I'm sorry!" she blubbered. "It's—it's up at the ranch."

"Well, now, that's a good place for it!"

Julia leaned against the Jeep and sobbed. "It's—Afton used to drive this Jeep, remember? And I drove the sedan, but this is what we always used in the field. It was on the books as part of the business. When we went through that financial bloodbath we called a divorce, I got the business and he got the ranch, and . . . well, he'd taken the spare out to make room while he carried some part for the wind generator up to the ranch, and he never put it back."

"Fine way to be ecologically responsible," I said sourly. "Use your wife's vehicle to make yourself vehicularly independent, if that's a word. All right, how far is it to the ranch?"

Julia looked up at the clouds with growing agitation. "You're not going to make it. Or you'd get there and be soaked to the skin coming back, and rolling a spare tire at least a mile even if you go straight across the hills there."

"Let's call a wrecker." I pulled out my cell phone. It read NO SER-VICE. I bowed my head, wishing the rain would start and cool my over-heated brain. "Okay then," I said, "what do you suggest we do?"

Julia looked past me at the road. "There's a car coming," she said. "Surely it will be someone who can help us."

22

MARY ANN NETTLETON LOOKED OUT THE WINDOW AT THE COMING storm. "I don't like the look of those clouds," she told her sister.

Rita Mae said, "Well, you wanted water."

"I want water in my well and I want this drought to break, but I don't want to be washed away by a flash flood."

"Do you think there's any worry of that?"

Mary Ann lifted her chin with determination to look at things in their best light. "That was the one thing Henry did tell me. He said that Dr. McWain told him that the dry wash beside the house is a place to stay out of if it got to raining hard. And he said those boulders out there might be troublesome, too." She pointed at one of the garage-sized rocks that nature had left perched on the mesa above the house. "They seemed so picturesque when we were looking at the place."

"Then let's drive into town," said Rita Mae. "I don't think you can take a whole lot more of this, and neither can I. We can have lunch, or even pack a bag and go up to my house in Denver. Take a nice, long bath. Relax."

"I'll go to lunch," said Mary Ann, "but then I need to come back here. I'll admit that this place has stopped being my dream home and become a nightmare, but still, it's all I've got, and I think Henry would have stayed, so I will, too. I'm going to join Helga Olsen's citizens' action group, Rita Mae. I'm going to join it and fight so no one else gets hurt like I did. And I'm going to sign up for that course at the community center. I want to know more about this world, and I want to be able to live in it without being such a sitting duck."

Rita Mae hurried off to the guest room to do her hair, then joined her sister in the master suite to help her decide what to wear. That was always the thin spot with Mary Ann, getting her set to be anywhere. She was brilliant as a homemaker, but as a citizen of the world, she was a flop. But maybe this catastrophe with her water supply was a cloud with a silver lining, just the thing to propel Mary Ann out into greater service. As she thought about it, she realized that Mary Ann would indeed be an asset to that group, bringing her fastidious organizational skills, her unflagging ability to stay on track, and her devotion to form.

Half an hour later, they were loaded into Rita Mae's Cadillac Coupe de Ville and rolling down the driveway toward the road. With satisfaction, Rita Mae noted that Mary Ann did not even look back, and when Rita Mae looked into the rear-view mirror, she was glad she hadn't because the clouds had taken on an ominous darkness. Maybe she'd be able to get her away to Denver after all, if only overnight.

At the end of the lane that serviced the development, Rita Mae turned out onto the narrow blacktopped road that led to the county road. Three-quarters of a mile along that road, they came across two women standing beside the road next to an old red Jeep. "I wonder what they're doing there," she told her sister.

Mary Ann looked up over the dashboard at the scene that had attracted Rita Mae's attention. "It's one of those sport-utility vehicles. Maybe they are preparing to drive it off-road."

Rita Mae said, "They aren't going anywhere with only three tires."

"Oh. Well, I hope the poor dears have Triple A."

Just then, one of the women turned toward the approaching Cadillac and waved at them with both hands, the universal "please stop" signal.

Rita Mae said, "I don't like to leave them out here to get rained on, but I wonder why they're dressed like that? Do you think it's all right to stop?" She glanced sideways to see if her sister was up to meeting these total strangers. What she saw surprised her.

Mary Ann was sitting up straight and smiling for the first time all day. "These women look like rugged individuals, and there's nothing wrong with that," said Mary Ann Nettleton. "Let's help them. It will be an adventure."

23

I TURNED TO SEE A CADILLAC COMING DOWN THE ROAD TOWARD US. Julia waved frantically and it pulled to a stop. There were two older women aboard, each neatly coifed and dressed like they were on their way to a party. The one in the passenger seat was wide-eyed with excitement. She had rinsed her hair a fetching shade of blue. The one behind the wheel was a bit huskier in build. Her hair was rinsed lavender. The one with the blue hair ran the little motor that opened her window and tipped her head toward the fresh air. "Are you two young ladies having a little trouble?" she inquired.

"Yes," I said. "We've got a flat. Could you give us a lift into Castle Rock perchance? Are you going that far?"

"I'm sure we could," said Lavender Hair. "Hop in." She concentrated on the task of pushing another button that unlocked the back doors of her car.

I turned to Julia. "C'mon, pardner, we got us a ride."

Julia locked the doors to the Jeep and followed me. She already had her valuables in the little pack that was cinched around her waist. She followed me to the Cadillac and lowered herself painfully into the leather seat beside me. When the door shut and the full force of the air-conditioning hit me, it almost gave me a brain freeze.

"Thanks for picking us up," I said. "I'm Em Hansen, and this is Julia McWain."

Both women swiveled their heads to look at Julia. The woman who was driving turned quickly back to her concentration on the road ahead of her, but the other continued to goggle at Julia with frank interest. "You aren't related to the late Dr. *Afton* McWain, are you?"

Julia managed to keep a calm face. "He was my husband until six months ago, when the divorce became final."

"Oh . . ." said Blue Hair, making a knowing song of that one syllable. "Well, I'm sorry for your loss anyway. It happens I once met your husband, dear. He was a fine man and very helpful to his neighbors."

Julia said nothing.

Lavender Hair said, "He was a geologist, wasn't he? And I notice that you are dressed for the wilds, too."

Julia said, "Yes, you can see by my outfit that I am a geologist." She folded her arms tightly across herself and stared out the side window.

I wracked my brain for a jolly topic to which I could change the subject, but Blue Hair spoke again before I could. She said, "Dr. McWain tried to explain to my dear, departed Henry where the water in our well was going."

Julia let out one of her sighs. "Yes, my former husband was a very smart, very knowledgeable man. You would be best served to believe him."

Lavender Hair said, "We haven't introduced ourselves. I'm Rita Mae Jones and this is my sister, Mary Ann Nettleton."

Mary Ann said, "How rude of us! How do you do. A Helga Olsen came by to talk to us about Dr. McWain's work. She was telling us about a development that's been proposed up here, that involves Dr. McWain's ranch."

Julia said, "Don't you worry your heads about that. My children are the heirs to that ranch, and as long as I am the trustee of that estate, I'm not giving in to any bully-boy tactics."

That got my attention. "What tactics are those, Julia?"

"There have been veiled threats. Suggestions that Afton might encounter some of the same problems the lady had who wouldn't give an easement to that project just south of here."

"Which were?" asked Rita Mae.

"She found her prize horses shot. One of them at point-blank range, through the anus." As if she'd just been discussing something no more distracting than a new hairstyle, Julia suddenly leaned forward, staring at something beside the road in front of us. "Hey, stop here. I just thought of something."

I swiveled my eyes to see what she was looking at, and then I recognized it: It was the landmark for the turn that led up toward the McWain ranch. Our friendly neighborhood Rhodesian Ridgeback came barreling down the hill toward us, barking his fool head off in his enthusiasm for this pinnacle moment of his day.

Rita Mae said, *"Here?"*

"Yes. By that turn there."

Rita Mae stopped the car but let it idle in the middle of the road. "Is that animal quite sane?" she inquired.

Julia said, "Ol' Barker? I wouldn't presume to pet him, but he's not angling for an early grave. He stays on his side of the fence."

Rita Mae sat twisted as far as her unathletic, past-seventy torso could go, looking at Julia with one eye. "What'll it be, Mrs. McWain?"

"I was just thinking where the spare tire to that Jeep is. It's up at the ranch, right up that track."

Rita Mae stared up the twin ruts. "I'm sure I can't drive this car up there, but how far is it? We can wait a short while if that would help."

Mary Ann added, "Even if you and Dr. McWain have had your parting of the ways, he helped my Henry, and I am glad to help you."

Rita Mae said, "That's the spirit, Mary Ann."

Julia said, "I have an even better solution. If you go just a few hundred yards farther along, there's the turn to the Johnson Ranch. It's graded. That driveway parallels mine—or should I say, Afton's—and that would put me within tire-rolling distance."

I said, "You're not rolling that tire with your knee all bunged up. I'll go get it."

Julia said quickly, "No, I can get Bart to drive me across over the connecting road." She pushed the button to lower her window and shouted, "Leave it, Barker!"

The dog stopped barking immediately and began wagging its tail. His big, pink tongue hung out around a happy-dog smile.

Rita Mae gave the steering wheel a pat. "I like a woman who can handle herself in a predicament," she said. She put the car back in D for DRIVE and drove.

As we neared the gate that led up to Bart Johnson's ranch house, a bank of red soil caught my eye. "What's that red clay horizon there?" I asked Julia.

"Paleosol," she said. "It outcrops all across this area. Why?"

I was grinning like a fool for no good reason. If that was the red clay I'd picked off of Afton's boots, it meant nothing whatsoever, because it only meant that he'd brought it with him from home. But it also meant that I could grab my sample, see if it truly matched the sheriff's evidence, and be done, truly done with this case. The more I heard about people shooting horses, the better that sounded to me.

By the time Bart Johnson's ranch house came into view, I had formulated a plan. We would retrieve Julia's spare tire and put it on the Jeep. Then, if the rain held off and Julia's knee recovered enough that she could drive home on her own, I could drive my rental car back out along this road and collect the samples, meet Michele for lunch, and be on my way to the airport and home by mid-afternoon.

Bart Johnson himself came out of the ranch house to greet us. He strolled around to the right front door, which was closest to his approach, nearest Mary Ann, who lowered her window to greet him. "Ladies," he said, tagging the bill of his King Ropes ball cap with an arthritic finger. He wasn't dressed for town today, so the Abercrombie and Fitch rig had been closeted in favor of a canvas shirt and a good old pair of Wrangler jeans.

Julia lowered her window, too. "Hi, Bart," she said.

Bart did a stiff demi-plié so that he could see her. "Julia. This is a surprise." His face was as stiff as his legs and hands. Bending was sufficiently difficult for him that he quickly straightened up again before he could notice me.

Julia said, "I have a favor to ask, Bart. I had a flat out on the road just now and . . . well, it's one of those messy little things that didn't get settled in the divorce: the spare tire to our . . . my Jeep is in the barn up at the ranch, or was last time I was there. I was wondering if you could run me over there to get it. This Cadillac is hardly the vehicle for the job, as I can see that Afton left the road ungraded until the last."

Bart put his gnarled hands on his hips. "Well, I'd like to help you, but, uh . . ."

I heard a crunching of the gravel beyond Bart Johnson. Someone else was walking toward the car from the house; in fact, two people. Johnson's son Zachary spoke first. He said, "Hullo, Julia."

Right behind him was the weasle-faced Todd Upton. "Why, it's Mrs. Nettleton," he said affably enough, but then added, "and Julia," his voice curling around a hard edge. "Sorry, Julia. You can't go there."

"And why not?" asked Julia, hotly.

Upton folded his arms across his chest. "Because the estate's been sealed until we can look after certain legal business."

Julia was out of that car like lightning and shoved her face right into the sneering face of the lawyer. "You sniveling, flesh-eating monster, how dare you speak to me like that? That trollop is not the legal heir to that ranch and you know it! My children are the heirs! It's explicitly spelled out in the divorce decree! You have no right to seal the estate!"

Upton was impassive. He spoke to her as calmly as if she were standing ten feet away from him and reciting nursery rhymes. "I'm so sorry to hear that your late *ex*-husband didn't take the time to inform you of his change of beneficiary."

Julia hauled off and slugged him. It was a roundhouse right, and a good one, and Julia is a woman of sufficient size that it had to hurt.

But Upton barely recoiled. He said, "Bart, you're a witness to that. And I'm sorry you *ladies* in the car had also to observe the behavior of a woman who can't control her impulses. Now, Julia, if you don't find your own way down the road and out of Douglas County right this minute, I'm going to press charges for assault."

Julia began to shake from head to foot, and I saw her begin to wind up for another go at Upton. I jumped out of the car and caught her around the waist with both arms before she could claw his eyes out and hauled her backward toward the car. It was a job stuffing her back inside, and my eardrums were ringing for ten minutes afterward, so loud were her epithets. But the thing I pondered most, as Rita Mae turned the car and sent it hurtling down the path again like she was born to motocross, was the look on Todd Upton's face when he saw me coming out of the car: His eyes widened not only with surprise but also fear.

24

RAY RAYMOND HAD BEEN NURSING A BAD FEELING IN THE PIT OF his stomach all morning, a sense of being pushed or crowded. By noon, it was beginning to tear at him, driving him to take action. He stalked through the police station in search of Eddie and found him in the locker room where he was putting on his uniform over black Jockey shorts and a black T-shirt that read 82ND AIRBORNE DIVISION and DEATH FROM ABOVE. Between the two lines of print a white skull bulged over Eddie's gut. The slogan sliced into Ray's consciousness, making a new cut along a well-worn path that always left him uncertain of his stature as a man. He had never served in the armed forces.

Eddie looked up from the bench where he was sitting. "Ray. Wassup?"

"I was wondering if your rumor mill had anything new on . . . Michele."

Eddie raised an eyebrow in appraisal. "Giving her some thought, are you?"

"No, I am . . . You got anything or not?"

"Don't get testy, man. Yeah, she went back to Colorado."

Ray waited, his jaws tight. When Eddie offered nothing further, he said, "And Em?"

"Yeah, Em's with her." He studied Ray with the eyes of a feral dog, evaluating his reaction.

Ray forced himself to breathe.

Eddie said, "They got backup there. It ain't like Colorado's got no boys in blue."

"I've got a bad feeling about this one."

"Welcome to criminal justice, Ray. We don't put people in jail because they're behavin' like model citizens."

Eddie's words were lost on Ray. He was already heading out the door, trying to think of a plan, searching mentally for the shortest route to his goal.

Eddie called after him. "Let Fritz take care of this, why don't you?"

Ray stopped. "And where might I find him?"

"At his house, most likely. I just played a game of tennis with him. If you hurry—" Eddie let his sentence hang. The door had swung shut behind his departing comrade.

Ray hurried into a squad car and drove quickly up the hill to the east, into the Avenues, where he'd seen the man named Fritz running. Time seemed to turn to jelly, impeding his progress. As he came down the block toward his house, Ray spotted Fritz coming out the door carrying a boxy black attaché, his hair still wet from his post-exercise shower. He was dressed in a pilot's uniform—all sharp creases and epaulets and aviator-framed sunglasses—and it gave him an air of crisp command that had lain hidden under his workout sweats.

Ray parked the police cruiser behind Fritz's SUV and got out. Then, having gotten this far, he couldn't get his mouth to work. His old reticence locked his jaws together, and he could not speak.

The pilot calmly put his case into his vehicle, then took off his sunglasses and turned to look at Ray. And waited for him to say something, the glasses dangling loosely in his left hand. In his gaze Ray found neither a challenge nor a welcome, but simply a quiet, alert openness.

"We haven't met, formally," Ray said.

Fritz extended a hand. "Fritz Calder. You're Ray . . ."

"Tom Raymond. Ray is a nickname."

"What can I do for you, Ray?" Now Fritz hooked his sunglasses into an epaulet and put his hands in his pockets, assuming a posture that spoke of elaborate ease.

Ray found this intimidating but knew that coming up to the man in his cruiser would provoke a move like this if the man was worth anything. Ray glanced at the pavement a moment to clear his head. "I'm worried about Em," he said.

"Now you have my undivided attention," Fritz said. "Is there news from inside the law enforcement community you need me to know?"

Ray met his gaze. "Yes. You know she's in Colorado."

"She was last Friday and Saturday, yes."

"She's there again now."

Fritz's eyelids flared wide and then tightened. "When did she go?"

"Last night. I can see you share my concern for her. She—"

"She flew commercially?"

"By public carrier? Yes. No, she didn't fly herself, if that's what you mean."

"She's with Michele?"

Ray let out his breath and only then realized that he'd been holding it. He needed to communicate the precise nature of his concern but could not isolate it from the chaos that suffused his being. Something was wrong, very wrong, that was all he knew for certain. "Michele is good, but she's green, and departmental politics are going against her. Hopefully they've made contact with the sheriff on the Colorado end, but knowing Em—"

Fritz's face had gone dark with anxiety.

Ray simultaneously relaxed and tensed. It was good that this man understood this complicated woman, but having his own anxiety mirrored back only increased it. "And you heard what I had to say about the nature of the case when I came to get her Friday morning."

"You said it was bad."

"It is. Whoever murdered Afton McWain was both violent and ruthless. And smart. The killer had thought it through. He took pains to confuse the identification and . . . well, it was ugly."

"How ugly, Ray? Come on, tell me."

Ray threw caution to the winds. "The FBI's already been alerted to the case because it's connected to some possible money-laundering schemes that could go straight to a drug cartel. The Feds say these guys hire professional hits when someone gets in their way."

Fritz now stood ramrod straight. "I'm on my way to Denver right now, if I can get through. The weather's bad. My client is a nervous flier, so he may scrub." He glanced at his black bag. "But if he doesn't go, that doesn't mean I can't. I'll find her."

Ray said, "May I offer you some advice?"

"Certainly."

Ray weighed his words. "Em is a . . ."

"Difficult woman. But a fine one. In her case, difficult is a pleasure."

Ray gave him the slight smile of sad agreement. "I couldn't have said it better. So you understand."

"If I challenge her, it can go the wrong way."

"You got it."

Suddenly Fritz laughed, a short, joyous burst. "Officer Raymond, sir, you and I might just become the best of friends."

Ray grinned as he tasted a swift, sweet moment of relief. "That's *Detective* Raymond, and I read you loud and clear and copy that."

25

MARY ANN NETTLETON TOLD US THE SAD STORY OF HER WATER well as her sister drove us to town and dropped us at the motel. Once there, I phoned around and found a cheap spare that would fit on the Jeep. Thus armed, I picked up my rental car and all but dragged Julia back toward Sedalia.

Julia insisted on stopping at a place called Bud's to get cheeseburgers. As a first bit of luck since leaving Salt Lake City the night before, I finally reached Michele just as she was heading out to the ranch and got her to join us.

I regaled Michele with the various upsets of our morning, emphasizing the confrontation with Johnson and Upton, while Julia swigged a beer and piled fresh cubes of ice into the plastic zip-lock bag the clerk at the hotel had supplied for chilling her injured knee. Michele took detailed notes. "Upton threatened to press charges against Julia for assault," I said, "but I think he was just trying to get us to leave. Fast. He wanted us out of there in a big way, but I can't believe it's because he's afraid of a punch in the nose. He didn't even flinch until he saw me. What is there about *me* that scares him when Julia McWain in full fury doesn't even make him blink?"

Julia winced as she rearranged her leg. "Hey, he's a congenital idiot. I'm glad we caught you before you drove up there, Michele. You shouldn't be going up there alone, and especially not now with this storm about to break."

"Why shouldn't I be going up there alone?"

"Because whoever killed Afton isn't working alone."

" 'Isn't working'?" Michele said. "You don't mean, 'didn't work'?"

I said, "Julia's right. I don't think it's safe to think the last drop of blood has been shed over this business. The one you like best for the killing isn't even here, but the shit's still hitting the fan. Every last one on your hot list had a reason to commit murder, if he or she is that brave or that stupid."

"Yeah," said Julia. "And if they'd kill Afton for those reasons, then they'd kill you as well."

"You have to be extra stupid to kill a cop," Michele said.

"Murder's never smart," I countered. "The people we're dealing with use brute force where the smarts run out. And it seems that half of this county wanted Dr. McWain out of their lives."

Julia took a particularly long drag on her beer and said, "Developers don't take kindly to hearing that they're running out of water. What's considered a well-founded opinion in the world of science and a fact in the world of engineering is seen as a threat to those who want to keep doing things the good ol' use-it-and-abuse-it way. Try getting them interested in building your house out of straw bales or rammed-earth construction while you live without running water in a glorified tent, why don't you?"

"You're talking about Dr. McWain," Michele said.

"Afton and I were divorced, but that doesn't mean I disagreed with his science. And I was aware of whom he was dealing with. They hated him."

"Turn this case over to the feds, Michele," I said. "The more I think about this, the more I think we're over our heads here. I'm just one borrowed analyst borrowing an SEM. The FBI has a whole lab in Virginia and at least three geologist-forensic examiners on staff full time."

Michele ignored my entreaty. To Julia she said, "Tell us about these people I don't want to mess with."

"Em just saw Upton in action. Johnson wants to cash in his ranch for a beachfront estate in Maui, and he 'don't take kindly to no hippy tellin' him he cain't do that.' And Attabury? If he can't develop Johnson's ranch, he's back to selling second-hand double-wides."

"And Gilda," I prompted.

"Gilda will be on the treadmill at the spa trying to get in shape for her next sugar daddy," Julia said bitterly.

Michele said, "Her next?"

Julia snorted derisively. "You think I didn't do a little research on her when I found out why Afton wasn't coming home? She's got a regular business going, that girl. She marries and divorces like some women change their shoes."

"But Afton didn't marry her," I pointed out.

"Nobody ever said he was stupid," said Julia. "Just horny, I guess."

I shifted uncomfortably at Julia's bluntness. I was used to her, but Michele was not. I glanced at the detective out of the corner of my eye. She had her game face on.

Julia muttered, "Hey, he was a good enough lay."

Michele said, "Tell me about the political end of things. Not all the county commissioners are all that fond of his citizens' group's proposed rezoning, and there's that curious matter of his association with Senator White."

"Oh, that," said Julia. "Yeah, White has to look after the business of getting reelected. She can't sound too anti-development or she'll be cutting off her revenue stream. And as for the county Mounties, not too many people are keen on changing the thirty-five-acre zoning to eighty, and Afton thought even that would result in mining."

Michele said, "Mining?"

"Taking water out of the ground faster than it can recharge. That's mining." When Michele still looked puzzled, she said, "Think of water as a resource, which is exactly what it is. An Earth resource. Just like oil or gold or copper. If you take water away faster than it's accumulating, that's called mining."

Michele said, "What about the wells people drill? Doesn't the state regulate that?"

Julia shook her head. "Water rights are governed by the state, but for well permits you go to the county. And they don't talk to each other a whole lot. Then you get a crooked county commissioner or two, or one that just can't understand this kind of stuff or won't take the trouble to learn it, and you're back to square one. It's as if people think it's an act of God whether there's water in their well or not."

I said, "That poor lady who gave us the ride into town sure got her education the hard way." I relayed Mary Ann's story to Michele, then asked Julia, "What do you think will become of her and her property?"

"Heaven knows," Julia answered. "She's not an isolated case. Every last house out that way has the same problem, and what if the Johnson ranch is turned into a resort? The developers will drive a well clear down to the bottom of the aquifer and show that he can flow nine hundred gallons of water per minute into a community water line, but then he'll be gone when the last buyer has moved in and the last drop of vintage water has been drunk."

Michele said, "Who was the Realtor when you two bought the ranch? And who's carrying the mortgage?"

Julia replied, "We bought it directly from the owner, Bart Johnson's brother, and he carried the paper."

"Wouldn't Bart's brother have made more money selling it to a developer?" I asked.

"Yeah, but he didn't want it developed. He thought a crazy cuss like Afton would love it the way he had, and every last elk and deer and wild plum tree on it."

I asked, "Can this brother call in the note now that Afton's dead?"

Julia shook her head. "The heirs have the right to assume the mortgage."

"So that's why Upton has his lawyerly hand on Gilda's thigh. But how could she make the payments?"

Julia grumbled, "Those boys would be only too pleased to help her out."

Michele was making notes. "Anything else we should know about these people?" she asked.

Julia let out her breath like a tired horse. "Upton cooked that will. He had to."

"How do you know that for sure?"

"Because it was part of the divorce decree that the kids inherit the ranch, or the value thereof. If it was to be sold, it was going to the Nature Conservancy or equivalent organization."

"Then Upton's bluffing," Michele said.

"Or the glorious Gilda is bluffing Upton," Julia replied.

Michele leaned back and stretched, her lack of sleep beginning to show. She said, "I haven't been able to locate Gilda. And the one I was looking for is still gone, too," she added, giving it to me without names so she wouldn't tip her hand to Julia. "And the others of interest are not answering phones. But at least now I know where to find Mr. Upton."

Julia stared into the neck of her beer bottle for several long moments, examining the suds that lingered in the bottom of the bottle. "I guess that's all I've got for you," she said. "I wanted to kick Afton's ass through his eye sockets, but I didn't want him dead."

"I believe you, for what that's worth," Michele said. She looked at her watch. "I'll meet you back at the motel at five, and we'll continue to check in before then."

"Continue?" I said. "I hadn't heard from you all morning."

"Sorry."

Julia began to droop.

Michele stuffed a last bite of burger into her mouth, dropped two twenties on the table, said, "Tip twenty percent and save me the receipt," and stood up to leave.

The waiter arrived. "Can I get you ladies anything else?" he inquired.

Julia said, "You got any Guinness? In a glass?"

"Sure." He looked at me.

I said, "We ought to get going. Get out there before it rains."

"Just one more," said Julia.

I waved my hand in a what-the-hell gesture. "Cup of coffee. Black."

The man picked up Michele's plate and glass and left.

I leaned back in exasperation. Up on Wildcat Mountain, Julia had been trying to hurry me, but now she seemed to be dragging her feet. I wondered if she was worried about her run-in with Todd Upton. If he pressed charges for assault, it could add serious complications if Gilda persisted in her claim against the ranch. I wondered if Julia was stalling, waiting until she saw Upton drive past the café, so that she would know that it was safe to go up toward the ranch.

The waiter came back to the table with Julia's beer and my coffee.

Julia lifted the beer to her lips.

The minutes ticked past. "We should get going," I said.

Julia stared at me over her glass with gimlet eyes. She said, "Three men walk into a bar, an Englishman, an Irishman, and a Scot. They each order a pint. Just as they are served, three flies fly up and one drops into the foam on each beer."

I said, "The Englishman pushes his beer away in disgust. The Irishman plucks the fly out of his beer and drinks it down. And the Scot—"

"Grabs his fly by the wings, holds it above the glass, and cries, 'Spit it out! Spit it out, ye thieving bastard!' Okay that's an old one."

Julia glared at me. She was in a darkening mood, and short-sheeting her joke had been a strategic error.

I had seen Julia in her moods before, but this one portended to be a corker. I wasn't sure that I could stand it. My nerves had begun to fry from lack of sleep and too many heavy issues bearing down on me. I itched to complete my tasks and turn my nose toward the airport and Salt Lake City. I decided that I would stop in at the sheriff's department offices in Castle Rock first and make damned sure they meant to back up Michele's movements, and then I'd be off. I said, "You sure you want to drink that? It may be raining by the time you get onto the highway. We still have to change your tire and get your Jeep back onto the road. That's going to take an hour at least."

"Then I'll take the old road. Eighty-five is such a scenic drive next to the construction on I-25."

"That could be worse. Watch out as you go under the trestle up by Littleton. It floods."

Julia said, "Three Scottish lassies are walking home from a celebration. They come across a lad who has passed oot in the ditch."

I heaved a sigh. "Okay . . ."

"The wind has blown leaves across the lad, so they canna tell who he is. You know what they do?"

"I can only guess," I said heavily.

"The first lassie picks up a stick and raises the hem of the laddie's kilt. And she says, 'Ach, that's not *my* husband!'"

"Okay . . ."

"Well, the second lassie, she then takes the stick, and does the same; lifts the laddie's kilt. And she says, 'Ye're right, that isn't yer husband.'"

The irony of her tale was not lost on me. "That's pretty good, Julia," I said, wishing I had heard it on a kinder day.

"And that's not all! The third lassie, she takes the stick and raises yon kilt and says, 'And neither is it any other lad from our village.'"

I wondered how Julia could even tell a story like that after losing her husband to a woman like lassie number three and knowing that she had been lassie number two. I downed my coffee and took a squint at Julia's beer. She appeared to be nursing it. "Bottoms up," I said.

She said, "A man walks into a bar with an octopus and says, 'I'll bet fifty quid this octopus can play any instrument in the house to virtuoso capacity.' And first the saxophonist—"

I cut her off. "And the octopus says about the bagpipe, 'Play her, hell! Soon as I can get her knickers off, I'm gonna have me way with her.' I told you that one, Julia."

"Okay, a lad from the regiment walks into the apothecary's and says—"

"We're burning daylight, Julia." Losing my last shred of patience, I said, "Besides, why are you still telling Scottish jokes? The man's dead. As I recall, you're of English extraction."

Julia stared into her beer. She said, "For all I know, he did figure out how to change his beneficiary."

"Afton?"

Julia's face crumpled with pain. Tears swam in her eyes.

I said, "You still want him. After all this—"

"I was always shooting myself in the foot around him," she moaned. She put her head down on the table and bawled.

I leaned back in my chair, resigning myself to a long conversation. "You're being too hard on yourself. He was a difficult man."

"That's what everyone says. And you're right, he was difficult. Damn it, Em, I should have just had my little affair with him and *skipped* the marriage."

I didn't want to hear about what went wrong in Julia McWain's marriage. I wanted to think that getting married could be a solution, not the beginning of a problem.

Julia took another long draft of her beer, set it down, and began to write on her cocktail napkin with her finger. "My friends kept telling me I was resisting change. La, la, la, you're resisting change, they'd say, 'It was time to move on. Let it go. It's his karma to run after younger women. It's his loss.' Bunch of New Age la-la freaks. But she had something I didn't, that's what he said."

"What do you think, Gilda was a better woman to him?"

"She's prettier."

"You'll find someone else," I said, chagrined that I couldn't come up with a less feeble platitude.

"Easy for you to say. You just float through life."

"Float? I haven't had a date in years."

This seemed to perk her up a bit. "None at all?"

I said, "Well, there *is* this guy I know."

"Yeah? A guy guy, or . . . a *guy*."

"Well . . . a *guy*. I mean, he's really, really attractive and all."

"Available?"

"Yes."

"Interested?"

"Maybe."

Julia put her bottle to her lips and aimed the bottom of it at me. She gave her eyebrows a quick pump. Lowered the bottle. "This is interesting. Em Hansen thinking about an attractive *guy*. I thought hell would freeze over first."

"Oh, come on, Julia. I've been involved with men before."

"Oh, sure. Once every decade, whether you need to or not. For five minutes, tops."

"Now, that's not fair! There've been guys . . . I just haven't brought them all around to meet you."

"Like who?"

"Well, since I've been living in Salt Lake, for instance, there've been two worth mentioning."

"Mention, then."

"Well, there was this guy Ray. He was a cop. Really good looking, and a solid guy, really. Wanted me to marry him."

"And?"

"Well, it didn't work out." I shrugged my shoulders.

"Why not?"

"Well, he's a Mormon, so he needed me to join his church, see, and—"

Julia cut me off with a snort that shot beer up her nose.

She had stopped crying, so I kept going with the topic. I said, "Okay, but it was serious. I really felt something for him."

"Something. Were you in love with him?"

"Oh, now, you've got to go and ask the difficult questions. I really, truly *wanted* him."

"You mean in bed." She shook her head. "That's sex. You'd know it if you were in love with him." She thumped her chest. "That you feel here, not the other place." She shrugged. "Or at least, that's what people tell me."

"Thanks for the anatomy lesson."

"Okay, you said there were two worth mentioning."

"The other was this guy Jack. Now, Jack was really something. Great in bed. Gorgeous. Funny. Full of shit, you know? With him I felt it both places."

"And what happened?"

"Well, he went away. But I guess you could say I was really in love with Jack."

"*Gonzo* for Jack is what it sounds like. All pressy-body and no stickum."

"That I can't argue. But for a while, it was really nice." I glanced at the Budweiser clock above the bar.

Julia said, "So tell me about this new guy. This *guy*."

"Well, this one is a really, truly nice guy. Wears well. Doesn't push anything on me. He has a sense of humor, but he's not just a joker. He can even cook, sort of. He's smart and likes to go for hikes and—"

"What's he do?"

"He's a pilot."

"Oh, a flyboy. Nice. Military? They've got an Air National Guard in Utah, don't they?"

"He *was* military. Navy. Flew an EA-6 in Desert Storm, but now that he's civilian, he's designing a new twin-engine prop-drive aircraft. He's got a jet-engine version of the same airframe on the drawing board. He's got the prototype together, and he's looking for investors to put it into production. Smart guy."

"What's his name?"

"Fritz Calder."

"So then, here's the twenty thousand dollar question: What do you need from Fritz?"

"I . . . well, maybe that is the question. I can't decide what I want with Fritz."

"*Need*, Em. My question was not what you want from him, but what you *need*." Her eyes clouded and focused inward. "It's so easy to want a man who can't give you what you need. Especially if you don't know what you want and need from yourself."

"Now you've truly lost me."

Julia stared into my eyes. "We go through the first half of our lives thinking that a man is the solution, but you know what? He's really just a mirror. When you think you're looking at the man, you're only looking at your own needs and longing staring right back out at you."

This was Julia: Half crazy but still half wise. I tried on her idea. What did I see when I looked into Fritz's eyes? And what did I want? I wanted a child, I knew that much, and if I didn't get going, it was going to be too damned late. I wanted a man to be with and love forever, who could love me. A love that would fill me to the brim. A love that would make me nuts with pleasure.

Julia said, "You're as crazy as I am, Em." She glanced out the window.

The sky was beginning to spit the first big drops of the coming storm. She said, "I don't know about you, but I gotta go." She stood up abruptly. "Just remember to look into the mirror, Em. Next time you see this man, look straight into him and ask yourself not just what you see looking back at you, but *who*."

26

Fritz Calder sailed toward the towering clouds in the twin-engine aircraft he had designed, pushing it to its maximums, cursing the lack of a tailwind. Under the hush of his noise-canceling headphones, it was totally silent except for the gentle whine of the engines. His attention was fixed on the far horizon, but he glanced repeatedly at his instruments. The weather radar screen glowed with concentrations of orange and red shapes along a line that ran north and south over Colorado's Front Range, directly across his path. In the distance the flickering lightning within the squall line bloomed with random strobes behind the cloud buildups. It reminded him of his months at sea in the Indian Ocean.

But on this day, he rode to war against an enemy whose face he could not see, and the targets on his radar screen told him that he must first evade the enormous dark clouds that stretched along the eastern flank of the Rockies from north of Boulder clear down past Colorado Springs. The cloud mass was forty thousand feet tall. Because—as the lack of tailwinds advised him—there were no winds aloft, a strange and ominous condition in itself, the tops of these behemoth thunderheads had not blown over into the classic anvil shape. Any pilot worth his salt knew what that meant. The hot, moist air was rising with terrifying force and probably carrying hail the size of golf balls. He'd have to divert far to the north or south to avoid them, continue east out toward Kansas and then turn west again before making his approach into

Centennial, rather than risk being thrashed to splinters in the titanic updrafts those clouds represented.

He focused his mind on the job of flying. He was flying to Centennial, where he'd pick up a car and continue to Castle Rock, where he would find Em. Find her and keep her safe, because each time he looked inside his own soul, he saw her, bright and shimmering, looking out at him.

27

THE BIG, SPLASHING DROPS OF RAIN COALESCED INTO A COLD, hammering downpour as I jacked the Jeep up to attach the spare tire. In no time at all, the air around us went dark with slanting lines of water. It covered the road until it glistened and began to run off. It hammered the roof of the Jeep. It wet us to the skin and chilled us to the bone.

With water coursing down my nose and dripping from my hair, I turned the crank as fast as I could, first up to get the blown tire off and the spare tire on, and then down almost too fast, dropping the Jeep back onto the road. Julia stood by helplessly, her knee so stiff and painful now that she held it straight.

"Get back in the car," I said. "There's nothing you can do out here."

Julia raised the back door of the Jeep and got out a jacket with a hood. "Here, wear this at least," she said.

I put it on to humor her, but I was already soaked to the skin. It was a faded red and had MCWAIN GEOLOGICAL CONSULTING embroidered across the right breast pocket, to match the logo painted on the doors of the Jeep. "When did you have this made up?"

"Just before we bought the ranch. I thought Afton would like it. It seems I didn't understand his ethic or at least the one he was changing to. Something about being made in a Third World country where they use child labor and adult semi-slavery."

"There's some truth to all that, isn't there?"

"Yeah, but as long as he's feeling so tender-hearted about children and overburdened adults, how about the ones he left behind in Denver?"

I shook my head as I cranked the second to the last lug nut back into place.

Julia huddled underneath the raised tailgate and shivered.

It began to hail. Big, white ping-pong-ball-sized lumps of ice came spitting out of the sky like a Dr. Seuss story gone deadly. I jumped under the cover of the open tailgate. Julia motioned for me to climb in with her so she could lower it in case the hail started breaking glass. When she managed to pull the thing down on her foot, she began to invent whole new combinations of swear words.

The drumming of the hailstones on the roof of the Jeep was deafening. The individual stones came larger and larger. A particularly large stone hit the windshield, breaking the glass into a perfect spider's web of cracks, and I could see them ricocheting off the rental car. I shouted, "Both vehicles are going to look like golf balls when this is over!"

"Sons of bitches, bastards all," growled Julia.

"How's your insurance?" I inquired.

"Passable. Big deductible."

"Life sure can suck."

"Amen, sister."

The hail passed, but the rain kept coming, even faster. The ruined windshield coursed with water, but held, letting only a thin stream of water through. "I'm going to finish up quick while I can," I said.

"If you insist on going back out there, use this," she said, handing me a hard hat emblazoned with the McWain logo.

I loosened the fitting band and put it on. "You might have given this to me earlier," I said. "It would have spared my coiffure."

"Yeah, you and the gilded Gilda. Hey, now that we have four tires under this thing again, let's drive up to the ranch and spin mud all over her fucking yurt."

"Whoa there," I said. "You want to watch that temper of yours, Julia. If that Upton guy doesn't file a complaint on you for punching him out, then mixing it up with Gilda will certainly do the trick."

Julia growled, "You're right. I'd better keep my distance. If I get within striking distance of that blood-sucking tick, she's dead."

"Watch who you say that around, Julia."

She broke into fresh tears. "You don't think I'd actually do something *that* stupid, do you?"

"No. You're stupid enough to marry a man so selfish he leaves you without a spare tire in a field vehicle, and you're stupid enough to drive up a dirt road without replacing it, but both of those are stupidity against yourself. You are not so stupid that you'd be stupid at someone else." I launched myself over the back of the seat and ventured forth again into the downpour.

A fresh onslaught of rain came rushing down the hill like an advancing curtain. Just before it drove down upon me, Julia rolled down the window and cried, "What's that?"

I turned to see where she was pointing, up toward the McWain ranch. "I don't see anything," I hollered.

"I thought I saw something moving up on the nearest ridge, just a couple hundred yards away."

I squinted into the rain but saw nothing. "Do you still see it?"

"No . . ." She was huddled in the car, shivering. Afraid.

I set to work, hurrying as I tightened the final lug nuts. In half a minute, I was done, and I climbed back into the Jeep, this time in the driver's seat. For a moment, I contemplated the mess the hail had made of the windshield. I could barely see through it.

Julia climbed forward over the seats. She said, "I'll drive."

"The hell you will. This thing has a standard shift."

"But—"

"I'll just pull up next to the rental car. You can drive that. You need to get back to Denver, right? It's your left knee that's messed up, but you can drive the automatic shift just fine."

"But I'm not listed on the insurance."

"I can phone the rental company and have you listed. What, would you prefer I drive you to Denver? And then figure out how you're going to come back and get the Jeep? No, we'll switch and I can drop the Jeep off and pick up the rental on my way to the airport." I started up the Jeep and eased it forward to pull up next to the sedan, watching through the right-hand window to make sure I wasn't getting too close, because I could barely see through the windshield. "The keys are in it," I said. "I'll meet you at your house in an hour or so."

She looked at her wounded leg. She tried to bend it. She winced. Then she grabbed her cell phone out of its cradle on the dashboard and prepared to get out. "You're following me, aren't you?"

"I have one more thing I want to do first."

"You've got to be kidding!"

"I've got to sample a few of those red clay soils, like just along here toward Johnson's ranch. And chert pebbles. I saw some sticking out of a cut bank down by where Jarre and Plum Creeks come together."

"N-n-no!"

"No?" I put a hand on her. "You're shivering, Julia. Get into that rental car and push up the heat."

"I can't leave you out here by yourself! What if you got hypothermic? And what if I have trouble driving that thing? Follow me, Em, *please!*"

"Come on, I'm a tough old ranch girl. I want to go home, and I can't go until I grab those samples. I'm already up here and soaking wet, so what do I have to lose? It'll take me five minutes and I'm out of here. You run along. If you have any trouble, I'll be coming along behind you. Take 67 to 85 and 85 to I-25. It'll be safest. You have trouble, call me on my cell phone."

Her eyes shone with anxiety and her teeth were bared in horror.

I said, "Julia, get out of here! Your lips are turning blue. Come on, the hail's stopped. I want to get those samples and get my butt home to Utah."

Julia at last did as I said, giving me one last bedraggled look and slipping quickly from one vehicle to the other. She started up the rental car and drove away.

I waited for a minute, listening to the rain, trying to let it be okay that I simply couldn't tolerate another moment of Julia's craziness. What had happened to my old friend? Had life become so damned disappointing that she couldn't pull herself together any better than this? Small thoughts trickled through my mind, the kind that point toward partings of the way, little justifications and rationalizations and one great big, nasty, in-my-face realization that some people move on with life and others fall behind.

The windshield wipers slapped back and forth, doing almost no good against the fractured glass. The clouds and rain had settled in so thickly now that I saw fit to turn on the headlights. I looked at the clock on the dash. It was only three in the afternoon, but it looked like dusk.

I took a deep breath and put the Jeep back in gear, but did not let out the clutch. Now that I was alone, I discovered that I was in fact feeling a little anxious myself. *Why would grabbing a sample frighten me?* I asked myself. *I'm simply saving an extra trip. I'm not nosing around on anybody's property. And it's not the storm; I've ridden horseback twenty miles in rains as hard as this. So what's my problem?*

Okay, I admitted to myself, *so the windshield's screwed up and three of your tires are bald. How's that so different from driving Dad's tractor to harvest alfalfa?*

I tried to calm myself, tried to think of something quiet and reassuring. The image of Fritz opened in my mind like a deck of cards fanning out smoothly, lined up by number and suit, except for one joker where a Jack should be, which made me smile. What had Julia said? I should look at him as a mirror?

Another bolt of lightning hit, followed within ten seconds by a crash of thunder. The center of the storm was moving closer. It was time to grab my samples or give up.

I glanced around to make certain that there was plenty of higher ground around me so that I wouldn't become a lightning rod. Twisting my face with the mental effort of trying to see through the small portion of the windshield that wasn't smashed, I headed up the dirt road that led toward Bart Johnson's ranch and drove along past the corner where the fence turned to the juncture with his entrance track. I was almost sad that the Rhodesian Ridgeback wasn't there to bark at me. The place was just a sea of running rain and mud, disconsolate and cold.

I set the brake and hopped out, leaving the Jeep in the center of the road so it wouldn't slide off into the ditch, the engine and the wipers running for whatever good they might do, and scratched quickly at the bank where it was dripping red like the blood of Mother Earth. Stuffing a wad of clay into the pocket of my jeans, I hopped back into the Jeep, closed the door, and removed the hard hat at last. My hair stuck to my forehead like paste. I thought of digging for another plastic bag for my so-called evidence but decided that it made no substantive difference whether it was hermetically sealed at the site anyway—this evidence was hardly conclusive of much of anything—so I left the muck where it was, cold and wet against my thigh.

As I eased the Jeep back into gear, I felt the tires slip. Cursing Julia for driving a car that not only lacked a spare but needed new tread, I put my foot on the brake and reached for the lever that would shift it into four-wheel drive. As my hand landed on the lever, I heard a horn sound behind me.

The lever wouldn't go into all-wheel gear. "Old-fashioned piece of junk!" I cursed, trying it a second and a third time.

The horn sounded behind me again, longer, more insistent.

I switched on the rear wiper blade, straightened up, and peered into the rear-view mirror. All I could see through the coursing rain and gloom was the muddy glow of a pair of headlights, high up like another SUV, but wider, like a truck. Cursing my luck at finding myself in front of a rancher in a hurry, I belayed the attempt to put Julia's Jeep in four-wheel drive and instead pressed down on the accelerator. The tires spun then caught and the Jeep began to roll forward. Racking it up through the gears, I glanced into the mirror again. The other vehicle was still close behind me, even closer now, and the driver again sounded its horn. I drove faster, then tapped the brakes to flash red lights in the driver's eyes, get him to back off. The truck careened in and rammed my rear bumper. Stunned, I glanced backward over my shoulder. In a flash of lightning, I saw two fists clutched across the top of the steering wheel of the vehicle behind me and above that, the brim of a hat. The driver was so intent on riding up my back that he was bent almost to the wheel.

My heart rattled in my chest. Half scared and half furious, I stepped on it, hurrying to get away from this idiot. The horn sounded again. In one last glance at the rear-view mirror, I saw the high headlights hurtling toward me. Again he rammed me, jerking my neck. No longer thinking about what I was doing, I stood on the gas pedal so hard my butt lifted off the seat.

Acceleration did not happen. Instead, I began sliding. Panicking, I racked the Jeep into lower gear and again floored it, hoping I could regain traction. The Jeep's wiper blades slapped frantically, but did nothing to clear the shattered glass. I felt the road pitch downhill. I was going at least forty miles per hour on an exquisitely slick surface with rocks to both sides. In a flash of lightning, I saw the vague outlines of the road swerving off to the right. I tapped the brakes then released them. I was caught between two hells, afraid to accelerate but certain that I should not stop. My back end swung out madly to the left. The big truck slewed wildly up on my right and turned toward me, ramming my rear wheel well. I felt the Jeep spin. It pirouetted crazily across the road, hit the ditch with a sickening lurch, and began to roll.

The world spun around me. I felt a giant's thumbs pushing into my ears and knew I was taking high G's. My neck snapped this way and that. Objects flew around the cab of the Jeep.

It took me a while to realize that the Jeep had come to rest. The world slowly spun down to a lazy, sickening swaying sensation. Precious moments passed. As I collected my wits, I noticed that the top of my head felt odd and with that, knew that I must be hanging upside down. I braced one hand downward against the ceiling and released the seat belt. I fell like a sack of wet cement, bruising my hip on the dome light, which for some reason had turned itself on. *That means a door is ajar,* I remember thinking, but I couldn't reason out which one.

I smelled gasoline.

I knew I couldn't stay in the Jeep—it could catch fire, and the other driver would be checking to make sure of his kill—but I couldn't get my mind to understand which way to go to find the window openers. *Are they hand-crank or electric?* I wondered and noted numbly that I had not taken the time to familiarize myself with the vehicle before agreeing to drive it. *Daddy taught me better than that,* a tiny little girl deep inside of me whimpered.

I rolled my head left and right and heard a nasty crackling sound in my neck but was at last able to ascertain which end of the box I was in faced forward. I aimed my feet that direction and kicked as hard as I could. The glass gave way softly, sending a painful jolt through my bruised body as my legs overshot their mark.

The space between the dashboard and the roof of the car seemed narrower than I remembered. I squeezed out into the sodden ground, trying through my shock to get my bearings. Water was running through the shattered windshield, carrying sand and bits of plants. Something sharp jabbed into the palm of one hand. I wiggled like an eel, squeezing through the space between the wrecked hood of the Jeep and the rocks it had landed on. The sounds of rushing water and rain and the slapping of feet sounded on the road. I broke free of my prison, sprang to my feet, and ran for my life.

28

I STUMBLED FRANTICALLY THROUGH THE SCRUB, NOW SMELLING sage, now something sweeter, climbing for high ground and the cover of a jagged outcropping of rocks that I could see above me. Once on top of the ridge I ducked in behind a line of boulders and kept on running, hoping I was heading toward Jarre Creek, the paved road, and the hope of finding the highway. The thought shot through my mind— *What if I flag down the guy who just rammed me?*—but I pushed it away and put everything I had into my clattering run over the rain-slick stones. I climbed, grit biting into my hands.

Burning lead filled my lungs, and I fell in between two boulders to catch my rasping breath. My saliva ran hot and burned my throat like acid. I gasped and wheezed, my rib cage working like a bellows.

I yanked in a breath and held it, listening.

Nothing.

Cautiously, I let out my breath and forced it to come in slowly, quietly. My head pounded and my hands felt like they were full of glass. I peered down toward the road.

I could not see the truck that had hit me. Where had it gone? Was the driver close by, out of sight below the rocks? Had he gone up a ranch road to come at me from another side? I listened. I could hear nothing over the driving rain, and it cut the visibility to a hundred yards or less.

My body was stiff with pain and growing colder by the instant.

Hands shaking, I dug through my pockets and found my cell phone and punched it on. The battery was three-quarters gone, but to my immense relief, I got a signal. I punched in 911 and hit SEND.

It rang twice and clicked to a connection. "State the nature of your emergency," said a phlegmatic voice.

My hands were shaking so hard that I had to hold the phone in both hands. I fought to control my voice around chattering teeth. "I'm on a ridge, west of Sedalia somewhere. Someone just ran me off the road. Please send help."

"You've reached Salt Lake City emergency. State your location relative to a highway."

"I'm in Colorado!"

"Are you on a cell phone?"

"Yes."

"Your service provider has put you through to the 801 area code 911 line. I can transfer you. What area code and jurisdiction do you wish me to dial?"

"Three-oh-three, I think. Sedalia, Colorado."

"Please hold." The line clicked over and rang and rang and rang . . .

I pulled the phone from my ear to listen again for pursuers. I could hear nothing but the pounding rain and the gurgling of water sluicing down the rocks.

When I put the phone back to my ear, I heard a recorded voice. It announced, "We are encountering an unusual number of emergency calls at this time. Please hold for the next available operator."

A bright flash lit the sky, almost immediately followed by a *crack!* and deafening *BOOM!* that rolled around me with a fully physical sense of concussion. The reek of ozone filled the air. I pressed myself tighter into the crevice.

The connection had gone dead.

I tried to harness my careening brain for another strategy. I was shaking now from head to foot and not just from the cold that was seeping in from my soaking wet jeans and socks and shirt. I knew that I was going into shock. Still crouching between the rocks, I stared into the illuminated dial of the cell phone, trying to imagine a solution to my predicament. Another bar in the battery-charge indicator had extinguished. The battery was old and weak; by the time it went down another bar, I would have less than a minute left. Unable to remember a single phone number of anyone anywhere, I pushed the button that would bring up previously dialed sequences. The first one was 801 area code, as was the second, and the third, and I realized that they all were. All Utah, not Colorado. I knew that one had to be Michele's, but I could not remember which it was.

I punched the lower button and scrolled downward through numbers listed by name. The names of the few people I had bothered to put into the memory flipped by. A for ADAM, B for BETTY, then F for FAYE—I almost punched that one in but remembered that it was her home number. The next name in memory was F for FAYE, CELL. I stopped. She rarely switched on her phone. Should I call that number and risk wasting precious battery time on another recorded message? I pressed the memory scroll button again. F again, this time for FRITZ, CELL.

Without another thought, I jabbed the SEND button. The line connected, rang, rang again, and then I heard the finest sound ever, the voice of a friend. "This is Fritz," he said, his voice strong and firm. I could hear road noise. He was driving.

I was afraid to raise my voice to be heard over the cell phone. So frightened, in fact, that I could not think what to say.

"Who is this?" he demanded.

"Fritz!" I called, anguish ripping the sound into pieces.

"Is this Em? Are you all right?" Alarm filled his voice, but then it deepened into a tone of command. "Em, tell me where you are."

"I'm . . . I n-need you," I stammered, trembling so hard that I could not control lips.

"I am coming, Em. I'm on I-25 coming south from Centennial. Tell me where you are!"

"W-west of Sedalia, on a d-dirt road off the road that goes to . . . Highway 67." I tried to remember which side of 67 the road turned off, but the universe seemed to pivot like a carousel. "Send the sh-sheriff to the Johnson Ranch. They'll know."

"Em, are you hurt?"

"I'm scared, Fritz."

"Are you in a car? Where exactly are you?"

Another flash and immediate *BOOM!* creased the air. I turned the face of the phone toward me to see if I was still connected, but I could no longer understand what the little symbols were telling me. I put it back to my ear and said desperately, "I'm hiding in some rocks. Find the J-Jeep and send the p-police. I'll s-see their lights, and I'll know I can c-come out. P-please hurry." The shock was deepening, and even the sense of cold seemed remote.

Fritz's voice filled my ear. "What Jeep, Emmy? What does it look like?"

"It's . . . can't remember."

"Is anybody with you? Do you need an ambulance? Damn it, Em, *tell me where you are!*"

Hearing fear twist through Fritz Calder's voice snapped me back to my senses. "My battery is almost dead. I'll be okay if you can just get here. Call the Douglas County Sheriff's Department and—" A sound needled my ear: *beep-beep!*

The phone had shut down, its battery dead. I was alone with the rain and the fear of death.

29

"It seemed like hours before I saw the red flashing lights of the emergency vehicles," I said.

"It was twenty minutes, exactly," Fritz replied softly, as he rubbed my hair with a towel in the warm bedroom of Trevor Reed's condominium in Denver.

"Only twenty minutes?" I asked, leaning into the force of his ministrations.

"Only? Only? It felt like forever to me. I've never been so scared in my life. I must have hit a hundred miles an hour in that damned rental car. I didn't have any trouble finding the sheriff's deputies," he said, laughing now. "They found me."

"No. It wasn't really like that."

"You're right, it wasn't. I had them on the cell phone, and I fell in behind them. Otherwise I could never have found you." He rubbed a little harder. "And that is not something I wish to contemplate."

Satisfied that my hair was as dry as he could get it with the towel, he grabbed a dry one off the stack he had put beside me where I sat at the foot of that gigantic bed. This towel he applied vigorously to my shoulders and back, even though I was wearing one of his big T-shirts and a terrycloth bathrobe Fritz had liberated from Reed's closet and I had dried myself before putting it on. But I didn't ask him to stop. It felt too good. The pressure of his touch was reassuring. It kept me focused on where I was and not the place where I had been.

"Now get up," he said.

"Why? I'm liking it here."

He stood up. "Come on, up!"

I did as I was told.

Suddenly Fritz was running in place. "Come on, run with me!"

He made it sound like so much fun that I started to move my feet, too, but they felt as heavy and hard as uncooked potatoes.

"No, *run!*" he insisted. "You won't break anything. The ER doctors said there's not a broken bone in your body, though having seen that Jeep, that's hard to understand."

I started to chuff a little faster.

He reached his hands out and tickled my ribs. "Run, Emmy! C'mon, there's a race to be run here!" His grin was infectious.

My face felt unnatural trying to smile like that, but my heart didn't want to be left behind, and I jogged all around the room, now waving my arms as Fritz had begun to do.

"Now over the bed," he announced, dropping to his hands and knees and scrambling over the covers, messing them up good.

I followed, wobbly but still game. My arms and legs ached, and the bandages on my hands and knees cut, but I made it without flopping onto my side even once. "Can I ask the purpose of this exercise?"

"Not yet. Now, I'm going to stand on the other side of the door here and you push with all your might, okay?"

"If you say so."

He stepped out of the room and closed the door to just a crack. "Now, push!"

Panic swept through me at having him out of sight. Stepping into the shower had been hard enough—taking my clothes off alone in the bathroom, even worse—but this was somehow unbearable. I lunged at the door, shoving frantically. I pushed and pushed, wondering why Fritz should leave me like this. I cried, "Let me out! Let me out, *please!*"

"*Push,* Emmy!"

I gave it everything I had. Sweat burst out on my upper lip. It was an out-swing door, and I was on carpeting and Fritz on hardwood. He began to skid, and I crashed through into his arms as he fought to regain his balance.

"That's my girl," he said proudly, gathering me up close. "Now you'll be okay."

My chest was heaving again, just like in the rain and the lightning, but now strong, protective arms surrounded me. My brain swung between the two sensations: shock and fear at what had happened that afternoon and the warmth and security of Fritz's embrace. I felt jagged energy drain from my body.

"There now," he said, stroking my hair. "There now."

I laid my head against his chest and put both arms around him in a tight embrace. "Why?" I asked. "Now tell me why."

"To release the trauma," he said. "Remember? The nervous system stores the fear and energy you need for escape until you release it by working your muscles. You know that. You've read the books."

"I've read the books," I told the fabric of his shirt.

He kissed the top of my head, then squeezed me tighter and swung me gently side to side.

About then I realized that we were hugging each other with both arms. I liked it.

I quelled the fear that rushed in behind that realization and closed my eyes.

Another wave of remembrance rolled across my brain. Lightning. Rain. The demon charging at me on the road.

"Open your eyes," Fritz whispered into my hair. "You're tensing up again. Open your eyes. What color is the wall?"

"Red. It's brick."

"That's my girl. Now tell me your favorite flavor of ice cream."

"Peppermint. No, green tea."

"Excellent. Green tea is magic. Okay, you can think about the trauma again for ten seconds. Ready?"

"I don't want to."

"Okay, wait for it to hit you."

"It's hitting me."

"Ten, nine, eight, seven, six, five—"

"That's enough!"

"Green tea ice cream!"

"Yum." I remembered now. Levine's book spoke of the vortex formed by the memory of trauma—the capacity of the horror to drag me under to relive the event—but also of the counter-vortex I could create that would balance and heal it. The game was to dip a toe into horror and then ground back in the present, give my brain something pleasant to fire on so it could spin things back the other way. Thus decoupled from the event, the latent energy bound up in the will to escape would be released to flow like a river between smooth banks. My mind bobbed sweetly on the currents, telling me, *What luck to know someone as smart as Fritz!*

"How are you now?" he asked.

"Better. Exhausted."

"I probably shouldn't push you so hard. The ER docs said to let you rest. But I can't stand—"

I was willing to lean against him all night if he wanted me to, but just then my cell phone rang.

"It's okay," I said.

"Ignore it," he said.

"Okay."

It stopped ringing, and twenty seconds later, Fritz's phone went off.

"Did you give Michele your number or something?" I mumbled.

"She would have broken my arm if I tried to resist."

I inhaled and let out a long, tired breath. "I suppose she won't go away until we answer it then."

Fritz's phone stopped its ruckus and ten seconds later, mine started up again. Fritz waltzed me over to where it lay on the recharger on the black stone counter, and I switched it on. "Hello, Michele," I told it.

"Are you alive?"

"No, I speak to you from beyond the grave. I was just getting into it with the worms."

"Nice image. Are you ready to talk?"

"If I have to."

"You'd prefer that whoever did that to you walks?"

"No. Go ahead then."

"What did the vehicle look like?"

"I already told the Highway Patrol. It was high and wide. I assume it to be a truck. Beyond that—" The image of that mass of metal hurtling toward me filled my mind again, and I tensed. Fritz returned the pressure, supporting my urge to fight with every ounce of my strength. The wave of fear washed over me and passed, leaving me once again rocked and slightly nauseous.

"What color was it?"

"Color?" My mind brought the image to life again, but saw nothing. No tint. Only the gray fury of slashing rain. "I don't see any."

"Call it white?"

"Could have been."

"But not black or red or green."

"No."

"A newer truck? Or older?"

"I . . . older. It had square corners. You know, like they don't make anymore."

"Describe the driver."

"I can't. I've already tried. I couldn't see the face because of the hat, and that was some drab ball cap, a dime a dozen."

"The driver's hands, then. Could you see them?"

"Yes—yes, they were white. Or white person hands. Tan, or whatever that color is. You know what I mean."

"Slender fingers? Thick?"

"Thick. So I'd say male. But it could have been deerskin gloves, for all that."

"Gnarly?"

"You mean like Johnson's hands? I'm sorry, the image isn't giving me that kind of detail."

"Then we'll say not, for the moment."

Fritz still held me, swaying gently from foot to foot. I said, "The steering wheel was dark."

"That's something, I guess." She exhaled her breath with frustration. "Tell me again how the vehicle came up behind you and hit you."

I repeated the sequence: the horn, the bumps, the quick cut into my right rear quarter, the awful spinning sensation before everything inside the Jeep turned to complete chaos as it rolled.

Fritz said, "That's an attack sequence used by professionals."

"He's right," said Michele. "They teach that trick to us cops, too."

"Explain," I said.

Fritz said, "The bumping was probably designed to get you moving faster, but the cut into the right rear wheel, that's textbook technique for getting a car to spin off the road. Part of why it's used is it usually doesn't leave a dent on the attacking car."

I tipped my head back to look at Fritz, "Are there a few things about your military career you haven't told me?"

He gazed into my eyes. "When they have us fly forty-million-dollar jets over hostile territory where men are shooting rocket launchers at anything with wings, they teach us what to do to avoid getting hit. And what to do if we get unlucky."

"They want you to bring it back in one piece."

"And it cost about a half million dollars to train me. I was worth something to them, too," he said huffily.

"And I thought it was your rakish charm," I said, giving him a dreamier smile than I had quite intended.

Fritz's eyes went wide. Ever so slightly he loosened his hug, and the gentle swaying stopped.

Michele said, "Em? you still there?"

I leveled my head so that I was eyeing his shirt front again and readdressed myself to the telephone. "Fritz is right, Michele, I don't think that maneuver was accidental in its efficiency. You should add that to your wish list for your background search of the suspects."

"What would that be? Guerrilla training?"

I said, "Military service. Special ops? I don't know, get creative. Where do you learn to be an assassin? You start out as a bodyguard and get cranky? Maybe he's law enforcement gone bad."

"So you do think this is a male of the species."

"God damn it, Michele, ask your questions as questions, okay? I appreciate your fancy training, but—"

"Sorry. It's become a reflex."

"And yes, I think it was a man, because the hands were not small and because I've never met a woman that kind of mean. Why, can you see Gilda doing that?"

"No, I can't. I think she's an opportunist but not that type and not that clever mechanically."

"What does that mean?"

Michele said, "Gilda is a leach. Leaches don't kill their hosts, it's not in their best interests. And it takes a certain capacity for cunning and mechanical ingenuity to put a scenario like that together. That's a little beyond your basic buy-it-with-sex, housebreaking, neo-Nature-Girl trollop. Whoever set this up was able to figure out the diagram of rain plus road plus Em Hansen in Jeep. And where in hell *is* Gilda?"

"Maybe she's dead, too. They killed Afton, so how about Gilda, and now let's go after another geologist, but it wasn't me he was after. I've told you that. I've told the state patrol that. I was in Julia's car, marked MCWAIN; I was wearing her jacket, marked MCWAIN; her hard hat, MCWAIN, MCWAIN, MCWAIN. She's the trustee of that estate until her kids turn twenty-one, am I right? I mean, read the tea leaves, Michele! Afton's gone, Gilda's hiding, and now someone's trying for Julia. It's not healthy owning land up there. Has someone checked on Julia? Maybe whoever did this finally saw that I wasn't Julia, and that's why they didn't follow me up that hill and finish me off!"

Michele said, "You've got to hope it wasn't you they wanted. But you told me Upton looked scared at the sight of you, not Julia."

"Yeah, but—"

"I'm letting the local law enforcement think it was you they were after, if you don't mind."

"Why?"

"Because you're law enforcement, and we have a thing about people trying to kill cops. It gets them more interested in the case, know what I mean?"

"I'm not law enforcement, I'm a geologist."

"You'd prefer we didn't count you as one of us? Oh great, then we'll just leave you out there to bleed to death next time."

"Exposure."

"What?"

"I would have died of exposure first."

"Doesn't matter; either way you're dead meat."

I still couldn't get my mind around what she was saying. "I thought they came because I'd had an accident, not because I was police!"

"You think so? How many emergency calls do you think were on the line just then, in that storm, with trees coming down over lines and people getting hit by hailstones the size of bricks and not just your car skidding off the road, and just how many officers do you think the state patrol has just hanging out in Douglas County waiting for some half-wit geologist to get herself in trouble? Huh? How many on duty in the Douglas County Sheriff's Department at that hour? Huh? Didn't think about that, did you, Miss forensic, dirt-in-the-dead-man's-shoes, I'm-done-now-and-I'm-out-of-here Hansen?"

She was wearing me down. I tried to laugh and think her words funny, but I was tensing again. Fritz was still holding me, even massaging the center of my back, but from a distance. Had I said something to offend him? Or had I, once and for all, completely misgauged the range of ways he might be interested in me? His solid presence was my anchor. I tightened my arms around him and held on for dear life.

To Michele I said, "You're right. Whoever did that probably knew the road and the lay of the land around it. But I don't think it was Johnson. His hands are pretty screwed up with arthritis."

"Your view was blurred and distorted by the rain."

Fritz said, "She's about done, Michele."

He was right, the strain of talking and trying to think clearly and worrying if I was somehow offending Fritz was exhausting what little strength I had left. I said, "I'm getting tired, Michele. What else do you need right now?"

"I need to find Attabury and his damned airplane, that's what I need! And I'd like to know where in hell Gilda's gotten herself to as well. She's gone, her electric cart's gone . . . so no, she's not dead, because I checked this morning and that cart was in the barn at the ranch, and now it's gone. The little creep has some kind of hidey-hole up there, or something. Guess she got nervous in the storm and made a run for it."

"She can't have gotten far in that thing." My voice was starting to sound frail even to me. I just wanted to get off the phone and collapse.

"That's what I thought, too. Damned strange behavior from a woman who's supposed to be aggrieved and plotting the theft of a valuable estate."

"Maybe she's shacked up with Johnson," I suggested.

"Now there's a fun couple. Why do you say that?"

Fritz took the phone out of my hand. "Michele, I'm putting Em to bed now," he said.

"Wait, you're coming back down here tomorrow, aren't you?"

"Talk to you in the morning, Michele," he said. His voice was still calm but as hard as granite. He switched off the phone and tossed it onto a couch.

I waited to see if he'd put both arms back around me now that he no longer held the phone. He did not. Instead, guiding me with just one arm, he led me into the bedroom. I let myself hope that he would lie down on the bed beside me. He did not. Instead, he turned back the covers, took away my robe, and indicated that I should climb in between the soft, silky sheets alone.

"My hair's still wet," I said. "I'll screw up these sheets."

Fritz grabbed a dry towel and laid it across the near pillow. "Satisfied?"

"Okay." I smoothed the T-shirt down around my hips, sat down on the bed, and stared up at him. I had no idea what my face told him. Did I look as fragile and pathetic as I felt? I looked into his eyes, searching for that mirror, but all I saw was the quiet center of a man I was beginning to realize that I loved. As he gently supported my head and shoulders and lowered me onto the bed, I wondered, *How long have I felt this way?* He brought the covers up to my chin, tucked them carefully around my face, smoothed my still-damp hair, and switched out the bedside light.

Soft light from the living room spilled through the doorway, lighting one side of his face. He looked at my forehead and touched it again, and then my cheek and chin. He smiled a sad smile. "How are you feeling?" he asked.

"Okay," I said, uncertain what that meant. Would ever mean again.

"I'll be on the couch," he whispered. "Call me if you need me. Anything at all." He turned and started for the door.

"Fritz."

He stopped. Turned and looked at me. "Yes, Em."

"I . . . I'm scared."

"You'd be damned stupid if you weren't."

"I mean, I . . . can I come sleep with you?" I blurted it out before I could worry that it might ruin our friendship forever. Suddenly, I could not bear the idea of life without him.

Fritz came back to my bedside and knelt beside it. He clasped his hands at the very edge of the mattress and folded his great frame so that his chin was on them, as if in prayer, his lips just showing above his strong fingers. "Em," he began, then fell silent again for a while. He lifted one hand to fiddle with the edge of the blankets, using that activity as an excuse to focus his eyes for a moment on something other than mine. "I care about you a lot. And you've just been through a terrible shock. I'm concerned that . . . you'll want things from me because of what's happened to you."

You mean sex, I thought, and, *But what if I'm really in love with you?* I said, "Sort of a Stockholm Syndrome."

Fritz gazed into my eyes. "Stockholm Syndrome describes the behavior of kidnap victims who become sympathetic to their captors," he said. He gave me a twisted smile. "I don't recall throwing you in a sack and dragging you here, Em, but it's true I didn't give you much choice about going to the emergency room. Are you sorry I did that?"

"No, you did exactly the right thing."

"You're afraid you won't sleep. Shall I see if Trevor has any sedatives in his medicine cabinet?"

"No. I just—"

Fritz put one hand to my lips, gently quieting me. "I'll sleep right here on the floor. I won't let anyone near you."

"You can't sleep on the floor!"

"Watch me," he said. He disappeared out the door only long enough to turn out the other lights and grab some cushions off the couch. These he plopped on the floor right by my side. He yanked the spare comforter off the foot of the bed and rolled up in it, making a joke out of it as if he were making a burrito out of himself, then made a very silly display out of lumbering down onto the floor thus attired. "Done," he said. "Now, I don't know about you, but I'm totally wiped." He closed his eyes and let out a horrific snore.

I laughed thinly. "Fritz! You don't snore, do you?"

In the thin light that found its way under the blinds, I could see his teeth appear as he smiled. "I am the worst! Why, are you changing your mind? I can still go out there and close the door."

I thought of taking one of the pillows and hitting him with it, but knew I was still just trying to provoke intimacy. Instead, I said, "No. Please stay."

My eyes were adjusting to the darkness. I could make out the rest of his face now. His smile was sublime.

30

FRIDAY MORNING, GILDA'S ELECTRIC CART WAS FOUND UPSIDE down and half full of wet gravel near the mouth of Jarre Canyon. The storm had done its work, wringing six inches of rain onto the Jarre and Plum Creek watershed in just over a two-hour period.

The runoff had had no time to soak into the soil. It had cascaded off the rocky summits in sheets and funneled into rivulets that sprang gushing from every fold and cranny. These fresh waters had in turn joined like thickening fingers into laden hands, continuing down the narrowing valleys and coalescing into one growing, strengthening body that rushed, churning and grinding with its sediment load, into the jagged slot of the canyon before it burst out into the wider flood plain beyond the foothills. At the speed of a locomotive, this flash flood had raised the sedate trickle at the bottom of Jarre Canyon into a thirty-foot wall of roiling, sand- and rock-choked water, surging like angry stallions over its upper banks, tearing out a bridge, and ripping away chunks of pavement the size of tennis courts from Route 67.

I was amazed that the cart was spotted as quickly as it was. The powers that be had done a good job of educating the residents of Colorado's canyons over the years following the Big Thompson flood. All permanent residents of Jarre Canyon had survived the deluge by leaving in time. But until the road was rebuilt, they would drive the long way around, climbing west over the first divide and connecting north along the Platte River toward Denver or south along the valleys of

Horse Creek, Trout Creek and Fountain Creek to Colorado Springs.

The authorities exhorted the local residents, newshounds, and disaster-stalkers to stay out of the afflicted drainages until repairs could be made, but some concerned citizen had flown over the canyon as soon as day broke looking for signs of distress and had called in a report over his radio. The FAA had relayed the sighting to the Douglas County Sheriff's Department, which deputized a ranch hand on a four-wheeler to drive down to the break in the roadway and take a look. The hand recognized Gilda's eccentric conveyance and remembered "the lady with the nice tits" driving it. His excited description launched a sheriff's helicopter, and soon the washed-out banks of Jarre Creek were dotted with searchers. They found bits of belongings scattered among the flood-washed willows and hung up on strands of barbed wire but no sign of the driver.

Gilda had therefore, and with dramatic buzzing that befitted a community that still counted itself small and closely-knit, been listed as missing and presumed dead.

All this I heard from Michele as she phoned three separate times, first asking and then begging me to return to Douglas County. Each time I said no. I considered turning off the phone, but I had left a message for Julia and was waiting for a return call. I had phoned her from the hospital and again when I arrived at Trevor Reed's condo, but had only gotten her answering machine. I was beginning to worry about her, and the news about Gilda's cart did not lessen my anxiety.

The fourth time Michele called, Fritz answered the phone and asked her politely what part of "no" she didn't understand. The fifth time, he evidenced his perturbation by asking her who had died and named her queen. Then he took matters even further into his own hands and himself turned off the phone.

We sat on the sundeck looking out across the Platte River Valley. If you think that sounds scenic, you've never been to Denver, or you like your scenery industrial, or you're some sort of transportation nut, because that's where Denver's railroad yards are and several viaducts that carry traffic in and out of town, not to mention Interstate 25. But even with the steady hum of traffic it was another sunny morning in paradise, the air washed clean by the previous day's storm, and if I hadn't ached from head to foot and had bandages all over the hands that held my cup of coffee, I might have thought I had hallucinated the entire previous day's events.

I turned to Fritz, who was leaning back in his deck chair with his eyes shut, lazily soaking up the sunshine, his thoughts a thousand miles away for all the trace they left on his face. I watched him for a while, wondering if there was any way his feelings for me were as strong or as sexual as mine now were for him.

I said, "What are your plans today?"

"I don't have any."

"Don't you have to get back to Salt Lake City?"

"Faye can fly him over."

"Reed?"

He nodded his head. "Something about not wanting to miss a party."

"But then who will mind the FBO?"

He shrugged. Clearly, he was not concerned.

"Fritz," I said, "you're not ditching work for me, are you?"

He kept his eyes closed and didn't answer.

"Fritz?"

"A long line of people have advised me not to have this conversation with you."

"What conversation?"

"Somebody's got to keep you safe," he said.

I picked at my bandages. "Thank you."

He opened one eye and looked at me. "You're not going to fight me?"

I shook my head. "In fact, I can't remember if I've even thanked you for yesterday. For saving my life."

He opened the other eye now but looked out across the valley toward the old brick buildings on the far side. "You seemed to have that well in hand," he said evenly, but I could see his jaw muscles tightening. "And . . . perhaps it's Ray you need to thank."

"Ray?"

"He came and got me. Said you were in trouble. And he didn't stop at that. He was on the phone with the sheriff's deputies when I arrived at the scene, telling them what kind of vehicle to look for."

"But how did he know what I was driving?"

"You'd have to ask him."

"*Ray* came and got you?"

Fritz nodded. "Nice guy. I'll have to buy him a beer sometime."

I wrestled with half a dozen possible next lines, but none seemed right.

The heat rising from the decking was beginning to make my head pound.

I said, "I'm going to go call Carlos," and went inside.

CARLOS WAS A little more emotional when I reached him at his office ten minutes and three phone calls later. "*¡Aiee!* Emily! Well, I'm glad you're alive, that's all."

"How did you know about all this?" I asked. I'd said nothing, only "hello."

"How? How? You think the law enforcement community has no interest in such events? Someone tries to kill one of us, it's one end of Colorado to the other before breakfast, *mi loca*. Hey, you at that fancy place again? I'm coming right now!"

I said, "Not now, Carlos. I just wanted to know you were near."

Silence.

"I'm with Fritz. I may as well be under lock and key."

Carlos let his breath out like a balloon. "Okay. But you call me. Anything you need. Anything."

"Yes, Carlos."

"*Mi amiga.*"

IT FINALLY OCCURRED to me that business hours had arrived and that Julia must be at work. Perhaps, like me, she had spent the previous evening at the ER—though I hadn't thought her knee was that bad—and then had picked up her children and had been too tired to even notice the light blinking on her answering machine.

I dialed the number for McWain Geological Consultants but got the answering machine there. No Julia. I was now officially worried about her, even scared. Considering the law enforcement community's reaction to the event, I could think of no reason why anyone would be stupid enough to go after me, so it *had* to be Julia the monster in the truck had been trying to kill. *Unless of course someone thought I was Afton . . .* But of course that made no sense. Who in such a small community would be ignorant that he was dead?

Where in hell was Julia?

I got the Denver white pages out of the drawer underneath the phone and dialed another number for a geological office in Duffy's petroleum tower—Tina, the woman I had called to tend to Julia a week earlier when this whole mess had first sprung screaming into life.

Tina was in. I asked if she'd seen Julia yet that morning.

"She's on a different floor, Em. I don't give out the hall passes around here."

"We were in the field together yesterday," I said, making it sound like nothing special, "and I was supposed to follow up with her today, but I'm not getting an answer at either her house or her office. Could you ask around?"

"I've got to pitch a prospect here in ten minutes. I really don't have time, Em."

"Then give me the name of someone on her floor."

She grunted. "Try Noel." She gave me a number.

Noel remembered me. He wanted to chat. I explained my problem, trying again to sound casual, but my urgency was beginning to leak through.

"Okay, okay," he said, laughing. "Hold your horses." He set the phone down. I could hear his swivel chair creak, and his footfalls as he walked down the hall and began to ask around. Presently he returned. "Hal says she trotted in here earlier, picked up her laptop and a few things, and hurried out."

"Did she say where she was going?"

"No."

"Would you please call me if she comes in?"

"Why don't you leave a message on her phone?"

Now, that was a perfectly reasonable question, and I did not have a ready reply. "I'm just concerned about her is all. I was supposed to hear from her, and I haven't."

"Okay, Em." Noel had a soft, kindly voice, and he used it soothingly. "Give me your number and I'll make sure to call you if I see her."

I gave him my cell number, told him to leave a message if I didn't answer, and ended the call. Then I sat there in Trevor Reed's big Denver condo and tried to sort out what I was going to do. Because not doing anything has never worked for me. I have, in the lingo of those bizarre people who make a profession of evaluating other peoples' personalities, a bias for taking action. Me, I just call it impatience. So there I sat, impatient as hell. Sure, a scant eighteen hours earlier I had been flipping through a colossal storm in a Jeep that had just been rammed by a homicidal maniac, but that didn't mean that I was ready to just say, *Oh, gosh, I must be in the wrong movie, I'll just stay home and do nothing.* In fact, frightening events invariably have the opposite effect on me. If I hold still, I feel trapped, as if the whole experience were some kind of snare that has me by the nervous system. It's more frightening—or shall I say, the experience of fear settles into me more absolutely—if I sit still and do nothing, like a rabbit who's waiting for the hunter to come finish her off. Like a rabbit, I wanted to be up running for it, but unlike a rabbit, running *away* wouldn't work for me; I wanted to run right straight *into* the object of my fear and blow it to smithereens.

Out of the corner of my eye, I looked out the sliding doors to the sun deck. Fritz was sitting there with his coffee, watching me.

I took three deep breaths and let each out slowly. Then I walked back out onto that sun deck and said, "Fritz, I know it's a risk, but I've got to go back down there."

Fritz nodded. "Risk I understand. Let's go."

31

We met up with Michele on the banks of Jarre Creek. She was in the middle of a confab with a sheriff's deputy, a big guy bristling with badge, walkie-talkie, and Sam Browne belt, and he was holding a metal clipboard. "Oh, here you are," she said. "Ernie, this is Em Hansen, the woman who got run off the road yesterday. Em, this is Deputy Ernie Mayhew of the Douglas County Sheriff's Department."

Deputy Ernie turned and shoved a meaty hand my way to be shaken. "I wasn't expecting to see you here today," he said. "We all thought you'd be sleeping it off."

"I'll catch up on my snoozing later," I said and introduced Fritz all around. "I've brought Fritz for two reasons: First, I don't think he'd have let me come alone. And second, he knows things we'll find useful. For instance, it was his idea to check the tower records to find out if anyone had flown from here to Salt Lake City a week ago."

Michele gave Fritz a look of appraisal. I scrutinized his return gaze: Did he find her attractive? Feeling my eyes on him, Fritz put his hands on his hips and scanned the river bottom.

Deputy Ernie said, "What's that got to do with trying to find the driver of that vehicle?" He smacked a printout on his clipboard with the backs of his fingers. It was an electronic photograph of Gilda's ill-fated electric cart, all bashed to hell.

I said, "There's no doubt that this is connected to Afton McWain's murder, is there?"

"That has not been determined," said Deputy Ernie. "I'll admit it's highly unusual that two people living together should meet with accidents within days of each other, 'cept for two things: They weren't the same kinda accident, and we don't yet have a second body." He jerked his head toward the creek bottom, where people in reflective vests were moving along with probes, poking newly deposited sandbars and prying under tangles of cottonwood branches that had fetched up among the willows. "The Douglas County Search and Rescue Team will find her if she's there."

"Where was the cart found?" I asked.

Deputy Ernie pointed toward a bend in the creek a quarter mile upstream. "About there, by that rock. It fetched up against it, kinda."

"Any idea how far upstream of that it went in?"

He stared at me blankly. "Not sure at all."

"Shouldn't we go look? There might be skid marks or something on the bank."

"Not sure why we'd need to," he said. He was beginning to sound annoyed.

"Because she might be upstream of the cart," I said. "She could snag on something and the cart could keep on rolling. Damned thing would probably float in all of that, but she'd go down like a sandbag."

Deputy Ernie's face grew an unpleasant tint of red.

Michele said calmly, "You just got here, Em. How do you know they haven't already worked that part of the scene?"

My eyes still locked on Deputy Ernie's, I said, "Sorry," but didn't mean it.

Fritz put a hand on my shoulder. He let it drop solidly in place, so I could anchor to it.

Deputy Ernie unclipped his walkie-talkie. "Seven? Come in."

"Seven," said a crackly voice.

"See if you can break a few loose to search up-crick from where that cart was, okay, Buck-o?"

"Check. How far, you think?"

"Just go to the spot we found it and start working upward."

"Ten-four on that."

"Number one over."

"Seven over and out."

Deputy Ernie returned his walkie-talkie to its clip and adjusted his aviator sunglasses.

Michele tipped her head toward me back behind his line of vision and rolled her eyes as if to say, *Try a little diplomacy next time, hotshot.*

I strolled over to a more private vantage point and went into a squat. It made my knees sting where the cuts were, but that was somehow reassuring. I picked at the bandages on my left hand with my right and ruminated on the fate of the woman who had invaded the privacy of my home.

Fritz had apparently decided that I could have at least that long a tether, but Michele did not. "As of half an hour ago, we have a lead on Attabury," she said as she strolled over toward me. "His tail number was spotted on a little airstrip south of Gallup. He borrowed a car from the guy who runs the FBO there. The FBI are on it."

"Good. The guy give a positive ID on Attabury?"

"No. Actually, it didn't sound like him at all."

"Damn. So you mean whoever flew the plane there borrowed a car."

Michele said, "Upton's got nothing to say. Johnson says his lawyer says to show due cause why he should be involved in any of this. Entwhistle says he's told us everything he knows, which is nothing. I explained to all three of them ten different ways that we've all noticed that McWain's lawsuit was in the way of their money-making scheme, but each and every one of them has pointed out that lawsuits are matters for the courts. Do they think I don't notice that they're all reading from the same script?"

I commiserated for a moment, then told her my concerns about Julia.

"Oh, I ran a check on her," Michele said. "She's at her house."

"When did you do this?"

She gave me one of those, *What, are you nuts?* looks. "Yesterday evening. I requested that the Denver Police have someone drive by her house. They reported your rental car parked in her driveway. When you mentioned this morning that you hadn't heard from her, I had them ring the doorbell. She's there. Something about a sick kid. Up vomiting all night or something."

"Oh."

"Yeah, oh." My concern for Julia turned instantly into irritation. I knew what it was like to be concerned about a sick kid—Sloane Renee's first fever had put both me and Faye in fits—but did that mean she couldn't give me a call to let me know she'd made it home?

I forced myself to focus on more present concerns. I said, "So you still like Attabury for Afton's murder, even though he's somewhere else when I get run off the road and this happens?" I pointed toward the creek.

"He's all I've got. He flew McWain to Salt Lake but claimed he'd never left home. When I hit him with the tower records and eyewitnesses at Million Air, he skedaddles. I have yet to crack anyone else's alibi. With your tumble yesterday and now Gilda's cart in the drink I've got the locals working overtime, but beyond Attabury, we've got a great big zero. So tell me what I've missed."

"The precise connections to the other four suspects."

"*Three* suspects. Who do you have in mind beyond Upton, Johnson, and Entwhistle?"

I waved a hand toward the creek bed.

Michele said, "Gilda?"

"Being dead doesn't mean she didn't do it," I said. "*If* she's dead. She sure as hell knew her so-called husband was dead before you told her."

Michele threw up her hands in frustration. "Who says Gilda didn't find her own way into the creek?"

"Plenty. She'd been gone or missing for two days before the storm hit, and that just four days after her so-called husband was murdered and one day after filing a court action to inherit the ranch. What would she be hiding from? Or whom? Coincidences of that magnitude simply don't exist. Turn it over to the feds, Michele."

"Okay, fine, I'll just go back to Utah with my tail between my legs. Might as well put in for a transfer to meter reading."

I pitied her. Her shoulders sagged. Her face was pinched with strain. I had to suppose that she'd had very little sleep in the week since Afton McWain's corpse was found. She had been battling for respect and assistance with two different county law enforcement jurisdictions—her own and Douglas County's—as well as digging for information through several federal agencies. And she was under thirty, female, and working alone. It can't have been a holiday.

I crouched down, picked up a stick, and began to scratch lines in the wet gravel on the stream bank. "We've just got to sort this out. We've got Afton's corpse in Utah," I said, drawing an arrow over to the west, "and now probably Gilda's here in Colorado." I drew an X for Afton but an open circle for Gilda. "He had everything to lose by dying, but she had everything to gain by staying alive. An odd couple. His death was her gain, or her loss if she had any real feeling for him, or if her claim was bogus. And then here's our Greek chorus of folks who hated Afton—the butcher, the baker, the candlestick maker, so to speak . . ." I set pebbles along the line. "Attabury, Entwhistle, Upton, Johnson, and let's not forget the politicians. How about Senator White? Let's give her a big ol' chert pebble." I picked up a smooth one and plopped it into place, then paused a moment, remembering the pebble found in Afton's pocket. Something about that went *tink* in the back of my head, some connection that wanted to be made, but I couldn't quite work it into consciousness. I stared fixedly at the arrangement of pebbles and lines, wondering what the picture was trying to tell me. "No, this pebble is Afton. I'll make this twig the senator." I placed her down below the line, making a shallow triangle.

"Why Senator White?" Michele asked.

"I don't know. But where there's greed, there's always some connection to politics."

"The politics of greed. But didn't she make a big fuss about what a great guy McWain was?"

"That would be the politics of looking publicly aggrieved, and the politics of not really addressing the issues."

"What do you mean?"

"People like Senator White have known right along that there's not enough water here to support development. It's her job to know these things, and even if she hadn't the wit to ask, people like Afton McWain beat a path to her office door to tell her. And we know he did. So let's look at the diagram." I began to scratch more lines in the dirt. "Here we have four men who are working together to develop land for housing. A developer, that's our deal guy; a banker, that's our money guy; a lawyer, he's the tricky one; and let's not forget our landowner. And of course there are all sorts of smaller players who also depend on this development to keep their local economy growing and therefore pink and happy." I picked up a handful of smaller pieces of gravel and sprinkled it across the diagram. "And along comes Afton McWain, trying to tell them their game is over."

Michele said, "Fine, so we have a group of people who don't want McWain giving testimony." She pointed at Attabury's pebble. "And this one looks like he got rid of the spoiler. Now what? Tell me why I shouldn't be on the next flight for New Mexico so I can be in on the collar."

The pebble. The chert pebble. It was almost there . . . almost . . . pebble . . . evidence . . . bingo! "The geological data!" I said.

"What?"

"In Afton's office. There was something there that was worth stealing. What?"

"That's your department."

"Whoever killed him saw him as an impediment to pushing the Wildcat Mountain development through."

"He was the expert witness. And?"

I picked up the bit of chert and warmed it in my hand. "This pebble is Afton, still alive. He knew that every last well was about to go dry. He knew that the water was irreplaceable in a human time frame." I dropped the stick right into the middle of the diagram. It went *splat* in the wet sand. "He made those cross-sections and those isopach maps.

He knew how very little water there was under Johnson's ranch. It was dry, dead dry. They couldn't let the investors know that! So you're right, it wasn't organized crime."

"How do you know that?"

"Because they're the investors," I said.

Michele picked up a smaller stick and showed how she could pry at the bigger stick. "But why kill Gilda? Perhaps she started demanding a bigger share, so they killed her too."

"But without her, they have no claim to the property. You see? That's the remaining snag. Was she actually trying to keep the land? Could she bar the easement?"

Michele shrugged her shoulders. "So then, maybe someone got mad at her and lost control. Her murder was accidental. So they throw her cart in the creek. Or she just blew it and fell in. Or she was distraught over McWain's death and committed suicide."

I shook my head. "Ticks don't commit suicide. They just hang onto their hosts and suck. But still, all of this seems so . . . cold. It's hard for me to believe that people would get this wound up over money. But what's harder for me to understand is how they can maintain the cover-up."

Michele said, "I've got Trevor Reed looking into that."

At the mention of Reed's name, Fritz walked over to join us. He said, "You've been talking to Trevor Reed about this case?"

Michele blinked. "Yes. Why?"

Fritz said, "Well, he's just . . . I'm surprised, is all."

The look of innocence on Michele's face was one for the ages. "I had him checked out. He's got a spotless reputation for honesty. And he agrees with me that it's always about money. Or sex. And here we have both. And besides, he says it was the Chinese mafia, not the Italians, or the Russians, or whomever else."

"May I make a suggestion?" Fritz asked.

"Sure."

"You two keep looking at the killer as the aggressor. Perhaps you have it backwards."

I frowned with concentration. "What do you mean?"

Fritz crouched down and started to realign the stones and sticks. "In

The Art of War, Sun Tzu says, 'Wild beasts, when held at bay, fight desperately.' McWain was holding the others at bay."

Michele blinked. "So you're saying we're dealing with wild beasts?"

Fritz nodded. "We can suppose that these people haven't thought through their motivations, or they wouldn't be so foolish as to take such a risk. But try thinking of them as warriors. They fight the way they train, and when they start to lose, their thinking can become quite primitive, a basic 'us versus them' mentality. When their established ways of doing things start breaking down, their reactions become like the reflexes of a predator when it feels it is in danger."

" 'Established ways of doing things?" Michele said.

I turned to her. "He means what people are used to. The systems we live by. This community is used to building a certain kind of house, and each person has tailored his or her livelihood around supplying that infrastructure or living within it. If you tell the wolf it can't eat caribou anymore you're going to have an argument on your hands."

Michele said, "This is getting off the point. One murder has been committed, and perhaps two. My job is to bring a murderer to justice."

I said, "You're looking at it as a crime, but Fritz is right, the killer or killers may be looking at it as a war. Wars are almost always fought over resources. A shortage of resources brings the stresses that lead to war. You talk about greed, but Fritz is right, this community is looking at deprivation, something taken away rather than something to be gained. We're talking about the human animal, whose sense of 'not enough' is tripped the moment things go level. We don't consider an economy healthy unless it's growing. Hell, we don't know what to do with ourselves unless we're growing something—food, wealth, a family. We don't know how to go backward. We only know how to go forward. Afton should have figured out how to make sustainable living look and feel high-tech and modern."

Michele stared down at the progress of the searchers along the creek bed. "You're sure not gonna see me driving around a territory like this in a glorified golf cart any day soon. It didn't work for Gilda." She snorted and walked off toward her car.

I turned to Fritz and shrugged. "So McWain fired the first shot," I said. "So how do we figure out who shot back?"

Fritz smiled cryptically. "A guy named Strozzi once said, 'When the predator fights back, he doesn't tell you where his weakness is.' "

BY NOON, THE search and rescue people were beginning to wilt with the heat. They had searched a mile downstream and half a mile up, and someone had taken a dog through the whole creek bottom from the place in the narrows where the flood had washed away the bridge and road clear down past the Sedalia Grill. They figured they had looked under every branch and had poked every fresh sandbar that might conceivably conceal a body. They advised the Douglas County Sheriff's Department that it was time to call off the search.

I flipped open my cell phone and called Tim Osner. "Hey, Tim, do you ever play with fluvial geomorphy on a crime scene?"

"You mean how rivers carve their channels?" he said. "Yeah, we get into that. If someone's dumped a body off a bridge, for instance, we throw a pig carcass with a radio tracking collar in from the presumed spot of entry and see where it comes to rest."

I suppressed the urge to ask if they had a luau afterward. I described the problem.

He said, "I can take off early today. I could be there inside of two hours, set up my software, do some figuring. You say they've already used dogs? We could go to plan B, figure it's a murder cover-up, and start looking for the grave site."

"You mean she was killed first and *then* the cart was thrown in?"

"Why not?"

"Tim, you're a genius! Bring air photographs of the area," I said. "The most recent you can get your hands on. You clever, clever man."

WITHIN THE HOUR, Fritz and I were in the air with a camera. Fritz had not designed his plane with air photo reconnaissance in mind. It has two propellers, but one's fore and the other is aft, so you can't shoot good pictures through the windshield, and it's low-wing, so it's hard to shoot to the sides as well, but Fritz knew how to stand it on one wing and somehow manage to keep it from falling out of the sky. Michele had loaned me a digital camera, so the only problem was knowing that the exposure was going to lag half a second behind each time I tripped the shutter.

We flew Jarre Creek three times at three different altitudes: three thousand feet up, fifteen hundred feet up, and Fritz's favorite, the low-level zoom. That last time he rocked it down through Jarre Canyon so low that we had the sheriff's deputies scrambling for cover. Fritz had a grin on his face so wide that I whipped the lens his way and recorded that too. Who says cowboys only ride horses?

I was back on the ground with the memory card from the camera in my hand when a van pulled up. "Which one of you is Em Hansen?" he asked. A nice-looking man with big, dark eyes climbed out.

"That would be me," I said, and handed him the card.

"Ah, you've gone digital, you lovely thing," he said. "Let me just shoot this straight into my machine. I've already downloaded the latest air photos, which were taken about a year ago." He led me straight to the back of the minivan he had arrived in and opened the door. Inside was a wealth of electronic equipment. When he saw my eyes widen, he laughed. "Hey, we come prepared. I've got complete equipment here— computer hooked up to microscope, scanner, fax, printer, geophysics, and the very latest in geostatistics software. You're gonna love us, baby!" He arranged himself on a seat that swung out from under a shallow counter and flipped a few switches, activating a keyboard and a big flat-screen monitor, then leaned back and rubbed his hands together in glee.

Deputy Mayhew was just walking up to the van. "Tim, long time no see," he said.

"Hey, Ernie, you in charge of this show? How's the wife?"

Tim got right to work. Inside of five minutes, he had overlain my images with his digitized air photos and normalized the two scales to match. "This flood did damage, all right. This bank has caved," he said, "and here we've got a fresh deposit of sand. Nice transverse bar, pretty as a picture. But wait! It *is* a picture!" He chuckled at his own joke. Then he set about analyzing the image for discrepancies, massaging the keyboard to develop probability maps. He pointed at the places where his maps indicated highest probability for transportation and deposition of an object the size and buoyancy of a human body. Then he overlaid the highway map and clicked a few more keys. The resolution of his map sharpened.

"What does that do?" asked Michele.

Tim chuckled. "Killers are just like water-well drillers. They like to make their hole at a place where it's convenient to back in their rig. So my software here weights the search for good access points." He put his finger on a bright red bull's eye. "So the S and R people already probed these areas?"

"Yes."

"How long a stick they use?"

I said, "Two meters. But I've been watching. If they hit a rock at three inches, that was it. They were looking for soft sand."

Michele asked, "And you are looking for . . . ?"

I said, "A burial, of course."

"You prefer an act of God or poor driving skills?" asked Tim.

I said, "Show me the bank that should not have failed in this storm, and I'll show you where the body is buried."

Tim giggled maniacally. "You sound very sure of yourself. Come on, you're taking all the fun out of this. Hey, Jerry!" he called, leaning toward the tailgate to get the attention of one of his colleagues. "You took Fluvial Geomorph from Stan Schumm up at CSU, right?"

"Yo." A lanky guy with blond hair that stood up in random tufts appeared at the tailgate. We explained the question to him. He climbed in next to Tim and went over several screens, turning his hands this way and that as he mentally reckoned the varying flow directions of the stream bed. "There," he said, putting a long, crooked finger on the screen. "That's an inside bank. The thalweg—the strongest part of the current—would have been on the opposite side of the creek at peak runoff—see, there's a fresh cut on that side, and it looks right, while this doesn't. It should have been depositing sand instead of eroding it. So unless you've got some kind of muskrat or beaver undermining that inside bank, that's it."

Tim tapped a few keys, putting the road overlay on the photographs using his GIS—geographic information system—database. "Like a spy in the sky," he said merrily. "Mm-huh, about a quarter mile upstream from this crossroads." He twisted in his chair and stared downriver. "Let's lock and load and put her in gear."

Deputy Mayhew said, "We didn't search there. Don't you think that's too far downstream?"

"For a flood deposit, maybe, but not for a burial," said Tim.

We drove in caravan to the site, Tim's van, Deputy Ernie in his cruiser, Michele in her rental, and Fritz and me in his. When we arrived at the site, we noted that while the scarp at the top of the bank looked fresh on the air photographs, it was hard to see from the center of the channel, where Jarre Creek was now settling back within its inner banks. There was in fact a screen of willows separating it from the area disturbed by the flood. I started to walk toward it, but Tim put out a hand. "We take it from here," he said and nodded to another man, who was just pulling up in a pickup with a very avid-looking dog riding in the passenger's seat. "Daisy, honey!" he called to the dog.

The dog stuck her muzzle out the open window of the truck cab. She had tall, pointy ears and a long, black snout. As her handler led her out on her lead, her narrow waist and long, sweeping tail danced with excitement. She already had an eye on the site.

I said, "What is she, some kind of German Shepherd cross?"

"She is pure Belgian Malinois," said her handler proudly. "They were bred for sheep but kept alive during the Second World War because they were so smart about carrying messages for the resistance." He took her to the bank, knelt beside her, removed her leash, and said, "Find, Daisy!"

The dog leapt down the bank and zigzagged across the ground, her nose down on the dirt.

"Can she find Gilda without even knowing what she smells like?" Michele asked.

The handler asked, "How long has this lady been dead?"

I said, "Anywhere up to three days."

He grinned. "A good cadaver dog can smell a corpse newer than that, and Daisy's the best."

On cue, Daisy yelped and scratched, looking up to her handler for the next command.

"Daisy, come!" he said.

The dog burst from her position, galloped up the bank with the long, liquid gait of a wolf, and came to a halt seated at his side.

"Good girl," he said, petting her and slipping her a treat.

Daisy raised her nose toward her master and gave him an adoring look.

"She found something?" asked Michele.

The man said, "Yes, something. It could be a deer, though such animals usually have better sense than to tarry by a creek bank when it's raining like that."

"Now what do we do?" asked Michele.

"We wait for the geophysicists and archaeologists," said Tim. "The geophysicists will use ground-penetrating radar to map the variations in density where the soil's been dug up. The archaeologists will do a careful excavation of the grave. They'll get infinitely more data than a couple of deputies with shovels can ever hope to get."

They arrived at six-thirty, having needed time to grab their gear after work. They went to work setting up cameras and grids and began mapping and digging.

Michele and I began a search through the weeds above the bank. It was there that Michele found the suggestions of footprints—about a men's size nine, or a women's eight—and I found what I was looking for: a twisted cylinder of plastic with a wire sticking out of it.

"What is it?" Fritz inquired.

"A blasting cap," I said. "Michele, would you get the good deputy over here please? I want him to watch me bag this thing for evidence.

But first, let's get Tim's surveyor to plot its position relative to the grave."

AT 7 P.M. I checked my phone for messages as my stomach began to growl with hunger for dinner. No one had called, not Julia, and not Noel calling to report on her. Where was she?

Michele's cell phone rang a moment later. I heard her say, "Yes, this is she. Yes. Thank you. Okay, I'm writing that down." When she'd ended the call, she announced, without looking at anyone, "The FBI found the pilot who flew the Baron to Gallup. They have voice recordings to prove which pilot made the calls, and eyewitnesses on the ground report only one man getting out at Gallup, and . . . it wasn't Attabury."

"Then where is he?" I asked.

"That has yet to be determined," was all she could stand to say.

◇

TIM OSNER'S CREW was rewarded for its painstaking efforts. At 7:49 P.M., just as we were arranging the vehicles to shine headlights on the site because it was beginning to get dark, the archaeologist in charge of the site struck something soft yet unyielding with her trowel. She switched to a brush and uncovered a hand and then an arm. As the excavation proceeded, the mortal remains of the woman known as Gilda emerged from their rustic grave, and, after the corpse was carefully photographed and removed, the search for evidence was carefully widened, revealing the telltale shapes of shovel marks left by the murderer, who had hurriedly dug her grave under the cover of the willows. The condition of the body indicated that it had been interred for several days.

"What a lucky killer," Tim mused. "What's the likelihood you're gonna get a storm like that so soon after, so you can toss the cart into the drink. I can see him thinking, if anybody finds her—a coyote digs her up, or someone digs in the bank for road metal—they'll ascribe it to the forces of nature."

"But why throw the cart in this creek?" Michele asked. "It brought us right to the corpse."

"Guilt," said Tim. "Killers may think they're trying to cover their crimes, but they often expose themselves in convoluted ways. They're like Lady MacBeth trying to get that spot of blood off their hands." He stared into the grave. "This one was clever, but not quite clever enough."

32

Saturday morning, Michele finally located Hugo Attabury. This did not require a house-to-house search of the continental United States. He turned himself in. He walked right into the Douglas County Sheriff's Department offices under the guidance and protection of his new lawyer, a hotshot defense attorney from Chicago. The man who flew his plane to New Mexico Wednesday evening had dropped him off at a private airport near Albuquerque, where he had gotten a cab to the main airport, showed proper identification but paid in cash for a flight to the Windy City. He was now ready to talk to Michele Aldrich and swore that this time, he'd be telling the truth.

I was allowed to watch his deposition through the one-way glass of the interrogation room. He stated that the situation was straightforward: He had in fact flown Afton McWain to Salt Lake City on the Thursday evening in question. He had gone there to have dinner with a man who wanted to invest in his development enterprise. McWain had heard that he was going there and had asked for a ride. With the thought that a little time together might provide the opportunity to persuade McWain to drop his case or at least tone it down, he had said yes. Attabury's investor had sent a man to pick him up at the airport and had given McWain a ride into town. They had dropped him at the south end of the Salt Palace Convention Center, where he said he was expecting to meet a friend. When Attabury had last seen McWain, he was very much alive. No, he had no idea whom he expected to meet there. And yes, he could produce the driver of the car, who saw him back to the airport three hours later to retrieve his airplane and fly home to Colorado. During the intervening time, he had been at the home of the investor, and if he damned well had to he would produce that man as well. Having said all of this, Attabury folded his arms across his meaty chest and refused to say another word.

Michele didn't even bother to ask any questions, let alone three times or in three different ways. She just sat and listened. She wasn't in charge of the interrogation. Attabury had specified that he would answer only to Deputy Ernest J. Mayhew. The whole party was over in less than fifteen minutes.

I was beginning to truly worry about Michele. She had dark circles beneath her eyes, and she seemed almost listless as she sat in that windowless room. I suppose she didn't know what to do next.

After Attabury and his high-priced lawyer left the room, Fritz and I stepped in. We had returned to Denver for the night, and this time he had slept on the couch, suggesting that I seemed well on the road to recovery and asserting that, even as cushy as the carpet was, he was in need of something softer.

But he stayed with me like a shadow, and he was there with me when I rejoined Michele. Deputy Ernie sat in a straight-back chair giving Michele a rather stony look. It didn't take a mind reader to know what he was thinking.

I said, "Deputy, I've been meaning to ask you a few things. You grew up here, am I right?"

He turned toward me, shifting his opinion from her to me. No longer was I a comrade in arms who had nearly been killed by the enemy; now I was just another interloper from out of state who didn't know the hearts and minds of the locals. "Yes, I did," he said slowly.

"Then you'll excuse me, but you must know all the other fellows we've been asking questions about. Misters Entwhistle, Upton, and Johnson. And then there's this group from away, the investors."

He looked away. "Oh, them."

Michele said, "Yes, them. I've been running checks on them with our colleagues over at the FBI. The principles of that organization are under investigation in two other states for money laundering and other suspected connections to drug running and racketeering. You're aware of all that."

"Yes."

I said, "It must be terribly distressing having this going on in your town."

"Spare me, Miss Hansen." Mayhew inclined his head such that he could look at me from underneath his eyebrows.

I said, "All right, I can see that you'd like us to make this quick, so would you please show Miss Aldrich your photograph of that evidence I entrusted to you out at Jarre Creek yesterday evening?"

He frowned but opened his clipboard and produced the photograph. It showed the blasting cap as it had been found lying in the grass, before anyone had touched it. He shifted heavily in his chair, frowning with growing annoyance. He could tell he was being put on the spot, and he did not like it.

I said, "You know what that is, don't you?"

"It's a blasting cap. You told me that. They're used by road crews, right?"

"I suppose they are, sometimes. Has anyone been working on the road out there any time lately?"

He shook his head. His hand was stiff on the clipboard, like a spider doing a protracted push-up.

I said, "Well now, I have another theory why that blasting cap was out there. You'll note that it's lying on top of every blade of grass and leaf it's touching, which suggests that it had not been there very long, but it's splattered with sand and clay from the surrounding soils, so it was there during the storm, right?"

He did not deny my logic.

Michele's eyes were beginning to widen. She was ahead of the deputy, miles ahead. "You use those things in gravel quarries, don't you?"

"Yes, you do," I replied. "Now the question I have for you, sir, is who among the men we've been trying to question has ever worked in a quarry?"

Deputy Ernest J. Mayhew closed his eyes. After a moment he let out his breath in a sigh. "He told me he was here all that day and night, and I believed him," he said.

"Who?"

"Johnson."

"Bart?" I couldn't believe it.

"No, his son, Zach." He hung his head. "We've known each other since we was kids."

Michele turned toward the door, ready to head for the courthouse to get a warrant for his arrest.

The deputy held out a hand. "Stop, Miss Aldrich. This crime is not under your jurisdiction." There was a phone on the table. He lifted the handset off its cradle and dialed a number. When the party answered, he said, "Sheriff, I'm afraid I need you to come down here. We got us some interrogating to do, and, well, it's an old friend of mine."

I waited patiently for the conversation to end, then said, with the respect due a man who could make an admission like he just had, "Ernie, may I observe while he's being questioned? It's just possible I've jumped to conclusions."

Deputy Mayhew lifted his great head and looked at me. "That would be fine, Em."

ZACH JOHNSON SAT in the chair by the table with his fingers twisting and one leg jumping like it was attached to an electric charge. His thinning hair stood in wild sheaves around his head, and graying whiskers sprouted around his chin. "No, Sheriff, I never did nothing like messing with no blasting caps outside no quarry. Sure, I know how to handle them things, but I ain't had my hands on none in years."

The sheriff of Douglas County was an affable sort who looked like he would be more at home in a T-shirt and sweats than the uniform he wore. He sat opposite Zach, all slouched down in a chair with his feet up on the table. Zach hadn't been formally charged, but he'd been brought in from the café in a cruiser and had been read his rights.

Next to Zach at the table sat Todd Upton, who had followed the police cruiser in his BMW. His hands lay on the table like sausages. He hardly even blinked. "You don't have to tell them anything, Zach," he said.

Michele stood next to me, itching to use her interrogation skills on such an easy subject. Her hands were twitching, and her lips moved with soundless words.

Fritz stood somewhere behind me. I could sense his quiet, rock-steady presence. I wondered what he was thinking. Did he find my line of work distasteful? Did he think I was taking undue risks? Could he ever be interested in getting together with a woman who lived my kind of life? With a sinking heart, I thought, *He wants more children. What kind of fool would want the mother of his children out mixing it up with criminals?*

The sheriff opened his hands to indicate that he was at a loss to explain recent events and needed help. "The thing is, we've got a corpse down there in the morgue, and the county coroner's taking a look at it, and we just thought that if you could tell us anything about this situation, it would be so much easier. You'd feel better, and we could take it easy on you, and we'd all stay friends."

On our side of the glass, Michele muttered, "Well, that's the short form, but he's got the general idea."

Upton said, "Zach, as your family's lawyer, I recommend you say nothing further."

Zach furrowed his brows. "Someone else is dead? Who?" He looked more mystified than scared.

The sheriff said, "We think you know. Come on . . ." When this didn't get a response, he said, "I hear your dad's been trying to sell the ranch. That would be a good thing for you all."

Zach said, "No shit. I could shit-can that job I work and live a little." He lifted one hand and rubbed the back of his neck.

"So if somebody tried to get in the way of that sale, you'd be mad at them, right?"

"Yeah . . ."

Upton said, "Zach, you don't know what you're saying."

The sheriff smiled and lifted his meaty hands into fists and did a little tight shadowboxing, which was a complicated motion to accomplish while slouching. He meant it to look goofy, and it did. He was saying, *Come on, I'm in on the joke. We're all pals here.*

Zach turned his head to one side and eyed the sheriff like a bull who's shying from the man carrying the cattle prod. "What you suggesting, Sheriff?"

"You tried to stop all this nonsense with ol' Afton, and then she got in the way."

"Afton? You think I killed Afton?" Zach was out of his seat with a jolt. "Hey, Sheriff, I don't know what kind of fool you take me for, man, but shit, I don't go whacking no neighbors!"

The sheriff dipped his head to one side and said, "Neighbors *plural*?"

Michele muttered, "He's good. Now go for the jugular."

Upton leaned back in his chair and folded his arms.

The sheriff's question turned Zach's outrage into befuddlement. "What's that mean?"

"What's what mean?"

"What you said."

"Plural?"

"Yeah."

The sheriff's face went slack. When he recovered himself, he said, "More than one."

"One what?"

"Neighbor. You said neighbor-*zuh*."

Now Zach looked hopelessly confused. "What are you talking about? Did someone else get himself killed?"

"He didn't do it," said Michele. "Nobody can be that stupid and pull off that level of deception."

I said, "I'm inclined to agree with you. How's a man live that far into his forties that stupid?"

Zach was waving his hands around in a mixture of aggression and childlike fear. "What you saying, man? Someone killing folks up our way? I gotta get back up there and look after Pa!"

I said, "How'd he ever survive working in a quarry?"

Michele said, "He could never have figured out how to get himself to Salt Lake County and back, let alone kill a man and drop a wall of gravel on his corpse without killing himself in the process. We're back to square one. I want Attabury's head on a pike!"

I said, "But why would Attabury kill Gilda? She was his last hope of getting McWain's property."

As if he'd heard my question, the sheriff said to Zach, "I got one more question for you, and then I suppose we're done. What you think of that lady Gilda that lived with ol' McWain?"

Upton tensed. "Zach . . ."

Zach eyed the sheriff suspiciously. "She's purty . . ."

"No, what I'm getting at is do you think she'd help you out, or do you think she's not such a good neighbor?"

Zach's face brightened a little. "Oh, she's fine, she is. Why, just the other day she paid a call on Pa and—"

"Zach!" Upton roared.

Ignoring the lawyer, Zach hurtled onward. "And she told him she'd be glad to pick right up where they left off with their negotiations to put the ranches together. Pa was real happy." He made a fist to emphasize his words. "*Real* happy."

AFTER ZACH HAD been dispatched back to his job at Bud's Bar in Sedalia, Michele and the sheriff compared notes to decide whether they had two separate crimes or one. They agreed that the two murders seemed inextricably connected. They reviewed a preliminary report from the county coroner, which stated that Gilda had been killed by a blow to the head, just like Afton McWain. The sheriff agreed to press further into the alibis given by Hugo Attabury and the other suspects and suggested that they both meet with the FBI agents who were looking into the investment group's questionable business dealings.

Michele's cell phone rang. "Yes? Wait." She got out her notebook and scribbled. "Okay. Okay, that is terrific!" She clicked off the phone and grinned. "Got him!" she squealed.

"Got who?" asked the sheriff.

"Upton," she said. "When Attabury confessed that he had flown to Salt Lake City the evening in question, that blew Todd Upton's alibi.

So I stepped up my search for evidence against him. Attabury's not the only one who knows his way to Salt Lake City. I've had friends with the Utah Highway Patrol checking filling stations all across Interstate 70. I've finally got him in Green River at 7 P.M. He paid cash, but a guy behind the counter liked the car."

"That puts him in Salt Lake City by ten-thirty," I said.

"Quicker than that, the way this observer said he was driving. *And,*" she said, now grinning ear to ear, "they dug into his service record for me. You know what he did for the army?"

"I've no idea," I said, "but does it involve explosives?"

"Give the lady a cigar," she said. "Demolition, specializing in setting off landslides."

ATTABURY CAVED QUICKLY under Michele's next round of questioning. He sang like a canary. He sang like a macaw. He shrieked like a buzzard.

The recital started soon after Michele walked into the interrogation room and put a hand gently on his shoulder. "I'm so sorry to have accused you. I was wrong. We know now that it was Todd Upton who killed Dr. McWain. And . . . I'm hoping you can help us with a few of the details."

Comprehension widened Attabury's eyes. He saw his ticket out of the everlasting stink of suspicion and grabbed for it. His lawyer nodded to him and he began to sing. "Anything," he gasped.

"Why did you say that you didn't take Dr. McWain to Utah?" Michele asked.

"Because Upton told me to say that! He said I'd do time, guaranteed."

"When did he tell you that?"

"The day we heard about McWain's being dead."

"Before I arrived?"

"No! I swear I didn't know McWain was dead before that!"

"But none of you seemed surprised by the news. Why was that?"

Attabury bowed his head and grabbed great hanks of his hair. "Because of what we'd just been talking about."

"Which was?"

"We were . . . we were discussing what to do . . . how to m-manage him. McWain." He buried his face in his hands. "We all wanted him to go away," he wailed, then peeked out from between his fingers and added, "Upton . . . he said McWain needed to be silenced." He watched for Michele's response.

She patted his shoulder again and settled herself on the edge of the table right next to him, an intimate, reassuring gesture. "Did Gilda feel that way, too?"

He shook his head. "No. She wanted the money, don't get me wrong, but she wasn't . . . she didn't know about . . . what Upton had in mind." His lip quivered. "She was a nice lady."

"But she'd just heard Upton say he wanted to silence McWain. What did she think of that?"

"She didn't hear him say that. Upton said that in the parking lot before we went in. Johnson had Gilda waiting in there to meet with us. Upton set the whole thing up. He had Johnson bring her up from Colorado Springs. We walk into the bar and she's on the phone. I realize now that was *you* she was talking to." He shook his head over the irony. "You were telling her you were coming, but she didn't tell us we were about to get company. She's a smart lady, Gilda. Didn't let on what she thought. Played her cards close. Poor Gilda." He hung his head.

"Yes, it's terrible. What else can you tell us about Upton's movements during the twenty-four hours before that meeting?"

"He phoned me that morning early, told me about the meeting at the Grill. I had to report to him about progress. We were trying to pressure McWain about the damned lawsuit."

"Giving him a ride to Utah was your way of pressuring him? I don't understand."

"He'd told Upton he was going to shout his story far and wide, and Utah was his first big step. Upton didn't like it. He said I should give McWain a ride to Utah so he could have someone meet him on the other end, talk some sense into him."

"Who was that someone?"

"He didn't say. I thought it was one of the investors." Attabury's face grew dark. "But it was him. He was there. It had to be him. He knew where I was dropping McWain and he was there waiting for him." He shuddered.

"But you dropped McWain at eight. Upton didn't reach Salt Lake City until ten at the earliest." Michele's tone was still soothing, matter-of-fact, as if talking to a child who had woken from a bad dream.

"Okay, so I lied about that, too. I took him to dinner. I dropped him at ten-fifteen." He put a hand to his face, probing a headache. "Upton said the investor was late. He called me on my cell phone, said to stall until then. What a patsy I was."

"Then you never met with the investor in Salt Lake City."

Attabury's face went hard. "No, I did not."

"You made that up about meeting an investor."

"Someone sent that car but no, I never saw anybody." He shook his head in exasperation. "I offered to rent a car, but Upton said no, he had contacts."

"Wasn't flying him to Utah taking a chance?"

Attabury suddenly smiled. "Not at all, considering that I had noth-ing to hide!" He threw back his head and laughed ruefully. "To think I bought Upton's jive about how you'd think I was the prime suspect! He said, 'I'll cover for you, Hugo. Just tell them we were playing golf to-gether. I'm taking a risk for you, old pal, so let's keep our story straight.' How dumb could I get?"

Michele smiled at him, rewarding him for his information. "This is very helpful information, Mr. Attabury. I have just a few more questions. Do you know anything about the geologic data that disappeared from Dr. McWain's log cabin shortly after that meeting at the Sedalia Grill? I'm talking about some maps and other diagrams, reports, papers."

Attabury folded his massive arms and nodded his head. "Sure. Upton didn't manage to hide that part from me. He had all that stuff at his house when I dropped by the day after. He was burning it in his outdoor barbecue. He shoved a bunch of it in quick when he saw I was there, but I knew what it was. He had some big, juicy steaks dripping down into it, really made the flames jump. And," he said, suddenly breaking down, big tears rolling down his shiny cheeks, "he had something else on that grill, little bits all on a skewer. He served it to me on crackers, with . . . with salsa."

"What was it?" Michele asked, her voice as soft as a child's blanket.

"He said it was Afton McWain's busy little fingers." He put his face down on the table and bawled. "I thought he was joking!"

An hour later, Michele had Todd Upton's fingertips where she wanted them: on an ink pad, giving prints, being booked and charged with the murder of Afton McWain. Upton said not a word under Michele's questioning. He had no lawyer present. Like many a criminal that had occupied that room before him, he knew his rights, and would cling to them until the last.

Michele shrugged. "That's okay, Mr. Upton. We've got everything we need without your confession, and it gives me pleasure that you'll pull a longer sentence because you aren't cooperating or showing remorse." She gave him a happy smile and traipsed out of the room.

Having tidied up the horrid little mess that had been entrusted to her detecting skills, Michele went to her motel, cleaned up, put on a lovely dress, and got into her car to drive up to Denver and meet Trevor Reed, who was waiting there to help her celebrate. "I've been meaning to thank you for making that connection to him," she told me as we met one last time in the parking lot, where Fritz had brought me to pick up my gear. She turned slightly, looking at me out of the corner of her eye. "And for sparking his interest in detection. Apparently you made quite an impression on him, but he said you had other commitments." She glanced at Fritz.

I shepherded her over to her car before she could start trouble for me. "So this is the celebration Trevor came to Colorado to attend. How did he know this would be the night?" I inquired as she buckled her seatbelt.

A new sort of smile played across her lips. "We've been in touch," she said. "Well, this leaves just one little puzzle unsolved. Gilda."

I nodded.

Michele opened her attaché and produced a sheaf of faxes. "Perhaps this will help. These are Gilda's cell phone calls for the week before her death. They just came in."

I quickly scanned the sheets. Michele had annotated the phone numbers so I'd know whom she had called and who had called her. I said, "Here's a call to Upton on that day we saw them all at the Sedalia Grill. But it's after that meeting, and after we took her to Denver. She must have phoned him from the tractor-trailer rig as she was barreling across Colorado on her way to Utah."

"To tell him that you'd seen what McWain had in his log cabin office?" she suggested. "And, perhaps, to tip him off that you're a geologist?"

"I suppose. Would that explain why he was frightened to see me appear at Johnson's ranch? But that doesn't make sense. Julia knows much more about those aquifers than I do, and he wasn't afraid of her."

Michele said, "Upton saw Julia as a legal adversary, not a geologist. And you are not just a geologist, you're a detective. You keep forgetting that. And we can't presume he was entirely smart, or he would have instructed Gilda not to contact him on her cell phone. The records are too good, and too easily subpoenaed."

"Murder is never smart," I said. "But even someone as cold-blooded as Upton couldn't control someone as self-serving as Gilda." I laughed. "Maybe she was even leaving a paper trail on purpose."

Michele smiled cheerily. "Maybe, but she's not my problem."

I reached out to hand the pages back to Michele.

Michele held up a hand to stop me. "But she might be yours. Keep reading."

I scanned further down the list of phone numbers. When I reached the last call Gilda ever made, my heart sank like a stone.

33

THAT LAST CALL ON GILDA'S LOG REQUIRED THAT I GATHER ONE last bit of trace evidence before I could leave Douglas County.

I asked the sheriff if he would accompany me and Fritz to the McWain ranch. "I won't require a search warrant. Just a quick glance at something will answer my question, but I want cover, and I want to do this straight up."

"You've got it," he said. "And we already have a warrant to search those premises."

It was a bouncy ride up the rutted road after that rain. When we arrived, the sheriff knocked on the door of the yurt and then the door of the log cabin just to cover himself, then asked what it was I needed to look at.

"Right over here," I said, hiking over to the barn. I pushed open the door. Just as I thought, that big, old white truck—the one I'd seen in there the day Michele and I drove Gilda up to get her gear—was there, but it had clearly been driven since my previous visit to the ranch. The concrete floor of the barn was tracked with mud, and there was a big bruise of red paint across the left front panel. Out on the loading dock, we found tracks and traces of mud left when Gilda's cart was pushed into the back of the truck, even though the rain had beaten hard on that evidence.

I explained the significance of my discovery to the sheriff, who nodded and agreed to help me with my next move. He got on the phone to call in an evidence team, and we got back into the cruiser and left before I could talk myself out of what I needed to do.

◆

FRITZ RODE WITH the sheriff the last mile to our destination so that I could appear to be arriving alone. They parked down the street and waited, both men watching me carefully. Carlos Ortega pulled silently in behind them in an unmarked car, representing his jurisdiction.

As I walked up to the house, I glanced back twice to make sure both cars were still there. My breathing had gone shallow. My stomach was in a knot. I wanted to be most anywhere else.

The blinds were drawn on the front of the house, so my approach would go unnoticed unless a dog had been added to the household in the years since my last visit, but I didn't hear a bark. I stopped for a moment at the foot of the walk and studied the front stoop. It was higher than I had remembered, which meant a longer drop, and there were junipers growing below it, a nasty landing if it came to that but better than concrete.

A half-grown girl answered the door when I knocked. "Hi, Samantha," I said. "Is your mommy home?"

The girl had Afton's dark hair and broad shoulders and Julia's long legs. "She's sleeping," she said. "You're Emily, right?"

"Yes, honey. I'm sorry, but I need to talk to her. Could you wake her, please? And then maybe give us a moment, okay?" I tried to wink at her, but it didn't work. I didn't have the heart.

Samantha shifted in the doorway until I could only see half of her face. "Okay . . ."

Just as she disappeared the rest of the way, Timothy appeared. I was shocked to see Afton's intense gaze coming from such a soft little face. He watched me while I waited, unabashedly observing me, scrutinizing my every fidget and twitch. He was his father's son through and through.

Julia arrived at the door, pushing her hair around as she shoved the sleep out of it. She paled when she saw who was waiting for her, then lifted her chin and came up with a smile. "Come in, Em. You're letting the heat in."

I cringed inwardly at the phrase. To Timothy, I said, "Run along a moment, okay?"

The boy gave me one last, lingering look and vanished.

I said, "I need to stay out here. It's better that the kids not hear this."

With a scowl, Julia stepped to my side of the doorway and yanked the door shut behind herself. She crossed her arms firmly across her chest, stiffened her carriage, and narrowed her eyes. "What's on your mind, Em?"

I shrugged my shoulders helplessly. "I just thought you'd rather tell it to me and get it over with," I said.

"Tell you *what?*" she demanded.

"About Gilda."

Her face was already hard, but now her eyes seemed to draw up into tunnels that receded straight to hell. "Fuck you," she enunciated, delivering the words precisely and with consummate contempt.

I opened my hands in supplication. "You almost killed me, Julia."

To that she did not reply. She hardened further.

I said, "Was that the idea? To kill me? Did you think I'd figured it out? Or did it start out as a ruse to make it look like Afton's killer had also killed Gilda and was trying to kill you? Shit, you dress me up in your jacket and hard hat, you put me in your Jeep. It was clever, Julia, but it didn't quite work."

Julia stood like a gargoyle: hateful, repulsive, and made of stone.

At that moment, I couldn't decide what hurt worse: that she had almost killed me or that she was no longer my friend. I found myself begging, "Tell me anything. Tell me you just lost control of that truck. Tell me you didn't mean to flip me into the ditch, *please*, Julia! Tell me you didn't mean to leave me there . . ."

Her eyes were still aimed at me but no longer saw me.

I said, "If you'd just left me to take my samples—do my *science*, Julia!—I would never have figured out what you'd done." I reached into those dead, dark eyes, searching for my lost friend. "I mean, that was clever, dumping her cart in the creek—I bought that hurt knee game, and the 'I want to sit in this bar and drown my sorrows' act, but did you really think I'd be so stupid that I wouldn't figure out the rest once you tried to kill me? That I couldn't figure out where you'd buried her body? Tell me you just panicked when you realized I was going near that creek. I mean, what was the game, stall me until those rains came and covered your tracks? How long ago did you bury her? Tuesday? Wednesday? She telephoned you. We have her cell phone logs. You talked for half an hour. What did she want? Quick cash? Did she want to cut a deal?"

Julia stared into space. I began to wonder if she could even hear me. Her eyes had no light in them, only darkness. I thought, *How much is it going to take to crack her?* I said, "Should I just leave this to the sheriff? His detectives are scrounging that truck for evidence right now, right this instant. If you wait until they come to you, you'll be lucky to get off with murder two. Come with me now and it's manslaughter, Julia! Reckless endangerment and manslaughter! I mean, *damn* it, Julia, I can understand how upset you were at that woman, but did you have to *kill* her?"

In my peripheral vision, I saw Carlos open his car door and leave it ajar. Fritz was already out of the cruiser, ambling casually toward us along the sidewalk as if he was out for a Sunday stroll. I wanted desperately to turn to him, to throw myself into his arms and bawl, but I kept my eyes focused on Julia. He paused, stooped to tie his shoe, straightened, lined himself up behind a fence where he could see me but Julia could not see him.

Julia's eyes bored into mine. It was like staring past death into the empty abyss of the damned, and all the brutal force of jealousy that had congealed into hatred came oozing back through.

I put a hand to my back pocket, making sure the short rope was there, and curled my fingers around it. She wasn't cracking. It was time to lie. I said, "I saw you in the rear-view mirror, Julia."

Nothing. Just darkness, the absence and antithesis of love.

I said, "I'm asking you to turn yourself in, so the law can go easy on you. This is it, your last chance, or I'm going to have to tell the sheriff what I saw."

Nothing.

I wished that I had Michele's training. What had she said? The trick was to sympathize with the killer, draw her out as if I were her friend. But I was her friend. Had been. Had tried as hard as anyone. Was still trying even after what she had done to me. What greater sympathy could she ask for? With sudden fury, I said, "I can see why Afton left you, Julia. You've gotten hard. At least Gilda was soft."

Julia's lips contracted, baring her teeth. "None of you understand!" she screamed. "You call yourself a friend, but you're just like everyone else, Hansen! You just stand there judging me!" Suddenly her hands shot toward me as her whole athletic body lunged toward my throat.

I dodged just enough to spare a crushing grasp to my throat, but her impact sent me flying backward and we landed, writhing like snakes, in the junipers. I braced one arm against her throat and arched backward against her battling strength to see where Fritz was. He was there, hovering over us, feet braced, his face intently focused, arms and hands at the ready to dive to my aid. His eyes locked on mine and spoke to me. *Now?* he was asking.

Not yet, I answered, shoving the heel of one hand against Julia's jaw. "You killed her!" I screamed, now slapping her face. *"Why?"*

"She *laughed* at me!" Julia roared, sinking a sharp elbow into my gut.

"But why kill her?" I panted. I had to get a direct and incontrovertible admission out of her before she did me real damage. We rolled off the junipers and across the lawn, she trying for a killing blow and I blocking with all my might. I caught a glimpse of the sheriff now, running toward us, and Carlos right behind him. Saw Fritz's hand come out to stop him. Caught a glimpse of his face again, as I kneed Julia in the stomach and ripped at the grip she now had on my hair. Her fingers gouged like talons across my face as I reached back and yanked the rope out of my pocket and wrestled her into a pin. Just like in my old calf-roping competition days, I wrapped the rope twice around her wrists, yanked them down to one flailing leg, gave all three a connecting hitch, and jumped away before she could kick me with the other, my hands flying up out of long habit fighting calves in the arena. I screamed, *"Why,* Julia? Was it to protect the kids' inheritance?"

Julia rolled onto her side, her anger at last dissolving into tears. "Because he loved her more than he loved *me,*" she howled from the ragged depths of her soul. "And I'd kill her *again* and *again* and *again*. . . ."

34

MARY ANN WALKED INTO THE COMMUNITY CENTER WITH HER HEAD held high. Helga Olsen was there to meet her, and greeted her with a hug. "Mary Ann! I'm so glad you made it," she caroled. "Come meet the others. Hey, everybody! This is Mary Ann Nettleton, a new hand!"

The heads of ten other citizens of Douglas County turned to welcome the new member of their group.

"Welcome!" said a young woman.

"Fresh blood!" joked a middle-aged man.

"This is hard work," said Helga. "Developers pay eighty percent of the county commissioners' campaign contributions, so it's an uphill battle, but we aren't easy to shout down."

"Pull up a chair," said a kindly faced elder gentleman. "I'm Fred Beauregard. Help me sort these envelopes, would you? I ran a law firm for forty years, but I must confess that I barely know how to alphabetize. Can't spell, either. My wife used to cover for me, but she's gone to her reward, where I can't embarrass her anymore." He winked at Mary Ann. "But they keep me around here because I understand the law," he added in mock confidentiality.

Everybody in the room laughed and introduced themselves.

Mary Ann laughed, too, and took her place within her community with a smile and a job to be accomplished. It was a difficult job that she knew would be filled with frustrations but also many joys as she learned more about her world and put her shoulder to the wheel with the other fine people who shared it with her.

◈

RAY AND HIS sponsor sat on the wall at the foot of the University of Utah campus enjoying the changes in the colors of the sky as day traversed into night, their stomachs contented with the sausage special from the Pie Pizzeria a half block down the hill. For a long time nothing needed to be said.

Ray's sponsor was an older man, stooped and careworn, and his face was pocked with the remnants of bad acne, but to Ray, he shone with the brilliance of Almighty God. The sponsor picked at a hangnail, releasing a stray piece of grit. "Is she okay now?"

"Who?"

"Em Hansen."

Ray smiled. "Yes, I think so. Yes, she is."

"What was it like, being with her in that moment? Please tell me again."

"You mean, when she was . . . when her Jeep was rolling?"

"Yes."

"It was terrible. I was driving a car myself when it happened, and I saw everything spinning around me. I had to pull over. It was just as if I was looking out through her eyes. It was terrible. Just like the night my wife . . ."

"But the other part, Ray."

Ray smiled. "You mean the light."

The man closed his eyes and smiled. "Yes."

"I knew Em was in trouble. I knew I was seeing what she was seeing. So I got on the radio and had the dispatcher patch me through to Douglas County, and I described the vehicle and which way to go to find her. Then I closed my eyes and prayed."

"And?"

"And I saw this lovely golden light, all shimmering."

"Ahh . . ."

Ray shook his head, smiling. "Life is such a mystery." He turned and studied the furrowed face of his friend. "What do you suppose that was?"

The man opened his eyes. "I don't know. But I'd like to call it a connection. You sent your love."

"Funny, it felt like I was letting go of her, not grabbing hold. And I could have sworn it was coming from her, not the other way around."

"Maybe that's the truest kind of love. The kind where we give with no need or expectation of return. And then, mysteriously, we find that we are still connected. A bond with no bind."

"Em and I have always had a connection. Always will. She saved my life once, you know?"

"You told me."

Ray smiled. "I suppose she's saved me a number of times, in a number of ways. Those guys on the radio out there looking for her thought I was nuts. They kept saying, 'Where are you calling from?' and 'How is it you know this?' but it was the least I could do for her." He laughed. "It's a good thing I'm with the Salt Lake PD, or they'd never have listened to me."

Ray shook his head in wonderment. "What do you suppose . . . you *must* have some notion, at least . . . that light! It was so beautiful!"

The man pondered this question a while before answering, "I used to think I knew, right down to a gnat's eyelashes, but I don't anymore." He shifted slightly, and stared into the sunset. "But a woman like Em, she burns bright. We want to draw close to them, to warm ourselves in their heat. It's comforting. It's life-giving. And then we get to fearing that we'll get burned. But here's what I sense: It takes one to know one, Ray. Life is the fire. We are the flame."

"And when we die? Does that fire go out?"

The man laughed. "You know the answer to that one, Ray."

"Some days I'm not so sure."

The older man picked at his fingernail again. "The best part of us never dies."

Ray smiled. "Not if memory is any guide."

They sat a while in silence, then the older man asked, "Is that why you joined the police force?"

"Is what why?"

"Her dying like that. Your wife."

"I guess. It's certainly *when* I joined." Ray threw a twig into the street and watched as the tires of a passing car crunched it into bits. "I wanted to help people. Protect people." He shook his head as if to rattle loose such wishes.

"You do help. You do protect."

"I see people hurt and dead all the time, and I can't seem to do much at all."

"But if you and others weren't there to enforce the law, more would get hurt, and more would die."

"I suppose."

"But none of that brings your wife back."

"That is correct."

The two men sat on the curb for a while longer in companionable silence, letting the relative coolness of the stone curb soothe them. Ray shot several more twigs into the street and was rewarded with two hits out of three under the tires of passing cars.

One twig had landed toward the center of the lane. It sat there, defying him; in harm's way yet magically safe between the murderous wheels of passing cars. He thought for a moment that he would name it Em, but then realized to his surprise that he didn't need to. In that small, silent *ah-ha*, a weight shifted off his shoulders that he had not noticed he had been carrying. He smiled.

The sponsor said, "What was her name?"

"I called her by her middle name. Amelia."

"That's a beautiful name."

Ray's smile widened into a peaceful grin. It was the first time he'd been able to let those silken vowels pass his lips in all the years since her death, and to his surprise and great joy, it tasted just as sweet as ever.

35

I FLEW BACK TO SALT LAKE CITY WITH FRITZ. HE DIDN'T SAY MUCH to me during the flight. He had said all he needed to say to me before driving me away from Julia's, which was, "Don't ever ask me to do anything like that again."

I had replied, "Okay."

I was tired, bone tired, and bruised from Julia's two attacks, but the worst hurt was not the kind that left a visible mark on one's body. I hurt in my heart. I hurt for Samantha and Timothy, who were as good as orphaned now, and I hurt for Julia, who wouldn't be able to see much of either of them for a long, long time. I hurt for every woman who ever poured out her love to a man who didn't love her in return. I hurt for people who couldn't understand that love is a forgiving thing that keeps on giving in the gentlest of ways even when there's been betrayal. I hurt for those who haven't discovered that the truest kind of love can never be taken from them, because it comes from within, welling up as the purest of gifts, with no requirement or expectation of return. And for the moment, I hurt for myself, because even in the intensity and shock of what she had done, I still loved Julia for all the times that had been better.

All these thoughts consumed me as we flew over the great, knotted spine of the Rockies on the way home to Salt Lake City. For it truly was my home now, the place I had chosen to send down my roots and make a life for myself.

When we landed at Salt Lake International Airport, I thanked Fritz one more time for his help and caring. He didn't say anything. He drove me around to the commercial aviation side of the airport, where I had parked my truck. And as he dropped me off, he didn't get out or say anything, only nodded and drove away.

I let him go. That's another thing love does, it gives a friend his space when he needs it.

But I didn't leave things like that for long. I gave myself ten days to recover. I walked with Faye, played horsy with Sloane, helped Michele wrap the case as the final evidence came in, and got back on the task of being just another geologist working for the Utah Geological Survey. I saw Michele and Trevor one evening, enjoying a meal at the restaurant across from the Salt Palace Convention Center in Salt Lake City where she had now located an eyewitness who was willing to testify that he had spotted Todd Upton the night of the murder, wearing dark glasses and a ball cap to obscure his bald head. Upton would eventually go to trial, as defiant and self-pitying as Julia. I wondered sourly if they might eventually have become friends if she hadn't punched him.

Over the next days and weeks, the horror of the two times Julia McWain attacked me ebbed, and I began, bit by bit, to feel normal again. I checked the mirror each morning, watching the scratches and bruises fade, and to counteract the vortex of trauma, I thought of Fritz. I thought of his calm presence, and, like the yin-yang symbol with the little bit of darkness in the light and the speck of light in the darkness, I began to find some calmness in myself.

When I was ready and hoped that he was too, I phoned him and invited him to go for a walk.

We met at dusk that evening and strolled under the spreading trees that lined the Avenues, passing quiet homes where families were tucking their children in with bedtime tales of princes and princesses who did heroic things. I ambled along beside him in companionable silence, listening to the small sounds our feet made on the sidewalk.

Fritz walked with his hands in his pockets, his eyes lost in contemplation. The air hung with the fading heat of summer. It would be fall soon, and the leaves above our heads would lose their vitality and drop away as the trees prepared to sleep through another winter.

We came at last to a small park and turned in to a place where the trees gathered together to form a space more private than the neighborhood around it. Fritz spied a bench and gestured toward it. I shook my head. "What I've got to say to you I'll say standing up," I said.

"Okay." He remained standing, too.

"You made a request of me, and I mean to keep it," I said.

"What was that?"

"About what happened in Denver, when I asked you to spot me while I tried to get that confession out of Julia. You said, 'Don't ever ask me to do that again.'"

He nodded.

"I won't."

His gaze didn't waver. It rested upon me like a feather, light yet strong and graceful in every detail. He said nothing.

"But I'll ask you to do something else instead," I said.

Fritz took a moment before asking, "And what is that?"

"Love me."

"I do, Em."

"I mean like a man loves a woman."

His voice caught in his throat like he was in pain. "I do. I always have."

I put a hand out and touched his face with my fingertips. "I'm so sorry that I hurt you like that."

He stared into my eyes a moment, then averted his gaze, but leaned toward me ever so slightly, pressing his cheek against my hand.

I found my voice again. "Fritz, I love you, too."

His eyes locked onto mine. He waited.

I said, "I needed time."

"I know."

"And you waited. Thank you."

His eyes swam with tears.

I said, "And I want to marry you and be with you always."

Every muscle in his body tensed.

I said, "I—I hope you'll consider it, anyway. Consider marrying me and taking me as your wife. I want to have children with you, one child at least, if I haven't waited too long. And I won't take on dangerous cases because that wouldn't be fair or reasonable to do if I'm somebody's mother and somebody's wife, and I'm real certain that I don't ever want to go through anything like that again anyway. But Fritz, I've got to do something that scratches my itch to dig into things, like maybe consult on cases but not actually go out on collars or anything, because . . . because, you see, I've looked into you and you're so still you're like a mirror. You're like a mountain lake first thing in the morning, the surface so smooth it's reflective. I look into you and I see your depth and your stillness and your incredible ability to face things that are scary. And in that mirror I see myself reflected back. That confused me at first because I was seeing my own uncertainty and I thought it was all of me, but now I see the other half, the warrior me, the part I'd like to knit back together with the rest by not being so alone, and that's why I love you so much, or a part of it, but also you're just . . . so . . . loveable. And I'm not making sense at all, but I'm afraid to shut up because if I do maybe that's the end of things, and I don't want them to end, ever."

Fritz had pulled his hands out of his pockets and put them on the small of my back and had begun, ever so slowly, to draw me into a hug that used both arms. "You're making perfect sense," he said, a huge smile curling his lips. "I'm with you—every word, every breath, every beat of your heart."

"Well, good, because I couldn't stand it if you thought I was crazy. Or if you didn't maybe want me as much as I want you!"

"Shhh . . ." He pulled me nearer, closing his arms tightly around me, now bending his body to meet mine, his hips tight against me and rocking gently, his heart pounding, his lips nuzzling against my hair.

"Fritz," I whispered, as I raised my face to meet his, time and space falling through the dark warmth he was creating within me. "I have so much to tell you."

His breath filled my ear with a whispered reply. "We'll have years and years to say everything we need to say, but first things first." His lips brushed my forehead, my cheek, my nose, then hovered so close to mine that I could feel their heat, and I fell into his kiss.